PRAISE FOR
THE CHICAGOLAND VAMPIRES SERIES

"I was drawn in . . . from page one and kept reading far into the night."

—Julie Kenner, *New York Times* bestselling author
of the Devil May Care novels

"Neill creates a strong-minded, sharp-witted heroine who will appeal to fans of Charlaine Harris's Sookie Stackhouse series and Laurell K. Hamilton's Anita Blake." *—Library Journal*

"The pages turn fast enough to satisfy vampire and romance fans alike." *—Booklist*

"Despite all that has and continues to be thrown at her, Merit's courage, guts, and loyalty make her one amazing heroine. Terrific!" —RT Book Reviews

"If you loved Nancy Drew but always wished she was an undead sword-wielding badass, Merit is your kind of girl."

—Geek Monthly

"Action, supernatural politicking, the big evil baddie with a plan, and, of course, plenty of sarcastic Merit one-liners. . . . Chicagoland Vampires is one of my favorite series."

—All Things Urban Fantasy

"Neill's Chicago is an edgier, urban Bon Temps."

—Heroes and Heartbreakers

"All I can say is *wow*." —Bitten by Books

"An absolute treat not to be missed." —A Book Obsession

"Delivers enough action, plot twists, and fights to satisfy the most jaded urban fantasy reader." —Monsters and Critics

Novels by Chloe Neill

The Heirs of Chicagoland Novels

WILD HUNGER

The Chicagoland Vampires Novels

SOME GIRLS BITE

FRIDAY NIGHT BITES

TWICE BITTEN

HARD BITTEN

DRINK DEEP

BITING COLD

HOUSE RULES

BITING BAD

WILD THINGS

BLOOD GAMES

DARK DEBT

MIDNIGHT MARKED

BLADE BOUND

"HIGH STAKES"
novella in *Kicking It*

HOWLING FOR YOU
(A Chicagoland Vampires Novella)

LUCKY BREAK
(A Chicagoland Vampires Novella)

PHANTOM KISS
(A Chicagoland Vampires Novella)

The Devil's Isle Novels

THE VEIL

THE SIGHT

THE HUNT

The Dark Elite Novels

FIRESPELL

HEXBOUND

CHARMFALL

WILD HUNGER

AN HEIRS OF CHICAGOLAND NOVEL

CHLOE NEILL

BERKLEY
New York

BERKLEY
An imprint of Penguin Random House LLC
375 Hudson Street, New York, New York 10014

Library of Congress Cataloging-in-Publication Data

Names: Neill, Chloe, author.
Title: Wild hunger: an heirs of Chicagoland novel / Chloe Neill.
Description: First edition. | New York: Berkley, 2018. | Series: An heirs of
Chicagoland novel; 1
Identifiers: LCCN 2018020583 | ISBN 9780399587092 (Trade paperback) |
ISBN 9780399587108 (ebook)
Subjects: LCSH: Vampires—Fiction. | Chicago (Ill.)—Fiction. | BISAC:
FICTION/Fantasy/Paranormal. | FICTION/Fantasy/Urban Life. |
GSAFD: Occult fiction.
Classification: LCC PS3614.E4432 W548 2018 | DDC 813/.6—dc23
LC record available at https://lccn.loc.gov/2018020583

First Edition: August 2018

Printed in the United States of America
1 3 5 7 9 10 8 6 4 2

Cover art by Tony Mauro
Cover design by Adam Auerbach

"In our youth our hearts were touched with fire."
—Oliver Wendell Holmes

WILD HUNGER

PROLOGUE

"Noooooo!" A little girl's voice echoed through the hallway. The cry was followed by footsteps, more yelling, and a petulant squeal.

"It's mine! You give it back right now, Connor stupid Keene!"

The dark-haired boy stuck his tongue out at her—the tiny blonde he relished torturing—then tore down the hallway, holding aloft the plastic sword he'd taken from his enemy. "Victory!" he said.

She followed him, Mary Jane shoes padding down the carpeted hallway, but he was nearly a foot taller, and she knew she couldn't catch him. Not by running. So she called in a reinforcement.

"Daddy! Connor stupid Keene won't give me my sword!"

Connor stupid Keene stopped and spun around, then leveled his best glare at Elisa Sullivan.

"I'm a prince," he said, sticking his thumb against his chest. "And I can take your sword if I want!" He was seven, and she only five and a half, so he was obviously the more mature of the two of them.

She jumped up to grab the sword but couldn't reach it. "Give it back, you . . . you . . ."

"'You' what?" he asked with a wily grin, spinning around to keep the toy out of her hands. "What am I?"

"You're . . . you're . . . you're a stupid boy—that's what you are!"

"Children."

They froze, then turned back toward the doorway to Elisa's father's office and looked warily at the vampire who filled it. "Is there a problem?" he asked.

"No, Mr. Sullivan," said Connor, scowling at his companion.

Green-eyed Elisa, just as wily as he was, stuck out her tongue at Connor, then batted her eyelashes at her father. "He took my sword," she said in a small, soft voice she knew was guaranteed to get her way. "And he won't give it back."

"Son, did you take her sword?"

They turned again, saw a tall man at the other end of the hallway.

"No, Dad," Connor said as his father walked toward him. Connor held out the sword and let Elisa take it back, but scowled when she stuck her tongue out at him. Again. *She is so spoiled*, he thought.

Gabriel Keene grinned wolfishly, crossed his arms over his chest. "I'm glad we resolved this peacefully."

Ethan Sullivan smiled, one hand braced against the doorframe as he watched his daughter and her nemesis do what they did best. "As am I. Do we need to talk about the House rules again?"

"No, Daddy." Elisa tucked the sword behind her back.

"Son?" Gabriel asked.

"No, Dad." Connor shifted from foot to foot.

"We talked about this."

There was a moment of uncomfortable silence in the hallway.

"I know."

As she bit her lip, Elisa looked up at Connor and saw the flush of embarrassment on his cheeks. She didn't like being teased—or not that much, anyway—but she really didn't like that look on his face.

She stepped forward, putting her small body between Connor and his father.

"It was my fault," she said.

Arching an eyebrow, Gabriel crouched down, hands clasped in front of him. "Was it, now?"

Worriedly, she looked back at Connor, then at his dad, and nodded once.

Gabriel leaned in and whispered quietly, "Is it your fault, or do you just not want Connor to get in trouble?"

In the just-slightly-too-loud whisper of a child, she said, "I don't want Connor to get in trouble."

"Ah." He nodded gravely, then stood again, Connor moving to stand beside him. "I think we've gotten things cleared up, then," he said, then ruffled his son's hair.

Connor grinned at him, leaned against his father.

And stuck his tongue out at Elisa.

ONE

Vampires were made, not born.

All except one.

All except me.

I was the daughter of vampires, born because magic and fate twisted together. I'd spent nineteen years in Chicago. Tonight, I stood nearly four hundred feet above Paris, several thousand miles away from the Windy City and the Houses in which most of its vampires lived.

Around me, visitors on the second level of the Eiffel Tower sipped champagne and snapped shots of the city. I closed my eyes against the warm, balmy breeze that carried the faint scent of flowers.

"Elisa, you cannot tell Paris goodbye with your eyes closed."

"I'm not saying goodbye," I said. "Because I'm coming back."

I opened my eyes, smiled at the vampire who appeared at my side with two plastic cones of champagne. Seraphine had golden skin and dark hair, and her hazel eyes shone with amusement.

"To Paris," I said, and tapped my cone against hers.

It had been four years since I'd last stepped foot in Chicago. Tomorrow, I'd go home again and visit the city and spend time with family and friends.

For twenty years, there'd been peace in Chicago among humans and sups, largely because of efforts by my parents—Ethan

Sullivan and Merit, the Master and Sentinel, respectively, of Cadogan House. They'd worked to find a lasting peace, and had been so successful that Chicago had become a model for other communities around the world.

That's why Seri and I were going back. The city's four vampire Houses were hosting peace talks for vampires from Western Europe, where Houses had been warring since the governing council—the Greenwich Presidium—dissolved before I was born. And vampires' relations with the other supernaturals in Europe weren't any better. Chicago would serve as neutral territory where the Houses' issues could be discussed and a new system of government could be hammered out.

"You look . . . What is the word? Wistful?" Seri smiled. "And you haven't even left yet."

"I'm building up my immunity," I said, and sipped the champagne.

"You love Chicago."

"It's a great city. But I was . . . a different person in Chicago. I like who I am here."

Paris wasn't always peaceful. But it had given me the time and distance to develop the control I'd needed over the monster that lived inside me. Because I wasn't just a vampire. . . .

Seri bumped her shoulder against mine supportively. "You will be the same person there as you are here. Miles change only location. They do not change a person's heart. A person's character."

I hoped that was true. But Seri didn't know the whole of it. She didn't know about the half-formed power that lurked beneath my skin, reveled in its anger. She didn't know about the magic that had grown stronger as I'd grown older, until it beat like a second heartbeat inside me.

Sunlight and aspen could kill me—but the monster could bury me in its rage.

I'd spent the past four years attending École Dumas, Europe's only university for supernaturals. I was one of a handful of vampires in residence. Most humans weren't changed into vampires until they were older; the change would give them immortality, but they'd be stuck at the age at which they'd been changed. No one wanted to be thirteen for eternity.

I hadn't been changed at all, but born a vampire—the one and only vampire created that way. Immortal, or so we assumed, but still for the moment aging.

The university was affiliated with Paris's Maison Dumas, one of Europe's most prestigious vampire Houses, where I'd lived for the past four years. I'd had a little culture shock at first, but I'd come to love the House and appreciate its logical approach to problem solving. If Cadogan was Gryffindor, all bravery and guts, Dumas was Ravenclaw, all intellect and cleverness. I liked being clever, and I liked clever people, so we were a good fit.

I'd had four years of training to develop the three components of vampire strength: physical, psychic, and strategic. I graduated a few months ago with a sociology degree—emphasis in suphuman relations—and now I was repaying my training the same way French vampires did, with a year of mandatory armed service for the House. It was a chance to see what I was made of, and to spend another year in the city I'd come to love.

I was three months into my service. Escorting delegates from Maison Dumas to Chicago for the peace talks was part of my work.

"How many suitcases are you bringing?"

I glanced at Seri with amusement. "Why? How many are you bringing?"

"Four." Seri did not travel lightly.

"We'll only be in Chicago for four days."

"I have diplomatic responsibilities, Elisa."

I sipped my champagne. "That's what French vampires say when they pack too much. I have a capsule wardrobe."

"And that is what American vampires say when they do not pack enough. You also have diplomatic responsibilities."

"I have responsibilities to the House. That's different."

"Ah," she said, smiling at me over the rim of her drink. "But which one?"

"*Maison Dumas,*" I said, in an accent that was pretty close to perfect. "I'm not going to Chicago on behalf of Cadogan House. It's just a bonus."

"I look forward to meeting your parents. And I'm sure they'll be glad to see you."

"I'll be glad to see them, too. It's just—I've changed a lot in the last few years. Since the last time I went home."

They'd visited Paris twice since I'd been gone, and we'd had fun walking through the city, seeing the sights. But I still felt like I'd been holding myself back from them. Maybe I always had.

"It's not about you or Cadogan or Chicago," I'd told my father, when we'd stood outside the private terminal at O'Hare, in front of the jet that would take me across the world. I'd been struggling to make him understand. "It's about figuring out who I am."

In Chicago, I was the child of Ethan and Merit. And it had been hard to feel like anything more than a reflection of my parents and my birth, which made me a curiosity for plenty of sups outside Cadogan House who treated me like a prize. And the possibility I might be able to bear children made me, at least for some, a prize to be captured.

I'd wanted to be something more, something different. . . . Something that was just me.

"You couldn't fail us by living your life the way you want," my father had said. "It's your life to live, and you will make your own choices. You always have."

He'd tipped my chin up with the crook of his finger, forcing me to meet his gaze.

"There are some decisions that we make, and some that are

made for us. Sometimes you accept the path that's offered to you, and you live that path—that life—with grace. And sometimes you push forward, and you chart your own path. That decision is yours. It's always been yours.

"I don't want you to go, because I'm selfish. Because you are my child." His eyes had burned fiercely, emeralds on fire. "But if this is your path, you must take it. Whatever happens out there, you always have a home here."

He'd kissed my forehead, then embraced me hard. *"Test your wings,"* he'd quietly said. A suggestion. A request. A hope. *"And fly."*

I had flown. And I'd read and walked and learned and trained, just like everyone else.

In Paris, I'd been just another vampire. And the anonymity, the freedom, had been exhilarating.

"We all carry expectations," Seri said quietly, her eyes suddenly clouded. "Sometimes our own, sometimes others'. Both can be heavy."

Seri came from what the European Houses called "good blood." She'd been made by a Master vampire with power, with money, with an old name, and with plenty of cachet—and that mattered to French vampires. Seri had been the last vampire he'd made before his death, and those of his name were expected to be aristocrats and socialites. Unlike in the US, French vampires selected their own Houses. She'd picked Maison Dumas instead of Maison Bourdillon, the House of her Master. That hadn't made her many friends among Bourdillon's progeny, who decided she was wasting her legacy.

"Are you excited to see Chicago?" I asked her.

"I am excited to see the city," she said, "if not optimistic about what will come of the talks. Consider Calais."

The most recent attack had taken place in Calais a week ago. Vampires from Paris's Maison Solignac had attacked Maison

Saint-Germaine because they believed they weren't getting a big enough cut of the city port's profits. In the process, four vampires and two humans had been killed.

The European Houses had lived together peacefully, at least by human standards, for hundreds of years. But after the GP's dissolution, all bets were off. There was power to be had, and vampires found that irresistible.

More than a dozen delegates from France, including Seri and Marion, the Master of Maison Dumas, would participate in the talks. Marion and Seri would be accompanied by nearly a dozen staff, including Marion's bodyguard, Seri's assistant, Odette, and me.

"Yeah," I said. "I don't know how successful it will be, either. But refusing to talk certainly isn't doing much good."

Seri nodded and drank the last of her champagne as two guards passed us—one human, one vampire—and silenced the chatter. They wore black fatigues and berets, and looked suspiciously at everyone they passed. Part of the joint task force created by the Paris Police Prefecture to keep the city safe.

The vampire's eyes shifted to me, then Seri. He acknowledged us, scanned the rest of the crowd, and kept walking, katana belted at his waist.

Vampires in the US and Western Europe used the long and slightly curved Japanese swords, which were sharp and deadly as fangs, but with a much longer reach.

Sorcerers had magic. Shifters had their animal forms. Vampires had katanas.

"There's Javí," Seraphine whispered, and watched as they kept moving, then disappeared around the corner. Javí was a Dumas vampire doing his year of service.

These weren't the only guards at the Eiffel Tower. Humans and vampires alike stood at the edge of the crowd below, wearing body armor and weapons and trying to keep safe the tourists and residents enjoying a warm night in the Champ de Mars.

We turned back to the rail, looked over the city. So much white stone, so many slate roofs, so many people enjoying the warm night. But the specter of violence, of fear, hung over it. And that was hard to shake. No city was perfect, not when people lived in it.

"Let us take a photo," Seri said, clearly trying to lift the mood. She put an arm around me, then pulled out her screen and angled the narrow strip of glass and silicon for a perfect shot.

"To Paris!" she said, and we smiled.

The moment recorded, she checked the time before putting the device away again. "We should get back. The Auto will arrive in a few hours." She slipped an arm through mine. "This will be an adventure, and we will be optimists. And I look forward to pizza and Chicago dogs and . . . *Comment dites-on 'milk shake de gateau'?*"

"Cake shake," I said with a smile. "You and my mother are going to get along just fine."

We'd only just turned to head toward the elevator when screams sliced through the air, followed by a wave of nervous, fearful magic that rolled up from the ground.

We looked back and over the rail.

Even from this height, they were visible. Five vampires in gleaming red leather running through the green space with katanas in one hand and small weapons in the other.

Not knives; there was no gleam from the flashing lights on the Tower.

What was shaped like a knife, but held no metal, and would turn a vampire to dust?

Humans had been wrong about vampires and crosses, but they'd been absolutely right about stakes. An aspen stake through the heart was a guaranteed way to put the "mortal" in "immortal."

I didn't know which House the vampires were from. I was too high to see their faces, and the gleaming red leather didn't give anything away. Leather was a vampire favorite, and French vampire Houses appreciated fashion as much as the French fashion houses did.

But their intent was clear enough. They ran through the crowd, weapons drawn, and took aim at everyone in their path. Screams, sharp and terrified, filled the air. I watched one person fall, another dive to the ground to avoid the strike, a third try unsuccessfully to fight back against the vampire's increased strength.

Paris was under attack. My stomach clenched with nerves and anger.

I wanted to help. I was stronger and faster than most humans, and trained as well as any vampire from Maison Dumas would have been. But there were rules. There were roles and responsibilities. The Paris police, the task force members, were supposed to respond to events. I was just a civilian, and only a temporary one at that. I worked for Dumas, and should have been focused on getting Seri safely back to Maison Dumas.

But the screams . . .

The guards who'd walked past minutes before ran back to the rail beside us and stared at the scene below in horror. And neither of them made a move toward the ground. It took only a second to guess why.

"Can you jump?" I asked Javí, the vampire.

He looked at me, eyes wide. "*Quoi?*"

I had to remember where I was, shook my head, tried again. "*Pouvez-vous sauter?*"

"*Non.*" Javí looked down. "*Non. Trop haut.*"

Too high. Most vampires could jump higher and farther than humans, and we could jump down from heights that would easily kill humans. But the trick required training, which I'd learned the hard way—believing I could fly from the widow's walk atop

Cadogan House. I'd broken my arm, but vampires healed quickly, so that hadn't been much of a deterrent. My mother had taught me the rest.

Javí couldn't jump, so he'd have to wait for the elevator or take the hundreds of stairs down to ground level.

But I didn't have to wait.

I squeezed Seri's hand, told Javí to take care of her, and hoped he'd obey.

Before anyone could argue, or I could think better of it, I slid the katana from his scabbard, climbed onto the railing, and walked into space.

I descended through rushing darkness. A human might have had a few seconds of free fall before the deadly landing. But for a vampire, it was less a fall than a long and lazy step. Maybe we compressed space; maybe we elongated time. I didn't understand the physics, but I loved the sensation. It was as close to flying as I was likely to get.

The first level of the Eiffel Tower was wider than the second, so I had to jump down to the first level—causing more than a few humans to scream—before making it to the soft grass below. I landed in a crouch, katana firmly in hand.

My fangs descended, the predator preparing to battle. While I couldn't see it, I knew my eyes had silvered, as they did when vampires experienced strong emotions. It was a reminder—to humans, to prey, to enemies—that the vampire wasn't human, but something altogether different. Something altogether more dangerous.

Two humans were dead a few feet away, their eyes open and staring, blood spilling onto the grass from the lacerations at their necks. The vampires who'd murdered them hadn't even bothered to bite, to drink. This attack wasn't about need. It was about hatred.

I was allowed only a moment of shocked horror—of seeing how quickly two lives had been snuffed out—before the scent of blood blossomed in the air again, unfurling like the petals of a crimson poppy.

I looked back.

A vampire kneeled over a human woman. She was in her early twenties, with pale skin, blond hair, and terror in her eyes. The vampire was even paler, blood pumping through indigo veins just below the surface. His hair was short and ice blond, his eyes silver. And the knife he held above the woman's chest was covered with someone else's blood.

Anger rose, hot and intense, and I could feel the monster stir inside, awakened by the sheer power of the emotion. But I was still in Paris. And here, I was in control. I shoved it back down, refused to let it surface.

"Arrêtez!" I yelled out, and to emphasize the order, held my borrowed katana in front of me, the silver blade reflecting the lights from the Eiffel Tower.

The vampire growled, lip curled to reveal a pair of needle-sharp fangs, hatred burning in his eyes. I didn't recognize him, and I doubted he recognized me beyond the fact that I was a vampire not from his House—and that made me an enemy.

He rose, stepping away from the human as if she were nothing more than a bit of trash he'd left behind. His knuckles around the stake were bone white, tensed and ready.

Released from his clutches, the human took one look at my silvered eyes and screamed, then began to scramble away from us. She'd survive—if I could lure him away from her.

The vampire slapped my katana away with one hand, drove the stake toward me with the other.

I might have been young for a vampire, but I was well trained. I moved back, putting us both clear of the human, and kicked. I made contact with his hand, sent the stake spinning through the air. He found his footing and picked up the stake. Undeterred, he moved toward me. This time, he kicked. I blocked it, but the force of the blow sent pain rippling through my arm.

He thrust the stake toward me like a fencer with a foil.

The movement sent light glimmering against the gold on his right hand. A signet ring, crowned by a star ruby—and the symbol of Maison Saint-Germaine.

I doubted it was a coincidence Saint-Germaine vampires were attacking the ultimate symbol of Paris only a few nights after they'd been attacked by a Paris House. While I understood why they'd want revenge, terrorizing and murdering humans wasn't the way to do it. It wasn't fair to make our issues their problems.

I darted back to avoid the stake, then sliced down with the katana when he advanced again.

"You should have stayed in Calais," I said in French, and got no response but a gleam in his eyes. He spun to avoid that move, but I managed to nick his arm. Blood scented the air, and my stomach clenched with sudden hunger and need. But ignoring that hunger was one of the first lessons my parents had taught me. There was a time and a place to drink, and this wasn't it.

I swept out a leg, which had him hopping backward, then rotated into a kick that sent him to his knees. He grabbed my legs, shifting his weight so we both fell forward onto the grass. The katana rolled from my grasp.

My head rapped against the ground, and it took a moment to realize that he'd climbed over me and grabbed the stake. He raised it, his eyes flashing in the brilliantly colored lights that reflected across the grass from the shining monument behind us.

I looked at that stake—thought of what it could do and was almost certainly about to do to me—and my mind went absolutely blank. I could see him, hear the blood rushing in my ears, and didn't have the foggiest idea what I was supposed to do, like the adrenaline had forced a hiccup in my brain.

Fortunately, beyond fear, and beneath it, was instinct. And I didn't need to think of what would bring a man down. He may have been immortal, and he may have been a vampire. Didn't matter. This move didn't discriminate.

I kicked him in the groin.

He groaned, hunched over, and fell over on the grass, body curled over his manhood.

"Asshole," I muttered, chest heaving as I climbed to my feet and kicked him over, then added a kick to the back of his ribs to encourage him, politely, to stay there.

Two guards ran over, looked at me, then him.

"Elisa Sullivan," I said. "Maison Dumas." Most vampires who weren't Masters used only their first name. I'd gotten an exception since it wasn't practical for a kid to have just one name.

They nodded, confiscated the stake, and went about the business of handcuffing the vampire. I picked up the katana, wiped the blade against my pant leg, and dared a look at the field around me.

Two of the other Saint-Germaine vampires were alive, both on their knees, hands behind their heads. I didn't see the others, and unless they'd run away, which seemed unlikely, they'd probably been taken down by the Paris police or Eiffel Tower guards. Fallen into cones of ash due to a deadly encounter with aspen.

Humans swarmed at the periphery of the park, where Paris police worked to set up a barrier.

Some of the humans who'd survived the attack were helping the wounded. Others stood with wide eyes, shaking with shock and fear. And more yet had pulled out their screens to capture video of the fight. The entire world was probably watching, whether they wanted to see or not.

I found Seri standing at the edge of the park, her eyes silver, her expression fierce and angry. She wasn't a fighter, but she knew injustice when she saw it.

I walked toward her, my right hip aching a bit from hitting the ground, and figured I'd passed my first field test.

I suddenly wasn't so sad to be leaving Paris.

TWO

Twenty-four hours later, I woke several thousand feet in the air, senses stirred by the whir of the automatic shutters. The jet's windows had been covered while we slept, protecting us from burning to a crisp in the sunshine.

Through the window, orange and white lights glowed like circuits against the long, dark stretch of Lake Michigan. And I could feel the monster inside me reaching out, stretching as if it could touch the familiar energy.

The monster had a connection to Chicago—to the city and the sword that waited in the Cadogan House armory—that made it harder to control here. That was one of the reasons I'd gone to Paris, and one of the things I couldn't explain to my father on the tarmac before I left.

My heart began to beat faster as the monster's magic rose, and I had to work to slow it down again, to stay in control. I breathed out through pursed lips, concentrating to send it back into darkness again.

I can do this, I told myself.

I wasn't the same girl I'd been four years ago. I was returning with more strength and experience, and four more years of practice in holding it down, keeping it buried. Which is where I meant it to stay. I'd be here for only a few days, and then I'd be on my way back to Paris, far from its reach. I would manage it until then, because there was no other choice.

Because I wouldn't hurt anyone else, ever again.

"Are you all right?"

I glanced at Seri, unclenching my fingers from the armrest and giving her what smile I could manage. "Fine. A little groggy."

Her brows lifted, and the expression said she didn't believe me. Seri was a Strong Psych, and had a sense about people, about emotions, about truth and fiction. And she'd almost certainly felt the magic.

"Jet lag," I said, which was mostly true. Vampirism and time-zone changes didn't mix well for me even in the best of times. I'd spent most of my first week in Paris napping.

She didn't look entirely satisfied, but she nodded. "I'm glad we have only the reception tonight." She smiled at the attendant, wiped her hands with the hot towel he offered. "I'm not ready to listen to hours of arguing."

"Me, either." And I didn't need to be a Strong Psych to know that no one on the plane was feeling especially optimistic. "But they'll have wine or champagne or both. And we'll only have to go back upstairs when the party's over."

The opening reception would be held at the Portman Grand, one of Chicago's poshest hotels—and our home for the next few days. I'd said no to Marion when she offered to let me stay at Cadogan House. There was nothing to be gained from baiting the monster.

"You could still change your mind about the hotel," Seri said. "Stay at Cadogan so you can see your parents more often."

I made myself smile at her. "I'll be working. Diplomatic responsibilities, remember?"

And a little more peace.

We landed safely, and half the passengers applauded the pilot, which I always found weird. The flight crew had done exactly what they'd been hired to do—get us safely across the ocean. Would we have heckled the pilot if the plane had gone down?

I unbuckled my seat belt and stood, then picked up my bag and katana. The scabbard was the marbled green of malachite, the handle corded with silk of the same color. The blade was pristine, the edge so thin and sharp that even Muramasa himself, one of the masters of Japanese sword making, would have approved. It had been a gift from my mother for my eighteenth birthday, the first sharpened sword I'd been allowed to wield. And I had learned to wield it—to unsheathe it, to defend with it, to attack with it.

I was well trained, and I'd been in skirmishes before. But I'd never killed with it. I hadn't seen violent death at all until the Eiffel Tower incident. Before then, I hadn't seen empty and staring eyes—the visible proof of how quickly and ruthlessly life could be stolen. And I had a very bad feeling those memories wouldn't fade as quickly.

The vampire seated in front of us rose and stretched, startling me from the memory.

He glanced around the plane, smiled in our direction. He was tall and lean, with taut, pale skin. His hair was silvery gray, his eyes pale blue and deep-set, topped by darker brows.

"Ladies," he said in accented English. "Did you enjoy your flight? It is better than flying across the Atlantic on the wings of the bat, no?" His smile was halfway between smarmy and silly.

His name was Victor, and he was of the high-ranking vampires from Maison Chevalier, another House in Paris. Unlike Marion, who liked to think and consider, Victor was a politician all the way through. Strategic, as all vampires were, and skilled at getting his way. But he was honest about it, and seemed to always be smiling, so it was hard not to like him.

"Our arms would be so tired," I said with as much smile as I could muster.

He grinned, pointed at me. *"Exactement!"* He pulled from a suit jacket a small box and flipped up the lid. A half dozen tiny and violently crimson macarons sat inside. "Would you care for a bite before we disembark?"

Seri shook her head. "No, *merci*."

Blood-flavored macarons were all the rage among French vampires. I could deal with the flavor; I was a vampire, after all. But I didn't like macarons even in the best of times. They were too indecisive. Were they candies? Cookies? I had no idea, and I didn't like snacks that couldn't commit.

"No, thank you," I said with a smile.

"You may proceed," the flight attendant said, allowing us to move toward the door. "Have a wonderful evening."

Victor gave a little salute. "Ladies, *au revoir*. I will see you at the party."

"*Au revoir*," Seri said, and lifted a hand to him. "You really shouldn't encourage him," she murmured when Victor disappeared ahead of us.

"He's charming in his way," I said, following her into the aisle.

"You should not have laughed at the bat joke. He will believe he is a great comedian, and we will never be done with his attempts at humor. I don't know if I can stand an immortality of it."

"We will persist," I said gravely. But his offer had me thinking— and worrying. "I didn't bring any souvenirs for my parents. Maybe I should have bought macarons at the airport."

"It is a rule," Seri said, "that one should not buy gifts at an airport."

"Okay, but which is more important? Buying gifts for your family at an airport, or showing up without gifts at all?"

She pursed her lips as she considered. "You should have bought macarons at the airport. But Chicago will be glad to have you home, macarons or not. You are the prodigal daughter returning!"

"I guess we'll see about that," I murmured, descended the steps, and breathed in the humid air of a Midwestern August.

*   *   *

I didn't recognize the cluster of humans who waited on the tarmac at the bottom of the stairs, but they introduced themselves as members of the mayor's staff. With apologetic and politic smiles, they explained delegates were arriving from all over the world, so the mayor simply couldn't greet every sup personally.

Given she was human, I didn't expect her to be literally in more than one place at a time.

A line of vehicles waited to take passengers and luggage to their respective hotels. Most were boxy and gleaming Autos that didn't need drivers, and would have been preprogrammed to send us to our destination.

In front of them stood my parents.

My father, Ethan Sullivan, was tall and pale, with golden blond hair down to his shoulders that matched my own. As on most nights, he wore a black suit and a cool expression. That was the result of four hundred years of playing vamp politics and having to learn early on to ignore the details to focus on the primary goal: the survival of his House and the vamps who lived there.

My mother, Caroline Merit—just Merit to most—stood beside him in slim-fitting black pants and a simple pale blue top, her hair dark and straight, her face framed by bangs. Her eyes were pale blue, her nose straight, her mouth wide, and she was pretty in an elegant way.

My dad called her Duchess, which fit until you heard her curse like a sailor or do battle against nachos. There was nothing aristocratic about that or her fighting skills. Give a trained dancer a katana, and she'll show you something spectacular. She now stood Sentinel for the House, a guardian for the organization and its Master.

My mother was over fifty, and my father more than four hundred. Neither had aged since I'd been born; they looked barely older than me. Humans usually found that weird, but to me it just *was*. They were my parents, and they looked the way they looked. Wasn't it weirder to have parents who looked a little different with each month and year that passed?

I'd eventually stop aging, too, or so we assumed. As the only vampire child ever born, we were writing the book about the growth of vampire children. For now, at least, I figured I looked exactly my twenty-three years.

Bag and katana in hand, I made my way down the stairs. And the second I stepped foot onto asphalt—onto Chicago—the monster reached for the ground, for the city and its magic. And the power of its desire nearly buckled my knees.

My parents didn't know about the monster. They knew only that I'd once lost control and a human had paid the price. I had a momentary flash of panic that I'd be overwhelmed by it, that they'd see that the monster was still inside me, caged but alive. Had probably been there since I'd been born, since I'd been magically fused to my mother. Because evil had been magically fused to me, or at least that's what I thought had happened.

Knowing would break their hearts, and I couldn't bear both the monster and weight of their grief. So I reached for every ounce of strength I had, forced myself to take one more step, then another. Four years of intense training, and cold sweat still trickled down my spine as I walked toward my parents. But they didn't seem to see it.

"It's so good to see you," my mother said, wrapping her arms around me the moment I put down my bag and placed the scabbard on top. She smelled the same, her perfume clean and crisp and floral. The scent made me think of our apartments in Cadogan House, where the pale and pretty fragrance had permeated the air.

"We missed you so much," she said quietly, her arms a ferocious band that seemed to quiet the monster.

Maybe the monster was afraid of her. If my theory was right, it had reason to be. . . .

"I missed you guys, too," I said.

"You look happy," my father said, giving me a hug and pressing a kiss to the top of my head.

When he released me, my mother held out a steaming to-go cup. "I thought you could use this after your flight."

"Thank you," I said, and took a sip. It was hot and sweet, with just a hint of hazelnut. I'd have sworn the grogginess started to fade immediately, but that might have been my obsession talking.

"This is perfect," I said. "Leo's?"

"It is," she said with a smile.

Leo's was my favorite coffee spot, a tiny box of a drive-through in Hyde Park not far from Cadogan House. The menu was limited, the servers were always surly, and it took only cash. But if you could get past the irritations, it was the best coffee in the city.

"If you're going to do something," she said, in a pretty good imitation of my father's voice, "do it right."

"You're hilarious, Sentinel."

"I know. I love your hair," she said, touching a long curl of it.

"Thanks." It had taken a while to figure out what to do with the blond waves I'd inherited from my father's side of the family. Too short, and it was a puffball of curls I couldn't pull off. Longer, the curls relaxed and became waves that were much more flattering.

"How was your flight?" my father asked.

"I was asleep for most of it." I held up my hand. "No burns, so the shutters worked. Private jet from Europe was nice. Free headphones and socks."

My mother's eyes lit. "Was there a snack basket?"

"You have an entire kitchen at your disposal," my father said.

"And Margot's too busy to walk around and offer me snacks all night." Her gaze narrowed. "Although that gives me some ideas."

"As you can tell," my father said with amusement, "your mother has not changed a whit since we saw you in May."

"I'm good with that," I said.

"We saw the footage from Paris," my father said, and put a hand on my mother's shoulder.

I'd prepared them, told them we'd been involved, so he wouldn't learn about the fight secondhand. But the fear and grief in his eyes was still keen.

Tears welled in my eyes, too. Suddenly swamped with the horror I'd seen the night before, I pushed the cup of coffee at my father and flung myself into my mother's arms.

"All right," she said, embracing me again. "It's all right. Get it out of your system. You'll feel better."

"It was horrible." I mumbled it into her shirt. "It was stupid, and it was senseless, and it was . . . so violent."

"It always is horrible," she whispered, rubbing my back. "It's not an advantage to be numb to terrible things. It means we can't feel. When we can feel, and we do it anyway, we show our bravery. And terrible times are when we need to act most of all. That's when we do the most good."

She held me while I stood there, crying onto her shirt, until I'd wrung out the worst of the emotion. Then I pulled back and wiped my cheeks.

"Sorry," I said, trying for a half laugh. "I'm not sure why I'm crying. That was . . . not very professional."

My father pulled an embroidered handkerchief from his pocket. I took it, swiped at my face. I felt childish for needing to cry, but a little better for having done it.

"You've had a long twenty-four hours," my mother said. "And you care about people, and you care about Paris. That's as professional as it gets."

"She's right," my father said, earning a thumbs-up from my mother. "You handled yourself well. We were very proud."

The tightness in his eyes said he was working hard not to re-play the discussion we'd already had about the risks of my Dumas service. He knew this was my story to write.

"Thanks," I said, and gave my face a final wipe, then stuffed the handkerchief into my pocket.

"Now," my mother said, looking around. "When do we get to meet Seraphine?" She hadn't been in town when they'd come to my graduation.

I glanced back at the jet, found Seri chatting with Odette at the bottom of the Jetway, and waved her over.

"*Bonjour,*" she said brightly when she reached us, slipping an arm through mine.

"Seri, these are my parents, Ethan and Merit."

"It is lovely to finally meet you!" Seri said, and exchanged kisses with them. "Your daughter is a jewel."

"We agree," my father said. "And we hope you enjoy Chicago as much as she's enjoyed Paris."

"I'm sure I will." She looked at my mother. "I understand we should discuss, um, cake shakes?"

My mother's face lit up like she'd won the lottery. "We should discuss them. Maybe we'll make good progress at the talks to-morrow, and we'll have time for a Portillo's adventure."

"Let us hope," Seri said with a smile, which quickly faded. "You have heard about the recent attack?"

"We did," my father said.

"Have there been any threats against the talks?" I asked.

My father lifted an eyebrow.

"I'm in service to Maison Dumas," I reminded them. "I'm working."

"No threats," my mother said, taking my father's hand and squeezing, probably giving him a signal. They could also com-municate telepathically—one of the common vampire skills I hadn't developed, probably because I hadn't been made in the traditional way of vampires—so it wasn't often I'd heard them disagree aloud about how to handle me or something I'd done.

Because of that, I'd had zero luck playing the "Mom said it was okay" card. Mom and Dad could check with each other without my even knowing it.

"Although the Spanish delegates are still arguing about seating positions," my father said, clearly not impressed with the behavior.

"You've seen the security plan for the Sanford?" my mother asked.

The talks would be held at the remodeled Sanford Theater. And while Chicago might have been peaceful, the event's organizers weren't taking any chances. There'd be barriers outside the building, guards inside and outside the facility, and security forces in the room in case anyone got brave. The forces would be a mix of human and supernatural—primarily vampires and members of the North American Central Pack of shifters, as the Pack had made its home in Chicago. Gabriel Keene was its wolfish Apex, no pun intended, and a friend of my parents.

Gabriel's son, Connor, and I had grown up together, or mostly. He was two years older than me—and figured he was two years hipper and wiser. He'd been the bane of my childhood, the irritation of my adolescence. We'd tolerated each other for our parents' sake, or at least as much as two kids could.

He thought I was bossy. I liked things the way I liked them.

I thought he was reckless. He said he was the prince and could do what he wanted.

And unlike everyone else in my life, Connor Keene had seen the monster.

"If you don't mind," Seri said, "I'm going to join Odette, as she appears frantic."

We looked back at the Autos, where Odette was gesturing angrily at the growing pile of luggage.

"I hope they haven't lost your bags," my mother said.

"I'm sure it is fine." She smiled, reached out to squeeze each of my parents' hands in turn. "It was wonderful to meet you, finally. I hope we will have time to talk!"

"We hope so, too," my mother said.

"She seems lovely," my father said, when she'd moved toward the car.

"She is. She doesn't take what she has for granted, which would be very easy for her to do."

"Then she's in good company," my father said with a smile. "Not many would agree to a year of service when it wasn't owed."

"It was owed in spirit, even if not technically," I said.

"You are your mother's daughter," my father said, with not a little pride in it.

"As if the thirty-eight hours of labor didn't prove it," my mother said with a smile.

"I recall them well," my father said flatly. "You were . . . very angry."

"Was it the cursing that tipped you off?"

"And the throwing of many objects," he said, counting them off on his hands. "And challenging an Apex shifter to a knife fight. And accusing your sister of being a Russian spy. And promising to stake the doctor if you didn't get drugs."

"Nonsense. I was a paragon of patience and gentility."

My father winked at her. "Of course you were, Duchess. And, to my point, you were also a very careful Sentinel."

"Why are you smiling?" my mother asked me, eyes narrowed.

"Just . . . it's good to be home," I told her. And I hoped it would stay that way.

"Good," my mother said. "Because we're glad you're here, too." She tapped a silver band on her right ring finger, checked the time. "You should probably get to the hotel. Someone from the

Ombudsman's office will meet you there, give you your badges, and make sure you get into the reception."

Relations between Chicago's humans and vampires were managed by the city's supernatural Ombudsman. My great-grandfather, Chuck Merit, had been the first Ombudsman, and the office had grown since his retirement ten years ago. William Dearborn held the office now.

"Sounds good."

I glanced over at the slate gray McLaren coupe parked between the Autos, and guessed it was my father's newest vehicular obsession. He didn't care to be driven, and much preferred to drive.

"Yours?" I asked him, gesturing to it.

My mother pulled a key fob from her pocket, smiled. "Mine. He's destroyed too many vehicles."

"In fairness, you were with me for most of those incidents."

"That's why I'm driving," she said, and pressed a kiss to my cheek. "The Auto will take you to the hotel. We'll see you at the reception."

I nodded. "See you there."

Odette met us at the Auto and offered small bottles of water. Like Seri, Odette had been made a vampire by a powerful and respected Master.

"Your parents are very much in love," Seri said, when we slid into the vehicle together.

"Yeah, they are." I looked as my dad reached out, took my mother's hand. They walked together toward her car. "It's pretty disgusting," I said with a smile.

THREE

The drive from the airport to downtown Chicago was like a weird dream from childhood. I'd seen the buildings and landmarks a thousand times before, but my memories had fuzzed around the edges like feathering ink.

The city had changed as I'd grown up, as supernatural tourism and creativity pumped money into the economy. The River nymphs had become fashion designers, and they'd made their eponymous headquarters in a gleaming gold building near Merchandise Mart that was nearly as large. The fairies, whose population had boomed after an evil sorceress spread magic through the city, turned a run-down block in South Loop into an undulating park with their new home, which was more castle than mansion.

The human parts of the city had changed, too. The newest buildings were topped by living roofs of plants and trees, and were dotted with wind-power funnels. Solar panels were mounted on cars, warehouses, and billboards with the city's "Zero Waste!" motto.

But some things hadn't changed at all. Even with Autos, traffic was snarled before we reached downtown. We headed east toward Michigan Avenue, passing the spot where that evil sorceress had tried to destroy Chicago. My grandfather, Joshua Merit, had owned the building where she'd made her stand, and it had been torn apart in the battle with her. It hadn't fared any better in the second round, but the architect probably hadn't planned for a dragon attack.

Since my grandfather would have given Scrooge McDuck a run for his money, he'd tried to rebuild. But no one wanted to invest money in what had been a lightning rod for magic. So he'd pulled down the building's shell, sold the scrap, and donated the land to the city. Now there was a pretty plaza where tourists and buskers gathered when the weather was warm.

The Portman Grand was just off State, a column of pale stone, with symmetrical windows and flags flying above the entrance. A crowd of humans had gathered to watch the Autos arrive, the sidewalk crowded with people who waved their screens in the air, waiting for a glimpse of vampires.

There were Cadogan House caps sprinkled in with the usual Cubs, Sox, Hawks, and Bears gear, and a few "Welcome to Chicago" signs that made me feel better after yesterday's attack. Peace was never guaranteed, but it was good to see allies in the crowd.

They screamed my name when I climbed out of the car. My parents were the closest thing American supernaturals had to royalty. That—and my unusual biology—made the media particularly interested in me. The attention had always made me uncomfortable, not least because I hadn't done anything to deserve it. But I waved and smiled as I followed Seri toward the door, letting the bellmen handle the luggage so I could get inside faster. And I didn't fail to notice the men and women in severe black suits positioned near the door. Security personnel keeping an eye on things. I relaxed incrementally.

Inside, the hotel looked European. Cool and quietly luxurious, with gorgeous art, lush fabrics, and soft golden light that left plenty of shadows for the wealthy and famous to lounge and whisper in and remain undisturbed.

"Elisa Sullivan!"

I turned, found a man with brown skin and short, black hair in twisted whorls. He was cute, with hazel eyes and a wide, generous mouth quirked in a crooked smile. Easily four or five inches over six feet, and fit for his height. His fashion sense was also quirky, if the bow tie and Converses he'd paired with the dark gray suit were any indication. A black canvas messenger bag was situated diagonally across his chest.

"That's me," I said, and took the hand he offered.

"Theo Martin. I'm one of the Assistant Ombudsmen."

"There are Assistant Ombudsmen?"

He smiled endearingly. "There are." His gaze shifted and he smiled at Seri.

"Seraphine of Maison Dumas," I said when she reached us. "Theo Martin."

"A pleasure," she said.

Theo pulled a packet from his bag, offered it to me. "Your badges, itineraries, maps, security information."

Seri and I took them. "The other delegates from France have arrived?"

"They have," he said. "They were escorted to their rooms on the secured floors. We've stationed security at the elevators and stairs, and throughout the building."

"Thank you," I said. "Any trouble?"

"None," Theo said, and his smile dropped away. "We heard about Paris. But we've had no concerns here. Hopefully, it will stay that way. And if not"—he lifted a shoulder—"that's why we're here."

By "we," he meant the Ombudsman's office.

My parents had had plenty of adventure before peace came to Chicago; they'd battled monsters, demons, sorcerers, and elves, among others. But while they'd saved the city several times over, those adventures—and the evildoers they'd battled—had damaged city property. Just after I was born, they struck a deal with the mayor: In the future, they'd let the Ombudsman's office handle the supernatural drama. In exchange, the damages to city property would be forgiven, and the Ombudsman got a bigger office, a bigger budget, and a bigger staff.

Theo's smile was still easy, so I didn't think he meant the comment as a rebuke. Just a promise to help.

"Sure," I said with a noncommittal smile. "And thanks for the packet."

"Enjoy your room," he said. "And we'll see you at the party."

Unless I fell into the minibar first.

I distributed the room keys and badges to Seri and her entourage and saw them to their rooms. We passed a half dozen guards on the way, which made me relax a little more.

They'd given me a suite with an amazing view of Grant Park and Lake Michigan. It was styled much like the lobby, but with Chicago flair. Expensive fabrics in pale gold and deep turquoise were paired with large, stark photographs of Chicago architecture: the nautilus staircase in the Rookery Building, the stair-step silhouette of Willis Tower, the lions in front of the Art Institute.

My suitcase was waiting and already propped on a stand. I stuffed clothes into drawers and toiletries into the bath, then hung up the fancier things I didn't want to have to iron over the next few nights.

I'd traveled in jeans and layers for the inevitable chill on the plane. The reception was semiformal, but still work. And it would require something more dramatic.

I'd learned early how clothes helped make the vampire, and that had only been reinforced in Paris. I'd brought a black cocktail dress—a simple column with a hem that ended just above the knees and long, fluid sleeves—and I paired it with black stilettos. Not practical for fighting, assuming that would happen at a supernatural reception, but they were kicked off easily enough.

I left my hair down, gave myself a quick makeup check, and added blush to cheeks made extra pale by travel, and mascara to green eyes that needed a pick-me-up.

After the party, I'd come back to the room, rehydrate, and try to squeeze in a few yoga poses. I'd started doing yoga as a teenager, because the stretches made painful vampiric growth spurts a little easier to bear, and I'd kept up the practice. I liked being flexible. But, most important, I liked being in control. Yoga gave me the focus I needed to stay that way. When I focused, I wasn't Elisa-and-Monster. I simply *was*.

I decided to leave my katana in the room. But I slipped a small knife into my clutch, just in case.

A vampire couldn't be too prepared.

Vampires were the only supernaturals officially participating in the talks, but the reception was open to all of Chicago's sups. Both sets—European vampires and Chicago supernaturals—were given the chance to make their own entrance into the party, a chance to show off their particular cultures. It was our version of the Olympic opening ceremony.

A wide wooden staircase led from the hotel's opulent lobby to the second floor, where the Red Ballroom awaited its guests.

There were metal detectors and scanners at the entrance, and a coat check for jackets, wraps, bags, and supernatural weapons that weren't allowed into the ballroom. I'd gotten an exception for my knife since I was there, at least in part, to keep an eye on the Dumas vampires.

A large man with broad shoulders, a short neck, and a pug-nosed face—one of Chicago's River trolls—offered a length of pipe to the young woman who manned the coat check, gum popping and apparently unfazed as she attached a tag to the pipe and handed the troll his receipt.

"Have a good night next please," she said, the words running together in a well-practiced song.

I walked into the ballroom, which was an impressive space. The walls were painted with sweeping murals of Chicago's history, the floor covered in crimson carpet patterned with gold filigree. Strings of tiny lights reached down from the ceiling like stars within reach.

There were bars and buffet tables along one wall that smelled enticingly of meat, a string quartet on the dais at the opposite end that played a low concerto, and a long aisle between cocktail tables where the supernatural parade would make its way through the room.

"Hey, Elisa," said a voice I didn't immediately recognize.

I glanced beside me, saw only shoulders. I had to look up to see the face of the Assistant Ombudsman I'd met earlier today.

"Hey," I said with a little wave. "It's Theo, right?"

"That's me."

He still wore the dark suit and bright gingham bow tie. "I like the tie."

"Thanks. I like the dress," he said, and gestured to his own arm. "And the sleeves."

"Thanks," I said with a smile. "Did you get all the delegates checked in?"

"Every last one of them," Theo said. "They're scattered around the city, of course, in the unlikely event anyone should attack. That was a challenge, and not just because of the egos."

"Complainers?" I asked with a smile.

"You have no idea. I won't name names—*Spain*," he muttered behind a fake cough, "but one delegate was angry about the size of his three-room suite, because he'd been promised a four-room suite."

"Obviously intentional to humiliate him."

He smiled knowingly. "Exactly. Another was mad because the

mini-bar booze wasn't top-shelf, and she wasn't going to drink swill."

I walked through my mental list of the European Houses, the delegates. "Germany?" I guessed.

"Nailed it," he said.

My parents walked in, my father in a crisp tuxedo, my mother in a sleeveless black sheath that fell to mid-calf, her hair around her shoulders. They were holding hands, my father whispering something that had my mother grinning. Her response had him rolling his eyes.

"They seem well matched," Theo said.

"I think they are." I looked at him. "Are you here with someone?"

"Me? No, I'm single." He smiled, but his brow was furrowed. "I'm not really looking. Career is first for me. What about you? The media loves to speculate about Cadogan's princess."

"That's just clickbait," I said. "I'm single, too, and not really looking, either. Ditto the career thing."

"Sounds like we have a lot in common."

I had a feeling he meant exactly that. No more and no less.

I hadn't known Theo for longer than an hour, but there was something about him I liked. Something honest and unpretentious. After living with vampires for twenty-three years, that was a characteristic I could appreciate.

"Yeah," I said. "It sounds like we do."

"Good evening," my father said when they reached us, then bent to kiss my cheek. "You look lovely."

"Thank you. You look very dashing, as always." I gestured to Theo. "Theo, have you met my parents?"

"Hello, Theo," my mother said, holding out a hand. "We met at the barbecue."

"Sure, sure," Theo said, and shook hands with her, then my father.

"Barbecue?" I asked.

"Your great-grandfather's annual event," my mother said.

The downside of living in Paris was missing family events. "Did he make the red coleslaw?"

"He did," my mother said with a grin, and I sighed balefully.

Theo slanted me a look. "That was a pretty serious sigh for coleslaw. I mean, no one actually eats the coleslaw, do they? It's just for show, right?"

"You obviously didn't try the coleslaw," my mother said, clucking her tongue.

Obviously baffled, Theo looked at my father. "But . . . it's coleslaw. What am I missing?"

My father slid his hands into his pockets. "I decline the invitation to debate coleslaw again. And I strongly suggest you walk away, as well. Debating food with the Merit family is a war you cannot win."

Theo still looked baffled, but he was smiling. Which I figured was just about the correct reaction.

"The coleslaw was fantastic as always," my mother said, ending the argument. "And the Pack supplied the meat this year. It was great. You should check out the new office while you're in town. It's impressive. And Lulu's painting a mural at Little Red."

"She told me," I said.

Lulu Bell was my best friend, and the daughter of my mother's best friend, Mallory Carmichael Bell. Unlike Mallory, Lulu didn't do magic. But she did art in a big way. She'd taken classes at the Art Institute, led her high school art club, and had gotten a degree from a fancy design school on the East Coast. Now she worked as a freelance painter and illustrator; the bigger the image, the better. Little Red was the Pack's bar, situated in a corner of the city's Ukrainian Village neighborhood.

"I let her know I got here safe, and I'm going to try to get over there tomorrow," I said. "Is Uncle Malik coming tonight?" I looked around again. I'd seen two of Chicago's Masters—Morgan Greer and Scott Grey—in the crowd. But the fourth was a no-show so far.

Malik had been my father's second-in-command until he'd gotten his own House three years ago. Malik and his wife, Aaliyah, had been the only other married couple in Cadogan House while I'd lived there. My father's siblings were long gone, and we hadn't visited my mother's side of the family very often, so Malik and Aaliyah had been my family.

"Not tonight," my father said. "He took point on preparations at the theater for the session tomorrow."

"He's with Yuen and Petra," Theo said, then glanced at me. "Roger Yuen's the second-in-command at the OMB—that's what we call the office—and Petra's our tech lead."

"And you got parade duty?" my mother asked with a smile.

"I wasn't about to miss this," he said. "It's the Macy's Thanksgiving Day Parade with fangs and fur."

"And there's your tagline," my father said with a smile.

Theo frowned and squinted at something in the front of the room. He mumbled something about flags, then offered his excuses and headed through the crowd. I watched until he reached a woman adjusting the flags of the represented nations at the front of the room, then worked with her to adjust their heights so they matched perfectly.

My father glanced at me. "I don't see Seri or Marion. I presume the French delegation is marching?"

"They are. I suggested they toss croissants from baskets, but Marion declined."

My father's brows lifted in amusement. "You suggested the Master of Maison Dumas throw pastries at a crowd of delegates?"

"It was funny in context," I said, and then wondered if I'd made some sort of international faux pas. But I remembered Marion's throaty chuckle, and decided I was in the clear.

"She actually thought *pain au chocolat* would be more festive," I explained.

"I suppose they won't be parading," my mother said, and gestured toward the door.

Gabriel Keene, shifter and alpha, stood just inside the ballroom, casting a wary gaze on the formal surroundings. His leather jacket and slacks were a contrast to the finery in the room, but his outfit was fancy by shifter standards.

At his side was his wife, Tanya. He was as tall and broadshouldered as Tanya was petite and delicate. He had dark blond hair, tan skin, golden eyes. She was pale with dark hair, her eyes green but sharp in a way that belied her size.

Shifters fell between humans and vampires on the mortality spectrum, getting longer life spans than humans but not the full dose of forever. So Gabriel and Tanya hadn't aged as much as humans, or as little as vampires. Time had put soft lines at the corners of their eyes, around their smiles.

They looked around, spotted us, and headed our way. And into the space where they'd stood stepped the prince of wolves himself.

The last four years had been good to Connor Keene.

He had his father's build and his mother's coloring. His wavy hair was nearly black, and just long enough to frame his springblue eyes. He had thick brows, a strong jaw, and a dimple in his square chin. His lips were generous and smiling. His nose was straight, except for a divot on the bridge from a high school fight.

He was undeniably gorgeous, but as cocky as they came. Absolutely sure of his place in the world, because he'd decided he'd take his father's position as head of the Pack, competitors be damned. And reckless, because he was a shifter. He'd driven me crazy, like an irritating burr. And because our parents were friends, he'd been a burr at Cadogan House entirely too often.

He was taller now, his shoulders broader, and the muscle

looked good beneath gray slacks and a gray vest over a white button-down shirt, the sleeves rolled up over strong arms.

He held himself differently. There was no teenage slouch, no lanky muscle. There was confidence, power, and awareness.

This wasn't the boy who'd stolen my toy sword.

This was a man on the edge of power.

So I prepared for battle.

FOUR

Connor glanced at me, eyes appraising as he looked me over, and took my measure. Then he strode toward us and joined his parents.

"Kitten," Gabriel said to my mother. "Sullivan," to my father. And then he looked at me, smiled. "Elisa. Welcome back."

"Thank you. It's good to be home."

"I'm sure you two remember each other," Tanya said, putting a hand on Connor's forearm when he reached us.

How could I have forgotten? "Of course," I said.

"Elisa." Connor said my name slowly and deliberately, like he'd never let the word cross his lips. Which was entirely possible, since he'd usually called me "brat" because it drove me crazy. I'd usually called him "puppy" for the same reason. Maybe we were playing nice.

"How are you?" I asked.

"I'm good. I didn't know you were coming back."

I smiled. "So you didn't dress up for me?"

His eyes warmed, a corner of his mouth lifting in a smile that had destroyed plenty of hearts. "I'm not wearing a cape. Isn't that the vampire uniform?"

Or maybe we weren't playing nice. "Only if it has the high collar," I said, pointing to my neck. "You aren't wearing the uniform of your people, either. Leather and motorcycle boots, right?"

This was our script of sarcasm. Older now than the last time we'd played it out, but we still knew our parts.

"I'm so glad to see nothing changes," Gabriel muttered, giving his son the side-eye.

Unfazed, Connor tucked his hands into his pockets. "I only wear leather for the really formal events."

"We'll have to make this fancier for you next time," I said with a sugary smile.

"How were things in Paris?" Tanya asked, interrupting the byplay. "We heard about the attack near the Eiffel Tower yesterday."

"It was . . . harrowing," I said.

"You were involved?" Connor asked, brows lifted.

"The vampires attacked humans, and I was closer than many of the guards."

"She jumped down from the second level of the Eiffel Tower to join the fight," Gabriel said with a smile that held a surprising amount of wolfish approval. "I'm surprised you didn't hear about it."

"I hadn't," Connor said, and I liked the narrowed consideration in his eyes. I didn't need his approval, but I liked the idea of shaking him up.

"Here comes trouble," Gabriel said, but he looked amused at the man who walked toward us.

He was a lot of man—nearly seven inches over six feet, and all of it hard-packed muscle. His skin was tan, his hair dark brown and shagging to his shoulders, his eyes hauntingly pale blue, and they crinkled at the corners when he smiled. They were topped with eyebrows that formed almost perfect Vs above his eyes.

"Elisa Sullivan," he said, "as I live and breathe."

Riley Sixkiller was a member of the NAC Pack, and he was Lulu's ex-boyfriend. While I was limited to nighttime tutors, Lulu had gone to high school with a good number of the NAC Pack, who lived in Ukrainian Village, not far from her parents' home in Wicker Park. She and Riley had dated for nearly a year. She was the weird and artsy girl; he was the athlete. They were from very different worlds, but had been inseparable for a time.

They'd broken up because it had been too hard for her to date a supernatural. Lulu had still been wrestling with her own demons, trying to come to terms with the magic she'd decided not to use but still had to live with. Riley and I had stayed friends afterward.

I let him embrace me, and was swamped by memories from the patchouli and sandalwood that clung to his clothes. He still smelled the same.

"You've grown up," Riley said, winging up his eyebrows. "Paris was good to you."

"It didn't suck. How are you? Been keeping the Pack in line?"

Riley snorted. "They don't need me for that." He gave Connor a considering look. "He's the one with his finger on the pulse. Usually of the hottest girl in the room."

Riley wasn't wrong. I was half surprised Connor wasn't here with a date.

A gong sounded, and we looked toward the dais at the end of the ballroom. Jessamine Franklin, the city's two-term mayor, stepped up to the microphone. She was a tall and athletic woman, with dark skin and straight, dark hair that just reached her shoulders and curved around her face. Her smile was wide and bright, her eyes sharp and canny. She wore a red sheath dress with an angular bodice that zigged across her shoulders, and her signature stiletto pumps.

"Welcome," she said, casting her gaze across the room. "Welcome. And once again, welcome. Welcome to Chicago. Welcome to this celebration of the diversity of our supernatural brethren, and welcome to this opportunity.

"For the past two decades, Chicago has experienced peace between humans and supernaturals. Vampires, shifters, humans, nymphs, fairies, and more have lived side by side. They have worked side by side. They have lived and loved side by side. That was not by chance, but by design. Because Chicago's humans and supernaturals saw past their own fears and concerns and looked to the future, to the needs of their children and their children's children, in order to make a city for all of us.

"The opportunity is here. The time is now. Let us act."

She stepped back from the podium, and the room lit into applause.

"God, I love her," Theo murmured, voice soaked with adoration.

"She is an impressive woman," my father agreed, and lifted his glass to the mayor.

She left the dais, waving as she was escorted through the crowd At the edge, she shook hands with a pale man with perfectly arranged silver hair, his suit a gray of nearly the same shade, with gleaming silver cufflinks, a knotted tie of pale blue silk, and a pocket square of the same shade that was folded to a nearly deadly-looking point. He put an arm on hers and made a show of guiding her through the ballroom.

This was William Dearborn, the Ombudsman. I didn't have any particular reason to dislike him or what he'd done with my great-grandfather's office. But there was something too slick about his look, about his mannerisms, that I didn't care for. A lot of showmanship, and that made me wonder how much substance lay beneath it.

The gong sounded again and the overhead lights darkened, and colored lights danced across the runway.

The crowd gasped as a sleek black panther trotted down the aisle. It was enormous—five feet of gleaming fur over taut muscle, tail flicking as it moved sinuously toward the dais.

I pulled out my screen and pointed it, recording video as the panther stalked away. Since Seri would be in the parade, she wouldn't be able to see the other delegates, so I'd promised I'd get video.

The big cat reached the end of the runway, hopped onto the dais, and circled back to face the crowd. The spotlights flashed, the air in the room electrifying as magic began to spin around the animal, creating a funnel of power as thick as fog that sparked like lightning and sent the tingle of power through the room.

Light flared again, then faded, revealing the stunning woman who'd been a predator only moments before. Her skin was pale, her eyes wide and blue, her hair a gleaming golden fall across her shoulders. She was utterly naked, revealing a body that was both toned and curvy in all the right places.

More gasps as the woman stood proudly, aware and unfazed by her nakedness, then inclined her head. The applause was deafening, the guests impressed by the magic, the panther, or the woman it had shifted into.

She walked off the dais, where Connor waited. I hadn't even seen him slip around to the front. An assistant helped the woman slip into a silk kimono while she gave Connor a feline smile that suggested they were more than just Pack mates.

I guessed he was here with a date after all. It figured. She was exactly his type: drop-dead gorgeous and entirely aware of it. I'd seen at least a dozen of his girlfriends, and they'd all been the gorgeous and hard-partying variety. Not unexpected for shifters, given the culture had a lot in common with a 1990s hair-metal video.

"Wow," Theo murmured. "That was . . . And she is . . ."

"That's Tabby," Gabriel said. "Your first time seeing the shift?"

"Second," Theo said. "But the first time wasn't nearly so . . . beautiful."

Gabriel chuckled knowingly.

"Shifters do know how to make an entrance," my mother said, and lifted her glass to Gabriel. "Well played."

"Just a reminder of our existence," he said. "In case any of these fine, fanged people forget."

They weren't likely to forget this.

The show had started with a bang, and that was only the beginning.

The international guests came first, groups of vampires who carried the standards of their Houses and nations. Spain, Germany, Ireland, Denmark, and a dozen more, most dressed like businessmen and women in suits and heels. I gave Scotland the prize for best costume, as their male vampires wore full Highland regalia while letting their fangs show. Iceland won my prize for innovation. They all wore hand-knitted sweaters patterned with blood droplets, crescent moons, and katanas.

The French delegation wore white and carried small French flags. There were no croissants, but they wore berets that looked better on the vampires than they probably ever had on humans.

And then it was time for Chicago's supernaturals. The River troll who'd stowed his pipe brought his enormous friends, and they walked down the aisle with a heavy, loping stride. They were followed by the River nymphs, small and voluptuous women with flowing hair, who used the aisle like a catwalk in their snug and tiny dresses.

Words turned to whispers as the ballroom doors opened again and the fairies made their entrance.

Claudia, their leader, looked very much the part of a fairy queen. Pale skin and wavy, strawberry blond hair; a body that was tall and lush and curvy. She wore a straight, sleeveless gown the color of candlelight and nearly translucent. Over it was a wide neckpiece of hammered bronze and gleaming cabochon jewels. Her dress was jeweled, too, with arcs of sapphire and citron and quartz that glittered in the spotlights. Her hair was knotted in complicated braids that spilled across her shoulders. Her magic was old, the cold vibration of power more like a slow, thick undulation.

I didn't know her companion—a tall fairy with dark, straight hair that reached his shoulders. His face was slender, his chin square, and his brows thick above dark eyes. There was something young and yet severe about his face. Or maybe it was the hard look in his eyes.

His body was lean and fit. He'd skipped the tuxedo, instead opting for a long, ivory tunic that draped past his hips, in the same candlelight tone as Claudia's and dotted with the same jewels, if less ornately than hers. So he was here to complement her, not compete. Her consort, not her king. She was to be the queen and the showstopper. He looked perfectly happy about the arrangement.

They murmured as they strode down the runway, heads held high, as if oblivious to everyone else in the room. Behind them strode a dozen of the fairies who'd once guarded Cadogan House, at least until they'd betrayed my father, turning their weapons against us because Claudia had changed her mind. They also wore tunics tonight instead of their usual black fatigues.

There'd once been thousands of fairies in England, Scotland, Ireland, and Wales. At least until humans exterminated some and extradited the rest. The fairies who'd survived the transition had lived together in a magicked tower in Chicago's Potter Park, which had insulated them from time, as fairies weren't immortal, and from the distance from their homeland. But the protective magic had diminished with time, so much that Claudia could barely leave her tower.

At least until Sorcha had inadvertently given the fairies a much-needed jolt.

Sorcha was the evil sorceress who destroyed my grandfather's building. She was a beautiful and wealthy woman who'd hidden her magic and then used it to make a bid to take over the city. Her first defeat at Towerline created a lot of powerful emotions in Chicago. Unwilling to accept her defeat, she figured out how to gather up those emotions, spark that collection with magic, and create a new being.

That creature was the Egregore. Then she'd made the Egregore physically manifest, putting it into the form of a dragon that my parents later defeated. Using a spell created by Lulu's mother, the Egregore's magic was bound into my mother's sword, the power imprisoned in the blade. The spell inadvertently bound me, then only a tiny nub of life, to my mother.

Sorcha's alchemy had been complicated, and one of its side effects was a wash of magic over the city while she gathered up all those emotions. Sups who were already healthy, like vampires and shifters, noticed the magic but hadn't been physically affected by it. But it had given fairies an obvious boost. They looked younger and stronger, they'd been able to have children, and they'd become more public because they had the strength to leave the tower. They'd abandoned their narrow tower for a home they'd built along the Chicago River, an enormous stone building modeled after England's Bodiam Castle.

I'd even seen Claudia naked and strategically positioned on the cover of *Vogue*. But they looked older now, too, as if the last few years had done damage. Maybe they were beginning to age again, or maybe the cover shot had been airbrushed and we were seeing the fairies tonight in their true and honest skin.

I was watching Claudia when her companion turned his head and met my gaze.

Magic rose, cold and heavy as iron. Magic that pulled and enticed, because that was the nature of fairy power, the reason why fairy tales always mentioned hapless villagers being lured away into the woods or across the moors. Fairies had drawn them near.

But for all that power, I had the distinct impression he wasn't looking at me, but through me—as if he could see past skin and bone and vampire to the magic that lurked there. I didn't want anyone, much less an enemy of Cadogan House, seeing that.

There was a sharp burst of magic—a slice of power—and the man's gaze slid back to the runway in front of him. Claudia, I guessed, hadn't liked his dawdling, and she'd snapped him back into line. And then they continued down the runway and disappeared into the crowd.

"Do you know them?" I asked Theo when they were gone and the magic had dissipated. "The fairies?"

Theo shook his head. "I've seen them at events, but haven't talked to them. They tend to stick with other fairies. Whatever her hierarchy, and you can bet she has one, humans aren't even close to the top. They're fascinating, though, aren't they? It's easy to understand how people were lost to the green land."

The green land was the fairies' ancestral home.

"Yeah," I said, and crossed my arms, still feeling the chill from the fairies' magic. And not sad they'd moved away.

My grandparents were wealthy socialites. My parents were diplomatic and well connected. Because of that, I'd been to plenty of parties over the years, and I usually enjoyed them. I liked the food, the chatting, the people-watching. But it had been a long night. Jet lag was giving me a headache, and my brain was getting logy. I watched Seri and Marion for some sign that they were slowing down, and hoped the party wouldn't go until dawn.

One more glass of golden champagne and I'd slump a little too far toward relaxed, so I switched to caffeine. There was a lonely silver tureen on a buffet table along the wall, so I flipped the spout and let coffee spill into a paper cup, added a splash of milk and sugar.

And I turned to find Claudia's companion standing beside me. I barely managed not to jerk and spill scalding liquid across my hand.

He stood, tall and lean, in a puddle of magic that spilled around our feet like fog, invisible but tangible.

"I am Ruadan."

"Elisa," I said.

"You are interesting," he said. "Unique among vampires."

"Not so interesting."

"Oh, I would disagree. You are the first bloodletter born of blood, not merely transformed by it. The first bloodletter who was never human."

Calling us bloodletters was derogatory, but not a surprise. It was the term that fairies used to describe vampires. And if a human had said I'd never been human, they'd likely have meant it as an insult. But his voice held curiosity and interest.

"I'm a vampire," I confirmed.

He looked me over again, and again I didn't care for the feeling.

"And you're Claudia's companion?" I asked, voice flat.

"We do not subscribe to human notions of romantic companionship. I am her consort, if she wills it."

I had the sense he didn't want to discuss it. Nevertheless, I persisted. "And does she will it?"

"I am honored to have been chosen for several cycles." His eyes flashed. "But that does not concern you, bloodletter."

"And what does concern me? You sought me out."

"I am curious about your biology. About how you managed to cling to this plane when all others before you failed."

I presumed he meant the fact that I'd been born, which hadn't been up to me. But most people didn't know the entire story—how my mother's biology had been enhanced by a binding spell created by Lulu's mother, Mallory.

My parents had explained it to me when I'd been old enough to wonder why I didn't have any other vampire children to play with. For everyone else, there was speculation—that I was an adopted human, or played by a very well-paid actress, or part of a vampire-medical conspiracy to create a new race of superbeings. A fang in every bassinet. Which would have been nice, because I'd have had more kids to play with.

"It wasn't up to me," I said, not interested in sharing the details with a stranger.

Ruadan didn't look convinced by the answer. "We were both of us born in an Age of Magic."

"Were we?"

"We made ourselves."

Now I was just lost.

"*Ruadan.*"

The word was sharp, a warning delivered by someone behind me.

I glanced back and found Riley, arms crossed and brows lifted, a flat expression on his face for the fairy.

"What do you want?" Ruadan asked through clenched teeth, disgust plain in his eyes. He did not like shifters.

"I need to speak with Ms. Sullivan," Riley said.

Ruadan's mouth thinned into a line, but he maintained control, inclined his head, then looked at me. "Bloodletter," he said, the word like a vicious promise, then strode away.

"That guy is creepy as fuck," Riley said quietly when he was gone.

"He's a weird one," I agreed.

"What's his deal?"

"He asked me about being born. As a vampire, I mean."

"He looking to date a vampire? I thought he was with Claudia."

"So did I. Which made it weirder." I smiled up at him. "Thanks for the interruption."

"You're welcome. I'd never say you needed rescuing, but figured I could do you a solid. I owe you one since I never made it to Paris to visit."

"You owe me a big one," I said with a grin. "I accept Leo's gift cards and Auto credits."

He patted down his suit. "I don't have either of those." He reached into his pocket, pulled out an old-fashioned butterscotch candy, offered it. "I don't know how long this has been in there, but you can have it."

"I'm not even a little bit tempted."

"Yeah, that's probably a good call." He grinned. "This is a borrowed suit."

I narrowed my gaze at him. "Were you going to tell me that before or after I ate it?"

His smile was slow and lazy. "Probably after." After a careful glance around, he dropped the candy into potted plant.

"Typical Riley."

"I play to type. You gonna be in town long enough to get in a game night?"

I grinned. "I don't know about my schedule, but I wouldn't mind taking a little of your money."

He winked. "Then it's done. And it'll irritate Connor, so that's a bonus."

I patted his arm. "Find your joy, Riley. Find your joy."

"It was a beautiful party," Seri said, strappy sandals dangling from a finger, a champagne flute in her other hand, as we rode the elevator back to the top of the Portman Grand.

I'd seen Marion up to her room an hour ago, after asking Theo to keep an eye on Seri, and was glad for the break. There'd been a lot of supernaturals crammed into the ballroom, a lot of magic swimming around, and the effect was dizzying. It was like a crowded party with too much perfume—except the perfumes were all deadly. And then there was Ruadan, who hadn't confronted me again, but whom I'd stayed uncomfortably aware of.

But considering the excellent champagne, meeting a new friend in Theo, and catching up with my family, all in all it had been a pretty good party.

"Chicago cleans up well," I agreed. "And nobody punched anyone."

Seri snorted, then covered her mouth delicately. "I believe I may be a little too relaxed."

"Jet lag and champagne," I said as the elevator came to a smooth stop, "are a powerful combination."

"*Oui,*" she said, and we stepped onto her floor. She hummed "La Vie en Rose" as we walked toward her door, then made a grand bow.

"Breakfast," she said, unlocking the door with her thumbprint. "Marion would like to speak to us at dusk, before the session begins."

Tomorrow was only a partial night of talks—a three-hour session to allow for opening statements and the beginning of discussions. Long enough to get people talking, but not so long that the frustrations they'd brought with them would boil over. They'd get to business in the second session, working with the host vampires and others from around the world to come up with a plan forward. Hopefully.

My parents were hosting an event at Cadogan House after the first session, another party intended to keep the atmosphere social and productive. And there'd almost certainly be great food and more champagne. I was going to have to pace myself.

"Sure," I said. "I'll be here at dusk."

"*Bonne nuit,*" she said, and closed the door again.

I walked back to my room, sending Lulu another message as I traversed the wide hallway: DAY 1 COMPLETE. TIME TO TALK TOMORROW?

Her answer was nearly instantaneous: GIRL YES. COME TO LITTLE RED!!!

I promised I would, then fell into bed without another thought.

FIVE

When the sun set again, I dressed in a black suit, added heeled boots and my katana, and headed down to Marion's room for breakfast.

Her suite was practically a palace. The living room was enormous and faced the river, with boxy leather couches that didn't interrupt the view. One wall was a window over Chicago, the city's lights piercing through the darkness like pinpricks. It looked magical. But darkness covered a lot of flaws. *That is,* I thought, *one of the reasons why vampires tend to be overly focused on politics and strategy.* It was easy to ignore the problems of the communities humans had built when we literally didn't see them.

I was vetted by the guards who flanked the door, which Seri opened when they allowed me to knock.

"Good evening," she said, looking perfect in a sheath dress with an angular neck and heeled boots. "Thanks for sending me the video. I haven't yet watched it, but look forward to it."

She gestured to the dining room table that stretched across another bank of windows in the adjoining room. The table was decked with platters of pastries and pitchers of blood, and the scent of bacon filled the air.

"Marion has assembled a feast for us," she said.

"Looks like it."

"Good evening, Elisa." Marion moved closer from the bank of windows, and offered a hand. Her skin was dark, her hair cropped into short curls, her eyes piercingly intelligent. Tonight she wore a simply cut black suit with block heels, and pearls dotted her ears.

Magic followed as she moved, putting a cinnamon-sharp bite into the air. It tangled with the magic of apprehensive vampires, gave it a bright but comforting edge.

"Good evening, Marion."

"You look very competent today." From any other vampire, that might have been an insult. But Marion wasn't one for sarcasm. She was a straightforward woman who appreciated critical thinking and a strong work ethic, and she was well-loved and respected by her vampires.

"Thank you. Any news from Paris?"

"The day passed peacefully, and I am grateful. Given the Masters who create the violence are here in the city of your birth, I hope we have not passed our problems on to you."

"I hope so, too. But even if so, Chicago is skilled at handling ornery supernaturals."

A corner of her mouth lifted into a careful and conservative smile. "So it seems." She gestured to the dining room. "Shall we break our fast?"

Odette and the rest of the vampires were already in the large dining room, sipping coffee at the table or putting plump fruit onto trays.

I took a croissant and poured myself some coffee, added cream and sugar, and took a seat beside Seri. When all the vampires had assembled their breakfasts, Marion tapped her water glass. The vampires turned their heads toward her in syncopation, like birds changing direction.

"Good evening," she said, when she had their attention. Her voice was soft and smoky, like a torch singer from another era. "I wanted us to have an opportunity to commune before the event."

She looked at us, then at the city silhouetted through the window, the blinking top of the Willis Tower, shining red for the occasion.

"Much trouble has been made to assemble us here. Cost. Time. Compromise. But we are an old people, and we are stubborn. We fear change, and we fear those different from us, even as we seek to live among them.

"But there is opportunity here." She looked at me, nodded approvingly. "There is a chance to make a new way in Paris, in France, in Europe, in the world—to find the same peace that they've found in Chicago. There is a chance for cooperation—if we can move past our own self-interest, our own prejudices. So, let us take a moment of silence to prepare ourselves for negotiation and debate and finding the path forward."

She nodded, and a hush fell across the room.

And in that quiet, hope rose.

The Sanford had been a theater with baroque style—vaulted ceilings, a golden dome, murals, and velvet drapes. It fell into disrepair, and was later saved by a very smart woman who realized that even if Chicago didn't need another theater, there were never enough wedding venues. She stripped out the chairs and the middle balconies, cleaned up the paint and gilt, and turned the main floor into the city's grandest ballroom.

Tonight, crystal chandeliers put a golden glow across the room, which was swagged with the banners of each vampire House participating in the talks. Tables had been politically arranged on the main floor, with a long, oval table in the middle, each seat marked with a placard. Behind it, another U of tables had been lifted by risers, so the delegates seated there had a clear view of the proceedings—or because those in the back row had complained their seats weren't good enough.

The energy in the air was enough to ramp up my adrenaline.

This was an important night. We'd gone through two security checks to get into the building, and the theater itself also had security. Guards stood at intervals along the wall—some who'd been brought by the delegates as security or escorts, and others who'd volunteered from Chicago's Houses and the Pack.

Dearborn wasn't here tonight, probably because there wasn't a photo opportunity. Cameras weren't allowed inside, and the mayor wouldn't attend the talks, so he'd probably moved on to greener pastures.

I didn't recognize many of the vampires or shifters, but found Connor on the opposite side of the room. He wore a black suit tonight that was perfectly cut to showcase his broad shoulders, narrow waist. Connor and I might not have had much in common, but I could admit he cut a powerful figure.

It was the first time I'd seen him looking so serious and focused. While his posture said he was relaxed—shoulders back, hands in his pockets—there was no mistaking the careful attention in his eyes as his gaze slowly slid across the room, back and forth, looking for threats.

He had grown up, and I was having trouble reconciling that with the cocky child who'd stolen my toy sword.

Connor's gaze lifted, met mine, and held. And there was as much power in the look as there was in his physical presence. There was strength in his gaze, like it had its own mass, its own weight. It was intense to be stared at with eyes so blazingly blue.

I wasn't used to a look from Connor having that much impact.

But before I could think too much about it, magic began to beat like a drum, like the warning of an army miles away. Except the pounding was in my chest—and it was growing louder.

The monster was reaching out again, and I understood immediately why it had awakened. Why it had stretched. This time, it wasn't for the city, but for the blade.

For my mother's katana.

She stood across the room in a dark suit, a white shirt beneath, her crimson scabbard belted to her waist.

I hadn't even considered that my mother would bring the sword here tonight. But of course she would. She'd be acting as host, along with my father. And as Sentinel, on behalf of his House.

My heart began to hammer in my chest. Not in fear, but in anticipation. In dread.

Her sword held the Egregore, the creature Sorcha had cobbled together from alchemy and the cast-off emotions of Chicago's citizens. When Sorcha manifested the creature into a dragon, my mother had the responsibility of bringing it down. Mallory had created the spell to bind the Egregore to my mother's sword, to confine the magic again. But the spell worked better than anyone had intended; it bound me to my mother. . . . And that wasn't the only thing.

I didn't know the monster existed until I'd become a teenager, until I was old enough to feel magic, to recognize the urge that was coming from inside me. I'd feared I was crazy, until the first time I'd walked into the House's armory.

I'd gone in with the other sups homeschooled at Cadogan to learn about weaponry, and the pounding had begun the second the armory door had been opened.

Her sword had spent most of the past twenty years hanging there, in part because of what it held, in part because she didn't carry it anymore. Chicago had been mostly peaceful, at least as far as sups were concerned. She'd taken a hiatus as Sentinel while I was young, and vampires had agreed not to carry visible weapons in public.

I'd moved toward the katana, and I'd felt the pull down to my bones.

That was the first time I realized that I wasn't crazy, that the monster was something other. I didn't know then or now exactly what it was—some fragment of the Egregore, or some new thing created by the binding magic—only that it yearned to be free from me, to be united with the magic in the sword.

And because I wouldn't let that happen, it was furious. That's why my anger often awakened the monster. Because it understood the feeling.

I'd made my mother and Lulu's tell me the story of the dragon over and over again, trying to ferret out some detail that would confirm whether I was right. I hadn't found that detail, and I still didn't know for sure. And I couldn't tell either one of them— couldn't bring myself to confess that Mallory's magic had hurt me and made me hurt others.

No one else, I promised. I was responsible for its behavior, and I would damn well *be* responsible.

Pushing through the mental haze of magic, I moved through the room to the double doors on the other end, slipped into the women's lounge. There were two walls of mirrored counters and stools, and no women in sight.

I moved to the closest mirror. My irises had shifted from green to silver, as happened to all vampires when their emotions were high. But along the edge, like the corona of an eclipsed star, was a thin line of gleaming crimson growing wider with each heartbeat. If I didn't take control, the red would bleed farther until my eyes gleamed like rubies. And there'd be no hiding that.

I was jet-lagged and tired, and the monster had sensed the weakness. So I made myself focus. Made myself bear down against it. I closed my eyes, slowed my breathing again, and counted to a hundred, and then again, until I could feel it recede.

When I opened my eyes, they were green again.

They were going to stay that way.

* * *

After the usual introductions and well-wishing, the first session of talks began with the airing of grievances, like an obscene vampire Festivus.

The European Masters were allotted four minutes apiece to introduce themselves and their House, and identify their singular goal for the discussions. Some spoke of peace. But most, being old and powerful vampires, spoke of power and recognition. They wanted to be part of the new order, whatever that might be.

"We were excluded from the Greenwich Presidium," the Master of the only Sicilian House said through his translator. "We demand a voice in the new regime."

The demand set off murmurs and whispers and a few outright rebuttals.

"Your House is the newest!" said one of the German delegates. "The Houses with longer tenures should have more power."

"Delegates."

My father pushed power into the word, and although it took a moment for the sound to spiral into silence, it was the only word he'd needed to speak.

"I would remind you that we are here to explore peace. We are here to speak our respective truths and listen to the truths of our neighbors. Respect is elemental, crucial, and mandatory." He turned his intense emerald gaze on every vampire in the audience. "If we do not start from that common thread, there can be little hope of progress."

There were more mumbles in the crowd, and his eyes went hard and cold. My father was a loving and patient man. But he did not tolerate idiocy.

"To those of who you believe progress is less important than your own self-interest, let me remind you what happened to the Greenwich Presidium. Self-interest does not serve the long-term interests of any House. Either you work together, as we have done in Chicago, or you fall together. And if you fall together, you will lose allies. You will lose coffers. You will lose reputation. . . . And you will lose lives."

He let those words echo through the room, and when silence settled again, he nodded.

My father had power and respect, and those words were likely enough for every vampire in the room.

But they weren't enough for the intruders.

I heard them before I saw them, the whistle that cut through the air. And then they swarmed into the ballroom, an army on the attack.

Fairies.

No longer in tunics, but black fatigues. Their hair, long and dark and severe, pulled back over sharp cheekbones and wide eyes.

As vampires rose to object and guards stepped forward with katanas drawn, they made a river of black around the edges of the room, a barrier between the vampires and the rest of the world.

My first thought was for the guards—vampire and human—who'd been engaged to protect the floor below. They'd been prepared for violence, could have combatted it. I hoped they'd succumbed only to magic and hadn't lost their lives to the supernatural ego.

With the vampires contained, this particular supernatural ego stepped inside. Her hair was down, waving locks that spilled across her shoulders. Her dress was white and gauzy, carefully embroidered with thread that glinted gold in the chandelier light. And in her eyes was fury that flamed as brightly as her hair, her magic sending the scent of salt spray and fresh grass into the air.

Ruadan stepped into the room behind her, also in his finery. Not a soldier, but a king. Or as close as he seemed likely to get with Claudia in power.

Some of the delegates looked afraid or confused. Others looked amused, as if this were part of some elaborate entertainment prepared for their benefit.

Chicago's Masters rose from their seats. They knew better.

My parents both looked back at me; the instinct to protect their child. I nodded, tapped the handle of my sword to signal I was fine, and was glad they couldn't hear the pounding of my heart. My fear didn't matter.

Neither looked entirely convinced I was safe—but, then again, none of us were at the moment—so they gave their attention back to the threat.

My father shifted his gaze to Claudia as the other vampires looked at him, still trying to figure out what was happening and what they should be doing about it.

"Claudia," he said. And in that word was an angry punch of power that rippled through the room like a wave.

My heart pounded with concern for him, for the risk he was taking, even though I knew he and my mother could handle themselves. I'd never seen them face down an army before—those days had been gone before I was born—and I didn't enjoy it now.

But there was something more dangerous yet. With each drip of adrenaline into my bloodstream, magic began to drum again, eager to join in the fight.

"Bloodletter." Her voice was hard, the word and tone an insult. "We are here to demand an end to this disrespect."

My father's expression showed no fear. He would show no deference to her. "What disrespect have you been shown?" He glanced around at the delegates, some of whom were showing their fangs, their eyes silvered with emotion. "How is a discussion about peace among vampires a threat to you?"

Lip curled, she looked around the room. "You gather your allies here to discuss revolution, to discuss that which bloodletters seek as much as they seek blood. Power over others."

She offered Ruadan a knowing smile, and he nodded back, eyes narrowed with satisfaction.

My father lifted an eyebrow. "That is incorrect. We are here to lay the foundation to end violence among the Houses of Europe. To discuss the peace we've found—or *had* found—in Chicago. Peace that you appear to be breaching, Claudia."

Claudia was either too egotistical to care that she'd angered him or oblivious to it.

"Then why were we invited to your party, but not to these serious discussions? It is insulting. And does it not prove you seek to hide your purpose from those who would bring it into light?"

"As the invitation explained," my father said, voice flat, "the reception was to celebrate our peace. The discussions pertain to European Houses, and, as far as I'm aware, fairies have no quarrel with the Houses in Europe. Do I misunderstand? Do you have grievances to air against Dumas? Against Solignac?"

For a moment, Claudia looked unsettled—and maybe a little confused—by the question.

"You are planning revolution," she said, her words as uncertain as her expression.

"We are not. If you have been informed otherwise, you have been misled."

"Wait." A vampire from Catalonia stood, a man with short, dark hair, tan skin, and suspicious eyes. "There is something suspicious here—shapeshifters in a room of vampires. If these discussions do not pertain to other species, why are they here?"

"Because they volunteered to provide security for this endeavor," my father said. "And I'd note they are showing substantially more grace than you about that fact."

This must have been Tomas Cordona, the Master of Casa Cordona. His House was one of the most conservative on the political spectrum, and generally believed sups shouldn't mix. The reception and shifters' presence was probably a challenge to that nonsense, which was likely one of the reasons the Chicago Houses had arranged it that way.

Tomas shook his head, pointed at my father. "Deny that you've sought to strengthen your position, to consolidate the power of the vampires in this city, or that you're content to share power with shapeshifters." He leveled a menacing gaze at Gabriel. "We do not believe in such things."

Gabriel's expression was cool and unruffled. There was no insult there, at least not that I could see, but a mild disdain that he'd probably showed to vampires before.

"Tomas, you are insulting your hosts," Marion said, disapproval clear in her eyes. "That is not befitting a vampire."

Tomas snorted. "You are plainly on the side of Cadogan, because you shelter its Master's child." He fixed his gaze on me, which lit a fire in my father's eyes.

"I would warn you, Tomas, to leave my family out of your raging. You were invited here today to seek peace. If you will act like a child, we would be happy to treat you like one." He looked around the room, magic lifting in the air. "There is no conspiracy. There is no revolution. There is no attempt to consolidate power. There is only an effort to help our brothers and sisters in Europe find a way to peace."

Silence fell and magic kindled, breaths bated for his next move.

My father looked at Claudia. "These talks do not pertain to the activities of fairies in Europe, nor to any supernaturals in Chicago. But if you wish to observe, to offer your expertise, it would be rude and injudicious of us to decline it. You may, if you wish, join us tonight as our guests."

I bit back a smile. My father was very good. Make the fairies an offer they couldn't decline without losing face—and one the vampires in the room couldn't complain about without looking foolish and ungracious.

"We will join you," Claudia said, chin lifted. "And we will see what trouble you seek."

Two chairs were located and placed in the empty gap in the outer ring of chairs, while my father sent vampires to check on the guards the fairies had managed to get past.

The chairs weren't fancy—armchairs probably borrowed from one of the hotel rooms. But Claudia and Ruadan seated themselves like royalty, her hand over his atop the rolled arm of her seat.

Unfortunately, the fairies' seating was the only problem solved during the first abbreviated night of talks. While most of the vampires agreed some kind of governing body was necessary, they couldn't agree on how that body would be formed, or how voting rights would be allocated. The oldest Houses argued they were the wisest, the most experienced, so their votes should carry more weight. Newer Houses with more money argued they had more value to society, so their votes should carry more weight. And everyone in between feared being swallowed by the larger fish.

Blood and food were offered an hour into the meeting. The fairies remained in their chairs—and well guarded—while the vampires partook. But the refreshment didn't make the second half of the session any more productive.

They'd barely gotten discussions started again when the Houses derailed them by arguing about how they'd contribute to paying the council's expenses when they were in session, and where they'd meet.

The European vampires faced some of the same questions America's founders had faced more than two hundred years ago, except that the vampires had centuries more ego and arrogance behind them.

We adjourned with little accomplished beyond identifying the real problem: how to get dozens of vampire Houses to sacrifice in order to come up with a plan that benefitted them all.

The fairies were escorted out first, and the room itself seemed to exhale with relief when they were gone. The shifters also disappeared quickly, and I couldn't blame them. They hadn't exactly gotten a warm welcome from the European Houses.

I spoke with Marion, agreed to talk to my parents about the path forward while she returned to the hotel, where the odds of a fairy attack seemed lower. And then I walked into the plush antechamber beside the ballroom to wait for their arrival.

I was checking the news on my screen when the door opened and my parents came in, followed by Theo and a tall, lean man with medium-brown skin, dark hair, and dark, somber eyes.

"Elisa," my father said, "this is Roger Yuen, the Associate Ombudsman."

We shook hands. "It is good to meet you, Elisa. Your great-grandfather is a good man."

"We think so," I agreed, then looked at my parents. "How are the guards?"

"Magicked," he said, and ran a hand through his hair. "We hadn't even considered the possibility magic—other than glamour—would be used as a weapon."

Glamour was the vampires' innate magic, the ability to lure humans and lower their inhibitions when it suited our purposes.

"So many hours of work," my father said, sounding uncharacteristically dejected, "with very little to show for it."

"It was unlikely the first round would result in a treaty," Yuen said kindly. "Perhaps now that the bad blood has been aired, so to speak, the real negotiations can begin."

"And we did avoid an apparent fairy revolution," my mother said, perching on the arm of my father's chair. "That's twice in two days we've seen Claudia in her finery."

"I could have done without the second," my father said, and looked at Yuen. "Thoughts?"

"She wants to be seen as powerful," Yuen said. "In control, and an important part of the city's leadership."

"Quite a change from their previous attitude," my father said dryly.

"Why would the fairies believe the talks were some kind of conspiracy?" I wondered.

"Claudia is unstable," my mother said. "She has been for a very long time."

"But why the sudden interruption?" Yuen asked.

"There hasn't been a gathering of vampires this large in many, many years," my father said. "Perhaps the fairies saw it as a threat."

My mother frowned. "But why not say something during the planning phase, or attack during the reception, or attempt to prevent the meeting in the first place?"

My father nodded. "The fairies have always been self-centered, but this was unusually specific. Like they'd only figured out our villainous plan tonight."

"Perhaps the scale of the issue is larger," Yuen said. "Their magic is fading again." He glanced at me. "You know about Sorcha? The Egregore?"

The word thrummed through me like a plucked string on a cello.

"I know," I managed, squeezing the words through tight lungs.

"Two decades have passed since magic was spilled over the city," Yuen said, "and it has largely dispersed. Chicago is nearly at level again, from a magical standpoint. Concern that they'll fade away again may have triggered their sudden interest—and the fear they'll be pushed aside by vampires."

"What about Ruadan?" I asked.

"We don't know much about him," Yuen said. "From what we understand, he's twenty-two or twenty-three, born after Sorcha's attack. There were several dozen fairies born in that timeframe, and we believe this was the first time fairies conceived children in the United States."

"How old is Claudia?" I asked, thinking of Ruadan's interest in her, romantic or otherwise.

"Older than me," my father said with a glint in his eye, reminding me that he had been nearly four hundred and my mother twenty-eight when they'd gotten together. I didn't want to think too closely about that.

"She looked older tonight than I'd seen her before," I said. "Worn around the edges."

"I thought so, too," my mother agreed. "Not by a lot, but noticeably."

Yuen looked at my father. "What is next, do you think?"

My father rubbed his temples. "I don't know. They seemed satisfied by what we offered today, and that was little enough. If they believe we're engaged in some sort of fanged conspiracy, I don't know what we could really do to appease them."

"They'll want seats again tomorrow," Yuen said, and my father rolled his eyes.

"I'm sure you're right. I'm inclined to let them in again to maintain the peace, but that's not helping the negotiations."

"And tonight?" Yuen asked.

I'd nearly forgotten: Cadogan House was hosting a party for the delegates. It would be fancy, since that was my father's style. And there would be food and music, since that was my mother's. Question was, Would there also be violence?

"We could cancel," my mother said, glancing at my father, but he shook his head.

"We won't be cowed by violence, threatened or perceived. That wouldn't serve Chicago or the purpose of these talks. We'll increase security. And make everyone aware that the fairies aren't above using magic to get their way." He looked at Yuen. "I'll be communicating with Kelley and the rest of my team as soon as we leave here."

Kelley was the head of Cadogan's guards.

Yuen nodded. "Very well. Then I'll leave you to your preparations, and get a report to Dearborn."

"He's going to be angry," my father said, but looked more amused by the possibility than disturbed. "He won't care that his promotional opportunity has gone south."

Yuen smiled. "We know who did the actual work in arranging this particular opportunity. But if the result is good, he won't care much about the details of how that came to be."

My father smiled, appreciating his dry tone. "You have a solid sense of him."

"I am well aware that part of my job is managing Dearborn's expectations," Yuen said. "And for all our sakes, I hope the result is good."

SIX

We had three hours until the Cadogan party, and I wasn't needed until it was time to escort the French delegation to my parents' House in Hyde Park.

I was trying not to think of the magic that awaited me, so I confirmed Lulu was still where she said she'd be, and took an Auto to Ukrainian Village.

The neighborhood on the west side where Slavs, Poles, and then Ukrainians had settled had a lot of town houses, plenty of dives, and several gorgeous churches. It was also home to Little Red, the Pack's Chicago headquarters.

When the Auto stopped, I found nothing left of the bar I'd seen four years ago: the scrubby little brick building that had squatted on the corner, a plate glass window in front so the Pack could keep an eye on the street. It had been replaced by a three-story building marked by horizontal stripes of steel and tinted glass. It hadn't occurred to me to ask Lulu if the Pack had moved, relocated to some other part of the city. The change was disorienting, and I turned a circle on the sidewalk to get my bearings . . . and caught the scent of roasting meat in the air.

Curious, I looked back at the new building, caught the tidy red inscription in the front door, also metal. "NAC Industries."

"I guess they upgraded," I said, and walked to the door and pulled it open.

The smell was even stronger here. Sweet and sharp and smoky, with a spicy kick. And behind it, the faint smell of fur and animal, and the vibration of powerful magic.

"Close door! You are letting out air."

The voice was rough, but one hundred percent recognizable. She rolled up to me in a red motorized scooter. Her hair was still dyed blond, her body a sturdy box on stick legs, her face lined with a few more wrinkles. But her eyes were still clear and suspicious, and her magic put a spice in the air that nearly overpowered the scent of food.

Her gaze narrowed. "You look familiar. I remember a little girl who came in here with her parents. Brat," she added with a sly smile. "And then a young woman. And then, poof, gone."

"Hello, Berna. It's been a long time."

Berna was one of the matriarchs of the NAC Pack, and Connor's great-aunt. Her particular corner of the Pack was from the Ukraine.

She clucked her tongue. "For years, you have not come by."

"I was out of the country."

"You have not seen our new building."

"I didn't even recognize it. It's so"—I looked up at the glass and steel atrium, and the mobile of metal parts that swung above our heads—"different."

"Modern," she said, lip curled like the word itself tasted sour. "Is not my style. But humans, they like." Her eyes narrowed, and her smile went sly as a fox's. "And they spend money."

"So I see. Smells like the barbecue business is doing well."

"Not just barbecue!" Before I could ask what she meant, she zipped her scooter around and headed down a hallway.

Deciding I'd better follow or be left behind, I hurried to catch up.

The floor here was shiny concrete, and the smell of fresh paint still tinted the air. But it wasn't strong enough to beat back the scent of food. And I hoped some of it was destined for the Cadogan House party.

"The kitchen," she said, pointing to a door. "Restaurant over there, bar over there."

"Over there" was behind what I thought was the same tufted red leather door that had hung at the old bar.

"Is still the Pack's place. For now," she added, her tone and narrowed eyes adding an ominous edge.

"For now?"

"Pack has been in Chicago for a long time. We are not as strong when we do not recharge. Some of us will return, be part of the woods and the air and the water. Join with the earth. And we will be stronger again."

"Only some of you?"

"We have business here," she said. "Industry. Many have started families, live as humans. But the Pack must be strong. So there must be a reconnection. A rekindling. That magic will be shared among us, and we will be whole again."

"Then I hope the Pack finds what it needs," I said with a smile. "I'm here to see Lulu," I added, before I ended up on another leg of the tour.

"She's in back, working." Her gaze narrowed again. "You will interrupt her?"

"No. I will just say hello."

There was an aching silence while Berna probably evaluated whether I was going to cost the Pack time or money. Then she nodded toward the far door. "Through there. She is working on the wall."

I left before she could change her mind.

I always forgot how small she was.

Lulu Bell was just over five feet tall, with a slender build and a thick bob of dark hair that scooped at an angle around her face, and that she was forever flipping out of the way.

She wore a sleeveless top in dark gray over calf-length leggings, and flats with toes so pointy they could probably be used as weapons.

She stood in front of an enormous wall—twenty feet long and at least fifteen feet high. Half the wall was filled in—streaks of wild color dancing around curvy female shapes. The other half was still what I thought was the base coat of paint, where light pencil marks created shapes that hadn't yet been filled in with color.

With a yellow pencil, she drew another waving line across the unpainted portion of the wall. "Thanks, but I don't need any more coffee, Berna," she said without looking back.

"Good," I said. "Because I didn't bring any."

Lulu glanced back, hair falling over her right eye. Her skin was pale, her eyes pale green in a heart-shaped face. Her lips were a perfect cupid's bow, and there was stubbornness in the set of her chin.

For a second she just stared at me, as if trying to reconcile the fact that I wasn't Berna. And then her scream cut through the air like a knife. She dropped the pencil, ran toward me, and jumped into my arms.

"Lis! You're here!" she said, wrapping her legs around my waist like a toddler.

I put my arms beneath her and tried to keep both of us upright. "You might be tiny," I grunted, "but you're way too heavy for this."

Even this close, I couldn't detect a hint of the magic I knew she carried as the daughter of two powerful sorcerers. Her parents had embraced their magic; Lulu was a teetotaler. I wondered if the apparent absence of it meant she'd lost her skill completely—or she'd just gotten better at hiding it.

"You're a vampire. You can handle it." She pressed a kiss to my cheek, then unfolded her legs and hit the ground again. "Let me look at you."

Before I could argue, she took a step back, gave me an up-and-down appraisal. "Your hair's long."

She'd come to Paris to see me a couple of years ago, but our communications had been mostly electronic since then.

"Yeah. It's better that way."

"So much. You trying for the *Sabrina* thing?" she asked with a grin. "The one with Audrey Hepburn? Full of newfound sexiness and charm?"

I gave her an arched eyebrow worthy of my father. "You're saying I wasn't sexy or charming before?"

"You didn't *believe* you were sexy, and you can't convince anyone else of something you don't believe."

"You're really good at backhanded compliments."

She patted my cheek. "Honesty is an undervalued commodity in this day and age, Lis. If people were a little more honest, the world would turn a hell of a lot smoother."

I didn't think this was the time to bring up her hidden magic, so I kept my mouth shut.

"Anyway, it looks like Paris did you some good. And I'm glad to see you."

"I'm glad to see you, too."

Then she held out a hand.

I looked down at it, then up at her. "What?"

"Where's my souvenir?"

Damn it. I should have gone with the airport macarons. "Still in Paris?"

She made a noise of exaggerated frustration. "You owe me a drink for that." She pointed at me with a paint-smeared finger. "And colcannon."

Lulu had discovered colcannon at Temple Bar, the official

Cadogan House watering hole. It also served Irish pub food, including the mashed potato–cabbage combination I didn't understand.

My lip curled involuntarily. "Colcannon is disgusting, and I'm not buying it. But I'll buy you a Guinness."

"Deal."

"This looks amazing," I said, hoping to change the subject from cabbage, and gestured at the mural.

She walked closer, flicked at a smudge. "It's not bad. Still a lot of work to go, but it's not bad. You want to help?"

"You know I can't draw my way out of a paper bag."

"I know. I was kidding. I love you, but I don't want you touching this."

I took a step closer, tilted my head at the four women, whose skin tones ranged from milky white to dark brown. Their limbs— some bent and some outstretched—flowed together like they were reaching for each other.

"What's the story?"

Lulu picked up the discarded pencil. "What do you think it is?"

Analyzing art wasn't my thing. But I stepped up, took a swing, and gestured to the woman on the far left. "Maybe something about women sharing their knowledge, their experiences?" I pointed to a swath of golden paint. "And how that helps them grow, enriches their communities."

She grinned. "That's not bad, Sullivan. Dead wrong, but not bad."

I was more disappointed than I should have been. "Then what is it?"

She lifted a shoulder. "Sexy hotness. The Pack wanted naked ladies, so I gave them naked ladies. Gorgeous, curvy, mostly naked ladies in a rainbow of shades and textures, and not a nipple in sight."

"Because a woman has to draw a damn line."

"Damn straight," she said, and made a small adjustment to one of the new lines. "They argued about this building, the plans, the design, for nearly a year before they finally broke ground. Ended up having to build the bar first, the rest of the building over it. It was a whole thing."

"Drama or not, it turned out pretty well."

"Yeah, it did." Lip between her teeth, she made another adjustment. "How was the shindig?"

"The reception was weird," I said, thinking of Ruadan. "I took some video to show Seri. We can watch it when you have time. The talks were a mess. The fairies interrupted, and it was a whole thing."

She glanced back. "The fairies? Interesting."

"They threw a fit about not being included, and then they were included, and vampires were still vampires."

"So, arrogance and arguing?"

"Pretty much. How's the family?" I asked carefully.

Lulu's mother, Mallory, had taken an evil turn before we'd been born. She'd gotten addicted to dark magic and wreaked her own havoc on Chicago. If my parents were seen as the saviors of Chicago, Lulu's mom was the sorceress who'd tried to bring it down. That she'd later helped save the city apparently wasn't nearly as sexy a memory, and people seemed to have forgotten it.

Lulu had her own guilt about what her mother had done, and it hadn't helped that she'd been teased and bullied by humans as a kid. They'd called her mother the devil or worse, and Lulu had wanted nothing more than distance from the magical.

"Dad is still bitching about 'all the weirdos,'" she said, "which makes me wonder why he agreed to move to Portland in the first place. Probably at least in part so he'd have something to bitch about. Mom's one hundred percent in her element. She's teaching classes, hosting 'Magic-Ins' for Wiccans. I think it was a good change for them. She'd wanted to start over. Even years after, she felt like she couldn't move on in Chicago."

I nodded. "Since I've been in Paris for four years, I can't really argue with that."

She snorted a laugh, glanced back at me. "For two people with pretty good childhoods, we're pretty screwed up about it."

I couldn't argue with that, either.

"How's the Mayor of Vampireville?" she asked.

That's what she called my father. "Diplomatic, as always. And Mom's good, although I think she misses yours."

"BFFs," she said with a shrug, as if that explained everything. "You been to the House yet?"

"Not yet," I said. "Diplomatic responsibilities. I'm going over there tonight for the Cadogan House party." And I declined the monster's invitation to dwell on that a little.

"Oh, right. I got an invite to that." She grimaced. "I wasn't going to go. That cool with you? You like people a lot more than me, anyway."

I smiled. "Your call. I'd love to wine and dine you on my parents' dime, but it's going to be fancy, and it's going to be vampires."

"You had me at 'wining and dining,' but lost me at 'fancy.'" She bobbed her head toward the mural. "The Pack wants this done by the end of next week, so I think I'm going to put in a late night. Speaking of which, have you said hi to Connor yet?"

"I saw him at the reception. Looked older, acted pretty much the same." And my dry tone should have indicated I wasn't impressed with that.

"You punch him?"

"Not yet."

"Good. He's coming around, you know."

I gave her a dour look.

"What? He's had four years to mature. And has to mature if he wants the Pack."

"There's a joke in there about animals being in charge, but I'm going to rise above it. I would like to talk to him, though." I hadn't planned on it, but since I was here, I wouldn't mind getting his take on the fairies. "Do you know if he's around?"

"I don't. But you can look." She used the brush, gestured to a door on the opposite side of the room. "If he's in the building, he's in the bar or the garage. Through that door."

"Okay," I said. "Maybe I'll see you tomorrow?"

"I'll check my schedule," she said, "have my people call your people." Then she turned back to her mural. "And Lis?" she called out, when I was halfway to the door.

"Yeah?"

"Be careful in there. It is a den of wolves, after all."

The bar portion of Little Red had been a dive, with dirty linoleum, gritty walls, and sticky, mismatched tables. The new version worked very hard to pull off the same level of comfortable grunge. And did a pretty good job of it.

The room was big, with concrete floors and brick walls. There was a stage on one end, an empty space in the floor for dancing or fighting, and a lot of mismatched tables and chairs.

The shifters watched as I walked through, eyes turning to me. Low growls and grunts mixed with the magic in the air.

They shouldn't have minded having a vampire in their territory, much less one who'd been raised with their crown prince. But none of these shifters looked familiar. Maybe the Pack had been recruiting.

"I'm looking for Connor," I said, and waited for someone to acknowledge me.

Two of them, big men with broad shoulders and leather jackets—like walking shifter stereotypes—rose and walked toward me. "Why you want him?"

"I need to talk to him."

"We don't like vampires in our place."

"I'm sorry to hear that. But this is a public place, so I can't help you."

One of them growled, began flexing his fingers. The other cracked his neck.

I figured they were bluffing—even if they didn't know who I was, surely they were smart enough not to start a fight with a random vampire—but I wasn't entirely certain. I was certain that shifters didn't much care for sups who cowered, so I amped up the bravado.

"I didn't come here looking for trouble," I said. "But I had to pass up a fight earlier, and I'd be happy to take one on now."

A woman walked into the bar, from a door on the other side. I guessed she was about my age. Light brown skin and a scattering of freckles across her nose. Dark eyes topped by thick lashes and brows, and a generous mouth. Her hair was a dark cap of soft, loose waves. She was petite, noticeably smaller than most of the men in the room, but her body was athletic, strong. She wore jeans and a tank top, a bundle of thin necklaces shimmering around her neck. And plenty of magic buzzed around her.

"Who's this, Jax?" she asked, striding toward us.

Her energy was different from that of the other shifters in the room. The vibration faster, like someone had plucked a different string on a violin.

"Vampire," Jax said.

"Vampire," she said, looking me over. "Elisa Sullivan. I recognize your face."

"I don't recognize yours."

"Miranda. North American Central Pack. I work for Gabriel. You don't."

"No, I don't. I'm here to see Connor."

Emotion flashed across her face, but she hid it away again before I could guess what it meant. "Why?"

"For reasons I'd like to discuss with him."

She took a step forward, and the fingers on my arm tightened. "You aren't in charge here."

"I didn't suggest otherwise. But I doubt you are, either. Do you want to tell Connor I'm here, or should we just start fighting and I can apologize to him later?"

I might have needed the bravado to get past the shifters, but beyond that, I really didn't like bullies. Standing up to them was one of my particular joys.

"Vampires don't own Chicago," Miranda said. "You can't just waltz into our place, expect to take control."

"I don't know." I looked at each of them. "Seems like this place could use a vampire. Maybe a class on etiquette and manners?"

"Bitch."

"Vampire," I reminded her. "So, yeah."

"What the hell's going on in here?"

I knew it was Connor before I turned around. Not just from the sound of his voice, but from the aura of scent and magic that sliced through the air and left behind a charge of its own.

It *commanded*.

It was impressive. And another surprising change for the prince of wolves.

I glanced back. Betraying nothing, Connor met my gaze. "A little out of your territory, aren't you?" he asked.

"I'm here to see Lulu, and while I was here, I had a few questions for you. You want to explain why these guys attempted to manhandle me?"

Connor's expression didn't change. "Attempted?"

I smiled slyly. "I'm better than I was."

"She was sniffing around," said the taller one, stepping forward beside me.

"I'm not a dog," I said with a brittle smile, my gaze on Connor. "I don't sniff."

"So you're just here to cause trouble, dead girl?"

The challenge in his eyes was marked by a glint of humor, and I guessed the performance wasn't for me, but for the shifters around us. No problem. I knew my part.

"I'm not dead."

"You sure about that?" He took a step closer. "You seem pretty frosty to me."

"Frosty" was one of the adjectives the media had liked to use about vampires generally, and about me specifically. I was pale and blond and careful, not the wild child they expected of young supernaturals. Like Connor Keene.

The shifters snickered, and I let my eyes silver, took a step forward that had them reaching for weapons to protect the crown prince.

I looked around the room, counted. "I mean, ten-to-one odds aren't great, but I'm willing to slow things down, give you a fighting chance."

Connor stepped forward, took my arm just above the elbow. And before I could argue, pulled me through the room to a door at the other end, then looked back at the shifters. "You hear any screaming, ignore it."

Then he shut the door.

SEVEN

We stood in a garage with flecked gray floors and towering ceilings, the walls covered in ancient Triumph and Harley signs. A muscle car was parked in one corner, and several motorcycles were parked here and there, including a beast of a low bike in matte black and gray.

I gestured to the closed door. "What was that all about?"

"A little performance for Miranda. She's one of the gunners."

"For your dad's spot?" Being the son of the Apex made Connor the most likely candidate to lead the pack when Gabriel decided to turn over the reins, but it didn't guarantee him the position. Still, I hadn't given much thought to his competitors.

Connor nodded. "She likes to throw her weight around. She's a mountain lion, comes from a family that's opposed to the mixing of the species."

That explained the unusual magic. "She is not charming."

"They lived alone for a very long time. Miranda and her brothers are the first to live in Chicago, participate in Pack activities."

"And how do you feel about having competition?"

"The Pack will do what the Pack will do." He crossed his arms. "Sounds like nonsense, but it's the truth. Doesn't matter how strong, smart, brave, capable an alpha is. What matters is what the Pack says. Miranda and those like her are looking to prove themselves, and there are others who want to befriend the potentials with wine, women, and song. That's the Pack way. Part hazing, part ass-kissing, part the promise of things to come."

"You poor thing."

"I love women and song, but not when they feel obliged, or when they're trying to prove a point, or when they're trying to make a score. I don't play that way." He gestured to the matte black bike on the other side of the garage. "You mind? I'm trying to finish the carburetor."

"Go ahead," I said, walking closer. "She's gorgeous."

I hadn't been a motorcycle person, had only ridden a couple of times with Riley, and he'd tried to terrify me on both trips. But there was no mistaking the appeal of this one. It looked powerful. Intense. Dangerous. It was a shadow, made for a man who could walk in darkness as easily as he could in light.

"It's Thelma," Connor said behind me.

"No way," I said, and squinted at her. Thelma had been his sixteenth-birthday present—a pile of rusted Harley bones spread on a blue tarp. And he'd been thrilled.

"Way," he said with a Valley Girl accent. "I've been working on her for the past four years."

"You've been busy." I ran the tips of my fingers over the quilted black seat, the leather as buttery as leather could be. "Looks like she's nearly done."

"I'm close," he said, and glanced up at me. "What brings you by?"

I sat down on a nearby chrome stool with a padded red leather top. Connor picked up a hunk of metal from the counter along the wall, began to work its fittings with a cloth.

"I wanted to talk to you about the peace talks."

His brows lifted. "You running security for Cadogan House now?"

"No," I said. "I'm working for Maison Dumas."

His gaze shot up. "You're what?"

"Mandatory service year. European vampires give a year of service to their Houses."

"You aren't a member of a European House."

"I'm not. But Dumas housed me while I was in school, so I'm paying it back."

He watched me for a moment, brows knit. "You're volunteering for a year? That's so unlike you, brat."

I will not let him rile me up. "I told you a long time ago that I wasn't spoiled."

"You did," Connor said with a sly smile. "But this is the first time you've had the evidence to back it up."

"You're hilarious."

"That's what the ladies say."

I rolled my eyes. "Shifters supposedly have the pulse of the supernatural community. Are there any rumblings about the fairies? Murmurs about something they're up to?"

"Rising fairy trouble?" he asked. "Aren't you the one with the sociology degree?"

I was surprised he knew, and was flattered more than I'd have expected. "Have you been following my academic career, puppy?"

"Word filters down, brat," he said, frowning at some bit of grime he couldn't reach. "I haven't heard anything specific, because we have a policy of noninvolvement. But there are some rumblings."

"Of?"

"Unhappiness." He unscrewed another part, cleaned that with the towel, screwed it back again. "Fear their magic is fading and they're powerless to stop it. Fear they'll end up like they were before—stuck in the tower."

That matched Yuen's thoughts. "And what do you think they

plan to do about that? Based on what little you know, because of that policy of noninvolvement?"

He smirked at my dry tone. "You aren't any funnier than you were before you left."

"Agree to disagree. Answer the question."

"But you're just as bossy," he said. "And I told you—it's just rumblings. Feelings. I don't know anything about plans. If we'd known, we'd have told your father before things started."

"What about Ruadan?"

He looked up. "What about him?"

"He seems . . . intense."

Connor didn't answer, just met my gaze evenly, waiting for me to say more.

"He approached me at the reception, after the parade."

"He approached you? A bloodletter?" This time he wasn't being sarcastic, but seemed genuinely surprised.

"Yeah."

Connor rose, put the towel on the counter, then looked back at me. "What did he want?"

"He asked me about how I'd managed to be born. I didn't get into the details."

"That's weird."

"It was." I shrugged. "Riley stepped in, and Ruadan scurried off. Which was fine by me."

Connor snorted a laugh. "Riley can play the badass when he wants to. I don't know anything about Ruadan other than the fact that he's Claudia's consort."

"Is he aiming for the throne?"

He lifted a shoulder. "Honestly don't know. That must have been some conversation to get you this curious."

"It's not him," I said. "Or not just." Feeling suddenly impatient, I rose, walked to the counter, picked up a screwdriver, and tapped it against my palm. "It's the fit they threw today. They decide there's this deep conspiracy against them, but we give them a meaningless prize and they're satisfied? As a strategy it doesn't make much sense."

"I'll grant you it's odd, but Claudia's crazy."

"So I've heard." I put the tool down, leaned back against the counter, and crossed my arms.

Maybe Connor was right and there was nothing to this beyond a fading queen's desire to matter, to have attention. That meant the talks would continue, the French delegation would be fine, and we might get peace in Paris.

"Maybe I'm just on edge," I murmured.

"Shocking. You're usually so calm and relaxed." Connor tilted his head at me. "Why are you asking me these questions? Why not talk to your parents? Or the Ombudsman?"

"The deal with Cadogan House."

"The deal with . . . Oh," he said, realization hitting him. "Cadogan House is supposed to stay out of it."

"That's the theory. We talked to Yuen after the event, and he had the same thought you did—that maybe the fading magic has them concerned." I shook my head. "I don't know. I've been out of the loop for four years. Maybe I'm just trying to adjust to the new sup order."

"You look different," he said, and I thought I saw appreciation in his eyes. "Still a vampire, of course, but different."

"Thanks for the evaluation."

His thoughtful expression didn't change. "You look happy."

The comment—so unsnarky—threw me off a little. "I am."

"Did you find what you were looking for in Paris?"

Another question that sounded legitimate—like he was actually interested in my feelings.

The answer, of course, was both simple and complicated. I lived, ate, slept. I walked cobblestone streets and tried macarons of every color (all of them equally gross), and no one knew who I was. For the first time in my life, I could figure that out—*who* I was—without an audience.

"I got to be myself," I said after a moment.

"And who is that?"

"Elisa Sullivan," I said, meeting his gaze again. "Not the daughter of someone else. Not the first child. In France, they didn't care who I was."

His brows lifted. "And here they cared too much?"

"You know how it was." I didn't want to get into that with him, so I changed the subject. "The wine, women, and song seem to have agreed with you."

He grinned. "Wine, women, and song agree with a lot of people."

I snorted. "That's why there's a trail of brokenhearted shifters behind you."

"Yours may be vampires," he said with a crooked grin, "but they're just as brokenhearted. Are you staying in Chicago?" he asked before I could contradict him.

I shook my head. "Heading back after the talks. I have nine months left of service, and then we'll see."

"We're leaving for Alaska in a few days."

The North American Central Pack was headquartered in Memphis, where the Keene family was originally from. But Aurora, Alaska, was the spiritual home of all the North American shifter Packs.

"The Pack's going back to Aurora?"

"Not the entire Pack. Just a group. I'm leading it. We're doing well financially, but we're feeling a little bruised after being in Chicago for so long. This city doesn't recharge us. There's too much steel, too much concrete, and too many people. The magic is diffuse. In Alaska, the magic is everywhere."

That must have been what Berna was talking about. I lifted a brow. "Is this about running around naked in the woods?"

"That's don't ask, don't tell. And, no. This is about feeling better, about healing. Our magic is worn down, literally. Scraped raw because we've been going, doing, fighting for so long. We aren't as strong. We don't heal as fast, even when we shift."

There was concern in his tone, and I realized he actually looked stressed. Connor had always seemed content to play the prince, having the prestige of the throne without actually having to worry about the job. Maybe he was taking that more seriously, too.

"That sounds serious," I said.

"It is. The trip's necessary, so the Pack will ride—and be prepared to fight."

I imagined a convoy of shifters in leather jackets, long hair streaming in the wind. Then I realized what he'd said. "Wait. To fight what? Road rash and sunburn?"

"There are conversations the Pack needs to have with sups outside Chicago's city limit. Incidents that need to be dealt with in person. Those conversations are necessary, but they aren't with allies, and some will take place in enemy territory." He gestured to Thelma. "But there are upsides."

"Then I'll let you get back to it. Thanks for the time, and good luck with Thelma."

"Thanks. Maybe I'll bring her out tonight. Give your fanged people a thrill."

I glanced back. "My fanged people?"

"The Cadogan House party. I'm expected to put in an appearance."

"Ah. Maybe encourage your friends to skip the leather."

"Shifters will be shifters," he said with a grin. "And it is a formal occasion."

As I walked back through the building toward the waiting Auto, I realized it was the probably the longest real conversation I'd ever had with Connor Keene.

* * *

Back to the hotel, and it would soon be time to get dressed and prepare for the next round of service to Dumas. For the party, and for Cadogan House.

But before that, I needed a break. Too many supernaturals and too much magic had me on edge, was wearing down the edges of my immunity against the monster. My hand had shaken when I'd pushed the button on the elevator, and I'd clenched my fingers into a fist so the humans I'd shared it with didn't think I was about to attack.

I checked in with Seri to confirm everyone was on schedule, then changed into leggings and a tank and sat down on the floor to stretch.

It had taken me a few years to find nighttime yoga classes that I liked and that gave me what I didn't know I'd needed: focus. Vinyasa, which focused on breath and flow from one pose to the next, worked for me. The practice made me stronger, more limber, and it helped me keep myself—and the monster—in check.

Still on the floor, draped so my nose touched my knees, I closed my eyes, waited for my limbs to warm, to loosen.

The drumming came suddenly, a warning played out in throbbing magic, and I fought it, sweat glistening over skin as I pushed against the intrusion. I began to move into poses, some in which my body was stretched, some in which my body was compressed. That required fluidity as I shifted from one pose to another, the movements between as precise as the poses themselves, as that was the hallmark of vinyasa.

An hour later, I was sweaty and exhausted. But my mind was quiet, and the drumming had stopped.

For now.

The snack and shower that followed had me nearly back at one hundred percent. I dressed, fancying myself up in the way of vampires.

Physically, I was turned out pretty well. My dress, found at a Paris consignment shop, was the color of emeralds, a sheath of bias-cut silk from the narrow halter-style top to the floor-skimming hem. It looked like the dress of a heroine from a 1940s mystery, worn to a fancy party where she'd pull a tiny, pearl-handled gun from her purse.

I paired the dress with strappy sandals in a metal that was half-way between silver and gold, and opted to pin my hair back into a knot, leaving a few waves loose around my face.

I liked feeling the weight of it on my shoulders—familiar, and almost like a cape of my own—but this dress deserved something more.

When I was assembled, my clutch and katana scabbard in hand, I locked up and headed to Seri's room. The guards at the door checked my identification, nodded, and let me in.

Seri stood in the middle of the room on a flat box while Odette, on her knees with a pin in her mouth, worked at the hem of Seri's gown.

If my dress was old-school American glamour, Seri's was French avant-garde. The skirt was long and straight, with a slit in the front that rose to the top of her thighs. There was a navel-baring bodice with mesh sleeves that started below her shoulders, leaving them bare. Her hair was piled up in a complicated braid around a silver diadem, and the same black mesh reached from the bottom of the band to the top edges of her sleeves, enclosing her face in a strange, cocooning veil. Her earrings were drops of diamonds long enough to brush the tops of her shoulders, and her eyes were dark and smoky.

"Lis!" she said, pressing her hands together with excitement. "You look exquisite. What do you think of this?"

"It's . . . amazing," I said, and walked closer, then around her. The fabric shimmered with even the slightest movement, so it looked like Seri had been draped in a starlit night.

"I am so glad we decided on the green," she said, swearing in French when Odette stabbed her with a pin.

"*Sois immobile!*" Odette said through her teeth, then pulled out the pin. "If you do not move, I do not prick you."

"She is a thorny rose," Seri said, sighing with relief when Odette sat back on her heels, surveyed her work.

"It will do," she said.

"*Merci,*" Seri said, stepping off the platform and giving the dress a spin. "It is beautiful, no?"

"It really is. Won't the veil thing get irritating?"

Seri laughed. "The ensemble is worth a bit of irritation."

"You look very vampiric," I said. "And very French."

She smiled. "Perhaps I will find a strong American vampire to teach me a thing or two."

"I wouldn't mention that to Marion. Are you ready to go?"

"Finishing touches," Odette said, adjusting the veil and fit of Seri's dress across the shoulders. Then she stood back, put her hands on her hips, and surveyed her creation.

"You are ready," she pronounced. And that was that.

Where downtown Chicago had become sleeker, Hyde Park had stayed pretty much the same. But several of the older homes and mansions had been renovated and rejuvenated, because peace brought new cachet to living next to vampires.

Cadogan House looked the same as it had four years ago. A big, stately stone building with an arch over the front door and a widow's walk crowning the top, in the middle of a gorgeous lawn big enough to be a park. There was a tall fence around the perimeter, a new guard house at the gate.

It had been my home for nineteen years. I loved the building and the park that surrounded it, and I loved my parents and the other House vampires who'd become part of my supernaturally

extended family. But I'd been ready to move on when I'd left for
Paris, and leaving the fortified House had been part of that. I'd
proven to myself that I could make it on my own. And coming
home again made the House seem somehow smaller.

Paparazzi waited outside the fence, but there were plenty of
guards to keep them away from the gate. They were positioned
every few feet, and I guessed they had repeated that precaution
all the way around the House. Unlike vampires, the humans
opted for guns, and there were matte handguns strapped to their
waists.

Our Autos rolled to a stop in front of the gate. A tuxedoed
guard with a clipboard approached the first Auto, opened the
door, and checked their credentials, then assisted Marion onto the
red carpet.

Seri squeezed my hand. "The House is lovely," she said. "Just
as you'd described." She leaned forward to look out the window,
take in the white lanterns that hung like moons over the cocktail
tables that dotted the front lawn. The tables were decked with
flowers. Servers bore trays of appetizers and crystal flutes of
golden champagne in the balmy August air, beneath a brilliant
waxing moon. Even in the vehicle, I could hear the hum of music
from a jazz band, probably on the other side of the House.

Our Auto pulled up into the spot vacated by Marion's car, and
the guard with the clipboard approached.

"Name?" he asked, giving me a pleasant smile.

"Elisa Sullivan, Seraphine, and guests."

The guard had been looking down at a clipboard, and his head
snapped back up quick enough.

"Yes, I'm their kid," I said with a smile. "We're here for the
party."

"Of course," he said, and stepped aside, offering a hand as I
stepped out of the car and onto the sidewalk. The song grew

louder, and the scents of wine and food and perfume added notes to the air.

When we were all out of the vehicle—eight vampires in assorted red-carpet wear—he stepped aside and gestured grandly toward the sidewalk. "Have a lovely evening."

"Thank you."

Shutters began clicking, screens pointed in our direction as the paparazzi caught the scent of blood, and they focused on Seri. She had an amazing way of seeming to ignore them while presenting exactly the right angle to their cameras, just the right expression of not caring and demanding their attention. She worked the dress, too, using her shoulders and hips and legs to show off its strange angles before sashaying toward the gate, Odette trailing behind her. There was a definite gleam in Seri's eye when she reached me.

"There is a time for politics," she said, "and a time for beauty."

I nodded, ignored the quickening of my heartbeat, the magical anticipation that rode beneath the skin. There was also a time for confrontation. And I had a feeling it would be sooner rather than later.

Paris was beautiful, and Maison Dumas was gorgeous. But there was something to be said for Cadogan House in late summer, when the trees were full, the air smelled of smoke and meat, and the lawn glimmered with torches. The House's lawn was enormous, big as a park with walking trails, copses of trees, and benches placed just so to take advantage of the views. Vampires from more than a dozen countries were enjoying the balmy air, walking across the soft grass with champagne flutes in hand as jazz filled the air, accompanied by the heady scent of August flowers.

"First," Seri said, "a drink." She glanced around the lawn. "Ah!" she said, and pointed toward a waiter with a silver tray. But when she began to walk in his direction, and I obediently moved to follow her, she stopped and held up a hand.

"Elisa, you are dear to me, and while I would be happy to have your company this evening, this is the first time you've been home in years." She put a hand on my arm. "You should take this opportunity to visit friends and family. I'm sure they have missed you."

"I'm working," I reminded her. "I'm your escort."

"Odette will be with me." She glanced around. "Besides, we are at your parents' home, surrounded by allies and guards. The talks proceeded without violence, if with a bit more drama than I'd have appreciated, and there's no reason to think there will be violence here tonight. Even if there was, there are plenty here to assist." She squeezed the hand already on my arm. "There is no need to be concerned."

"You're sure?" I didn't mind a good party, but I didn't want to shirk my duties.

"I am sure. I spoke with Marion, as well, and we agreed you should be able to visit with your loved ones."

"All right," I said, figuring I'd do both. I could enjoy the party, but stay within sight of Seri and Marion in case I needed to intervene. And she was right: The guards and vampires here were more than capable.

"In that case, I'll see you later."

And I walked toward Cadogan House to face the monster again.

EIGHT

It had been four years, but Cadogan House smelled exactly the same: like wood polish and fresh flowers, the scent from the enormous vase of wildflowers on the pedestal table in the foyer. There were parlors off to each side, a curving oak staircase that led to the first floor, and a long, central hallway that led to the cafeteria and offices.

I walked to the pedestal table, let fingers trail across slick and smooth wood. And the memory crept into view like a photograph.

I'd been sixteen, coming downstairs to the foyer to wait for Lulu; she was going to sleep over.

I'd found Connor slouched on a wooden bench—back against the wall and long legs stretched out in front of him. He wore snug jeans and a T-shirt beneath a black moto-style jacket. His arms had been crossed over his chest and his eyes were closed, so a fan of dark lashes brushed his cheeks. His hair had been longer than it was now—thick, dark locks that brushed his shoulders—and his lips had been curved in a smile.

He'd looked, I'd thought, like a very wicked and happy angel.

"What's up, brat?" he'd asked, without opening his eyes.

"Do you call all vampires 'brat' these days?" I'd asked, walking closer.

"I can smell your perfume."

I'd blinked. I'd worn the same fragrance for years—a pale pink liquid in a square bottle that smelled like spring flowers—but I'd never have thought he'd noticed.

"Wolf," he'd said, opening his eyes drowsily. "Predatory sense of smell."

"So you say. Making yourself at home?" I'd asked, nudging the toe of his boot.

"The Pack's an ally," he'd said. "Aren't we supposed to make ourselves at home?"

"You want a drink and a snack plate, too? Maybe a blanket?"

"Sure," he'd said with a grin, sitting upright and clasping his hands between his knees. "You going to get that for me?"

"Not in this lifetime."

He'd actually clucked his tongue. "That's poor vampire hospitality. And before you can interrogate me, Mini Sentinel, my dad's talking to yours. I'm waiting."

"Not interested enough in the Pack to join in?"

That had hit the mark, and something flashed in his eyes. But before he could answer, the front door had opened and Lulu had walked inside.

"What's up, other brat?"

"What's up, Labradoodle?" She dropped her bag on the floor with a resounding thud.

Connor had hated that name, which is exactly why Lulu used it. But his expression stayed the same—lazily confident.

"What will you two maniacs be doing tonight? Alphabetizing the books in the library?"

"At least we know how to alphabetize."

Gabriel had walked into the foyer, smiled when he'd seen us. Connor sat up straight, which had had me biting back a grin. "Elisa. Lulu."

I'd offered a wave. "Hey, Mr. Keene."

He'd given me a wink, then looked at this son. "Let's go, Con."

Connor had risen from the bench, offering us a salute as he'd followed his father outside again.

"At least you get 'brat,'" Lulu had said when the door closed again. "You're the original. I'm the other."

She walked to one of the windows that flanked the door, watched the pair walk down the sidewalk. "It's a damn shame he's such a punk. Because he would be stupid hot if it wasn't for the attitude."

"Maybe," I'd said. That Connor Keene was gorgeous was undeniable. "But he'll always be a punk."

Seven years later, I ran my fingers along the table, then headed for the staircase that led to the third floor.

He was still hot. And maybe, surprisingly, a little less of a punk.

The apartments—our home within Cadogan House—opened into a pretty sitting room. My parents' bedroom was to the left. To the right was the smaller suite they'd created for me: a bedroom, bathroom, and closet I'd learned later had been carved out of the House's "consort" suite. TMI, but there you go.

I walked toward my bedroom, wondered if it would feel the same to be surrounded with stuff from another part of my life, or if everything would feel distant, strange.

There was nothing pink, no photographs under the mirror, no freeze-dried roses or trophies. Striped bedspread, matching lamps on the nightstand, and a desk with everything arranged just so, which is how I'd liked it. A small table held the turntable I'd saved my allowance to buy, the vinyl organized alphabetically beneath it.

A bookshelf held a few books and a lot of coffee mugs from my favorite spots in Chicago. There were mementos, but they were organized in the scrapbooks on the second shelf. Plenty of photos of Lulu in those, occasional shots of Connor. Family trips to amusement parks and cities with enough nightlife to give us something to do when the sun was down.

I walked back into the sitting room. And that's when I felt it.

The katana, pulsing with magic, was only a few yards away.

I knew it would be in the House, had hoped the fact that I hadn't sensed it the moment I'd walked in the door meant the calm I'd managed at the hotel was giving me the cushion I'd needed. But just like that first step into Chicago, I'd guessed wrong again. I was susceptible. Vulnerable.

And I didn't like being either.

I moved closer, walking toward my parents' bedroom, and the magic pounded harder, so it felt like concert-worthy bass rattling the floor to a song I couldn't hear. But everything was still—the frames on the wall, the vase of flowers on the table, the inkwell on the secretary in the corner.

I stepped over the threshold. The walls here were pale blue, the wood dark brown, the accents white and silver.

The package of red brocade silk lay on my parents' bed, a shock of color across a crisply white duvet. It was tied with a braided and tasseled ivory silk cord, and it was close enough to touch.

My mother had taken the sword out of the armory again. Probably because of the fairies' interruption, and just in case she needed to protect the House. She wasn't wearing it tonight; the rest of the guards would be protecting the House, and I was part of the Dumas contingent. And she had diplomatic responsibilities.

Magic throbbed in my chest, pulsing like a foreign heartbeat.

I moved into the bedroom, untied the cord, and unwrapped the fabric, revealing the gleaming red scabbard.

Visually, it looked exactly like what it was—a sheathed katana. There was nothing especially unusual about the lacquer or the cord around the handle, and I knew the blade would look well crafted and lethally sharp.

It was the magic that mattered, the power bound to the sword, and the trace of it that had bound itself inside me.

I was here, alone with it. If there would be a reckoning, this was the time. So I squeezed my hands into fists, closed my eyes, and relaxed the mental barriers I'd erected against the magic's cries.

They called to each other. Not because they wanted to be bound together inside me or inside the sword, but because they wanted to be free so they could spread their anger around the city.

"Not going to happen," I gritted out.

Its reaction was instant and painful. The monster lashed out, fury flashing across my skin like fire, hot enough to singe.

I stumbled backward, reaching out to the wall behind me to steady myself, green silk pooling around me, my heartbeat racing as magic tried to fight back. I swallowed hard and bore down, then stood up again. "You aren't in charge," I said, and took a step forward.

Anger spread again, and I breathed through pursed lips to deal with it, but tears still sprang to my eyes.

"You don't own me," I said, taking another step forward and staring down at the inert metal. "And you never will. So do us both a favor and give up the fight."

I'd come to say my piece, and I'd said it. It took the rest of my strength to wrap the scabbard in silk again, to knot the cords, to straighten the blanket beneath the package. That seemed important somehow, that the blanket was straight.

I stepped back, the tightness in my chest easing up as I put distance between myself and the sword. But I could feel the pulse beneath my ribs, the refusal to give up.

I'd won this battle. But the war would continue, and we'd all see who won.

* * *

In the bathroom attached to my bedroom, I pressed a damp cloth against my neck until my heart had slowed and my eyes faded to green again. Until I felt like Elisa.

Then I tossed the towel into the laundry and walked out of the room, giving the apartment one last look before I closed the door. The monster hadn't bothered me as a child, not until I'd been old enough—or it had been old enough—to reach for my attention. That wasn't true anymore.

I wasn't entirely sure what I was going to do when my service for Maison Dumas was complete. I'd thought about it, and had nearly nine months to keep thinking about it. But one thing seemed certain.

I couldn't live in Cadogan House.

Not while the magic lived here, too.

My father's office was as elegant as the rest of his House. It held the carefully curated souvenirs of his life amid the pretty furniture: a desk, a conversation area with armchairs, and a long conference table where he could hash out issues with his staff.

He sat at his desk, frowning at something on the sleek glass screen perched there. He wore a black tuxedo, perfectly fitted, his hair tied back at his nape.

"Burning the midnight oil?"

He smiled but kept his gaze on the screen. "Just finishing up a project," he said, then swiped a finger against the glass and looked up at me. "And don't you look lovely?"

He rose, came over, and pressed a kiss to my forehead. "My smart and kind and beautiful girl."

He liked to say that, had been saying it for years, and had always put "beautiful" last. Whether it was true or not, he'd tell me it was the least important of the three. "You are smart," he'd say. "You should be kind. And if you are, you'll always be beautiful."

"Thank you. The House looks great. Luc did a very nice job getting things ready."

Luc had been Captain of the House's guards, and he'd been promoted when Malik became Master of his own House. Kelley had taken over for Luc.

My father grinned. "He has an unusually good hand with decorations. And Kelley has done an excellent job in his stead on security."

"Do you think there'll be trouble tonight?"

"I don't know. The Ombudsman's office doesn't believe so."

"And what do you believe?"

A sly look crossed his face. "I believe the issue is in their hands, and I trust them to handle the investigation. And in the meantime, we have guards posted in and around the House."

"So I saw." I looked around the room, at the mementos he'd chosen to keep in sight. A few stood on glossy white floating shelves under glass covers. "Do you ever miss it?"

"Miss what?" he asked.

"The adventures."

He smiled, tucked his hands into his pockets. "They didn't always feel like adventures. More often, they were terrifying or constraining or infuriating. It is hard to be an enemy, Elisa. It wears."

"And you're less of an enemy now?"

"It would be more accurate to say we don't involve ourselves in situations in which we could cause harm—even collaterally—to the city. And, more important, we found a different kind of adventure." He smiled at me. "But no less terrifying . . . or infuriating."

"Is this your segue into the trials and tribulations of parenthood?"

He raised a golden eyebrow, my dad's signature move. He'd scared off a couple of human boyfriends with that one. "Fewer trials than tribulations, but yes. We wanted to be parents, and we wanted to keep you safe. We tried to do that."

He looked at me, considering. "Have you given any thought to what you'd like to do after Paris?"

"I'm thinking about it," I promised.

"The House is always hiring," he said with a knowing smile. "And you have an in with the Master."

"No nepotism. We've talked about that. I earn my way or I don't."

He walked toward me, took my hand. "I didn't think I could be prouder of you, and then I saw you fighting at the Eiffel Tower for someone who wasn't able. That's who you are, Elisa. You just need to figure out what you'd like to do with it."

"Am I interrupting?"

We looked back and found Malik Washington in the doorway, wearing an impeccable navy suit, a gingham square tucked into the pocket. His skin was dark, his head shaved, his eyes pale green.

"Uncle Malik!"

We strode to each other, met in the middle.

"Congratulations on the House!" I said as we embraced. "And sorry I couldn't make it to the reception."

He smiled. "Thank you. We appreciated the card and the macarons. They were truly excellent."

At least I'd gotten that present right. "Paris is very good at macarons. How's life as a Master?"

"There is, somehow, more paperwork. Vampires and bureaucracy are strange bedfellows."

"So Dad always said. How's Aunt Aaliyah?"

"She's good. On a deadline."

"She always is," I said with a smile, which he returned.

"She sends her best, and hopes we can get together before you leave again."

"That would be great, if you can keep the fairies and vampires in line."

"We'll do our best," he said earnestly. "How are you? How is Paris?"

"I'm good, and Paris is great." I pointed to the ceiling. "It's been a while since I was upstairs, so I gave the apartments a walk-through."

"That must be a very strange feeling, to walk through your childhood room."

"It was . . . odd," was all I'd admit to.

Since I'd faced down my old monsters, it was time to go watch the new ones. Leaving my father and Uncle Malik to talk, and leaving my katana in his office for safekeeping, I took the House's main hallway through the cafeteria—which was empty, given the spread on the lawn—and out onto the brick patio that stretched in a half moon along the back of the House.

Urns of white flowers scented the air, and while there was an abundance of magic along with it, the mix stifled the thrumming of my mother's sword, so I wasn't about to complain.

Vampires and other supernaturals strolled in the grass and near the long buffet tables set up a few dozen yards away near an oak tree whose branches nearly skimmed the ground.

I found Seri and Marion speaking with Scott Grey and Morgan Greer, Chicago's other two Masters, who laughed as they watched the screen Scott held out.

Probably puppy videos. Even vampires liked puppy videos.

Having confirmed they were safe and sound, I looked for the waiter with the champagne I'd seen earlier. I'd earned a little re-laxation.

And I turned to face down a wolf, albeit one in human clothes.

Connor stood behind me in a black tux that enhanced every bit of hard and sleek muscle and seemed to make his blue eyes glow. One dark lock curled across his forehead, and a day's growth of stubble darkened his jaw. He looked, somehow, even more dangerous. Even more wicked.

That probably suited his escort just fine. Tabby stood beside him, gorgeous again tonight in a gold sequin dress with a deep V-neck and long sleeves that reflected sparks of light across her amazing face and carved cheekbones.

"Hello," Connor said.

"Hello." I shifted my gaze to his girlfriend. "And hello."

"Brat, this is Tabby."

"Hey," Tabby said, fingers tangling in a lock of Connor's hair in a way that looked more irritating than seductive. And the expression on her face was one of absolute boredom.

"It's nice to meet you. Your magic at the reception was impressive."

"Just part of what we do." She dropped her hand, propped it on her hip. "I want something to drink. You?" she asked, glancing at Connor.

He held up a beer. "I'm good."

"I'll be back," she said, then kissed him lavishly and slunk toward the bar.

"She is . . . really beautiful," I said. It was the only compliment I could think of, and I didn't think "She seems super comfy with PDA" would come off very well. Not that it would have been intended to.

"She is," Connor said, and we watched as the waiter offered her a short glass of amber alcohol.

She downed it, held the glass out for another. And when a vampire approached the bar for a drink, she snapped her teeth at him in a show of . . . ferocity?

Beautiful. But maybe not very classy.

"That's not leather."

I shifted my gaze back to Connor. "What?"

"Your dress. It's not leather, but I still like it. Green's a good color on you."

"Thank you," I said slowly, suspicious at the compliment. "I like the tux."

He shifted his shoulders with obvious discomfort. "Suits are for humans and vampires."

"You're pulling if off just fine. And you know you look good in it."

The words were out before I knew I'd said them, and the surprised look on his face said he'd noticed.

"I should probably dial that back or your ego will be out of control. Let's say you look acceptable for a shifter."

"But not quite as good as a vampire."

I just grinned at him. "I don't want to insult you at my ancestral home."

He snorted. "This is a good shindig for a vampire party."

"It is nice," I agreed. "What would a shifter party look like?"

"Leather, like you said. Muscles. Cleavage. Thrashing guitar. Broken beer bottles, supernaturals thrown through plate glass windows, axe-throwing contests."

"That was a thing?"

He squinted as he remembered. "Couple of years ago. Berna decided the bar tables looked too new. They pulled a few off the bases, hung the tabletops, and threw axes at them." He took a drink. "They did look better afterward. She has a good eye."

"The bar looks good," I said. "But the floor's too clean."

"If you only knew how many conversations we've had about that. I keep threatening to roll Thelma out there, change the oil right in the bar floor."

"But you don't, because Berna terrifies you?"

"I admit nothing." He smiled, his eyes crinkling at the corners.

He was in a better mood now than he had been earlier today. Maybe it was the date or the booze, or just the fact that he was at

a party instead of thinking about the Pack's future and the enemies he might meet on the way to Alaska. Whatever the reason, I
liked seeing him like this.

"What?" he asked, eyes narrowed.

"Nothing. Just thinking that you're in a good mood."

"Am I not usually?"

"Not in my direction," I said with a grin.

Connor cocked an eyebrow at something behind me.

I looked back, found Riley grinning as he carried a three-foot-
high stack of aluminum trays toward a buffet table. He'd also
worn a tuxedo, and it was working just as hard as Connor's to
hold in the muscle and magic. He'd pulled his hair back into a
man bun, and it showed off the interesting lines and angles of his
face.

"You're staring," Connor said.

"He's worth it," I said, and grinned back at him. "Does it
bother you that you're the second-prettiest shifter these days?"

His gaze narrowed dangerously, and that made my blood race
a little harder. Probably some ancient vampire reaction to shifters.
"I'm neither pretty nor second place for anything."

"Mmm-hmm. You're plain and retiring, as every man in want
of a wife should be."

This time, he grunted. "I'm not in want of a wife."

"All Tabby to the contrary. Doesn't the Pack want you have a
partner?" I frowned, trying to remember. "Isn't there something
in the code about the Apex being married?"

They might have liked the rock-and-roll lifestyle, but shifters
had pretty conservative opinions about relationships. It was re-
lated, or so Connor said, to their relationship to the earth and the
belief that even an alpha occasionally needed a second opinion.
Shifters partnered with shifters, and generally of the same animal
variety, although Gabriel's aunt Fallon had loosened that rule
when she'd married a shifter who transformed into a white tiger.

"I'm not Apex," he said. "Yet."

There was a high whistle, then a ringing of silver against crystal. All eyes turned to my father, who stood beside my mother (also in sleek Cadogan black—an off-the shoulder column that skimmed the ground, with long, fitted sleeves of black lace on tulle) on the brick patio at the edge of the House. The crowd quieted, turned to face him.

"I don't want to interrupt the party," he said. "I just wanted to take this opportunity to express our gratitude for the steps you've taken tonight toward a lasting peace. The road to that peace will not be easy. It will not be smooth. But it is worth the effort." He lifted his glass. "To peace."

"To peace!" the crowd echoed.

"And I'd be remiss," he continued, "if I didn't mention how proud we are to have our daughter home once again, even if for a little while."

I smiled politely at the supernaturals who all turned to stare at me.

"Just imagine the rest of the crowd is naked," Connor murmured behind me. "It'll help."

Spoiler alert: It didn't.

NINE

Eventually my father moved on, and the guests' attention went back to the food and drinks and other guests.

Theo walked toward us with a woman in a long-sleeved dress of emerald green. Her skin was tan, her hair dark and straight with golden highlights, her eyes wide and dark under long, dark brows.

"Hey, Elisa," Theo said.

"Hey. Theo, do you know Connor Keene?"

"Sure," Theo said, and stuck out his free hand. "I mean, I don't think we've met officially, but I know who you are. Good to meet you."

"Theo works for the Ombudsman's office," I said.

I glanced at the woman he was with, and memories fired. She seemed familiar, but it wasn't until I saw she wore satin gloves in the same shade as the dress that I realized why.

"Oh, my god!" I said. "Petra!"

She smiled and held up a hand. "Hey, Elisa."

"I barely recognized you!"

"Yeah, I got a lot taller," she said with a smile. "My dad's six-two. And it's been like"—she lifted her gaze, counting to herself—"eight years?"

"About that," I said, then looked at Theo and Connor. "Petra and I were tutored together until she moved. Wyoming, wasn't it?"

"Wisconsin," she said. "Dad's an accountant with a big firm. We got transferred."

And we hadn't done a very good job of keeping in touch with each other. "Are you back in Chicago now?"

"Have been for about a year."

"That's great. How's the aeromancy gig?"

"Aeromancy?" Connor asked, brows lifted.

Petra turned her wide smile to him. "I can commune with the weather. Hear it, influence it a little. Lightning and I have a unique relationship."

"Thus the gloves," I said, and she nodded.

"That's . . . frightening and impressive," Connor said, which I figured was about the correct reaction. "Can I see?"

"Sure," Petra said, and pulled off a glove. "Hold out your hand, palm up."

It made me smile that our brave and muscled shifter hesitated before offering his right hand.

She put her ungloved fingers over his, then blew out a slow breath. And a brilliant blue spark sizzled between their hands.

"*Shit,*" Connor said, eyes widening as he was literally shocked by power.

"How cool is that?" Theo asked enthusiastically.

"It's pretty fucking cool," Connor said, looking at the palm of his hand, then rubbing the skin.

"Injuries?" Petra asked, putting her glove back on.

"No, not at all," he said, lifting his gaze to hers. "It was a little like shifting—the same sizzling power. But concentrated."

"And that's one of the reasons why Dearborn hired her," Theo said. "She's also an Assistant Ombudsman. Head of the tech crew."

"Small world," I said. Although it had been a long time since I'd known Petra, she'd been smart, funny, and kind. That she worked for the OMB, as Theo called it, made me feel a lot better about Dearborn being in charge.

"Speaking of small worlds," Theo said, "did you get a load of the panther?" He gestured toward the woman currently draped on William Dearborn. "Or maybe a cougar would have been more accurate."

I just managed not to choke, given the woman was Tabby. "That's Connor's date," I said with a very forced smile.

"Well, she seems . . ." Theo faltered, obviously grasping for a compliment. Then he shook his head, apparently giving up. "Like something you could improve upon?" he offered to Connor.

"She's vivacious."

"She's vivating all over the Ombudsman," Petra said dryly.

"It's fine," Connor said. His voice had tightened, and I wasn't sure if that was because he was irritated by the activity, or our questions about it. And it wasn't, frankly, any of our business—any more than Tabby's sex life was.

"You're a good-looking man," Theo said appraisingly. "I go for chicks, but I'm sure there are plenty of ladies who'd be interested in you and have a little more to offer in terms of loyalty." He looked at me speculatively. "You're single, aren't you, Elisa?"

"*No,*" Connor and I said simultaneously, and with just as much emphasis. Which wasn't flattering to either of us.

"Not my type," I said with a mirthless smile.

"Not even in the same universe," Connor agreed. "And I have a girlfriend." He sipped his drink.

"Oh, okay," Theo said. "Your protestations are totally convincing." He looked at me with a grin. "Do you have any hobbies, Elisa? What do you do for fun?"

"She doesn't," Connor said.

"Sick burn, puppy," I said. "Just because I don't party twenty-four/seven doesn't mean I don't have hobbies."

"Is it stamp collecting?"

"No."

"Do you literally watch grass grow?"

As my irritation grew, my eyes silvered, and I let him see it.

"Come at me, brat."

"Seriously," Petra said with a nod, "you two are very cute."

Connor actually growled.

And it was time to change the topic. "I have hobbies. Yoga. And there's martial arts training, katana practice, blah, blah, blah. It's hard to find time to just do things. I think I'd like to learn calligraphy."

Connor blinked. "That is not what I'd have expected you to say."

I shrugged. "I like letters. They're very . . ."

"Orderly?" he asked with a grin.

"When you're facing down immortality," I said, "order is important. Rules are comforting."

"Rules are constricting," he countered.

"My parents are aeromancers," Petra said. "And hobbies are hard when you're the kid of a sup. There are expectations."

I thought of the discussion I'd had with Lulu, how our parents' abilities had affected us. "No disagreement here."

"I played baseball as a kid," Connor said. "Third base, and had a fantastic arm." He flexed his biceps, and the muscle strained against the slick fabric. "But the old man wanted me at Little Red, at the House, at wherever the Pack happened to be. So that was the end of that. Pack comes first. Always."

"I don't understand the point of baseball."

Theo looked at me, blinked. "What do you mean, you don't understand the point of it? What's to understand? It's a sport."

"If there's time for the players to have snacks, it's not a sport. It's recess."

Connor rolled his eyes. "Seeds aren't a snack."

"Agree to disagree," I said, holding up a hand, and was glad to finally speak my truth about baseball. My mother was Cubs fan, so dissent had not been allowed in Cadogan House. "But I understand your point. I took piano lessons until it was time to take katana lessons."

"Didn't you hate piano lessons?" Petra asked.

"I did," I said with a smile, impressed that she'd remembered. "With a passion. I like music, but I can't make it. And my teacher— Mrs. Vilichnik. God, I hated her. She was like the villain from a Victorian orphan story."

"They just wanted us to be prepared," Connor said. "For, you know, Juilliard or supernatural warfare."

"I know."

"I'm actually feeling moderately better about growing up human," Theo said. "I'd figured it was boring—homework, anime, baseball and basketball, trips to Challengers Comics to grab the new releases. Maybe I had it easy."

"I wouldn't say human is easy, either," Connor said. "Mortality, illness, bullies. Being a sup makes those things easier, at least some of the time. Except when it doesn't. Except when it makes life harder."

I froze, shocked into silence by the possibility that he was going to say it aloud, talk about my monster, the evidence he'd seen.

But he didn't even look at me. Just brushed his shoulder against mine. It was so light, so casual, that I wasn't sure if he'd done it on purpose—an acknowledgment that he'd felt the magic that accompanied my fear—or if it was accidental.

"Well, if it isn't Elisa Sullivan."

I turned back. The vampire behind me was handsome, with wavy blond-brown hair that nearly reached his shoulders and was tucked behind his ears. Tall and muscular, with broad shoulders that narrowed to a tapered waist. He wore a pale gray suit over a white button-down, and he'd skipped the tie.

"Welcome back to Chicago, Elisa," he said, and pressed a kiss to my cheek.

His accent was British, and his name was . . . something with a D. *Darren? David?*

"Dane," he said. "Grey House."

I made the introductions, ending with Connor.

"Of course." Dane smiled. "The prince of wolves."

"Not exactly," he said. He sipped his drink, watching me over the rim. "How do you two know each other?"

"We met before I went to Paris," I said.

"You wound me, Elisa," Dane said with a grin, putting a hand over his heart. "We had dinner shortly before she left."

The memory, or what there was of it, clicked into place. There'd been a dinner I didn't much remember. I'd liked his accent and his sarcasm, and hadn't given anything else much thought. I'd also been focused on Paris, and not especially interested in dating a vampire who looked my age but was decades older.

"How did you find Paris?" he asked.

"Halfway between X and Y."

Connor grinned. Dane's smile was a little more forced.

"It was lovely and complicated," I said.

"Sounds like Chicago," Dane said, then looked at Connor. "I understand the Pack's leaving us soon. Heading back to Alaska, are you?"

"Some of us," Connor said.

"Of course. Shame to leave now when things are getting interesting."

"Interesting?" Connor asked.

"After years of peace, I mean. The fairies' bursting into the peace talks. The violence in Europe." He looked at me. "There are many videos of your heroism at the Eiffel Tower. You handled yourself well. It was impressive."

The sudden flash of interest in his eyes, that deeper ring in his voice, didn't win him the points he probably thought they would. I hadn't been trying to play hero. I hadn't been playing at all, and neither had the vampires who'd attacked.

"It was what needed to be done."

Dane seemed surprised I hadn't taken the bait, hadn't been flattered by his approval. And Connor looked pleased by my answer.

As if looking for an exit, Dane waved at someone across the yard. "Well, I should make the rounds. Good seeing you again, Lis."

He squeezed my hand, making me think I'd been downgraded from a kiss on the cheek, and walked away.

"I think I just got dumped."

"Good riddance," Petra said. "He seems like an ass."

"I don't think he's an ass. He's just . . . a vampire."

Connor made a grumbling sound of agreement I wasn't sure was flattering. "And what about that vampire?" he asked, gesturing with his glass toward Seri. She was standing on the lawn near the pool, a semicircle of supernaturals around her, watching as she posed like a model in an old *Vogue* ad. One foot forward, hands on her slender hips, shoulders tilted back.

"Vain or insecure?" Connor asked.

"Neither," I said with a smile. "She just really likes that dress." For reasons that still eluded me.

"Maybe you should give Dane a shove in her direction," Petra suggested.

"No, thank you. I'm not playing matchmaker," I said. And I didn't need to, since Dane walked to her and made a courtly bow before pressing his lips to the back of her hand, which put a glowing smile on her face.

"Solves that problem," Connor murmured, and took a drink.

"Four years, and your jokes aren't any better. You should have practiced in the interim."

"My jokes are just fine. But I have to work with the material I'm given."

I rolled my eyes, and Petra and Theo shared a look.

"What?" Connor asked, gaze narrowed.

"Nothing at all," Petra said, then tapped her glass against mine. "To supernaturals and friends."

Glass shattered. For a second, I was afraid I'd put too much strength into the gesture and cracked our champagne flutes. But the noise had come from elsewhere.

"Get your hands off me." A vampire's voice, pitched high and angry, echoed across the yard.

I looked back. Tomas, the vampire who'd agreed with the fairies during the opening session of the peace talks, faced down Riley a few yards away. And there was hatred in Tomas's eyes.

"You should step back, vamp," Riley said. His expression was calm, but his eyes were just as hot as Tomas's, magic swirling gold in his irises.

We reached the scuffle just as my father did.

"Problem?" he said, so that it was less a question than an order, a demand that any problem be immediately resolved.

"This animal attempted to strong-arm me."

Riley's expression was a mix of bafflement and sheer rage. "I didn't lay a hand on you. You were about to run into me, you dick, and I put my hands out to keep you from making contact."

"You're all alike," Tomas muttered. "Animals."

"Tomas," my father said, and the word was a warning. "You are a guest in this city and, for now, a guest in this House. But if you cannot find your manners, you'll find yourself a guest of neither."

"I don't take 'animal' as an insult," Riley said, gaze unwavering on Tomas. "But I don't care to have my intentions questioned."

"I'm surprised," my father said, glancing at Tomas, "that, being a vampire, you'd find a shifter intimidating. You've your own strength, and you certainly don't seem impressed by the Pack."

Tomas's eyes fired. "I am perfectly capable of handling myself, Sullivan. The fact that you'd take their side over mine confirms what the fae said. You've forgotten your loyalties."

"Loyalties?" my father asked, a single eyebrow lifted. It was one of his favorite expressions, and this time it managed to convey both surprise and anger. "Cadogan House is allied with the North American Central Pack. Cadogan House is not allied with Casa Cardona, as you refused our offer. Moreover, despite our efforts to organize these peace talks—for the direct benefit of your vampires—you have done nothing but attempt to derail the process. I am very aware of with whom my loyalties lie, Tomas. And you'd do well to remember that."

Furious magic pumped off Tomas in waves. But however petulant his behavior, he was at least smart enough to know when to fold. Facing down my father and his allies at my father's House was apparently that time.

"We are not optimistic about this process or the intentions behind it," he said, lifting his chin. "But the vampires of Catalonia are not cowards. We will not abandon this process to those who would seek to do us harm."

He turned on his heel, his short black cape twirling as he moved, and stalked away.

The entire crowd seemed to exhale. As magic and the threat of violence faded, the other vampires drifted away.

My father looked at Riley. "I apologize for his behavior. I hope you know it does not represent the attitude of this House."

Riley smiled, offered my father a hand. "He's just a stuck-up asshole. I know you're good people." He looked at me and offered a wink that had Connor stiffening beside me, which just made Riley's grin spread even more.

And with that, the crisis was averted and peace returned to the land.

Hunger I'd been ignoring for hours suddenly blossomed; I

couldn't remember the last time I'd eaten. "I'm going over there," I said, pointing to the buffet. "And I strongly suggest no one get in my way."

They didn't get in the way. Instead, they followed me through the line, then over to a table where we could sit and eat—and I could keep an eye on Seri and Marion.

There'd been no other outbursts, no other hints of violence. I'd glimpsed a few fairies—in addition to all the other supernaturals my father had invited—but they'd mostly milled around like everyone else. Except they hadn't eaten any of the food, but that was a cultural thing. Fairies only ate food they'd prepared themselves, because they didn't trust what they called "Others" enough to share their grub. Ironic, given that fairies were historically known for their trickery and theft. Maybe they were projecting. Convinced Others would try to harm them, given the fairies' penchant for doing just that.

We ate and chatted, and when the party began to wind down and Seri failed to stifle a yawn, I rose from the table.

"I'm going to go check on the Maison Dumas delegates. Looks like they're about ready to go."

"Couple of hours until dawn," Theo said with a nod, checking his watch. "The party will probably be wrapping up pretty soon, anyway."

"My father will politely begin to shoo them toward the door," I agreed, then glanced at Petra. "It was good to see you again."

"You, too, Lis. I hope we see more of you while you're in town."

"We'll see how the talks go." Because that would figure largely in whether I had free time.

I glanced at Connor, was prepared to offer a polite goodbye, but he was chatting with Tabby, who'd rejoined him when she'd given up on William Dearborn.

"He wouldn't hear you, anyway," Theo said with a grin.

"Can't argue with that," I said. I grabbed my glass and headed toward the empty tray standing at the edge of the tables.

The crowd was thinning some, delegates having returned to their Autos and hotels, the Cadogan vampires returning to their rooms upstairs.

I lost sight of Seri, turned a circle to find her again, and detected the scent that vampires were most familiar with.

Blood. And a lot of it.

I picked up my dress to keep the silk from dragging along the dewy grass of early morning, walked toward the brick patio that surrounded the House's outdoor kitchen.

Tomas lay on the ground, blood soaking into the brick beneath him.

He'd been divested of his head, which lay two feet away from the rest of his body.

Standing over both, eyes wide, tuxedo shirt splattered with blood and clutching a blood-smeared knife, stood Riley Sixkiller.

TEN

I stared at the scene, tried to process what I was seeing. "Riley. What the hell—what did you do?"

My heart was racing, and not just because of the blood on the ground. The hunger was ruled, fortunately, by the part that had no interest in the blood of a dead man.

Riley looked at me, then down at the body, and his eyes went huge. "Elisa. What is—" And then he seemed to realize he was holding a knife and took two halting steps backward, as if he could simply walk away from it.

"Riley," I said again, my throat so tight I could barely manage a whisper. *"What did you do?"*

Before he could answer, a scream split the air. I spun around, found a female vampire—one of the German delegates—shrieking behind me.

Metal struck stone, and when I looked back again, Riley had dropped the knife, was backing away. He made it two steps before he ran into Connor.

"What the fuck?" Connor said, his voice harsh. And then he turned his eyes, huge and cold, on Riley.

"I didn't do this," Riley said, but there was more than a little uncertainty in his voice. "I didn't kill him. I don't even—I don't even know him. He popped his cork earlier, and that's it between us. I didn't fucking touch him."

All evidence was to the contrary, which made my stomach roll in greasy waves.

Connor nodded, but put a hand on Riley's shoulder, and his fingers were white with tension. Riley wasn't going anywhere.

The German delegate screamed again, and people began running over, creating more noise and more chaos. I scanned the crowd for Kelley or my parents, or someone from the Ombuds' office. But while there'd been plenty of people to meet earlier, no one had yet appeared to handle this crisis.

"Ma'am," I said, "please stop screaming."

But she didn't stop, and the sound triggered more rounds of yelling from the people who joined us.

"*Step back!*" Connor yelled over the din. His hand was still on Riley's shoulder, but this time the move looked protective. "Everyone step back and shut the hell up."

The vampires closest to us, to Tomas, were smart enough to follow the angry shifter's instructions. But the other delegates from Spain arrived, and the ear-piercing screams—this time joined by wails—began in earnest again.

"*¿Que paso?* Who did this? Who has hurt Tomas?"

Someone tried to pull a delegate away, but he yanked his arm back, making contact with another vampire who stood nearby. Thinking he was being attacked, the second vampire struck out.

I cursed and ran toward them, grabbing one by the arm and pulling him away from the crime scene and the fight.

What should have been a moment of quiet reflection became—because of fear, shock, language barriers, and the vampire ego—a comedy of errors.

"That blond vampire is attacking!" someone screamed, and someone else tried to wrench me away from the fighters I'd been attempting to separate.

"I'm not the one attacking!" I said. "I'm the one trying to break it up!" While my katana might have been handy, it was probably better that I didn't pull it on visiting vampires.

The vampires behind me were shoving each other, which pushed me forward so I nearly tumbled into the spreading blood on the patio.

"Elisa!" Connor called my name, but he'd shoved Riley behind him and jumped into the fray to separate two more fighting vampires.

The fight was all around us, chaos spreading like a rippling wave through the party my parents had so carefully arranged.

A male vampire with platinum hair and pale skin ran toward Riley, malice in his expression. I moved to intercept them, grabbed the arm he raised to strike Riley's back, and twisted.

The vampire was old, and he was strong. He swung around and backhanded me, and would have sent me to the ground if I hadn't kept my grip on his free hand.

Pain sang across my face, and the monster decided it had waited long enough. It was heat in my bones and fire across my skin, and it slammed against the edges of my consciousness, trying to break through.

I fought back against two opponents—avoiding the vampire's next strike and bearing down to keep the monster contained, to keep it from rising up and taking me over.

The vampire snatched his arm away, and this time I let him. He had to shift his weight to stay upright, and I took advantage—a front kick that connected with his chin. A snap of his head, and he fell back to the ground.

Someone grabbed me from behind, pinning my arms. I screamed and kicked backward, fought my way free, and punched the vampire who'd held me, sending him stumbling backward and radiating pain through my arm.

Pain was a drug that fed the monster, and it grew stronger still. If it couldn't have freedom, it would take blood.

Its rise pushed me down, as if I were sinking slowly to the bottom of a pool, watching the world through sun-dappled water. My body still moved, but the monster was in control. And it was far more bloodthirsty than me.

The vampire I'd punched climbed shakily to his feet and aimed furious quicksilver eyes in my direction.

The monster stretched through my limbs, rolled my shoulders, and then plunged forward. A side kick to put the vampire off balance, and then a front kick to put him down. He hit the ground and grabbed my ankle, and I used my stiletto-clad foot to stomp on his hand.

He screamed, and the monster reveled in it.

Memory flashed—of the man I'd left bruised and bloodied on the sidewalk, my knuckles cracked and raw . . .

Not again, I told myself. *I won't let it happen again.* I mustered every ounce of strength, worked to push up, to swim through the monster's magic.

"Stop this now!"

My father's words were an earthquake of power and fury. And they were enough to freeze every supernatural in the scuffle—and send the monster back to its depths. I sucked in a breath like a diver breaking the surface, and felt my fangs retract. . . . And I hoped to god my eyes weren't crimson when my father got a look at my face.

He stood behind us, eyes silvered and fangs gleaming, absolute fury in his eyes, in the set of his jaw. The crowd parted as he moved forward, the first sensible thing they'd done.

He gave Tomas a long and somber look, but moved to me first.

"Are you all right?" he asked when he reached me.

"I'm . . . fine." I rubbed my forehead, which had the benefit of covering my eyes. "Just a little dizzy. I don't know who slapped me, but he had some power. Just stings."

I wasn't too dizzy to be nervous that my father had seen the monster, to be worried that I'd been discovered. That others would have seen it peeking through and would be just as horrified.

"I'll be fine in a few minutes. Dad, this was like . . . mass hysteria."

"So I see," he said, then turned his gaze back to Tomas.

Around him, the scene began to order itself as onlookers stepped back, moved away. As if keeping vigil, my father kept somber eyes on Tomas until Theo and Petra joined him and began working to preserve what they could of the scene.

"I'm going to take a minute," I said to no one in particular.

Still holding myself in check, I walked into the grass, kept going until I'd reached a copse of shadowed trees. I reached out to touch one, dug fingers into the bark, and found focusing on the sensation—and the pain—made the anger and fury recede.

When my heart slowed, I pulled my hand back. I'd left deep white gouges in the bark.

"Those look like claw marks."

I spun around, found Connor standing behind me.

"Just some extra energy to burn off," I said, hating the monster for the necessity of the lie.

His expression didn't change. "Your eyes. They were red. They're silver now," he added, probably having felt the punch of my suddenly panicked magic. "And I doubt anyone else noticed given the chaos. This was . . . what happened before?"

Another memory flashed—this time, the reason the monster had first overpowered me. Because she'd lain on the sidewalk like a broken doll. One of the men had held her backpack. The other had looked down at her with sickening interest, his smile twisted. And I hadn't even tried to hold back the rage.

There was compassion and concern in Connor's eyes. I'd have understood admonishment or horror, and they might have made me feel better. I could stop being angry at myself, let someone else take over. But I hadn't earned anyone's compassion, and I didn't understand what to make of the sentiment coming from him, of all people.

"I don't know what you're talking about," I said, refusing to engage. But when I started to walk away from him, he grabbed my arm.

"It was the same thing," he said. "It still affects you."

"It doesn't matter."

"It does matter. You can tell me."

I looked up at him for a long time, into a face that was almost unfairly handsome and eyes that looked like they'd seen their share of darkness.

Ironic, wasn't it, that the boy who'd driven me crazy for most of my life—and vice versa—was the only one who knew the truth? The only one I could unburden myself to.

And much as I wanted to pretend that what had just happened hadn't actually happened, the secret—and the power—was eating me alive from the inside. So I let myself say the word, and it still felt heavy on my lips.

"Yes."

He nodded, gaze shifting from me to the gouges in the wood. "Did that help?"

"Not really," I said, and nearly smiled.

"Here," he said, pulling off his tuxedo jacket, revealing his own torn and bloodied shirt beneath. "You're shaking."

"I'm okay," I said, and couldn't manage to tear my gaze from the sweeps of blood, the magic that drifted into the air from them. "You're hurt."

"I'm fine. Just scratches." He held out the jacket. "Put this on until you can get fixed up."

I looked down, realized my dress was ripped, one of the halter straps torn and unraveling, so the top was little more than a flap of fabric waiting for an opportunity to fall.

I took it from him, our fingers brushing across dark wool.

"Thanks," I said, and slipped my arms into the sleeves and bunched it around me.

The jacket smelled like heat and cologne and a hint of animal that reminded me of wildness and freedom. It smelled like Connor.

I looked up at him, trying to get my bearings. "Are we friends now?"

"Don't go crazy, brat," he said with a smile. But his eyes were dark when he looked back at the vampires clustered on the patio and surrounding his Pack mate, accusation in their eyes.

The fairies' interruption at the peace talks had been strange but nonviolent. They hadn't managed to break the peace, only to bend it a little. But this was real violence, an undeniable breach of two decades of peace. This was murder. And how could we help Europe's Houses with a cease-fire if we couldn't even manage it in our literal backyard?

I was a witness to some of it, and knew I'd need to stay and make a statement—and help my parents, if I could. I talked to Marion, got her permission to stay behind, then found two Cadogan guards to escort them back to the hotel.

I hadn't taken all of my clothes to Paris, so I went back to my room on the third floor, changed from the stained and ripped dress into jeans, a T-shirt with a scoop neck, and a pair of well-worn suede boots with a low cuff. I stuffed the dress, clutch, and shoes into a tote bag, carried that and Connor's jacket downstairs again.

The House swam with magic, the nervous energy of vampires and the other sups at the party. And it grew stronger as I passed the silent vampires who milled in the foyer, watching me as I walked to my father's office.

My parents were already there, along with Dearborn, Theo,

Gabriel, and Connor, everyone in small species-specific clusters. The room was quiet, and my mother's sword lay on the conference table, unsheathed and gleaming.

I wasn't sure if the monster was tired from the outburst or unwilling to challenge me now, but it barely surfaced. I pushed it down until the magic was a pulsing ache in the back of my head. At least that only hurt me.

I walked to Connor, held out his jacket. "Thank you," I said softly, and still the words echoed through the room like a gunshot.

He took it but didn't put it on.

I put the tote with my katana, then walked back to my parents, who both reached out to touch me, as if to reassure me and themselves that I was safe.

"Dearborn wants to speak to you," my father said quietly.

"I figured."

"He'll have an agenda. And I suspect that agenda will be cleaning up this matter as quickly and quietly as possible, so he can report to the mayor that it was an aberration, it was handled, and it doesn't involve the city's Houses or the talks. The evidence, at present, only points to Riley. Based on what I know about Dearborn, I suspect he'd be more than happy to rely on that evidence and let the blame fall on the Pack."

"Even if it's a setup?" I asked. Because I still couldn't wrap my mind around the possibility Riley had done this. And yet . . .

"Even if," my father said. "Because resolution is faster than investigation. So be careful of his questions. He'll be looking for particular answers."

"I'll be wary," I promised.

"Are you ready?" Dearborn asked, the words echoing across the room. He wore a slim tuxedo, his silver hair gleaming, sterling cuff links gleaming. Even the shine on his shoes was perfect. Once again, the perfection bothered me. Maybe because his were the only immaculate clothes in the room. Everyone else's were bloody, muddy, mussed, or torn, because they'd been part of the fray or cleaning it up. He apparently hadn't lowered himself to get involved.

"Sure," I said.

"Why don't we sit?" my father suggested, gesturing to the sitting area on the left-hand side of the room. I took the end of a leather sofa, and my mother sat beside me. My father stood behind us, a unified front. Although I wasn't the one who needed protecting.

Gabriel took a seat across from me. Connor didn't sit. He stood behind his father, arms crossed and a grim expression on his face.

Dearborn, unsurprisingly, took the club chair at the end—the "head" position. Theo stayed on his feet and looked nearly as uncomfortable as Connor did. Except one of his own hadn't been accused of murder.

Dearborn pulled a screen from his pocket, made some adjustment, then set it on the table. A small green light pulsed hypnotically in the middle, signaling it was recording. Dearborn sat back, crossed his legs, and looked at me. "Your version of events, please."

A steadying breath, and then I told my story. "I was going to check on Seri and Marion. Before I reached them, I could smell blood, so I went to check it out. I saw Tomas, lying on the ground. His head . . . was a few feet away." I glanced at Connor, apology in my eyes. "Riley stood nearby, and the knife was in his hand. There was blood on his shirt."

There was perverse satisfaction in Dearborn's eyes. "You saw him holding the murder weapon, covered in blood, and standing over Tomas's dead body?"

I saw the shifters flinch, but I focused on Dearborn—and the facts.

"I saw Tomas on the ground," I said matter-of-factly. "I saw Riley standing nearby, and Riley was holding a knife. I don't know if it was the murder weapon, and I don't know what happened before I got there."

Dearborn's gaze went hard. "Did you see anyone else?"

"No. One of the German delegates found us, screamed when she saw Tomas. And then chaos broke out, and everyone began fighting. My father arrived and broke it up."

"The German delegate was Gerda Kreitzer," my father said. "She's waiting in Luc's office."

Dearborn nodded.

"Riley didn't do this," Connor said, and his gaze on Dearborn was hot. "He wouldn't kill a vampire he didn't even know."

"Connor," Gabriel said quietly, a warning to his son to tread carefully.

"All evidence to the contrary," Dearborn said. "While I appreciate that some of you, at least, are loathe to jump to conclusions, it seems obvious to me what happened."

"And what's that?" my father asked.

Dearborn gave my father a weary look, as if bored by his refusal to accept the obvious. "I'm told the victim expressed concern about shifters, including Sixkiller, during tonight's session. They had a public altercation at the party in which blows were exchanged approximately an hour before Tomas was killed. Sixkiller stewed over it, and his anger got the best of him. That, you all have to admit, is the simplest explanation for Tomas's murder. 'Killer' is in the shifter's name, for god's sake."

I glanced at Connor. His eyes were on Dearborn, and the fury on his face wasn't any better masked than that on his father's.

"It's a family name," Gabriel said shortly, magic drifting in the room as he spoke. "There's history behind it that has nothing to do with this."

"Noted," Dearborn said coolly.

"You believe this was an attack on Tomas," my father said, "and not on the talks generally."

"Tomas is the only one dead," Dearborn said. "And despite the fairies' intervention at the peace talks, which was handled and concluded, the talks continued unimpeded. What purpose would be gained from killing one delegate here?"

"Shifting our focus?" my father suggested. "Creating animosity between the delegates to preclude the possibility of peace? Many prefer war."

"Occam's razor," Dearborn countered. "The simplest explanation is usually the correct one."

"*Usually,*" my father qualified. "Perpetrators are aware of that concept, too, and can alter their behavior to fit it."

"If Riley did it," my mother said, and slid an apologetic gaze to Gabriel, "and I'm not saying he did, maybe he didn't have a choice. Maybe someone made him do it. Someone drugged him. Or magicked him."

"He'll be tested for drugs," Dearborn said. "But a positive drug test would hardly excuse homicide."

"Magic might be more likely," I said, and thought of the vampires' reaction to finding Tomas. "Riley looked really dazed when I found him. He seemed confused, kind of out of it. And the crowd's reaction was also weird. It makes sense that they'd be shocked, that they'd be angry. But they started fighting, and not just Riley. They fought me."

Maybe that's also why I hadn't been able to hold back the monster.

"He wouldn't kill anyone," Connor insisted.

"And your friend is entirely innocent? He has no violence in him?" Dearborn's gaze was cutting.

"If you have questions about the background of a Pack member," Gabriel said, "direct them to me. I assume you're aware of Riley's history given the question, and the fact that he overcame substantial odds to become the man he is today."

"Or he didn't overcome them," Dearborn said, turning off the recorder and slipping the screen back in his pocket. "But that's the purpose of the investigation. To find the truth."

"What happens now?" Connor asked.

Dearborn rose. "He'll be taken in and questioned by the CPD and our office, per the standard protocols. We'll keep him at the supernatural facility until his preliminary hearing, after which he'll be remanded back into our custody. Bail is unlikely given the nature of the crime and his"—he looked at Gabriel—"background."

There was scuffling in the hallway as five CPD officers moved Riley through the hall, hands tied awkwardly at his back. Riley's expression was absolutely deadly.

"Theo, accompany them back to the office."

Theo glanced at me, then headed for the door, his expression as grim as Gabriel's had been.

"You should postpone tomorrow's session," Dearborn said to my father. "Presuming anyone wants to continue the talks, given the breach of the peace."

"Perhaps, instead of focusing on Riley," my father said, "we should consider who would have wanted that breach?"

"It hardly matters, given the deed was done," Dearborn said. "As to the delay, announce it's not because we're afraid of further attack, but because we wanted to honor the delegate who was killed. It is . . . an opportunity for reflection and consideration of the reason for the talks."

"Good spin," my father said dryly.

Dearborn seemed to miss the sarcasm and walked to the door. "We'll be in touch." He stopped and turned back, adjusting his cufflinks before looking up. "I expect none of you will attempt to interfere with our investigation. That would be viewed by myself and the mayor as a violation of the spirit of cooperation my office has come to embody"—he lifted his gaze to my father— "and the specific deal previously negotiated with Cadogan House.

This is our matter to handle, and handle it we will. Without interference."

With that, he disappeared.

"That man is no Chuck Merit," Gabriel said, derision obvious in the tone.

"No, he is not," my father said, taking my mother's hand. "He's a political operative with more interest in staying in the mayor's good graces than in finding the truth. He's had a very easy tenure up to now, and he took a great deal of pride in the talks, in the shine they brought to the city. He won't like his blemish on his record, and he'll want to close this quickly."

"And damn the consequences?" Gabriel asked.

My father inclined his head. "But he's the Ombudsman, so he's the one we have to deal with. Do you have an attorney you trust? If not, I can make a recommendation."

"Emma Garza," Gabriel said. "Tanya's sister. She's an attorney, and she can handle this."

"Good." My father frowned. "You know we have to stay out of the investigation, let the Ombudsman handle it. That was the deal we struck."

"I'm aware," Gabriel said dryly.

"The Ombudsman will likely keep us updated, given the crime occurred here," my father said. "And whatever we learn, we'll tell you. In the meantime, be careful." His eyes were cold and hard. "Because peace has apparently become too much of a burden for some of us."

"Let's go," Gabriel said, and headed for the door. Connor followed him out, and didn't so much as look at me on the way.

So much for friendship.

"Riley wouldn't have done this," I said, looking back at my father when the shifters were gone, their magic receding behind them.

"It certainly doesn't seem like the kind of thing he'd do," my father said, but his tone was soft. "But our feelings about him didn't sway Dearborn, and they probably wouldn't sway a jury."

Kelley stepped into the doorway, screen in hand. She was tall and slender, with pale skin, dark eyes, and gleaming ebony hair that fell just past her shoulders.

"But perhaps this may," my father said, gesturing her into the room.

Kelley walked to the television, pointed her screen at it. The monitor filled with a color shot of the brick patio.

"Surveillance video," my father said, and we all walked closer to get a better look.

I glanced at him. "You waited until Dearborn was gone to watch this."

"I wanted to see what happened at my House first," he said. "Then we'll report."

Being the kid of Ethan Sullivan was a masterclass in political strategy.

Kelley advanced the video, and we watched as sups silently milled around the patio, chatting, checking out the barbecue grill and burners, and nibbling hors d'oeuvres. Tomas walked into the frame—and the video shuddered, shook. When it cleared again, Tomas was on the ground, dead. Riley stood over him, bafflement in his expression.

"There's no video of the incident," my father said, and looked at Kelley.

"There is not," she said. "And no other camera caught this particular spot."

"That's . . . interesting," my father said.

"Isn't it, though?"

I looked between them, then back at the screen. "You think someone altered the video."

"The camera was fine until it wasn't," Kelley said with a nod. "And Tomas was alive until he wasn't."

"What about the other parts of the yard?" I asked. "Whoever killed Tomas would have been covered in blood, and he or she would have to make an entrance and an exit. Surely some other camera captured it."

"They did not," Kelley said. "Conveniently enough, there appears to have been a cascading failure among certain of the House's cameras." She futzed with her screen, and the video footage was replaced with an overhead view of the House and lawn. A series of red dots made a path from between the patio and the fence on the west side of the House.

"They came in over the fence?" my mother asked.

"And left again that way," Kelley said with a nod. "We checked the area—carefully so as not to disturb any evidence—and found no implements, no blood trail, no discarded clothes."

"The perpetrator left," my father said. "And was very careful."

Kelley inclined her head. "Now we have to determine why the cameras failed in the particular way that they did."

"What are the options?" my mother asked. "Someone hacked into the system?"

"Or temporarily blocked the camera," my father said, "although this doesn't look like a visual break."

"No, it does not," Kelley said. "I have an idea, but I'd like to flesh it out a bit more before I advise you."

"You're the expert," he said. "Let us know what you can, as soon as you can."

"Of course, Liege. What about Dearborn?"

My father considered. "It might be most helpful to the Ombudsman if we were to provide the video along with our conclusions regarding . . . we'll call it the 'blip.'"

"That's a very good idea." Kelley's smile was sly. "If we have our answer first, we can tell them we've eliminated the possibility of a mechanical failure. And you just never know about technology. I'll be in the Ops Room," she said, then pocketed her screen and disappeared into the hallway again.

"Give me something to do to help," I said when she was gone. "Riley's my friend."

"You can't get involved," my mother said. "That's the deal."

"I can't just sit around while people blame him for murder. He didn't do it."

"There's an agreement," my father said. "I understand you made a promise to Maison Dumas, but we made a bigger one to the city of Chicago, to the people who live here. This time, that agreement has to win. It's for the best, and not just because the Ombudsman's office is trained to investigate."

"I can handle myself."

"We know, Elisa. But we've worked hard to keep Cadogan House safe, to keep the vampires protected. If we breach the deal, we lose our charter."

That was the other penalty of the deal made with the mayor, the other promise exacted from Cadogan House. Cadogan, Grey, Navarre, and now Washington had been recognized by the city of Chicago. They were official. They were licensed. They were, basically, allowed to exist. Ironic, considering the House had been in the city longer than any of its humans had been alive.

His voice softened. "If I said I was sorry that you're being excluded from the investigation, it would be a lie. You're my daughter, and I want you safe and sound."

I made a sound of frustration.

"I also wish we could do more," my father said. "But that is the agreement we made. We will not break it. Not even for the Pack. And not even when it happened at my House."

His tone had sharpened, and I guessed he was facing his own struggle.

"We're doing what we can," my mother said, putting a hand on his shoulder. "The rest is outside our control."

"I don't find that acceptable," he said.

"I know." She smiled, just a little. "Because you prefer to lead, not follow, and because you'd never take a life to prove a point, whatever point this might have been. But this battle isn't yours. You were just unlucky enough to own the battleground."

"I really wish you'd stop being so reasonable," my father said after a moment.

"I'm angry, too. But anger won't help us, and it won't help Riley."

My father looked at me. "You should warn the delegation to be careful until we know what's happening here. It seems unlikely they'd be targeted, but until we know precisely why Tomas was targeted, we can't be sure."

"I will," I promised. "I'm sorry this happened here. I'm sorry the House was violated, that this was brought to your door."

He nodded, put an arm around me. "It has turned out to be a horrible evening all around. I'm sorry this is what you found when you returned home. It's not what I wanted for you. Maybe when dusk falls again, we'll find it a little better."

The guests had left, and the cleanup had begun. But the lawn was still dotted with overturned furniture, empty champagne glasses, and abandoned linen napkins. The excited magic that had sparked in the air had been replaced with sadness, grief, and confusion.

Since I made it back to the hotel with less than an hour to go before sunrise, I left a message for Seri, confirming I'd give her and Marion an update at dusk.

I also got Lulu's voice mail, so I also made a promise to her to give an update tomorrow.

Once in my room, I stripped off my clothes, left them in a pile on the floor, and fell face-first onto the bed. And then tried to figure out how to get around the deal my father had made.

I didn't have any reason to doubt what I'd seen—Riley holding a knife over Tomas's body—except for the ten years I'd known Riley and every instinct in my body. He wasn't a killer. Either he'd happened to be in the wrong place at the wrong time, or someone had made sure he'd been in the wrong place at the wrong time.

The Ombudsman was looking for proof that he was guilty.

I was going to find proof that he was innocent.

ELEVEN

I dreamed of knives, of spinning blades that sliced tiny nicks in my skin, until every inch of my body felt like it was on fire.

I woke in a sweat, pushed my hair out of my eyes, and tried to slow my breathing.

I was also starving, so I walked to the mini fridge to check out my options. Booze, soda, fruit juice. Four bottles of Blood4You, the old-school bottled blood my parents preferred. Four bottles of Hemo, my favorite. I thought Blood4You tasted like plastic, and the flavored varieties tasted like plastic plus imitations of actual food. I preferred the unadulterated variety, probably because I'd been drinking blood since birth. My parents had scared plenty of humans by handing me bottles of pink milk during evening walks—when the humans got past wondering why a baby was out of the house at midnight.

I grabbed a bottle of Hemo, flipped the cap, and drank the entire bottle in seconds. Then I grabbed another and did the same. After three, I finally began to feel level again.

I'd gotten sleep and nourishment, so it was time to get on with my evening—and figuring out a way to help Riley. I wanted to see what the humans were saying, so I plugged my screen into the hotel's monitor and selected the twenty-four-hour news station.

A panel of humans speculated about Riley's motives. They stopped short of calling him a murderer, probably not because they believed him, but because they didn't want to get sued. They called him a suspect, and I could all but hear the air quotes around the word. The photographs they'd picked just helped their narrative. They emphasized how large he was, how strong, how *other*. Not delicately handsome, but a hulk. A thug of a man. A man who obviously could have killed.

They didn't know Riley and didn't care to. That it was totally out of character for him to hurt anyone wouldn't have made a good story. Kindness wasn't thrilling.

But until there was evidence the Ombudsman would believe—that all of us could believe—nothing was going to change. And in the meantime, the real murderer was still out there with a motive we didn't understand.

Before I could turn it off, the image switched to a photo of Connor and Tabby arriving at the party, then shots of couples talking—Connor and me, then me and Dane, then Seri and Dane. They were stacked above a headline that read, "Love before Violence?"

I rolled my eyes. Never mind that Connor and Tabby were the only ones actually dating, and the rest of us had just been chatting. Casual conversation at a party also apparently wasn't thrilling enough.

Irritation layered over the impotence and frustration I already felt about not being able to help Riley.

But by the time I emerged from the shower, an idea had begun to blossom. A way that I could avoid breaching the mayor's deal with Cadogan House so I could do some investigating, and my parents wouldn't get tagged for it.

Yes, I was Ethan and Merit's daughter, and I'd lived in Cadogan for most of my life. But I wasn't *officially* a Cadogan vampire. I'd been born into the House, so I hadn't been officially Commended into it—the process through which Initiate vampires became Novitiates. I was technically a Rogue, a vampire unaffiliated with any particular House.

If I wasn't a Cadogan vampire, any deal with Cadogan House didn't affect me.

Was it a technicality? Maybe. But Riley was worth the argument.

I got dressed, opting for jeans, boots, and a long-sleeved, flowy black top, and pulled my hair into a knot that I hoped made me look moderately professional. I had a report to give, and plenty of questions to ask.

And if my parents and the Ombudsman learned what I was doing, plenty of explaining to do.

I rose, walked to the door. It was time to do my part.

Two human guards stood outside Seri's hotel room. They wore head-to-toe black and eyed me suspiciously as I walked closer.

"Elisa Sullivan to see Seraphine and Marion," I said, and pulled out my identification.

They looked at it, then me, then the ID again, just as they'd been instructed to do.

Good. I liked it when people followed instructions.

"Ma'am," one of them said, then unlocked and opened the door.

The suite was full of vampires and heavy magic. Seri saw me first, rushed over. She wore jeans and a striped top, her feet in red ballet flats and her hair in a messy knot that somehow managed to look fashionable.

As she pressed kisses to each cheek, I could feel the frizzle of her nervous magic. "You are all right, Lis?"

I nodded. "I'm fine. How are things here?"

"They are . . . concerned," she said quietly, sliding her gaze back to Marion and the others. They sat on couches near the large windows, talking quietly as they looked over the dark city.

"Yesterday didn't turn out the way any of us had planned."

"No, it did not."

Marion glanced back and rose, walking toward us with the other vampires in her wake.

"Developments?" she asked.

"I haven't yet spoken to my father this evening. I wanted to speak with you first. We're anticipating the Ombudsman's office is going to be difficult to deal with," I said, and explained what we'd heard last night from Dearborn, and how prickly we expected him to be.

"Riley wouldn't have killed Tomas," I said, giving the words as much confidence as I could, and meeting their gazes as I said it.

Marion tilted her head. "He was found with the murder weapon."

I had a feeling I was going to be having this same conversation a lot in the near future.

"He was," I agreed. "And he'd had a public altercation with Tomas at the party, which was after Tomas insulted shifters at the talks. But Riley wouldn't have cared about any of that, and even if he'd been irritated, he wouldn't have killed over it. Yes, his past is checkered. But I know him, and I've known him for a very long time. This isn't his way."

"If you believe Riley is innocent, who do you think did it?"

"I don't know. Not yet."

I wasn't sure how much to tell them, but decided my loyalties to Maison Dumas were at least as strong as those to Riley, if not stronger. So I told them about the missing video footage, the killer's escape route, and the possibility magic had been used to skew Riley's memory.

"You think he was influenced?" Marion asked, gaze clear.

"I think there was magic in the area of Tomas's death," I said carefully. "I think someone killed Tomas, and Riley made the perfect fall guy."

"Why kill Tomas?" she asked.

"I don't know that, either. But I don't think it's a coincidence that there are no talks today, that the session was canceled."

"You believe someone wanted to disrupt the entire peace process," Marion said.

"That's the only link we know of at the moment."

"The fae interrupted the session yesterday," Marion said. "Were they were involved in the murder?"

"There's no evidence of that so far," I said. "There were fairies at the party, but they didn't cause any trouble that I know of."

"I had the same thought," Marion said, nodding as Odette handed her a cup of tea. "Thank you, *ma chère*." Marion took a heartening sip, then set the cup down in its matching saucer. "And how can we assist in helping your friend?"

The question nearly brought tears to my eyes, and reminded me once again why I'd felt such a connection to Dumas.

"You could give me time," I said. "I realize I'm here on behalf of Maison Dumas, but I'd like your permission to look into this, to try to find out what happened. Not just for Riley, but because the killer is still out there—and willing to kill—in order to get what they want. That makes them dangerous to all of us, including your house."

Marion sipped again, considered. "You have my permission to make inquiries," she said, then grinned. "And how, pray tell, do you plan to get around Cadogan's arrangement with the city?"

I smiled back. "I'm still working on that one."

The Ombudsman's office was located in the abandoned brick factory that also housed Cook County's supernatural prisoners. The factory's offices had been renovated, and a second building had been converted into a space for supernatural mediations and educational events. That had been my great-grandfather's doing: adding a learning component to the office's mission. The city's politicians had, for once, done some long-term thinking and agreed with him.

The property was fenced, but the gate was open, the entrance edged with shrubs and a sign bearing the office's logo. That was also part of the deal my great-grandfather had made for rehabbing the factory. He'd agree to move his HQ from the South Side neighborhood he'd worked in before, but the gate had to stay open, the offices had to be inviting, because he'd wanted humans and supernaturals to feel comfortable visiting here. Now it looked more like a campus than an industrial relic.

I walked to the admin building, waved at the guard who sat near the entrance. Clarence Pettiway had guarded the office since I'd been old enough to visit, and always had a book in hand.

This time he looked up from a faded paperback and lifted a hand in a wave. His dark skin was liberally wrinkled, but his eyes were still sharp.

"Well, if it isn't little Elisa Sullivan. Although not so little now."

"Mr. Pettiway, it's good to see you." I gestured to the book. "What's in the queue today?"

He turned it over, revealing the creased cover of Homer's *The Odyssey*. "Hope to get in a little classical reading this week. Working on one of those Top 100 Reads lists. What brings you by?"

"I'd like to speak with one of your prisoners. Riley Sixkiller."

The smile disappeared, and his face went hard. Mr. Pettiway was retired from the CPD, but he was still a cop at heart. "He's in lockup. And Mr. Dearborn didn't authorize you through."

That was a tricky one.

"He doesn't know I'm here," I confessed. "But Riley's been a friend for a really long time, and I think someone set him up. I'd just like a few minutes to hear his side of the story. I know I'm asking you for a lot. But I promise I'd only need a few minutes."

It took nearly a minute for him to relent, to rise and put down his book, then walk me down the hallway to the dismal concrete corridor that led to the holding facility.

Mr. Pettiway pressed a hand to the security plate, and the door popped open with a loud, mechanical *click*. He held it before it could close, looked back at me again.

"I'm allowing this because of your great-grandfather, and because I figure you're a pretty good judge of character. But you'll be careful?"

"I promise."

And I could handle myself better than Mr. Pettiway imagined.

The room was enormous, big as a football field with walls twenty feet high. And it was empty except for the glass-and-concrete cubes arranged in a tidy grid. No steel, no bars. But cages all the same.

The first cube in the first row was empty, as were most of the others. Riley's cube was second from the end.

I found him pacing behind the glass wall. He wore pale gray scrubs and white socks, and the thin fabric somehow made him seem smaller. Behind him, the cube was empty but for a slab bed built into the wall, a sink, and a toilet. The ceiling was glass, but the other three walls were concrete, to provide a little privacy. And like most prisons, I guessed, it was depressing.

I waited until he lifted his gaze—and then saw hope flare and fade again. I was instantly sorry I'd put it there.

"Elisa. You come to stare at the animal in the cage?"

There were dark circles under his eyes and a bruise on his jaw, probably from fighting back against his arrest.

"I came to check on you. And ask you some questions."

"I've already talked to the cops. The Pack." His voice was dismissive, his words short. I couldn't exactly blame him for being angry.

"I know. And I know you didn't hurt him, Riley. I know you didn't kill Tomas."

His eyes widened, softened.

"Tell me what happened," I said.

"I don't know." He squeezed his eyes shut, rubbed his temple. "And trying to remember makes my head scream."

"Okay," I said, filing that away. "Then tell me what you do remember."

"Brisket."

Not what I'd expected him to say. "Brisket?"

"The Pack supplied the meat for the party, including brisket we'd smoked at Little Red in the new kitchen—there's a mesquite pit, but I guess that doesn't matter. I got to the party same time as the van, helped unload the trays." He held out his arms in a rough rectangle. "You know those big aluminum pans?"

"Sure. The catering pans. I saw you carrying them."

He nodded. "I brought them in, got them situated."

"And then what?"

"I went out to the party. Had a whiskey—Cadogan has the good stuff—and walked around, talked to people. I ate and drank and listened to the music, talked to my Pack mates about the Sox, this problem Cole is having with one of his cams."

"Cams?"

"On his ride. Engine cam."

"Ah. Got it. Keep going."

"We thought about asking if we could take a dip in the pool, after the party died down. I figured Sullivan would be game. I wanted to check the water, so I kneeled down, put my fingers in. It was warm, but not too warm. And then"—he winced, rubbed his temple again. "And then I saw something. Or heard something? I don't . . . I don't remember."

"Something caught your attention?"

"Yeah. But I don't know what. And then I smelled blood, and I looked around—" He stopped, brow furrowed, and pressed a clenched fist against his forehead. And, like he'd been holding in pain, exhaled loudly.

I moved closer to the glass. "Do you need me to get someone, Riley? For the pain?"

"No. I can handle it." But he walked to the bed, sat down, and cradled his head in his hands.

His size made it even harder to see him hurting. He was strong, so pain that brought him down would have probably been unbearable to me.

"The next thing I knew," he said without looking up, "you were standing in front of me, and the woman behind you was screaming. Then the cops showed up." He looked up again, misery and anger warring in his eyes. "And here we fucking are."

"Have you ever had gaps in your memory like that?"

"No. When my brain was working again, I recognized the man on the bricks. The delegate from Spain. The one who raged about shifters and vampires working together, then nearly ran into me and tried to blame me for it."

"Did you know him before the event? Had you talked to him before?"

He lifted his head and his eyes seemed clearer, as if the pain had vanished because we'd switched topics. Could magic have done this? Affected his memory, and made it painful to access?

"Neither. His name, photo were probably in the security dossier." He tried for a grin. "But I don't pay much attention to vampires who live a continent away."

Since I hadn't given much thought to shifters while I'd been in Paris, I couldn't fault him for that.

"Would anyone want to hurt you?" I asked.

"I'm a shifter," he said, as if that explained it completely. "I've got enemies like everyone else." His eyes darkened. "But my enemies would come after me. They wouldn't kill someone else."

"Who are those enemies?" I asked.

He rose, walked back to the glass. "You know I did time—before the Pack."

"Yeah." Lulu had explained it. Riley was born in a small town in Oklahoma, but left when he was sixteen, looking for excitement. He ended up in Memphis in an independent band of shifters—the Rogues of the shifter world—who didn't recognize the authority of any Apex outside their own family. Unfortunately, it had been less a family than a gang, and he'd done time for assault and larceny before he tried to pull a con on the wrong shifter. Gabriel hadn't fallen for it, and he'd apparently seen past the grift. He pulled Riley into the Pack, and Riley had been on the straight and narrow—or as straight and narrow as shifters' paths got—since then.

"Some of the family weren't happy about my decision."

"They aren't in Chicago, though, are they? Weren't they in Memphis?"

"Yeah, and I don't see them traveling all the way out here to make trouble for me. They were pissed, but I wouldn't say they were invested, if that makes sense."

I nodded. "It does."

"Lis, I don't have any idea why someone would have killed that vampire, or made it look like I did it. I can't remember what happened, and I'm in this goddamned cell for no reason except, as far as I can figure, I was in the wrong place at the wrong time."

"I know, Riley. And I'm sorry. We're all working to figure out what happened."

He nodded, but misery swam in his eyes.

"If you think of anything, let me know. Or talk to Connor or Gabriel. Just—tell someone."

"I will."

I nodded and turned, guilt following me like a shadow.

"Elisa."

I glanced back at him. He'd moved closer to the glass, flattened a hand against it.

"Animals shouldn't be caged."

The magic and pain and budding fury that swirled in his eyes had me shivering.

The grounds of Cadogan House were darker than they had been the night before. The party gear was gone and the sky was overcast, the air warm and damp and still, like misery itself had been trapped in the humidity, ready to suffocate. A swag of black taffeta and crepe hung from the front gate and the front door, a memorial to the immortal killed within.

It was quiet inside, too, and the air was still thick with the smell of yesterday's flowers.

I found my parents in my father's office. They stood together, watching the screen my mother held out.

"Good evening," my father said, glancing back when I stepped into the doorway.

"Hi," I said, moving to them. "How are you doing?"

"We are . . . concerned," he settled on. "We had a moment of silence at dusk in honor of Tomas, but that still feels insufficient."

I reached out, took his hand. "I'm sorry."

"So am I," he said. "I was no fan of Tomas. He was pompous and a little paranoid. But that doesn't excuse murder."

"Is there any news about the investigation?" I asked, wishing for some smoking gun that would prove Riley innocent—and that I hadn't entirely misjudged his character.

My mother glanced at my father, then at me. I didn't take that as a good sign. "We've got bad news and odd news," she said.

"Give me the bad news first."

"Riley's fingerprints were the only prints on the knife. And they were in the right place." She held up a fist like she was gripping an invisible knife, ready to strike.

"The perpetrator could have wiped off the other prints." And would have done just that if this was the setup it looked like. But the absence of other prints still tied the knot in my stomach a little tighter.

"And the odd news?"

"The blip in the surveillance video," my mother said, "was magical."

"I don't understand what those words mean together."

"I told you," my father said with a smile for her. "I didn't get it, either, the first time."

"Kelley says the missing video wasn't caused by a technological problem," my mother said. "It was magical in origin."

I frowned. "Someone spelled the camera?"

"She doesn't know, and there's nothing before or after the blip that shows who made the magic."

"A shifter couldn't work a spell," I said. "And even if they could, it's not a very shifter thing to do. To kill someone at a party, in public, and then blank out the footage?"

"It's pretty passive-aggressive," my mother agreed. "Shifters tend to take more ownership of their behavior."

"What about the fence where the killer came over? Have they found anything there?"

"Nothing," my mother said.

"The Ombudsman continues to investigate," my father said, and I could hear the irritation and the warning in his voice—that I wasn't supposed to get involved.

I wasn't going to argue with him, especially since my best argument involved telling him his daughter wasn't a real member of his House.

"I'm going to see Lulu," I said. "I don't know if she'll want to talk about this or not, but I figure I could make the offer."

"Of course you should," my mother said. "Do you want to take her something from the kitchen?"

It was just the kind of thing my mother would ask. "No, but thanks. You'll let me know if you find out anything else?"

"We will," she said. "And give our best to Lulu."

"I will." And hoped that would be enough.

I wanted to talk to Lulu, and I wanted to talk to Connor, not necessarily in that order. But first, I wanted to take another look at the scene of the crime.

Tonight, the House's cafeteria was full of vampires taking their first meal of the day before heading out to their jobs in- or outside Cadogan. The smell of bacon permeated the space, and I was half-surprised my mother didn't mention it was a bacon day. She and bacon had a special relationship.

It was humid on the back lawn, the torches and lanterns gone, the yard dark but for the occasional path lights and moonlight that filtered through the trees. No vampires, no humans, no CPD crime-scene techs. The site of Tomas's death was empty of people tonight, which seemed equally fitting and sad.

Even if I hadn't known the way to the patio, the scent of blood would have drawn me. It had been washed away, the scene already photographed and imaged, but it still stained the air.

The patio bricks were laid in a hexagon. There was a kitchen on one side, and a low brick rail on the other that provided seating.

I walked across the brick from one end to the other, gaze sweeping the ground for anything unusual, anything that might have been missed. I found nothing. If anything had been here, it had probably been taken by the forensic team or determined to be insignificant and washed away, just like the blood.

I checked the grass nearby, found nothing but the divots where supernaturals had scuffled in soft grass. But then something crunched underfoot. Half expecting to find a squished bug, I lifted my shoe to find something shiny wedged between grass and brick at the edge of the patio.

I crouched down. It was a brooch, a complicated knot in a careful gold filigree. I didn't recognize the piece or the design. But it was near the site of the murder, so I figured that made it worth another look.

I reached into my pocket, pulled out the handkerchief I'd borrowed from my father the night I'd arrived and had meant to give back. I picked up the brooch, wrapped it carefully, and put it away again.

Maybe it was evidence; maybe it wasn't. But at least it was something.

TWELVE

I contacted Seri and Marion when I was in an Auto again. Based on their expressions on my screen, the information about the fingerprints and magical tampering of the surveillance video didn't thrill them.

"A shifter could not affect electronics with magic," Marion said.

"No, they couldn't."

"But that does not exonerate your friend. It indicates only that there was at least one other party involved in the murder. Someone with magical skills and the intention to use them to cover up a crime."

That made it sound like a conspiracy, which didn't bode well for the peace talks or peace in Chicago. "Or one person who wanted to cover their tracks," I said.

"Yes," Marion said. "That is possible." But she didn't sound convinced. "What are your next steps?"

"I've talked to Riley, and I'm going to talk to Connor Keene, Gabriel's son. He's Riley's friend and would know if Riley had enemies."

"Or a temper?"

It was a logical question, but it suggested she wasn't buying my theory. "If he has a temper, I've never seen it. But I understand and respect your concerns. That's why I'm going to talk to Connor. If I learn anything else, I'll let you know."

"That is as much as you can do," Marion said. "But I fear for this process. Someone wished to interrupt it. And they have succeeded."

I could hear the music a block before I arrived at Little Red, the low bass line, throbbing drums, and thrumming guitar. Either the Pack had turned up the jukebox or there was a concert tonight at the bar.

I guessed the answer by the dozens of gleaming bikes lined up outside.

I skipped the bar entrance, went in through the office. Berna sat in the lobby on her scooter, staring intently at an e-reader beneath an enormous pair of pink and rose gold headphones. I guess she didn't like the band. She looked up when I walked in, gaze narrowed.

"Connor," I mouthed.

"Garage," she said, returning her gaze to her book.

Permission enough, so I headed through the hallway she'd led me down before. When in doubt, I turned toward the noise.

The door to the bar vibrated on its hinges with each strum of the bass guitar from a band covering Jimi Hendrix's "All Along the Watchtower." I pushed open the door and was nearly pushed back by the deafening sound. The tables were full, the air smelled of smoke and spilled beer, and the room buzzed with magic strong enough to raise the hair on my neck. Shifter magic was a powerful thing, and there were a lot of shifters here. That gave it a dangerous edge.

There were also plenty of humans in the crowd, mostly twenty- and thirty-somethings who probably hadn't come to the bar for the music but for the magic. For the power and the possibility something might happen.

The door to the garage was closed, but shifter free. I walked inside and closed the door, which muted the sound of the band to a dull roar.

I didn't see any shifters. But the magic in the air said I wasn't alone.

A low stool rolled through the bikes on the other side of the room with a squeak of rubber on linoleum. On it sat a narrow-eyed Miranda.

She wore skinny jeans, black boots that laced up to her knees, and a black bra beneath a distressed black tank. Her hair was curlier today, soft, dark waves that framed her face perfectly.

The boots said she was ready to fight. And so did the expression on her face.

"You aren't wanted here," she said, rising. "You arrested our Pack mate."

"The CPD arrested your Pack mate because he was literally holding the murder weapon." But I held up a hand before she could argue. "And I know he didn't do it, so save us both the lecture. I'd like to talk to Connor."

"He's busy trying to take care of Riley. And it's two days before Alaska."

It took me a second to get the reference. "Oh, right. The road trip."

"The *return* trip," she said. "It's important for the Pack."

"I'm sure it is." But I didn't move. "I'd still like to talk to him."

She rolled her eyes.

"Look," I said. "I get that you have a problem with me, although I don't know how that's possible, since we don't actually know each other."

Lips pursed, she looked me over. "I know enough about you and your kind. *Brat.*"

"That word doesn't do the damage you think it does. But good try."

Irritated magic rolled across the room.

The door opened behind me, and she looked over my shoulder at someone who'd entered.

"Connor," she said, "you have a visitor. The vampire's here again."

"I see that," Connor said, walking toward us. He wore jeans and a gray Little Red T-shirt that snugged against his sculpted abdomen. "Give us a few minutes."

"She wants to talk about Riley. He's important to me, too."

"Miranda."

Anger boiled in her eyes, but she kept her mouth closed. She walked to the bar door, music spilling into the room like a cresting wave when she opened it, then slammed it behind her again.

"She doesn't much like me," I said.

"No, she doesn't. You're not her type."

"Meaning?"

"Meaning Miranda's a good Pack member. You're not Pack. And like many shifters and vampires, she has very specific ideas about loyalty." Connor kept his gaze on the closed door. "She's also worried about Riley."

"Were they together?"

"No," he said.

He looked back at me, eyebrows furrowed, dark slashes over his blue eyes. Like a man who had things to say but wasn't ready to say them. It wasn't hard to guess what he was thinking. "We don't need more vampire involvement where Riley is concerned."

"What happened to friendship?"

He gave me a flat look. "He was arrested at Cadogan House."

"Not by vampires. You know why they had to arrest him. The evidence was there, Connor."

"He's in a cage."

"I know. I went to see him."

Connor wasn't the type to show surprise. He generally rolled with the current, whatever it might have been. That was the upside, I guess, of not being too focused on rules. But he definitely looked surprised now.

"You went to see him?"

"I'm not your enemy, and I'm not his enemy. I don't know how or why he ended up holding a knife, but I know he didn't kill Tomas. So I went to talk to him, and to find out if he knew anything else."

"What happened to the deal with the mayor's office? The ban against Cadogan involvement? I thought you stuck to the rules."

"I do. But I'm not a Cadogan vampire."

He blinked. Whatever he'd expected me to say, it wasn't that. "What does that mean?"

I offered my theory, watched confusion change to disbelief, then appreciation. "You think the Ombudsman will buy that? Or your father?"

"Fifty-fifty on the Ombudsman. And if I have to use it, it's going to hurt my father. But my father's not being framed for a crime he didn't commit."

Connor watched me again for a long moment, then nodded. "All right. What did you learn by talking to him?"

"That he doesn't remember anything. That he blacked out or he's missing time, and he has one hell of a headache when he tries to remember."

Connor's brow furrowed. "He told me about the headaches—he was obviously in pain, and I asked him about it. But I didn't make the connection to his memory."

I nodded. "Someone was very careful to hide their tracks. Unfortunately, that means Riley can't tell us what actually happened. And I didn't get anything else specific—nothing about Tomas or anything weird that happened at the party that might have triggered someone to frame him. Did you get anything else?"

"No."

"Is there anyone who'd particularly want to hurt him? Not just Pack enemies, but personal ones?"

He walked to Thelma, whisked an invisible spot of dust from her leather seat. "Not that I'm aware of. You know Riley, Lis. He's likeable. Big and a little gruff, but—and I'll deny it if you tell him I said this—a teddy bear. He'd chew off his own arm and offer it up if you needed one. That's why he's one of us."

"What about Tomas?"

Connor sneered, and still managed to make the expression sexy. There was, apparently, no expression that didn't look good on the prince. And that was just irritating.

"My only knowledge of him comes from his displays at the theater and the party. He's not a man I'd ever want to know, or know more about."

I couldn't really argue with that. "Okay," I said, and pulled the handkerchief from my pocket, showed him the brooch. "Do you know what this is?"

He glanced at it, lifted his brows. "No. Should I?"

"I don't know. I found it on the patio at Cadogan House."

"Did someone drop it at the party?"

"I don't know," I said. And this time, looking at the brooch tickled a memory I couldn't fully access. But before I got any further down that path, the door opened, more waves of music following the big man who walked inside.

This was Eli Keene, Connor's uncle. He was tall, with tan skin, broad shoulders, and dark wavy hair that skimmed the shoulders of his shirt. There were strands of silver in his hair and the scruffy beard that covered his jaw, and they made him look more experienced, more powerful.

Eli looked at Connor, then at me. If he thought anything was odd about a vampire standing in the Pack's garage, he didn't mention it.

He gave me a nod. "Elisa. Heard you were back."

I nodded back, tucked the handkerchief back into my pocket. "Hey, Eli. Building looks good."

"It does," he agreed. There was pride in his eyes, but his expression stayed somber. "You're needed," he said to Connor.

"I'll be there in a minute."

Eli looked at him as if debating whether to repeat the order, then slid me a glance before looking back at his nephew. "Make it quick."

He disappeared again, leaving the cry of a squealing guitar in his wake.

"The show must go on," I said, when the door closed.

"That's what they say. Responsibilities."

"Alaska?"

"Alaska," he said, but his eyes were shadowed. "He was supposed to go with us."

"Riley?"

Connor nodded.

"I'm sorry. And that someone is using the Pack for this."

"Why do you care?"

The words put me on my guard, but the tone was quiet and seemed honest. "Because as much as you drive me crazy, I know you. And I know Riley. And it's not fair."

He watched me for a minute. "That's some of it, but not all of it."

I didn't like that he'd seen something I wasn't entirely ready to talk about. But I'd already crossed that threshold with him once. "Because of the Eiffel Tower."

He frowned. "The attack?"

I nodded. "It was bad, Connor. The vampires walked through a park where people were just hanging out, being happy. And they killed them because they were pissed at someone else. Vampires are fighting like damned children, and they're hurting other people to do it."

"You think vampires are behind this?"

"Not necessarily. But I think it's wrapped up in the peace talks, and that's a big, messy bundle of supernaturals. I know Riley wouldn't do it. And I don't like people using my father or his House for murder."

There was something deeply considering in his eyes, and I nearly looked away from the intimacy of his evaluation. "You've gotten kind of impressive, brat."

I narrowed my gaze. "I'm not sure that's a compliment."

"It is." He gestured toward the door. "Fascinating as it is to see this other side of you, I need to get back to work. But you'll let me know if you find anything?"

"Sure," I said, and I left him to prepare for his journey.

Lulu had grown up in a house in Wicker Park not far from Little Red. When she got a place for herself, she changed neighborhoods, moving to the Near North Side and a loft apartment. Since I'd failed on the souvenir front, I stopped for coffee on the way.

I climbed out of the Auto to look up at the unassuming brick building, the long rows of windows. It looked like a warehouse, which was the architectural calling card for this particular neighborhood.

The other tenants had names listed beside the buzzers for their apartments. The one I assumed was hers, since her name wasn't listed, bore a splotch of red paint. I mashed the button with an elbow.

"What? I'm working." Her voice was irritable.

"It's me," I said, and the locks disengaged with a *snick*. I rearranged the coffee cups and yanked open the door before it locked again, then slipped inside and climbed the wide and beaten stairs in the unassuming lobby.

She was on the fourth floor, and one of only two doors in the long hallway. I walked to hers, and since my hands were full, knocked with an elbow.

"It's open!" she yelled out.

I managed it awkwardly, found myself looking down at a slender black cat. It stared up with green eyes, a swishing tail, and a very suspicious expression.

"A cat is giving me dirty looks," I said.

"That's Eleanor of Aquitaine."

"Hi, Eleanor." I gave her a smile.

In response, she hissed at me.

"She doesn't like nicknames," Lulu called out. "It's Eleanor of Aquitaine or nothing."

I lifted an eyebrow at the cat. She stared back, unblinking and unmoved.

It occurred to me that I didn't know any vampires who had cats. Maybe cats didn't like vampires. But I was an adult, so I'd try again.

"Hello, Eleanor of Aquitaine."

Her tail stopped flicking, but her expression didn't change. Then she turned and walked away, tail still swishing as she moved.

"Rude," I murmured, and kicked the door closed.

Lulu's loft was a rectangle of space with a cluster of rooms in the middle. The floors were wide planks of well-used wood. The walls were sandblasted brick, and were hung with enormous paintings in brilliant colors, art show posters, and weavings of tufted yarn. She'd put some kind of colored plastic over the glass in the long row of casement windows, so a rainbow spilled into the loft from the streetlight outside.

There was a low couch along one wall, a plank coffee table in front of it. In the middle of the room sat a long table topped with rolls of canvas, cups of paintbrushes, and tubes and jars of paint. Part of the table slanted up to hold a work in progress at an angle for easier painting. Lulu stood in front of it, dowsing a brush in clear liquid.

There was a kitchen along the wall in the middle, a long bank of open shelves and cabinets with an island in front. And on the facing wall, an old-fashioned secretary cabinet with an aluminum chair in front, a pile of bills on the open desktop.

"This place is . . . amazing."

"Thanks." She went to the sink, washed her hands.

"I brought coffee from Leo's. Mocha for you; double espresso for me." I put hers on the island, took mine, and opened the tab that kept liquid from sloshing in the Auto. They deducted extra funds from your account if you dirtied up the interior.

Lulu laughed. "You made it nearly forty-eight hours without a Leo's run."

"Not even," I said. "My parents met me at the airport with a cup."

"Addict."

"Loud and proud."

Lulu snorted. "Either way, thank you, because I need the jolt. I've been at this for hours." She rolled her shoulders as she dried off her hands, then moved toward the coffee.

I walked to a bookshelf made of plumbing fixtures and un-painted boards, surveyed the photographs spread across the top. There was one of Lulu's parents, one of the cat, and one of us. We'd been in junior high—made up almost entirely of knees and elbows—and convinced we were badasses.

"A lot of leggings in this picture," I said lightly.

"And pointy eyeliner. We must have been going through a phase."

"Evidently so."

"Riley didn't kill anyone," Lulu said suddenly.

So much for the preliminaries.

I looked back and found Lulu at the island, one leg crossed over the other, the drink cradled in her hands. And misery in her eyes.

"No," I said, walking back. "I don't think he did. I think someone else did, then set him up for it."

She looked up. "Why would they do that?"

"I don't know yet. Have you talked to him recently?"

"No." She adjusted in her seat, obviously uncomfortable. "Not since the breakup, when we had to exchange some stuff. But other than that, no. I haven't talked to him."

She sipped her drink as if looking for something to do, something to fill the quiet that she couldn't fill with words.

"He's at the brick factory," I said. "If you want to go see him, I mean."

"I don't think that would be a good idea." But the look on her face said she was conflicted.

"Okay." I climbed onto a stool, sipped my coffee. "What about the Pack? Do you know of anything weird going on with them? Anything someone might target Riley about?"

"No, or not that I'm aware of."

"Would you be?"

She frowned. "I don't know. I've been at Little Red more in the last few weeks than I have in the past four years. So I'm around." She lifted a shoulder. "You know they're going to Alaska?"

I nodded. "Yeah. Riley was supposed to go with them. He won't be going now—at least not until this is cleared up. But I don't see how that would matter enough for someone to kill over it."

"Me, either."

"Okay," I said, and put down the coffee cup. I shifted on the stool to pull out the bauble I'd found at Cadogan House. "What about this?"

She didn't take the handkerchief or the object, but leaned over to peer at it. "There's magic in this," Lulu said. "You don't have to use magic to recognize it."

I didn't detect any magic, so it must have been faint. "Does it look familiar to you?"

"No. I mean, it's pretty, but not familiar. What is it?"

"I don't know. I found it at Cadogan House. Near where Tomas was killed."

"Maybe someone dropped it," Lulu said. "I mean, there was a party, right? Doesn't mean it came from the killer."

"No, it doesn't." But there was still something about it that seemed familiar, and that bugged me.

"Didn't you take video of the reception or something?"

"Yeah, for Seri," I said absently, peering at the gold. There was dirt in some of the filigree, but that might have been from my stepping on it. "Did you want to watch it?"

"No." She chuckled. "Aren't there supernaturals in that video? You know"—she waved a finger at the brooch—"dressed up?"

I looked up, stared at her for a moment. "Oh my god, you're a genius."

She huffed, sipped her drink. "You may be the Watson to my Sherlock."

"Who's your Moriarty?"

"TBD," she said. "Let's see some fringe and fangs."

There wasn't much of either in the reception. Plenty of silk and sequins, a dryad with skin patterned like birch bark, and, of course, Tabby, who was too sexy for her shirt.

But we didn't see the brooch. Not pinned to a sash or a bodice or a hat.

"Maybe you're right," I said. "Maybe it's a total coincidence. A bit of jewelry dropped sometime between 1883"—that's when Cadogan House was founded—"and earlier tonight."

"Or it could be a fairy."

I tossed my empty cup in the recycling box. "Yeah, there were a few fairies there. But more vampires."

"No. Not any fairy. *This* fairy."

I turned back. "What?"

With a satisfied smile, she pointed at the screen. "I found your brooch wearer."

"You are kidding."

I hustled back to Lulu and the screen, watched the video she'd pulled up and enhanced. Something glinted on the tunic worn by one of the fairies—tall and pale, with sleek, dark hair and chiseled cheekbones—who followed Claudia and Ruadan in the procession down the runway. As he moved, the glint resolved. The gold knot was pinned at his throat.

"You were not kidding."

"Nope. Do you know him?"

"No." I hadn't seen him at the party, but that didn't mean he hadn't been skulking around.

Of course, the fact that a fairy had worn the pin found near the crime scene didn't mean it had been used to commit murder. It could have just fallen off the tunic.

"Why would a fairy have killed an ambassador from Europe?" she asked, when the parade wound to a close.

"I don't know. The fairies were dicks at the first session, and so was Tomas. Both of them railed about vampire and shifter conspiracies."

"And then a shifter is accused of killing a vampire. That's convenient."

I looked at her. "Yeah," I said slowly. "That is convenient. Maybe they did want to disrupt the peace talks. I mean, that mission was at least partially accomplished by the fairies when they barged in yesterday, but the murder got tonight's session canceled, too. But it still seems really indirect. Why not just attack the talks themselves—literally, not in the fairy-interruption way? Or take credit for the murder because you think it will get you some political traction?"

"I don't know." She put down the screen, folded her hands on the island, and looked at me. "Maybe we should ask them."

"Ask who?"

"The fairies. I have a car." She held up her fists and mimed a steering wheel. "We get into it, go to the castle, and ask them."

"No," I said. "Absolutely not. That's too dangerous." And a violation of so many rules that even Connor might have balked at it.

"It's not a risk-free idea," she admitted. "But what's the other option? We sit around while Riley's in lockup?"

"We could end up dead."

"That's true for you every time the sun rises. The only thing that matters is what you do in the dark."

I narrowed my gaze at her. "That was really philosophical."

She lifted a shoulder. "I've been reading more since you've been gone. I've even got a card for the Cadogan House library."

"How did you get a library card?"

"I'm a friend of the House," she said dryly. "Supernatural parentage has some advantages."

"Doesn't that violate the magic ban?" I asked.

"We aren't talking about magic," she said, hopping off the stool and emptying her cup. "We're talking about murder and a friend of mine. Why do you think I'm painting that mural?"

She walked to the kitchen counter, plucked a key fob from a silver bowl, looked back at me with a dare in her eyes. "Are we doing this?"

I tapped fingers against the granite. I shouldn't have been considering it. I don't want this blowing back on my parents.

But I thought of Tomas, of blood spilled at my father's House. I thought of Riley in his sad gray scrubs and the desperation in his eyes. And I thought of the future. If the perpetrator was willing to kill at Cadogan and frame a good man, what else were they willing to do? How could I just stand by?

"This has to be low-key," I said, decision made. "No snark, no sarcasm. We just ask polite questions. I'd really prefer the Ombudsman not hear about this."

Lulu winced. "Shit. I forgot about that—the deal with Cadogan House."

"I think I have an out there," I said, and told her my theory.

Her whistle was long and low. "Your dad is not going to like that—you not being an official Cadogan vampire."

"No, he is not. And the Ombudsman might not buy it. So we need to be really, really careful." And when it came to supernaturals, even "really careful" could go bad.

I tried to figure out how to politely phrase the next question without expressly mentioning her magic avoidance. "If things go bad, can you take care of yourself?"

"I've been learning Krav Maga. And there's also this." She moved to a narrow door, pushed aside a broom and mop that tried to escape, and pulled out a black duffel bag. She brought it back, put it on the counter, and unzipped it.

"Damn, Lulu."

It was filled with weapons, mostly bladed. Sheathed knives. Throwing stars. Handguns. Even a wakizashi, a smaller sword carried by samurai as a companion to the longer katana.

"Dad taught me a few things," she said.

I'd forgotten Catcher had been an expert, had given my mother her first katana lessons. From what I knew about him and his particularity where weapons were concerned, I didn't think he'd approve of Lulu's Everything in the Duffel Bag method of storage.

She pulled out the wakizashi and a handgun, then rezipped it and put it away again.

She belted the short sword expertly, checked the handgun expertly to see if it was loaded, then slipped it into her pocket. "Ready to go."

"I can see that."

"One thing," she said, then held up a finger. She pulled a sticky note from a pad on the counter, scribbled something, and stuck the note to the refrigerator door.

I stepped closer to read it. GONE TO QUESTION FAIRIES, it read, then listed the date, followed immediately by, IF NOT BACK IN 24 HRS PLZ RETRIEVE BODIES.

"You've also gotten more morbid in my absence."

"I dwell in darkness," she said flatly. "The ravens are my minions and the moon my master."

"I know I haven't lived in Chicago for a while, but do you really think we can just drive right up to the castle and ask for an invite?"

"We'll find out," she said, then looked down at the cat. "Eleanor of Aquitaine, guard the door. We're going hunting."

THIRTEEN

Calling Lulu's vehicle a car was too generous. It was, at best, a caricature of a car. A soup can rolled onto its side, with pasted-on tires that had more in common with doughnuts than road-ready wheels.

"An Auto could be here in minutes," I said with a grimace.

"Autos are corporate; corporations lie." She unlocked the door, began to wedge her way inside. "It's small and it's ugly, but it runs on used cooking oil. Zero Waste, remember?"

That explained why it smelled like peanuts and fried chicken. I folded myself—origami style—into the front seat. "No point in paying for aesthetics or space."

"Exactly."

She hit the ignition, which I assumed released a snack to the hamsters under the hood.

I hoped to god we wouldn't need a getaway car.

The moon was nearly full, only a fingernail of shadow along the edge, and it cast an eerily strong glow over the gravel where we'd parked across the street from the fairies' home.

When they'd followed vampires, shifters, and sorcerers into the public sphere twenty years ago, they'd bought an unused tract of land in South Loop along the south fork of the Chicago River. The strip of land had been an empty lot for years. They'd built a fence around the property and a castle in the middle.

A narrow path of crushed white stone led onto the grounds beneath an arched gate in the iron fence. At the end of the straight drive was the dark stone wall of the castle. There were round, crenelated towers at each corner, square towers at the midpoint of each side, and a gatehouse in front.

"You have to go through the gatehouse to get in," Lulu said. "The courtyard's behind that—it's called a bailey—and it circles the building that holds the living quarters. That's called the keep. There will probably be a lot of guards."

"You really looked into this fairy-castle thing."

"I'm nosy. We could skip the steel," she said, looking down at the wakizashi in her hand. "Reduces the odds of the OMB finding out about it."

"No weapons is not an option. We both go in with what we can carry. And are people really calling it that?"

"OMB? Yes. Fewer syllables."

"I don't approve."

"Color me shocked."

"Let's go," I said, casting a final glance at the moon. Not even full, and it was still nearly bright enough to read by. We wouldn't exactly be making a secret approach; they'd see us coming up the path. But maybe that would make them feel more secure about our visit—and less likely to freak out.

My chest tightened when I considered the possibility the monster would show itself on this little field trip, which was already a bad idea. But there was nothing I could do about that now.

"Elisa?" she asked, as we walked down the path.

"Yeah?"

"Why are you really doing this?"

I looked at her. "What do you mean?"

"I know this is risky for you. Why are you doing it?"

"Because he was nice to me, important to you, and part of the Pack. That makes him important to me."

She blew a breath through pursed lips like she was working to control tears. But she held them in.

"You know you don't have to do this, right?"

She looked at me, then looked away, chin set. "My family and friends are magic. Saying no to it—" She paused, as if searching for words. "It's hard. I don't regret avoiding magic. But I regret the other things I have to give up because of it, because I'm afraid of what I might do. Of that damn slippery slope."

I reached out and squeezed her hand. She squeezed back.

"Someone needs to help him, and right now, I can be that someone. I owe it to him. And I've given up so much that I owe it to myself. Just to see." She looked back at me and smiled. "I'm glad you're back, even if for just a little while."

I smiled at her. "Let's go talk to some fairies and try not to get killed. 'Cause this is a really bad idea."

"Yeah," Lulu agreed with a smile. "But at least we're getting out of the house."

The grounds were quiet, the lawn immaculate and rolling, the stone crunching softly as we walked toward the gatehouse and its enormous doors—two halves of a twenty-foot-tall arch, with black hinges holding them in place.

There was magic here, a faint buzz that left a chill in the air. I wasn't sure if that was castoff from the accumulation of the fairies themselves, or because they'd magicked this building just as they had the tower.

The door on the left opened before we could knock. A male fairy in black fatigues looked through. His hair was dark and straight; his body tall and lean. His eyes were dark jewels among his pale, angular features.

"You are a bloodletter," he said.

"I am," I said. "She is not." No need to get into the details about Lulu's magic if she wasn't using it. "We'd like to speak to Claudia."

"Claudia does not commune with bloodletters."

"Okay," Lulu said, "then how about you answer a few questions?"

The fairy shifted his gaze to her, his movements methodical and his face expressionless. "You do not have permission to encroach upon our land. And yet you seek to ask us questions."

"We have come peacefully to your door, and we have questions to ask," I said. "If you don't want to answer them, we'll leave. It's that simple."

He looked at me for a moment, and then the door slammed with enough force to blow the hair back from Lulu's face.

"Friendly," she murmured, but didn't take so much as a step backward.

Magic began to pepper the air and my heart began pounding in response, adrenaline beginning to flow. I could feel the monster stirring, a moth drawn to flame.

Not going to happen, I warned it, and pushed down against it. It was like trying to ignore an ache, trying to flex a muscle in spite of it. You could still move, but the pain didn't go away. And the monster didn't, either.

"If I'm mortally wounded," she whispered, "you have my permission to change me. But make sure I get a good room in Cadogan House."

"Third floor has the best views," I said, flipping the thumb guard on my katana.

Ten seconds later, both doors opened, and we were beckoned inside.

The gatehouse's walls were as high as a two-story building. The ceiling was open to the sky, to moonlight that speared through to illuminate the stone floor. A second set of double doors mirrored the first and led through the wall.

Torches hung from the walls, sending flickering firelight across the space. But for the snap and sputter of the torches, the room was utterly silent—despite holding nearly a dozen black-clad fairies who stared back at us, all of them holding staffs or straight swords.

They stood in a perfect semicircle, Ruadan in front of them. He wore a tunic today in gleaming emerald, locks of his long, straight hair knotted into complicated braids. Gold filigree gleamed along the edges of his tunic, gold thread had been braided into his hair, and his fingers glowed with rings.

This wasn't the subdued Ruadan from the reception, the man whose purpose had seemingly been to complement his queen. This looked like a man who'd taken control. And I wondered if it was a coincidence that Claudia wasn't among the fairies.

"Bloodletter," he said, in a tone that was equally insulting and curious. But not surprised. He'd either watched our approach or had been informed of it.

He shifted his gaze to Lulu. "And . . . not human."

"Human enough," she said, but her voice was quiet.

I moved incrementally closer, so my shoulder bumped hers in a show of support and solidarity.

"Ruadan," I said. "We'd like to ask you some questions."

"About?"

No point in screwing around, I thought. "About Tomas Cardona. The vampire killed at Cadogan House. Do you know anything about his death?"

"Why would we? He was a bloodletter. Our involvement with bloodletters has been minimal." But his lips curled into a smile. "You have come into our castle, so perhaps that will change."

"Our friend was wrongly accused of his murder," I said. "We're trying to help him."

His gaze darkened to storm clouds, and there were quiet murmurs around him in a language I didn't understand.

"You believe we have information regarding the murder of a bloodletter. Or information that would acquit a shapeshifter."

"We don't know. Do you?"

"Be careful you do not put your trust in those who shift and change. Their inconsistency proves they are untrustworthy."

"Riley didn't kill Tomas." Lulu's voice was hard and certain.

Like a well-oiled gear, Ruadan's head turned slowly toward Lulu. "Are you making an accusation?"

"No," she said, and I felt her trembling beside me.

I shouldn't have let her come, I thought, regret and guilt twisting in my gut. That I shouldn't have come, either, wasn't the point. I was immortal, had a biological shield against my own stupidity. She didn't have the same protection.

The murmurs rose to mutterings, to shifting feet and irritation. The curiosity that had gleamed in Ruadan's eyes evaporated, and they went hard as stone. Frankly, I preferred the anger to the creepy interest.

Lean jaw clenched, he took a step forward, the scent of astringent herbs lifting into the air around him. "You come into our territory without our permission to inquire if we have committed a crime."

I took a step forward, trying to draw his attention back to me. "We didn't ask if you'd committed a crime. But now that you've brought it up—did a fairy kill Tomas?"

"You are rude and presumptuous, not that we would expect more of the Others."

"You're right," I said. "It was rude and presumptuous to come here. Murder is also rude. I'll ask again—did a fairy kill Tomas?"

His eyes flashed and his voice went low. "We killed no one."

I noted the pin at the neck of his tunic. "Did any of your fairies lose a gold pin, by chance, at Cadogan House?"

He jerked. Covered it quickly, but I'd seen the movement. He might not have known the pin had been lost, but he knew what it meant that it had been found.

"You didn't know they were sloppy, did you? That they didn't just kill the vampire, throw magic over Riley, escape over the wall. They left a little something behind."

"You will return it."

I shrugged. "Don't have it," I said, and was glad I'd thought to leave it in the car, just in case they tried to take it back. "It's locked safely away."

"You dare threaten us."

"No threats. Just questions. And the only way questions could be a threat is if you're hiding something."

Ruadan's jaw worked, as if chewing back angry words. Magic lifted again, this time cold and dark and angry. The mood had changed, and I knew there'd be no more conversation.

I caught movement to my right. The semicircle of fairies was stretching, attempting to surround us. I stood a step backward, and pulled Lulu back with me, just a little closer to the door.

Someone screamed words that were more song than battle cry. They were all fighters, and they all wanted their turn.

My heart began to pound like a war drum, too eager for battle. I wrapped my right hand around the corded handle, ready to draw.

"You've gotten more vampirey in my absence," Lulu murmured behind me.

"Yeah," I said with a sunny smile. "I'm a regular Dracula. I'm going to distract them, and you're going to run back to the car."

"Fuck that," Lulu said, stepping beside me, rotating her wrist to spin her own blade. "I'm not letting you have all the fun."

"All right," I said. "But be careful."

"No promises."

I looked back at the fairy in front of me. He was thin like the others, tall and willowy, with dark skin and eyes. The blade of his sword gleamed in the moonlight.

He stepped forward, and I met him. I unsheathed my katana and used it to push his away, then spun it back to slash horizontally across his chest, but didn't break skin. He jumped back, as spry as he was strong, then came in again with another overhead blow.

I stopped it, but felt the impact echo through my arms.

He lunged. I went low, kicked in a sweep that dropped him to the ground and sent a ripple of disappointment through the crowd of fairies who watched.

He managed to hold on to the sword, flipped onto his feet again. He swung the sword, stepping into it to increase the power. I rotated at the last second, and his blade still whooshed closely enough that I could feel the breeze on my face.

I stayed in the spin, kicked his leg, sent him forward. The fairy pulled his sword up sharply, sent the blade singing against my shin.

Fire erupted as the scent of blood filled the air.

"First blood!" someone shouted.

The injury hurt and I didn't like the precedent, but I was glad that they'd shed my blood first. If we survived long enough to deal with the fallout, it would help prove we hadn't intended the violence.

I pushed down the pain and tried to ignore the monster's sudden interest in the battle. And then another fairy joined the fun.

A dagger sliced through the air. This time I kicked up, hitting his wrist and sending the weapon skittering through the air. My second kick made contact with his jaw, snapped back his head.

But he shook off the impact, then dove on me, sending us both to the ground. We grappled, blades clattering away, both of us trying to find the right grip, the superior move. In the scramble, his elbow connected with my face, and my knee caught his kidney. But neither of us found the move that would stop the other, and we both ended up on our feet again.

On my left, Lulu was fighting another fairy in close combat, blades glinting as they spun. Her father had trained her well; she fought like a champ. But she wasn't immortal, and it was easy to see she was getting tired. Her arms were shaking from the effort of lifting the blade. I needed to get her out of here.

"Get back to the car," I yelled, hoping she'd hear me over the noise of the fight.

"Fuck you, too," she said, and blew hair from her face as she brought her sword down on a fairy's forearm. He turned, but not fast enough. The blade sliced across his arm, raising a beaded line of blood that made the air smell of green things.

The temptation was sudden, and it was strong, like blood and magic were combining to compel me to drink. My eyes silvered and my fangs descended, my fingers suddenly shaking with want. I had to clench my hands to hold myself back, to keep from falling at his feet to drink the blood right from his veins.

This was the lure of fairy blood, and I wasn't the only one interested. As if propelled by the desire, the monster broke through the barrier I'd erected to keep it quiet, to keep it secreted away. It rose like a flame, brilliant and hot in the darkness, burning away everything around it.

A red haze covered my vision, and I knew my eyes had turned the same color—a side effect of the monster's magic. As it took control, hatred rose in my stomach like bile. I heard a scream, realized a moment later—when my throat felt like I'd swallowed broken glass—that I'd been the one who'd made the sound.

With the monster in control, I jumped forward toward the fairy. I fell on him, and we hit the ground together in a tangle of arms and legs, trying to get in a strike. I made contact first, landed a punch on his cheekbone that made his head thud dully against the ground. And because that wasn't enough for the monster, I hit him again.

"Lis! Lis! Elisa!" I heard Lulu's voice but couldn't pull myself to the surface. The monster was too strong.

"Snap out of it!" she said.

The fairy beneath me, his gaze still unfocused, grabbed my hands. And then my ankles were drawn together, my feet tangled. I was dragged backward, and the shock was enough to shake the monster loose. It wanted freedom, but it didn't want me dead. Because that wouldn't serve its purpose. That wouldn't set it free.

I looked back. Thin green vines had snaked around my ankles and were working their way up my calves. And others were rising from the ground like a nest of snakes, headed for my wrists.

I shifted, pulling the tendrils around my ankles. A few snapped, putting more of that vegetal scent into the air. But more vines pushed through the stones to replace them and shackled me like iron.

"Elisa!" Lulu was on her knees a few feet away, vines around her ankles, her wrists bound together. This time there was fear in her eyes.

Ruadan knelt beside me, pulled a dagger from a leather holster at his waist, held it up in the moonlight. And then the blade was at my throat, and I stopped moving. I knew what fairies with blades did to vampires.

"It would be a shame to kill you," he said. "You are an interesting specimen, and I wish to know more about you. And your magic."

"I'm just a vampire."

"Oh, I don't think that's true." He angled the blade just enough to prick, and I felt the trickle of blood at my neck.

The look in his eyes made my stomach clench harder. Surprise and shock. Interest and intrigue.

Ruadan dabbed a droplet of my blood with a long, pale fingertip, then flicked his tongue to taste it. "Power," he quietly said, and there was too much interest in his eyes.

My blood chilled as I realized he'd recognized something about the monster. Maybe not all the details, about the history or the origin. But he knew there was magic that wasn't just vampiric.

Before I could respond, there was a howl outside the gatehouse. And the sound was full of anger and rage.

It came at a full run, earth pounding beneath huge paws. Silver fur and ivory fangs glinted in the moonlight, and the scents of pine and smoke and animal lifted on the wind.

It wasn't until it reached us—until I saw its ice-blue eyes—that I knew we weren't in danger from him.

Connor.

My heart pounded with a new kind of ferocity.

He bit through the tangle of vines at my feet. There was an answering scream in the crowd of fairies, as if his teeth had met their flesh. There must have been some magical connection to the one who'd woven the magic.

That was enough to have the other tendrils around Lulu and me shrinking back. She ran toward me, helped me to my feet. My legs felt heavy, shaky. Maybe because of the fairy magic. Maybe because of the fight. Maybe because of the monster.

Connor looked us both over, eyes narrowed, then moved in front, putting his body between us and the fairies. He surveyed them, then paced in front of them, anger rumbling in his throat. His ears lay flat, his stance slow. He was big and dangerous, and he was ready to fight.

I was shocked, awed, and a little unnerved. Not just because he'd found us and was obviously trying to protect us, but because he was showing us who he was. Letting Lulu and me see his animal form, the sacred part of himself only other shifters would normally see.

Connor reached Ruadan and bared his teeth, made another threatening growl that lifted goose bumps on my arms.

"Animal," Ruadan spat, lip curled in obvious disgust. He clearly didn't have any love for vampires, but he seemed to loathe shifters even more.

Connor growled again, and Ruadan inhaled sharply, nostrils flaring.

Two fairies stepped forward, one on each side of their leader, and drew their blades. This was no longer fairies versus vampires. It was fairies versus Pack.

And that, I thought, *might make the difference.*

"You have a decision to make," I said, my voice hoarse from screaming. "Do you want to hurt the prince and take on the entire Pack? You know they're dangerous. Untrustworthy," I said, throwing his word back at him. "And very, very powerful. I doubt you'd enjoy that fight. And I doubt your queen would, either."

There was a hot burst of magic as insult spread around the room. They might have obeyed Ruadan, protected him, but Claudia was their still queen.

Ruadan's lip curled, his fingers fisted so tightly, his knuckles were white. But he didn't make a move. It probably wasn't a coincidence that he hadn't made any moves except when I'd been bound.

He murmured something softly, the sounds shifting between soft vowels and hard consonants, the language old and powerful.

Whatever he said, his fairies got the point. The tension of their bodies, their stances, loosened. But their eyes grew no kinder. They were angry, partly because of the intrusion, partly because Ruadan had leashed them again. He'd riled them to a fight, and they wanted the satisfaction.

"We're leaving," I said, and Connor stepped closer to me, his fur—so soft—brushing against my fingers like a whisper.

I picked up my sword and turned Lulu so she went first, so my back was to the fairies. Connor padded behind us, and we ran down the path toward the car.

FOURTEEN

Thelma, low and menacing in a spear of moonlight, sat beside Lulu's car. The wolf padded onto the road behind us, then circled around to face us, lips curled back over gleaming teeth.

Connor was still a wolf, and he was pissed.

"I don't recall inviting you along on this little adventure," Lulu said to him. "So we aren't the only ones who have explaining to do."

It was the driest look I'd ever seen on an animal.

Maybe that's why he didn't warn us before light filled the darkness, searing across my retinas as magic engulfed him. It whirled around his body, sending energy and the scents of pine needles and fur into the air. I'd never stood in the sun, never felt sunshine on my bare skin. But the scent of him made me think of those things.

The light spun like a cyclone and dissipated just as suddenly, lights streaking into darkness and leaving Connor Keene completely, utterly naked.

"Clothes are on my bike," he said, running a hand through his hair, and walked toward Thelma.

I'd never seen Connor with so much as a shirt off—and that had been my loss entirely. His body was perfection. Wide shoulders that led to a flat stomach and narrow waist, strong arms and legs, every inch of him toned from hard work and activity.

I couldn't look away . . . and didn't want to. Muscle rippled and shifted as he moved, and I had to fight back against the instinct to reach out and touch, run fingers down the taut skin that covered his abdomen or the sleek curve of his back.

Connor glanced back at me, and there was plenty of ego in the look.

Having seen the product, I couldn't argue with the ego. But the realization that I'd just fantasized about Connor unsettled me. Who was I?

Lulu gave him a two-fingered whistle. "The ensemble is fantastic."

He flipped her off.

"I mean, he is just delectable," Lulu said quietly.

"He's not bad," was all I was willing to give him. I was still too disturbed by the fact that I found him attractive.

"You could bounce a quarter off his ass."

"I can hear you, Lulu," he called back, pulling on jeans and a T-shirt. He glanced back, and there was no hiding the masculine pride in his eyes. "Wolf hearing, remember?"

"Yes, I know," Lulu said with a thin smile.

Connor sat on the edge of the bike to pull on his boots, then ran a hand through his hair. I figured his transformation was complete enough for us to talk again.

"What the hell are you doing here?" I said when we walked toward him.

"Saving your ass, apparently. What are you doing here? You're supposed to be the good one."

"The good one?" I asked. "What does that mean?"

"It means you're supposed to be smart enough to do the right thing, to follow the rules. And not walk into a fight."

"I did the right thing," I told him with barely veiled fury. "We didn't come to argue. We came to ask questions. To help Riley. We didn't ask you to barge in."

Boot laces still hanging, his shirt not quite snugged down to cover the strapping muscle over his hips, he glared at me. "The rules don't say anything about barging into a fairy castle."

"They opened the damn doors," I gritted out. "And since when do you come riding to vampires' rescue?" I asked, brow arched as high as I could make it. "I thought shifters stayed out of politics."

"You'd better be glad I made an exception."

"We were handling ourselves," I said.

"Oh, good," Lulu muttered. "Connor and Elisa are fighting. Shock. Surprise."

"Can it, Bell," Connor said, but didn't spare her a glance.

"How'd you know we were here?" I asked, gaze narrowed.

"I followed you from the loft."

"You did not," Lulu said.

"I did. Need to learn to spot a tail, witch."

"Don't call me witch, puppy."

Connor's lip curled.

"Focus," I said, and looked at Connor. "Why were you at the loft?"

His jaw worked. "Because you seem to think you're Sherlock Holmes."

"I'm Holmes," Lulu said. "She's Watson."

He closed his eyes for a moment, as if gathering patience. "If you're willing to dig in the dirt at Cadogan House," he said, opening them again and arrowing in on me, "I thought you might do something else stupid." He gestured toward the castle.

"Riley wouldn't have done this," I said. "But we're the only ones who seem to understand that. And until we prove it, the real killer goes free."

"He's my friend, too," Connor said. "He's my friend, my Pack mate. He's family. And my responsibility."

"You aren't Apex yet," I said.

"*Yet,*" he said, his gaze so intense it might have bored into me.

"Here's an idea," Lulu said. "Let's get the hell out of here, and

you two can continue arguing somewhere else." She looked back
at the tower. "I don't think we're guaranteed they won't try for
round two."

Connor nodded. "There's a diner up the road. The Carpathian."

"The Carpathian, as in the mountains in the Ukraine?" I wondered. The Pack had strong connections to the Ukraine.

His smile was wolfish. "The mountains are in the Ukraine, and
the restaurant is here. It's one of ours. Meet me there." He pointed
a finger at each of us. "And no detours."

He pulled on his helmet, climbed onto his bike, kick-started
the engine. The bike growled to life, and it sounded as sexy as it
looked. With one last glance at me, he drove off into darkness.

"Is it irritating that he expects us to follow him?" Lulu asked.

"Yes," I said.

But it was our best option.

"On the way, can we discuss in detail how good he looks naked? Almost makes it worth his testy teenage years."

Shaking my head—and more than a little flustered to find I
agreed with her—I followed her back to the car.

I checked my injuries in the car. The cut at my neck was nearly
invisible, the slice along my shin deeper, but knitting together
nicely. My cheekbone was bruised, and the mark would take longer to disappear. Bruises always did.

The Carpathian wasn't the typical shifter hang, if there was
such a thing, given that the NAC Industries building probably
blew the curve on what was typical. It was a train car, long and
silvery blue, its metal gleaming in the moonlight. The roof was
curved, the sides pinstriped, the narrow windows glowing between crisp white curtains. Hydrangeas with white clouds of
flowers lined the metal staircase that led into the entrance door.

The bike was already there when we pulled into the gravel lot.
Connor leaned against it, helmet propped on the seat, screen in

hand. He put it away when we walked toward him, then reached out, ran a thumb lightly across my cheekbone.

"You're hurt," he said, tilting my chin into the light. "Your father will see that."

I ignored the frisson of heat from his touch. "I'll heal."

"I'm sure you will. Make sure he doesn't do anything rash."

"He never does," I said. My father was the most controlled person I knew.

We walked inside, found a dozen narrow booths lining the walls and a kitchen at the other end. Four of the tables were occupied. One by a single, three by couples old and young, who talked quietly and clearly enjoyed their food. There was a small stand at the other end of the train car, nestled between the wall and the door to the kitchen, where a turntable spun a violin concerto that rolled softly through the air.

"It's . . . intimate," Lulu whispered.

"And friendly," Connor said, watching a woman walk toward us. She was slender, with pale skin, dark hair, and enormous eyes set in a heart-shaped face. She wore a white apron over trim, dark pants and a dark shirt, and kept her gaze on Connor.

"Keene," she said when she reached us, then looked us over.

"Natalia."

She said something in what I guessed was Ukrainian. He responded in the same language. More talking, and a glance at the smears of grime on Lulu's clothes, the bruise on my cheek. Her eyes narrowed.

"There will be no trouble here," she said, voice thickly accented.

"None," Connor agreed. "The trouble was left behind."

Another moment of hesitation, and she relented, pointed to a booth, asked another question.

"*Tak*," Connor said with a nod. Natalia walked to the bar, and he put out a hand, gestured us into the booth.

Lulu slid in, and I slid beside her. Connor took the other bench.

"It's been a long time since we've done a late night in a diner," Lulu said, gaze tracking across the restaurant's interior.

"I'm sure that was entertaining for everyone," Connor said.

I crossed one leg over the other. "We didn't have money, so we'd order black coffee and eat the free crackers and jelly."

"How did you not have money? Your parents *are* Cadogan House."

"Not a lot of part-time jobs for teenagers who could only work at night. I did chores in the House, but that money only went so far."

His smile was dubious. "Because you had a staff to pay?"

"Because she has a coffee habit," Lulu said, and pulled a paper menu from the holder at the edge of the table, handed one to me. Only a few items were on the menu, and all of them had at least one indecipherable ingredient. There were four kinds of artisanal water.

"You still picky?" Connor asked.

With a vampire metabolism, I'd wanted nothing but blood, grilled cheeses, and chocolate chip cookies growing up. Thankfully, I'd grown out of that stage.

"I usually eat what's available," I said, giving him a thin smile. "No one likes a hangry vampire."

Natalia came back, put glasses of water—artisanal status undetermined—in front of us on the table. Then she looked at Connor expectantly. *Because he's the shifter,* I wondered, *or the only one she trusts to order from their very particular menu?*

"Three burgers," Connor said. "Set us up."

"Of course." She nodded, then turned and walked back to the kitchen.

"Are you under the impression we can't order for ourselves?" Lulu asked testily.

"Shifter place, shifter rules. If I order, they think I'm in charge. Makes it easier for everyone."

"Because you're you?" I wondered. "Or because I'm a vampire?" The incident at Little Red had made it clear that antivamp prejudices still ran through the Pack.

He watched me for a moment, as if carefully considering his answer. "Both," he finally said. "And the burgers are good."

Lulu crossed her arms. "We'll see."

"He's a wolf," I pointed out. "Probably knows good meat from bad."

"One of my many skills. And now that we're out of danger, please explain to me why you two decided to start a war by storming a literal fairy castle in the middle of the night."

"The pin belonged to one of the fairies," I said. "The one I found near the Cadogan House patio."

Connor's brows lifted. "How do you know?"

"She took video of the reception," Lulu said. "We reviewed the evidence and reached a conclusion based on the same."

"Thank you, *CSI*." His tone was dry as dust.

Lulu saluted. "And bee-tee-dubs, your girlfriend is a firecracker. That panther routine?" She mimicked wiping sweat from her brow. "Impressive."

"She's not my girlfriend. We aren't together anymore."

"Oh, well, damn," Lulu said. "I will cease harassing you on that topic, and congratulate your good decision making."

Connor rolled his eyes, shifted his gaze to me. "So, the pin belonged to a fairy. Was the fairy at the party?"

"I don't know. If he was, I didn't see him." We'd have to talk to Kelley—or maybe Theo—about that. See if the Cadogan surveillance video revealed anything else.

"Why did they let us go?" I asked, working that over.

"Because they're smart?" Lulu said. "They realized they don't want the wrath of Cadogan House and the Pack raining down upon them."

Maybe, I thought. They had backed down after Connor had arrived. But that look in Ruadan's eyes, that interest, made me wonder if we'd been allowed to leave because he had something else planned. I had no idea what that might be, but I had a sinking feeling—after that talk about power—it had something to do with me.

Didn't matter. I'd handle it, just like I'd handled the fight.

Natalia returned, put plates of food in front of us. A waiter behind her added glasses of beer.

"Diakuju," Connor said, and she nodded, left to check on the other patrons. Her expression changed completely when she reached them. She smiled, which softened her features, put a hand on their shoulders, chatted with them quietly. It took me a minute to realize why, to recognize the magic that lingered in the air.

I looked at Connor. "Are we the only non-shifters in the restaurant?"

He pulled pickles, onions, tomatoes, lettuce off his burger, piled them on the side of his plate. They barely had time to settle before Lulu grabbed them, piled them onto hers.

"Yes," he said, then took a bite. "And the salad is unnecessary."

"Textures," Lulu said, then sawed at the entire pile to cut it in half, then in quarters. Then she picked up a wedge, bit off the pointed end.

"You still do that."

She looked at Connor, chewed. "I don't like putting my face into food. I'd rather bring the food to my face."

"You're an odd duck, Bell."

"At least I'm not literally a duck, Keene."

"You're well aware what I am, Bell."

"True," she said, winging up her eyebrows.

I hadn't yet tasted the food, so I grabbed a fry from Connor's plate, chewed.

He stopped chewing midbite. "What the hell, Sullivan?"

Lulu smiled, shook her head. "You think I'm a weird eater? She prefers to eat other people's food. Freaking fry thief."

"Fries from someone else's plate always taste better," I said, finishing off the one I'd stolen. "You can have some of mine."

"That is empirically false," Connor said. "And I don't want your fries. I want my own fries."

I shrugged, reached unapologetically for a fry from Lulu's plate. She slapped my hand away. "Bad vampire. Eat your own food."

"Fine." I gathered up the burger, took a bite. "Not bad," I said, and took another. "I'm surprised this place doesn't make the Chicago top-ten list."

"It does," Connor said. "Just not the human list. Riley eats four of these at a time." His smile fell away with the memory.

"Maybe the Ombudsman would let you bring him one?"

"I doubt it," he said sourly. "Dearborn's a dick. If he wasn't, Riley wouldn't be in prison right now."

"It's because he looks big and dangerous," Lulu said. "He has plenty of muscle and power to back that up. But he has an enormous heart."

"So why did you break up with him?" Connor asked.

Her gaze lifted. "He didn't tell you?"

Connor shook his head. "I know it wasn't what he wanted, but he didn't talk about it. Riley's easygoing, but he's not one for talking about his emotions."

She looked up at the ceiling, as if wishing for strength to get to it. "We were getting serious. And it was getting harder for me to, I guess, *avoid* his magic."

"To avoid it?" Connor asked.

"I made a conscious decision not to do magic. Dating a shifter is like . . . being ensconced in it. A lot." She looked at me. "More than just vampire magic, because with vampires, the magic is mostly driven by emotions. You get nervous or excited or really hungry, and you throw off a little magic. But with shifters, it's all the time. It's in the air."

"And the ground," Connor said. "It's part of our connection to the natural world—or the result of it."

Lulu swirled the beer in the glass, watching the liquid spin. "It was becoming more difficult to be around him and still say no to using my magic. I loved him," she said. "It just wasn't right for me."

"I'm sorry, Lulu," Connor said, and I saw only compassion in his eyes. Maybe for Lulu, maybe for his friend, maybe for a relationship broken because love hadn't been enough.

"It's all right," she said with a smile she was obviously fighting to keep in place. "It was hard. It sucked. And we both lived through it."

She looked up at Connor, at me. "Get him out of this. Whether we work together or not, he's being used, and that's not fair."

"Working on it," I said, and put my hand over hers, squeezed. But when I went to pull away, she didn't let go.

"I love you," she said to me. "And I tolerate you," she said to Connor. "But I'm going to bow out of any further fairy-related adventures."

"You held your own," Connor said, which was high praise from a shifter. But Lulu wasn't moved.

"Oh, I know. I'm a Bell, and I can handle a blade. And tonight I did what needed to be done. Hopefully it actually gets us somewhere." She glanced at me. "But I think I got it out of my system. I just want to make art and drink good wine and binge unhealthy television. Is that so wrong?"

I smiled at her. "That's the cool thing about being a grown-up. You get to set your own boundaries."

"A novel idea," she murmured, and I guessed she was thinking about our parents. Then she pushed back her plate and slid me a glance. "I think we also need to talk about the elephant in the room."

"What elephant in the room?" I asked. But I could see it in her eyes, the concern and worry . . . and the thread of fear behind it. They mixed shame and guilt in my belly.

Her fingers stayed tight around mine. "The . . . berserker thing." She dropped her voice to a whisper. "Your eyes went red. Really, really red."

I had a moment of panic. She'd just told us she didn't want to be involved in any more magical drama. I couldn't tell her now, couldn't confess that I was brimming with magical drama. Wouldn't that just push her farther away?

"Fairy magic," Connor said, looking completely unruffled by the lie. He'd always been very good with a bluff. He stretched his legs under the table and nudged my foot with his to keep me from talking—and to offer comfort.

She tilted her head. "What?"

He lifted a shoulder, the move utterly casual and confident. "It does freaky things to vampires."

Connor Keene, former teenage punk, had lied to protect me. I stared at him—equally shocked by the action and suspicious that it was part of some ploy.

But then again, he'd protected me the first time, too.

We'd been in high school—or Connor and Lulu had. I was still homeschooled by tutors at night at the House. There'd been a party at Cadogan our parents were attending, so we'd gone to get pizza at a place called Saul's, one of my mother's favorites.

Lulu had left her phone in the Auto, and she'd gone outside to grab it. "Two minutes," she'd said, and made us promise to order her favorite twisty breadsticks if the waiter returned while she was outside.

Five minutes later, she wasn't back yet.

I'd gone outside to check on her. And I'd found her on the ground, eyes closed and skin pale.

I'd had a bad moment of panic, thinking she'd been killed. But her chest was still rising and falling, so she was still breathing.

A man had stood over her, rifling through her backpack while his partner in crime yelled through the window of the apparent getaway car for him to hurry up and get in. But he didn't move. Just looked down at Lulu with lust in his eyes as his fingers rifled blindly through her bag.

The rage rose so suddenly, so blindingly, that there'd been no way to fight back against the monster. I'd jumped forward, sent us both to the ground. I'd ripped Lulu's bag out of his hands, tossed it aside. And then I'd pummeled him. Beaten him for hurting her, for stealing her stuff, for the look in his eyes as he'd surveyed her small form. And for whatever reasons the monster had had, whatever had fueled and driven its rage.

I couldn't stop.

Connor found us outside, pulled the driver out of the car, then pulled me off the attacker. And he'd held my arms while I screamed and writhed, until the monster receded and I could breathe again. Until I was just me again.

And then the shock set in as I'd stared down at the man on the concrete with a mix of horror and fear.

Connor hadn't been horrified, only worried about Lulu, about me. "You protected her," he'd said as he'd waited for me to calm down, and then as we waited for the cops.

In the hospital, the attacker had raved about monsters attacking him, and the CPD assumed he'd meant vampires and shifters. He'd been partially right.

Connor was the only one who'd seen my eyes, who'd seen my rage. And for seven years, he hadn't spoken a single word about it.

Lulu sat back and crossed her arms, looked between me and Connor. "I think I knew it did something, but not to this degree."

"It was the blood," I said quietly, hating the omission but making it, anyway. "The fairy blood. It has a different kind of lure to vampires. It's more powerful, harder to resist." That part, at least, was absolutely true.

"Could be your genetics, too," Connor said. "Magic helped make you, after all."

Possible contender for Understatement of the Year. "Could be," I said, sipping my beer and hoping Lulu hadn't noticed the blood had probably drained from my face.

Connor still hadn't shifted his legs, broken that connection between us.

"He's into you."

I jerked, looked up at Lulu. "What?"

"Ruadan."

It took a moment for my brain to switch gears. And when it did, her confirmation of my fear didn't make me feel any better. I'd seen his interest, too, of course. But I knew it wasn't romantic, even if I couldn't explain to her how I knew.

"Explain," Connor said, with more than a little force behind the word.

Lulu studied me, gaze narrowed in concentration. "I don't know. He just looks at her . . . I guess, maybe, covetously? But I thought he was with Claudia."

Connor's body wasn't relaxed anymore. He shifted, too, sitting up and leaning over the table, icy blue eyes intent on mine. "Covetously?" he asked.

"It's the same old, same old," I said. "He's political, and probably thinks there's something I can get him." And that was all I was willing to say aloud.

Connor clearly didn't believe me, but he was wise enough not to push the issue.

"We have to talk to the Ombudsman, my parents. Tell them what we've got, and what happened tonight."

"We don't have anything," Connor said. "We have a pin, some speculation"—he glanced up, gaze settling on my face—"and a bruise. None of that is going to free Riley. None of it is going to convince the Ombudsman that he's got the wrong man, especially if the other option is creating a supernatural war."

I didn't disagree that our case was weak, but we couldn't sit on this.

"Your dad will freak out," Lulu said.

"She's twenty-three," Connor said.

Lulu snorted. "Like that matters. You've met him before, right?"

"He's more than four hundred years old," I said. "A lot of ego accumulates in that time. And, no, he won't like it. But he'll get over it. Something's going on. Something bigger than Riley or the talks. Something involving the fairies. They need to know."

Then it would all be out in the open. Which I realized I'd prefer. I didn't mind investigating carefully. But this was an entirely different kind of sneaking around, and it felt beneath all of us.

"I think we're ready to go here," Lulu said, glancing around.

"I'm ready," I said.

"I'll pay," Connor said, and pressed the credit chip on his key fob against the circle on the table. It beeped, then glowed green.

Lulu frowned at it. "I wonder if the chip reader finds satisfaction in its life."

"Would you?" Connor asked.

"That's a pretty profound question for a shifter." But when Connor narrowed his eyes at her, Lulu lifted her hands. "All in fun, my friend. All in fun. You're like the protective older brother I never had. And never really wanted."

FIFTEEN

"The burger was good," Lulu said, when Connor joined us again in the parking lot.

"They have a good hand with food," he said, then looked at me.

Time to do the right thing, I told myself, *even if it stings a little.* "I'm not admitting we needed you, but thanks for helping us out there. It was . . . moving toward ugly."

"You're welcome," he said.

I nodded, feeling like there was more to be said, but not entirely sure what that should be.

"Lis will be right there," he said, and walked a few feet away, gravel crunching underfoot. Apparently, I was supposed to follow obediently. Which I did, eventually.

Lulu watched us with lifted brows, but went to the car, climbed inside.

"Thanks for being cool about Lulu. About the breakup."

His expression was amused, but there was mild insult in his eyes. "What did you think I was going to say to her?"

"I don't know. The point is, you didn't."

"I like Lulu," he said. "She's like the little sister I never really wanted."

"Well, thanks. I'm still getting used to mature Connor."

"You're hilarious."

"Thank you."

His expression went flat. "That's not what I wanted to talk to you about."

I didn't think it had been. And I braced myself for a conversation I didn't want to have.

"Does it hurt you?"

I blinked. That's not what I'd expected him to ask. "No. It's fine, and I'm handling it."

"Are you? Because you aren't acting like you're handling it. If you were handling it, you wouldn't be hiding it."

I looked back at Lulu. She'd pulled out her screen and was making a big effort to look everywhere else except at us.

"I'm handling it," I said again, each word a battle that I struggled to win. I turned away, but he grabbed my arm.

"I don't think so," he said, eyes shifting as he searched my face. "Even I can see that you're walking a very dangerous line."

I just looked away.

"Trying to ignore it, to push it down, isn't going to help you. Not in the long run. But maybe you could learn to control it."

Irritation began to buzz along my skin. I knew he was trying to help, but that didn't make me any less angry at his polite suggestions. I'd been living with the monster, had been *fighting* the monster, since I'd been old enough to recognize its voice. To understand that I wasn't just angry or psychotic, but . . . invaded.

"You don't know what you're talking about."

His eyes went dark and he moved a step closer. "I know better than anyone, Elisa. I've seen what it can do to you."

Memory flashed, sharp as a dagger, and I could all but smell blood in the air. "Destruction is what it can do for me. Pain."

"That's true of any power. It just has to be managed. Look," he said, his voice softening, "if you don't want to do that, maybe there's a way to strip it out again. Someone who can use magic to remove it."

That someone was dead. Sorcha—the one who'd created the Egregore—had been killed by her own creation.

"I don't need advice, and I'm not going to apologize for who I am." Not when it wasn't my fault.

His eyes went hard, jaw tight with frustration. "No one asked you to apologize. And there is no mistaking who you are. You're stubborn and brave and goddamned dumbfounding at times. And it's not like you to give up."

The anger turned up to a full boil. "I'm not giving up anything, except this conversation. But next time I'm looking for magic advice, I'll be sure to give you a call."

I walked back to the car, leaving him standing behind me.

"You all right?" Lulu asked when I climbed into her car. "That looked like a pretty heated argument."

"Just a difference of opinion."

The car was silent and still while she looked me over, evaluated.

"That's what you're going with?"

"Yep."

"All right, then. Buckle up, buttercup, and we'll hit the road."

"Can you take me back to the hotel? I need to check in with Seri."

"Sure thing."

We were halfway back when my screen beeped, signaling an incoming message.

I pulled it out, found Seri's number. "Hey, Seri. What's up?"

"We're leaving, Lis."

"What do you mean, leaving?"

"We're going to the airport. Leaving Chicago tonight."

"Who is we?"

"The delegates of France."

I was floored. If the delegates walked away, that was it for the talks and the chance for peace. And I didn't know where it left me.

"Seri, you can't leave. Not now. If we want peace, we have to keep working at it. We can't just walk away. That's probably what they want, anyway—to break up the talks. We can't give in, even if it's dangerous."

"Lis, there was no peace to find here. But there is work to be done at home."

I needed to do something, although I had no idea what that would be. Because even if I wanted her to be wrong, I understood her fear. I had to believe she wasn't right, that there was always a chance Europe's vampires could put aside self-interest and think about the future.

"Just hold on, Seri. Okay? Wait for me at the airport." I didn't know what I'd do at the airport, how I'd make them change their minds. But I had to try.

There was silence for a moment, then: "I'll stall as long as I can, Lis. But I must go."

The call ended, and I stared at the screen for a moment, my mind racing like my emotions. Then I looked at Lulu. "I need a favor."

Fifteen minutes later, Lulu squealed to a stop outside the private terminal. I climbed out of the car, a little shocked we hadn't gotten crushed along the way, and ran inside.

It was late, and the building was empty. The plane waited outside. Seri and Odette, the only vampires in sight, were climbing the stairs.

"Ma'am?" asked the desk attendant as I blew past toward the door, then rushed outside and into a plume of heat and wind. "Ma'am!" she yelled, and I heard her chair squeak as the door slammed behind me.

I ran toward the plane. "Seri!"

She turned, a black pashmina around her shoulders, leather

leggings and black stilettos below. A dark ribbon held her hair at the nape of her neck, the long ends of grosgrain blowing in the wind.

"*Attends,*" she said, and offered her bag to Odette, then climbed down to the tarmac.

"Marion and Victor believe it is best to return," she said. "The French delegates have voted, and we must abide by that decision."

"Seri, I know this is hard for everyone. But if you leave, the other delegates will follow. The entire summit will fall apart, and Tomas's death will have been for nothing." I looked up at the open door. "I should have reported to Marion sooner, but it's been a long night, and I haven't had a chance. I could talk to her, explain what's happening, what I think the next steps should be—"

Seri leaned in close to look at my face. "You are injured!"

"I'm fine. It's nothing. It was . . . there was . . ." How was I supposed to tell her that the thing she feared—more violence— was exactly what had happened?

"A difference of opinion," I settled on. "And we're getting closer to figuring out what happened. We've been investigating and gathering evidence. Riley didn't do this."

She looked surprised. "You have another suspect?"

I had a video of a fairy who looked nearly exactly like every other fairy. "Not exactly," I said. "But we're working on it. Just— talk to Marion and ask her to give me some more time, to give the process one more chance. I stayed in Paris," I reminded her. "Even when there was violence, I stayed. Because I wanted to help."

For the first time, I saw guilt in her eyes. "I am sorry. You are braver than me, Elisa. Perhaps you are braver than all of us."

I dropped my arm, stared at her. "And what about me?"

They weren't just leaving Chicago; they were leaving me be-hind. I was the escort, the vampire who was supposed to accom-pany them here and back again safely. But they hadn't given me a heads-up, or time to pack, or a ticket for the ride. I didn't know exactly what this meant for my service, my tenure with Maison Dumas. But it surely didn't mean anything good.

This time, Seri's smile looked forced. "You will follow us when you are ready, of course." Then she leaned forward, pressed a kiss to my cheek. "We will see you in Paris, Elisa. Be safe."

"Seraphine!" One of Marion's assistants, a skinny man in a dark suit, leaned out of the door and waved his hand. *"Allons-y!"*

With an apologetic smile, she strode quickly back to the plane, offered a wave as she took the first step, then disappeared up the stairs.

I made myself walk back inside, forced my feet across the terminal and back to Lulu's car.

"Bad news?"

"They're leaving. Going back to Paris. The entire French delegation."

"Didn't you fly over here with her?"

"I did."

"And they're going home without you?"

"They are."

"And . . . how do you feel about that?"

"I don't entirely know. *You are braver than me,*" I muttered, even doing a pretty good imitation of Seri's accent.

"She said that?"

"She said that."

Lulu tucked her hair behind her ear. "Is it wrong if I say there's something bitchy about that? Like she's using it as an excuse. 'Oh, you're just braver than me.'"

"Seri's a good person," I said, but I didn't disagree with what Lulu said. And I thought of Connor's thin line. "And how do you know when you've stepped from brave right into reckless?"

"When you can change into a wolf?"

I dropped my head back to the seat, closed my eyes. "They're going to tank the talks. If they go, there's no way we're going to get everyone together again. There's no way we're going to get peace in Europe." Right now, it seemed like even peace in Chicago was in danger.

Was that why this mattered so much to me? Because my parents had managed peace here?

"I'm pretty sure the talks were already tanked."

I opened my eyes, gave her a piercing look.

"You know it's the truth, Lis. Murder doesn't exactly whet the appetite for peace. And now the question isn't how to get the talks moving again. It's figuring out who wanted to derail them in the first place. Who wanted to ruin what we have? To change the balance of power?"

I was fired up and prepared to argue with whatever she'd said. But she was absolutely right. My job was no longer escorting the French delegates.

It was figuring out who had sent the French delegates home.

Twenty minutes later, we pulled up in front of the Portman Grand.

A knot of paparazzi waited outside, their gazes avaricious. They were waiting to question me about murder, about the peace talks' failure, and, depending on how long they'd been out here, the fact that the French delegates had taken their luggage and run.

I sucked in a breath, put my hand on the car door. "I'm the brave one," I murmured, but Lulu jerked the car away from the curb before I could get out.

"Nope," she said, continuing through the circular drive. "Can't do it."

"Can't do what? Where are you going?" I checked the side mirror, watched the possibility of a hot shower and minibar binge disappear behind me.

"I'm getting you away from this hotel and all those bloodsucking reporters—no offense. You'll stay with me."

"Stay with you?"

"In the loft. There's a second bedroom. Well, it's storage, really. And it's small. And Eleanor of Aquitaine might have peed on some stuff. I mean, I check in there and keep the door shut, but I think she does it out of spite." She waved it away. "I'm sure it's fine. We'll just Febreze it."

I weighed cat pee against going back to Cadogan House and facing down my mother's sword again. "Actually, that would be fantastic."

"Good. Because traffic is a bitch. Autos were supposed to clear this nightmare up," she said, laying on the horn.

"What about my stuff? My luggage?"

"You can grab it tomorrow when the reporters have slithered back into their pits. You can borrow some stuff tonight."

"I don't deserve you," I said, marveling at how generous she was being, especially after I'd been dumped by vampires. For possibly the second time this week.

With a half-cocked smile, she adjusted her rearview mirror. "I'd say we probably deserve each other."

This time, I tried to pay the proper respect as soon as I walked through the front door.

"Hello, Eleanor of Aquitaine."

She just blinked and stared. And looked generally judgmental.

"I don't think she likes me."

"Probably not," Lulu said. "But she doesn't really like anyone. I'm here because she allows it, and we both accept that." She reached down, scratched the cat between the ears. The cat leaned into her hand and made a weird little bark when Lulu stood up again.

"She barks."

"She *talks*," Lulu corrected. "In her own particular accent."

As if offended by the comment, Eleanor of Aquitaine trotted away, tail in the air.

"Where did you get her?"

Lulu walked into the loft, pulled off her jacket, tossed it onto a stool at the kitchen island. "Honest to god, she was sitting outside my door one night, just staring up at it. No tags, no collar, no microchip. Just four pounds of attitude and expectation."

I lifted my brows. "Black cat just randomly shows up at the door of the daughter of two famous sorcerers?"

"She was a kitten at the time," Lulu said. "And she's just a cat. She's not a sorceress in disguise, or a familiar, or shifter, or whatever. She is particular, though. Keeps me on my toes. I bought her a cheap catnip toy one time and she could tell. Left a dead mouse on the kitchen counter. Found her sitting in front of it when I got up to make coffee, like she was daring me to clean it up."

"Maybe it was a gift?"

"She hissed when I touched it. I had to wait until she was out of the room before I tossed it."

"She might be evil."

"Oh, she's definitely evil." She smiled broadly now. "That's why I respect her space and her privacy."

"How much privacy does a cat need?"

"You'd be surprised." She yawned, stretched her arms over her head, then swiveled side to side. "Hell of a night, Sullivan."

"Yeah."

"Insomnia will not be a problem tonight. Let's go take a look."

"At the cat-pee room?"

"At the cat-pee room."

We passed a bedroom and surprisingly large bathroom, and reached a closed door on the back side of the loft, farthest from the windows. So far, so good.

She opened the door, flipped on the light.

"Ta-da," she said weakly.

It was a decently sized room, maybe ten feet by twelve. But it looked like the set of a horror movie, right before things go bad. There was a four-foot-high ceramic clown, and a headless male mannequin wearing a pair of lacy underwear. Lulu rounded out the collection with some kind of taxidermied albino rodent and a long board punched with dozens of rusty nails.

But the nightstand and bookshelf were fine.

"Sidewalk finds for future art projects," she said, dragging the clown toward the back wall. Then she put her hands on her hips, looked around. "At least it doesn't smell like cat pee," she said brightly.

"No, it doesn't." But I eyed the mannequin warily.

"His name is Steve."

"Where would you suggest I sleep? And that's not sarcasm."

She wheeled the mannequin to one side. The wheels made a rusty grinding noise Eli Roth probably would have appreciated. Then she pulled down a panel of wooden slats that hung on the side wall. I'd thought it was an art piece, but it descended to the floor, making a neat platform bed.

"Murphy bed," I said. "That's handy."

"I had a roommate for a few months. It didn't take."

"What was wrong with her?"

"She was . . . chipper. I don't mind laughing, appreciate quality sarcasm. But she thought the world was a happy and wonderful place."

"And you know better?"

"Parts of the world are great; parts of the world are garbage. I can't abide optimism."

I pointed down. "Those are Snoopy sheets."

"Snoopy was a realist. Much respect for Snoopy. Woodstock was the asshole."

I had no response to that.

"You still a T-shirt sleeper?" she asked.

"Yeah."

She gestured me to follow her, and we walked to the other bedroom. Unlike the rest of the space, it was nearly colorless. The walls were pale gray, and there was a low platform bed, the bedspread white with dots of a slightly paler gray. A nightstand held a windup clock, water glass, and magazine. The only thing on the walls was a large painting of the curvy women I realized was her signature style, this time in shades of white, black, and gray.

"Very different look in here," I said.

"Need it quiet when I sleep, loud when I'm awake." She slipped around the bed to a gray chest of drawers, pulled one open.

She pulled a bright pink "Magnificent Mile" T-shirt from a drawer and tossed it to me. The tags were still attached.

"Haven't gotten around to wearing this yet?" I asked, holding it up by the little plastic tie.

She shrugged. "It was in a gift bag, I think, from some deal my mom talked at."

I walked to the painted canvas. Up close, I could see textures in the paint. Ridges from the brushstrokes. A grid from some sort of plastic embedded in the acrylic. Tiny spikes I really wanted to test with a fingertip. But I knew better than to smear my fingerprints all over her work.

"I like the layers in this one," I said. "You're really good."

"I'm . . . determined," she said. "I think sometimes that's more important. Just putting a little bit out there, every day. You do the work or you don't. The externalities don't really matter." She yawned. "The fight wore me out. I'm going to crash hard. I'll be around tomorrow. I have a commission to finish up before I can go back to the mural. It's for the Near North library branch."

"You're famous."

"In a very different way than I figured," she said gravely. "Anyway, I'll be around."

I nodded. "I'll probably go to Cadogan tomorrow. Tell them about the French Houses if they haven't already heard, see if they've got any more information."

"And you're cool with doing that on your own?"

"I mean, you're welcome to be my sidekick anytime. But, yeah, I can manage. You have a painting to finish."

She seemed relieved. "If you learn anything, let me know."

"I will." I walked to the doorway, Eleanor of Aquitaine moving into the bedroom as I headed into the hall. "I really appreciate this, Lulu."

"Damn right you do."

SIXTEEN

I was not murdered in my sleep. I couldn't be sure Steve hadn't moved in the night—had he been turned toward the bed?—but he hadn't pushed me into the loft to face the sun, so I wouldn't complain.

I got dressed and found Lulu with arms and legs akimbo on the bed, her hair spread like a dark halo. I considered waking her up, but figured she could use the rest. She'd fought hard.

And then there was her guard. Eleanor of Aquitaine eyed me suspiciously from the end of the bed. "We don't have to be friends," I whispered. "It's good enough that you're a friend of hers."

One tail swish, then she closed her eyes.

I guessed I'd gotten all the time and attention she'd been willing to give.

I took an Auto back to the hotel, jumped out half a block before the entrance, and slid into the lobby before the paparazzi realized who I was. I showered and changed clothes, pulling on a green V-neck T-shirt, skinny jeans, and boots, and repacked my one and only suitcase again. Twenty minutes later I was in another Auto, headed to Cadogan House.

I'd done the right thing, asked my parents and Theo to meet me at the House to discuss what had happened the night before, what we'd learned from it, and why I hadn't violated the Ombuds' deal.

It was going to be ugly all around. I'd left the hotel early, hoping I could get some time with my parents to warn them about my theory. They'd be angry enough about the fairy visit. Telling them I didn't consider myself a Cadogan Novitiate wasn't going to help things.

"It can't be helped," I murmured, trying to reassure myself.

"Please repeat command," the Auto said, in a stiff female voice that tried to thread the needle between comforting and authoritative.

"I didn't give a command. I was having an emotion out loud."

"Increase motion sensitivity?"

"No. Do not increase motion sensitivity." I didn't even know what that was, but it proved Autos weren't all created equal. "Continue to destination, please."

"Continuing to destination."

I thought about applauding her, but didn't want to risk it.

The House was quiet. There were vampires in the foyer and front parlor, whispering as I walked through. They smiled or offered nods but didn't speak.

I could feel the Egregore as I got closer to my father's office, and knew my mother's sword was there. The monster called to it, trying to push through me to move closer to the magic contained there.

· When I stepped into the doorway, the throbbing of power was nearly loud enough to drown out my heartbeat.

It doesn't matter, I told myself. *It can't matter.*

My mother leaned over the conference table and a spread of paper, katana belted at her side over jeans and a black top. My father was at his desk in his typical suit.

"Hey," she said, standing straight. The word was an echo behind the pulse of magic, and I made myself concentrate on the lingering buzz of power my parents put into the room, which was lighter and brighter than the sword's.

The monster wasn't interested in that, so it receded. For now.

"I was just looking over the proposed security updates," she said, but her smile faded as she squinted, looked at my face. "What happened?" She strode toward me, steel in her eyes. Not just my mother, but Sentinel of Cadogan House.

My father frowned and moved around his desk. "What happened to your face?"

"My face?"

When he reached me, he brushed fingers over my cheek.

Damn. The bruise hadn't faded completely, and I'd totally forgotten about it. "We'll get to that."

He arched an eyebrow. "Will we?"

There was a knock at the threshold. Theo stood in the doorway, Yuen behind him. Yuen wore a dark suit; Theo, jeans and a fitted button-down shirt in pale blue gingham.

I gave Theo a hard look. He was supposed to show up alone, then report back to the Ombuds and save me the trouble of having to face them directly.

And I still hadn't briefed my father. I opened my mouth to ask them to give us a minute, but Yuen strode inside with fury etched into his face.

"Ruadan called the Ombudsman's office," he said, settling angry eyes on my father. "Complained that Elisa visited them, attacked, instigated violence among the fairies."

My first reaction was fury at the lie, but my father's gaze—cold and icy—kept me silent. And the seconds that elapsed while he turned that gaze on me seemed to take a lifetime.

"Are you out of your mind?" His words were chilly and as sharp as his gaze. It wasn't the first time that I'd angered him, and might not be the last. But even at twenty-three, I didn't care for the feeling.

Then Gabriel stepped into the room, Connor behind him.

"And she was joined by Connor Keene," Yuen said.

"I guess we've come at just the right moment," Gabriel said, but my father's eyes stayed on me.

"We didn't attack the fairies," I said. "Lulu and I went to the castle to talk to them—just to talk." I pointed to the fading bruise on my face. "They took a different position."

"Why did you need to talk to the fairies?" My mother's eyes had silvered with emotion.

"Because of this." I pulled out the handkerchief and the pin and handed them to my father. His eyes widened.

"Fairy made?"

Of course he'd know that, I thought ruefully, wishing I'd shown it to him first. "As it turns out," I said, then pulled out my screen and showed him the still I'd saved yesterday. "Worn by a fairy at the reception. I found it near the patio after we talked yesterday."

My father's expression didn't change as he tucked the handkerchief away, handed the pin to Yuen. But my mother's went thoughtful. "You inspected the crime scene."

"Sentinel," my father warned, probably detecting the hint of approval in her voice.

"Yes," I said, looking back at him. "I found it, and we found the fairy wearing it in the video."

"And you didn't report this because?"

"I didn't know if it had anything to do with the murder. He could have been at the party as a guest, and it happened to fall off. We wanted to see if it meant anything first." I glanced at Yuen. "Especially if the Ombudsman's office already thinks Riley's guilty.

"We decided we'd ask them about it," I continued. "So we drove out there. And they were . . . less than accommodating."

My mother snorted a laugh, then covered her mouth at my father's glower. "Sorry. Inappropriate. That was just . . . such a Sullivan thing to say."

The glower deepened. "Sentinel."

"And so is that," she said, and made an effort at a serious face.

"They attacked you," my father said, looking at me again.

"Yeah. We didn't see Claudia, but Ruadan was there."

"What instigated the violence?" Yuen asked.

"They're sociopaths?" Connor said dryly.

"They were fine at first," I said. "Ruadan seemed interested that we were there. But we asked about Tomas, if they had any information about his death. It went downhill from there. I asked about the pin, and they attacked."

"They attacked you?" Yuen asked.

"They made the first move. Lulu and I defended."

"Lulu?" my mother asked.

"Wakizashi," I said. "Catcher trained her."

"Of course he did." I could tell she wanted to ask more— probably about her skills, the dance of the battle, and how I'd handled myself. But she managed to hold her tongue.

"We fought," I said. "And we were outnumbered. And then Connor showed up."

"That's awfully coincidental," my mother said, glancing at him.

"Right place, right time," Connor said.

My mother looked dubious, but didn't object.

"You could have been killed."

I looked at my father. "I'm fine. But Riley's in a cage."

"You were given express instructions not to interfere with this investigation."

We all looked at Yuen. The anger or frustration he'd been holding in had apparently boiled over. I'd figured him for calm and collected, at least in comparison to Dearborn. But there was no calm in his eyes right now.

"We didn't interfere with your investigation," I said. "You

weren't investigating the fairies because you've already decided Riley's guilty. We've found a new suspect."

Yuen stepped forward. "That is beside the point. You violated Cadogan's contract with the city. Penalties will be assessed, financially and legally."

Damn it. There was no way to avoid this now, no time to prepare my father. "The deal doesn't apply to me."

"As a member of Cadogan House—"

"I'm not a member of Cadogan House," I interrupted, and steeled myself, made myself look at my father. "I'm the daughter of its Master, but I'm not a Novitiate. I was never Initiated or Commended. I'm not a member of any particular House. That makes me a Rogue. And Rogues didn't sign the deal."

The room went absolutely silent. And my father's expression went absolutely blank. And a little bit lost. My heart clenched uncomfortably.

Gabriel walked to Yuen, put a hand on his shoulder. "I'm going to get some coffee, and you're going to go with me." He all but pushed Yuen out of the room. Connor and Theo followed, Connor giving me a supportive nod over his shoulder.

They closed the door and left us in silence.

It was a full minute before my father spoke.

"You are as much a member of this House as anyone ever has been or will be," he said. And I could plainly see the hurt in his eyes.

"I'm sorry," I said. "I wanted to talk to you about this before I said anything, but there hasn't been time. Cadogan House is my family," I said, wanting to take a step toward him but not sure if that was the right thing to do. "It always has been. I didn't grow up feeling excluded." That would have been impossible in a House that had basically adopted me as its mascot.

"But you weren't Commended," he said. "Not officially. And you consider yourself a Rogue."

"I don't consider myself anything," I said, not realizing it until the words were out. Maybe that's why I'd felt such a strong kinship with Maison Dumas. Because I hadn't had the same connection to Cadogan, at least not like my parents had. And maybe that's one of the reasons Seri and Marion's leaving had hurt so much. Because Dumas had been my House as much as any other. But when it had been time to run, they'd left me here.

"I'm not sure I agree with your argument," my father said. "But there's no precedent to measure our behavior against. You were the first child. The *Canon* had nothing to offer." The *Canon* was the collection of vampire laws. "But if you're right," he continued, "I'm sorry. I'm sorry that we didn't think to make it official."

His voice was colder now, controlled in a way that only a Master with experience could manage. He stood apart from us, and my mother looked between us with concern, trying not to take sides.

"I didn't feel excluded," I said again. It was the only thing I could think so say. "And in this particular situation, it's handy."

My father nodded. "Tell them we're done here, will you? And ready to discuss the rest of it."

I nodded, knowing I'd been dismissed. And left my parents alone, with a cold ball in my stomach.

"She's right," my father said when the others were back in the room. Theo came in with coffee, offered me a cup. But my appetite—even for caffeine—was gone. Connor watched me carefully, as if trying to gauge how the talk had gone. I didn't meet his eyes; I wasn't ready to dive into those feelings.

"She wasn't Initiated into the House or Commended, and the *Canon* doesn't provide for membership based solely on a genetic or familial relationship."

"That's a technicality," Yuen said.

"No," my father said, "it's a contract. If you want to enforce the deal so carefully negotiated according to its terms, then you have to adhere to those terms."

I thought I saw appreciation in Yuen's eyes.

"This isn't you, Yuen," my father continued, his voice softer now. "I'm sure Dearborn is angry, but you know better."

"Could I trouble you for a drink?" Yuen asked after a moment, and my father smiled.

"That bad, is it?"

"Dearborn's pissed," Theo said as my father went to the bar, poured two fingers of Scotch, neat, into a chubby glass, then offered it to Yuen. Yuen sipped, lifted his brows.

"Very nice."

"Very old," my father said. "And it does the job."

Yuen nodded. "Dearborn is furious. He had convinced the mayor the peace talks were his idea, rather than yours," he said, looking at my parents. "He cares less about their effectiveness in reducing violence than the political reward of hosting a well-received event in Chicago."

"He's a player," Gabriel said. "Or imagines himself to be one."

"Yes. Ruadan's call was routed first to him, and his . . . *displeasure* was passed to the rest of us, with orders to fix the situation immediately."

"With your magic wand?" Gabriel asked with a smirk.

"Something like that. I suspect he wants Riley locked away, literally and figuratively, so he can assure the mayor and the rest of the delegates that Tomas's death was an unfortunate act by a lone wolf—pun intended—that won't affect the talks going forward."

Yuen looked at Gabriel. "He'll use Riley as a scapegoat if he can. Even if that means the rest of you go down, too."

"Alaska cannot come soon enough," Gabriel muttered, but the fury in his eyes belied his casual tone.

I'd put their trip out of my mind, and was disappointed to remember it now. Not just because Connor had helped us last night, but because it seemed like we were starting to interact like adults, were putting aside our history. We were becoming friends, or something like it.

"My hands are tied," Yuen said, "as are those of Cadogan House." He shifted his gaze to me. "But perhaps Elisa has some flexibility. If you want to secure Riley's release, you'll need evidence—solid evidence—that he's not involved."

I smiled thinly. "Then let's get to business."

We sent the reception video footage to Kelley, asked her to run the fairy's image against the House's surveillance video of the party.

While that was underway, we talked through the visit to the castle again to see if there was anything we'd missed. We didn't come up with anything new, but I did wonder about the effect of our visit.

I looked at Yuen. "You said Ruadan called you? Why not Claudia?"

He blinked. "I presumed she delegated the task to him. He's younger, more comfortable with technology."

"Claudia wasn't in the gatehouse," Connor said. "Maybe Ruadan was handling the matter himself under her orders, so it was his duty to complain." He frowned. "But it didn't have that feeling—like he was there solely to protect her interests."

"It didn't," I agreed. "It felt like he was playing king."

"And perhaps the phone call was another example of that?" Yuen asked, nodding. "That's a possibility. He might have designs on the throne."

"Fading magic," Gabriel said, and we all looked at him. "Ruadan is young. He was born after the Egregore. Fairies have been powerful his entire life, and that's changing now." He lifted a shoulder. "Maybe he's angry about that process and blames Claudia for it."

"What could she have done differently?" my mother asked.

"That's the question, isn't it?" Gabriel said. "Possibly nothing. But maybe Ruadan has other ideas."

"They let us leave," I said. "At least in part because they didn't want to incite the Pack's wrath, but I don't think that was all of it. I think they have something else planned, and it must have something to do with the talks, right? That's when all this started. Maybe the question isn't who killed Tomas. It's who wants the peace talks interrupted—and to breach the peace in Chicago in the process."

"And why," Yuen said, then glanced at my parents. "You've had experience with the fairies."

"We hired them," my father said. "They were called mercenary fairies then, because that's how they presented themselves. They were skilled and merciless and available for hire. They guarded the House during daylight hours, when we were asleep, for many years, until they turned their weapons against us. They are capricious. And as the 'mercenary' moniker should have warned me, they were, apparently, available to the highest bidder."

"The Greenwich Presidium," my mother said. "Cadogan House held an artifact Claudia wanted. They turned on us to obtain it. Gold and jewels are especially alluring."

"They don't believe in romantic love," my father said. "But Claudia had an apparently meaningful relationship with what we'd have called a demon. And she was the one who told us about the spread of Sorcha's power across Chicago."

"Her behaviors are inconsistent," Yuen said.

"Externally, yes," my father said. "But internally, they're entirely consistent. She is the center, always. She wanted coin, so she offered the fairies to the House as security. She wanted the jewel, so she offered her services to the GP instead."

"And then there was the green land," my mother said, reaching out to take my father's hand. She breathed in slowly, as if preparing herself, and then looked at Yuen.

"Before they lost their power, the fairies lived in what they called Emain Ablach, the 'green land.' They came to Chicago but retained their connection to that realm. When Claudia came to Cadogan House to talk to us about Sorcha, she made the green land"—she made a waving motion—"sweep over us. It was a beautiful place. Hilly and green and cool. We could smell the ocean on the breeze, hear the grass rustling. And there was a little girl."

She looked at me.

"This wasn't long before we got pregnant. But it hadn't happened yet, and we didn't know if it would ever happen." Her gaze lost focus as she walked through the memory. "We heard this laugh—a child's laugh—but there was no one around. No parent she might have belonged to, except for us. I don't know how we knew it, but we knew she was ours."

Her voice softened to a whisper. "In that moment, there was absolute happiness. But it was only for a moment. Claudia brought us back here. Or maybe it's more accurate to say the green land was taken away from us. The sense of loss was . . . devastating. It felt like we'd lost her for real."

She looked at me again. "It hurt to come back. To leave that—and her—behind, especially when we didn't fully trust the prophecy. What if that had been our only chance with her? With you?" She breathed out heavily through pursed lips, obviously working to control her emotions.

"I'm here," I said, and smiled.

"I know. And we're glad. Usually," she added with a grin, her way of diffusing the emotion in the room. "I guess the point is, the green land is a powerful place for fairies. I don't know if they were able to increase their connection to it after Sorcha, when their power was stronger. But either way, I'd bet their connection is less now." She looked at Yuen. "Maybe that's what this is all about—thinking political power is how they obtain the magic they need."

"Unclear," he said. "But the more information we have, the better the chance we can deal with them before they get out of hand. Or further out of hand."

"Maybe insinuating themselves into the peace talks is an effort to get the power they need." I looked at my father. "You heard about the French delegation?"

"What about them?" Yuen asked.

"Chevalier and Dumas went back to Paris near dawn," my father said.

Good, I thought. *At least they'd done him the courtesy of telling him directly.*

"What did Seraphine have to say about this?" my mother asked, frowning as she walked to me, then took my hand.

"That the talks had been disrupted and there wasn't a reasonable chance they'd work, so Marion and Victor voted to go home and deal with problems on the ground."

"I'm sorry," my mother said. "I'm so sorry they left the way they did. I believe I'd take that very personally."

"It's hard not to," I admitted. "But Lulu's letting me stay at her loft, so that helps."

My mother smiled. "I left Mallory's to come here, and now Lulu's taking you home to her place. That seems about right."

"There will be no talks without France," Yuen said.

"I told Seri that. She was apologetic, but . . ."

"But they still got on the plane," Connor said.

I nodded.

"The delegates from Spain left early yesterday evening. The other delegates remain in town," my father said. "They opted to cancel tonight's session, given the absences, but I understand some of the delegates will be meeting together in smaller groups."

"So there's still hope," my mother said.

"Fading hope," he said. "I don't blame Spain, and I don't blame France. I don't know who to blame." He looked at me. "But the fairies seem to be at the top of that list."

The room got quiet, all of us probably wondering what would happen next.

"You should find Claudia," I said to Yuen.

"Claudia?"

"Either she's directing Ruadan, so this is her fault, or she doesn't know what he's doing and she needs to. She has to be the key here."

Yuen looked at Theo and me. "Go back to the castle and demand to talk to Claudia. Tell them you're there on behalf of the Ombudsman, and you have CPD support. Take a couple of officers with you if you need to. But talk to her."

Theo nodded. "And Dearborn?"

"He might see your communicating with the fairies—because it's inconsistent with Riley's guilt—as a rejection of his authority. So you can say no to the task, and I won't hold it against you."

"No, I'll go," Theo said enthusiastically. "Dearborn can shove his authority up his pompous ass."

"Oh, I like him," my mother murmured.

"I'll go with you," I said. "You don't want to go in there alone." I looked at my parents, tried to reassure them with a glance that I could handle myself. My mother nodded back. I might have been her child, but I was an immortal and I was strong. And they'd have to let me take my chances.

I looked at my father, and his expression was still carefully blank. He was very good at that. I chalked it up to four hundred years of experience.

"We'll focus on the peace talks," he said. "Try to keep the remaining delegates in the country. Perhaps they would be amenable to discussions here."

"The ballroom," my mother said with a nod. "It's a good thought, presuming we can keep the fairies out."

My father's voice was dry. "We will keep the fairies out." He glanced at Yuen. "And we'll advise you of the results of the video search."

"Then I'll leave you to it," Yuen said, glancing between me and Theo. "Be careful out there. And report in frequently."

"Will do, boss." He looked at me. "You ready?"

I glanced at my parents, then back at Theo. "Can you give me a few minutes?"

"Sure, I'll be outside. Head out when you're done." And he looked back at the door. "Okay if I grab something from the kitchen?"

"Go for it," I said.

In the time we made those arrangements, my father was gone, leaving my mother and me alone in his office.

"He went to talk to Kelley," my mother said. "I think he needed a few minutes."

I nodded.

"You could have handled it better," she said. "You could have talked to him first."

"I meant to—I was going to. Yuen got here earlier than I thought he would." Or the Auto had gotten me here later. But, really, neither of those mattered. It was my doing, my fault for not taking him aside first.

"You're right," I said. "I should have." And the thought that I'd hurt him curled my stomach again. "Should I talk to him about it?"

"Why don't you give him a little time?" she suggested. "This isn't just about Cadogan House, but about his being your father. He'll be hurt that you didn't talk to him, and guilty that he failed you by not making you a full member."

"He didn't fail me."

"But he'll think he did," she said, not unkindly. "He loves you,

and he loves this House. And your being part of the House—
that's important to him, too."

I nodded, feeling miserable and hating that there was no quick
fix for it.

She put an arm around my shoulders. "You've had a hard
homecoming. I'm glad Lulu's there for you. And that Connor was
there."

"Not for long. He's taking the Pack to Alaska."

"I know. How do you feel about that?"

I gave her a narrow-eyed stare. "What do you mean, how do I
feel about it?"

She just looked at me for a moment. "How do you feel about
his leaving?" she finally asked. "You've been spending more time
together since you've gotten back. And he helped you out last
night."

"Leaving is what he has to do," I said, not comfortable digging
into my feelings about Connor any more than that. They were
complicated, and he was leaving, anyway, so they hardly mattered. "The Pack has been planning this for a while."

She nodded. "I'll talk to your father. And when things have
calmed, you should talk to him, too. Apologize."

I would. As soon as possible. Because walking around with a
bellyful of guilt was going to get very old, very fast.

"Be careful tonight," she said, wrapping her arms tightly
around me before I could respond. "We both want to handcuff
you to Cadogan House, keep you safe. But that wouldn't do anyone any good."

She pulled back, brushed fingers against my cheek. "We are
very proud of who you've become. But never forget where you
came from."

With those words in my head, I walked back through the House,
found Connor waiting outside, one leg slung over Thelma. His

arms were crossed, and there was a very serious expression on his face.

"What's wrong?" I asked.

"Nothing." He uncrossed his arms. "I've got work to do for Alaska, but I wanted to talk to you first."

I didn't like the second mention of Alaska, and still didn't want to think about it.

"I wanted to talk to you, too. About last night—I'm sorry about the attitude. You were trying to help, and I wasn't ready to hear it."

He looked back at me, brows lifted. "Is Elisa Sullivan, the bossiest of the bossy, apologizing to me?"

"I'm not bossy. I'm decisive."

At that, Connor rolled his eyes.

"But yes, I'm apologizing. I know you were trying to help, and I appreciate that you're on my side. It's just hard to take advice after dealing with this for a long time on my own."

"I'm sure it is. The bigger point still stands: You don't have to deal with it alone."

I didn't believe that for a second—especially since he was the only person who knew the truth and he was leaving—but I could appreciate that he cared. "Thanks."

"Listen, Lis . . . Theo seems like a good guy, but the fairies are dangerous."

"He'll be there on behalf of the Ombudsman," I said. "They may not respect me or Lulu, but I imagine they'll think twice before going up against the entire city."

"And Theo?"

My brows lifted. "What about him?"

He looked at me quietly for a moment. "Can he handle himself?"

Given the pause, I wasn't sure that was the question Connor really wanted to ask. And it occurred to me—maybe a little late—

that I didn't actually know the answer. Surely Yuen wouldn't send Theo to the castle if he couldn't handle it.

I settled on, "We'll find out."

"That's not a very good answer."

"It's the only one I can give you. We have to go to the castle because we don't have any better options. Riley's still behind bars, and my parents' House is being used to further someone's violent agenda." I gave him a halfhearted smile. "Don't worry, you won't have to rescue me again."

"I didn't mind rescuing you the first time," he said. And there was something different in his eyes. Emotion I hadn't seen before and wasn't entirely sure what to do with. "But you don't really need rescuing, Lis. You just need a good partner."

I wasn't prepared for the intensity of his gaze, and my instinct was to turn away, to put space between us that would give me time to think.

"You don't need rules for this," Connor said, and grabbed my hand before I could turn.

I looked back at him, watched his eyes darken like storm clouds over a cold, deep sea, his gaze so intense he might have seen through to my soul—and felt the sudden, wild hunger that rose up in response to it.

Connor watched my face, thumb stroking the sensitive skin on the inside of my wrist.

Magic pulsed in the air, and it had nothing to do with my monster or the fairies. It was shifter magic, wild and rough and barely tamed. And it was vampire magic, dark and careful and dangerous.

When he finally released my hand, which prickled from the residual magic, the intensity in his eyes had changed, evolved into satisfaction at whatever he'd seen in my eyes—or the pounding pulse he'd have felt in my wrist.

It took a full minute to find my voice again. "I have to go."

Connor looked at me quietly for a moment, and this time his face was unreadable. "Be careful."

I nodded and stepped back, then watched him pull on his helmet and start the bike with a roar of engine and exhaust. And then he drove off into darkness.

SEVENTEEN

It was a balmy night, and although Theo wore short sleeves, the air-conditioning in his vehicle—a former Auto with ZERO WASTE and OMBUDSMAN stickers on it—was turned up to arctic levels.

"Warm, are you?" I asked him, climbing inside.

"Sorry," he said, and turned it down. "I'm from Texas. Hard habit to break. Everything all right back there? With you and Connor, I mean?"

"There isn't a me and Connor, so yeah, everything's fine." Wanting to change the subject and get this particular show on the road, I glanced at him. He looked cool and collected, if excited. "If things get bad in there, you can handle yourself?"

"I don't have your blade training, but yeah." He lifted up the hem of his shirt, showing the gun holstered at his waist. "I was with the CPD before I joined the Ombudsman's office. I'm a certified marksman."

I blinked. "What? How old are you?"

He smiled. "Twenty-six. I've been shooting since I was ten. My parents thought it was weird, but I was good, so they dealt with it."

"And why the switch to the Ombuds' office?"

"You ever read comics?"

"Not really."

"Being a human, supernaturals are kind of 'other.' We didn't really have access to them—the Houses aren't zoos—so you make

assumptions. Immortality, magic, strength. Comics, graphic novels, are how we know about those concepts. That's how I got interested. I started as an intern, then worked the reception desk
when Marge decided to retire."

"And do you still think we're superheroes?"

He grinned. "Most of the time, you're a little more Bruce
Wayne than Batman. But the lure's still there."

I tilted my head at him. "You looking to join a House?"

"No. My ma's religious, and that would pretty much kill her."

"Huh."

"Yeah, she's old school, despite my efforts to the contrary."

"There's only so much you can do."

We drove to the castle and parked outside, found the gate open
again. The castle was dark, and the neighborhood was silent but
for the whistle of a train in the distance.

"It's quiet," Theo said, pulling out his weapon, turning off the
safety, and checking the chamber. When he was satisfied, he holstered it again. I belted on my katana.

"It was quiet last night, too," I said, and we stepped through
the gate, walked in moonlight toward the gatehouse. "But not this
quiet."

One of the doors was open several inches. Theo looked inside,
then pushed it open all the way.

The gatehouse was empty, the room lit only by the shaft of
moonlight. Even the torches were gone, their holders empty.

"The torches were lit last night," I whispered. "This is where
they met us."

"You didn't go any farther?"

"No."

Theo nodded, pulled out his screen, began taking photos.

I walked to the doors that led into the courtyard and pushed.

I expected them to be barred from the inside, for the gatehouse's emptiness to be a trick or a trap, so the weight nearly pulled me inside when the door swung open, revealing a wide avenue of space around the keep, which stood in the middle. There were squares of grass and stone, raised gardens filled with vegetables and flowers, planted trees, and sitting areas where the fairies might have enjoyed the weather.

Like the gatehouse, everything was dark and quiet. The torches were gone, every window in the building dark, with only the moonlight casting shadows across the stone.

I took photos, then slipped back into the gatehouse.

"Anything?" Theo asked. He crouched near the wall, ran a swab along the ground, then slipped it into a clear bag.

"Nothing. No fairies, no lights. There are garden plots that still have food, so they didn't take everything. But they seem to be gone. What do you have there?"

"Fairy dust."

"You're joking."

He rose, slipped the bag into his pocket. "Entirely," he said with a grin. "I'm just pulling a forensic sample." He looked up and around. "It's not often we have an opportunity to inspect a fairy house."

"Glad I could help." I glanced back toward the doors. "We need to check the keep."

"Yeah," he said, and followed me into the courtyard, then let out a low whistle. "This is impressive."

"Yeah." The tower loomed in front of us. It was difficult to estimate stories given the irregular windows sprinkled across the front facade, but I guessed at least four.

"You want to take the building or the courtyard?" Theo asked.

"I'll take the keep," I said, too curious to pass up the chance to walk through the fairies' home.

"You okay going alone? And I'm not saying I doubt your skills with what is probably a really sharp katana." He cast a wary glance at the door. "I wouldn't want to go in there alone."

"There's no one in there."

He looked back at me. "How do you know?"

"Magic," I said. "There was a lot more of it last night just because there were so many of them here. I wasn't sure until I walked into the courtyard. But they're gone." I looked up at the tower. "I mean, still creepy. Still possibly haunted and booby-trapped. But I can deal with that."

I'd dealt with worse monsters.

"Here," he said, and pulled a small flashlight from his pocket, then checked the time on his screen. "Twenty minutes. You aren't back by then, I'm coming to find you. And don't make me do that."

"I'll do my best." I checked the time, then flicked on the light and headed toward the keep.

Theo didn't need to know my hands were sweating.

The doors were unlocked. I pushed one open, slipped the flashlight into the gap, and spun the beam around the space. No movement, no sound, no fairies, so I slipped inside but froze just inside the door in case of a booby trap. Once again, there was only silence.

The room was tall—two stories of stone, the walls covered in embroidered tapestries, the windows covered by long velvet curtains. There were alcoves on both sides of the room, stairs disappearing as they curved upward. There were woven rugs on the floors, a long table in the center of the room flanked by benches, and an enormous fireplace with a hearth that was nearly ten feet long. At the other end was an ornate throne in gorgeously carved and gleaming wood. This was probably the central gathering room, the place where the fairies ate and socialized and took their instructions from Claudia.

But there was no sign of the fairies now, only the things they'd left behind. That included a fine layer of dust that had settled sometime within the last twenty-four hours, probably stirred up when they'd gathered their belongings and left the property. And it smelled green, like asparagus and freshly cut grass just beginning to decay.

I flipped a mental coin and took the staircase on the right, a spiral of stone steps cantilevered into the wall. No rails, no bannisters. I kept a hand on the stone and stayed as close to the wall as possible, then made my way up to the second floor. A passageway curved away from the stairs, and I stepped through and into a narrow hall with several doors on one side and windows on the other.

The window glass was wavy and bubbled, and I figured that was an artistic choice to better match the medieval feel of the place. They looked over the courtyard, and I watched Theo's flashlight bob here and there as he searched it.

The doors were open to small bedrooms that weren't unlike the dorms at Cadogan House. More gorgeous wooden furniture, including several beds with posts carved into climbing vines and flowers. Fairies might have been assholes, but they had really good taste in home decor.

The passageway curved again, and after a stretch of twenty or thirty feet, dead-ended in another arched wooden door. This one was nearly as tall as the gatehouse doors, which made me think I'd reached the queen's room.

I listened for a moment, trying to ignore the thud of my heartbeat. And when I confirmed the room was silent, I opened the door.

The other rooms had been mostly empty, but orderly. This one was chaos.

The ceilings were higher than in the other bedrooms, two stories of stone that soared to a grid of wooden beams, with golden flowers painted between them. There were two tall windows, once covered by thick curtains. But the velvet, in deep and shimmering blue, lay in piles on the floor.

One of the bed's carved posts was broken, silk sheets and thick blankets tossed aside. An armoire stood in the corner, the doors open, the contents torn out and spilled onto the floor, including a white dress that shimmered with jewels.

The dress Claudia had worn to the opening-night session.

I needed to find Theo.

I took photographs of the room, and made it back to the court-yard with only seconds to spare in my twenty-minute allotment.

"No fairies," I said. "I didn't have time to search the entire keep, but I found this." I showed him the pictures I'd taken of Claudia's room. "Someone trashed it."

Theo studied them, brow furrowed. "Why would someone do that?"

"Maybe she had a tantrum. Or maybe she didn't want to leave and fought back against it, and this was the result."

Theo nodded. "Maybe they were angry at her." He looked back at me. "You said you didn't see her last night? That Ruadan was playing at being in charge?"

"Yeah. You're thinking he wasn't just playing?"

"I don't know," he said. "I don't get why they'd have left all this. The castle is basically new, and they built it to their own specifications. It's theirs and it's fortified. There's no reason for them to leave."

"They could have been afraid Cadogan would retaliate."

"Because they're suddenly afraid of a fight?" Theo asked, and he had a point.

"They don't make decisions based on fear," he said. "They're smart and calculating narcissists. They're sociopaths that hold grudges. That's what drives them."

They hadn't looked like they'd planned to pack up last night, which meant they'd made the move after we left. And probably because of us.

"They left this place because they wanted to be—physically—somewhere else," he said. "We need to find that location and figure out what they wanted with it."

"Do the fairies have other residences in town?"

Theo shook his head. "Other than the tower, which they abandoned, not that we know of. But they've gone somewhere, so we'll start scanning the satellite feed, try to nail down their new home."

He looked around. "Still a lot to go through here, but I'll get CPD officers to sweep the rest of it. Let's go back to the car. I want to update Yuen. Then we can decide what to do next."

"Get me coffee," I said, "and you can call whomever you want."

The scent of roasting beans poured through the skinny drive-through window at Leo's, and I thought it was possibly the best thing I'd ever smelled.

"Chicago dogs. Pizza. Hot beefs. You have an entire city at your disposal, and you want cheap, drive-through coffee?"

"It's not cheap, and it's the best coffee in Chicago," I said, closing my eyes at the first sip of sweet and hot and sharp.

"There's a barista serving civet coffee in a hipster café in Wicker Park who's weeping right now because of what you said."

"I'm okay with that." And I took another sip. Civet coffee seemed like the kind of twisted punishment Eleanor of Aquitaine might have come up with.

My needs fulfilled, Theo pulled the vehicle into an empty parking lot. Yuen's image appeared like a hologram above the dashboard. The car might have been a recycled Auto, but it had a few tricks up its sleeve.

"Trouble?" Yuen asked.

"Not the kind you're thinking of," Theo said. "The fairies are gone. The castle is empty."

Yuen's brow furrowed. "What do you mean, empty?"

"They've abandoned the castle entirely. Left the furniture behind, but taken everything else. And they trashed Claudia's room. Elisa will send you some pics."

Yuen was quiet for a moment as he considered. "They trashed her room," he quietly said, and his gaze shifted to me. "Thoughts?"

That he'd asked for my opinion made me sit up a little straighter and choose my words more carefully. "I don't think she'd have destroyed her clothes. She's too vain. That makes me think someone else did it. Ruadan, or his fairy allies, seems like the best candidate. But until we find them, we won't know."

He nodded. "Agreed." He held up a hand, then looked to the side at something we couldn't see. And his eyes widened.

Petra's face appeared beside Yuen's, as if she'd moved to stand beside him. "We've got something weird in Grant Park. You're closest."

"Something weird?" Theo asked.

"A power surge. Vibrations, and they're magical in nature. This isn't weather or geology or underground construction someone forgot to tell the city about."

I frowned. I didn't know anything about magical vibrations, but guessed humans wouldn't be able to feel them. "Who reported it?"

"River nymphs," Petra said. "Two near Buckingham, communing with the water in the fountain." Her voice was dry. "They felt it, reported it to a meter maid, who thought they were drunk bachelorettes."

High heels, strong makeup, short dresses. That checked out.

"Where in Grant Park?" Theo asked.

"All of it," she said. "The vibration's got a good spread. But start near the fountain."

"Copy that. I'll take a look and report back." He looked at me. "You up for another adventure?"

I was up for a bucket of wine and a chance to apologize to my father. Or a bucket of wine *before* I had a chance to apologize to my father. But since I was unlikely to get either right now, I figured I might as well do the city some good.

"Sure," I said. "Let's do it." I'd just need to tell Lulu that I wouldn't be home for dinner.

I'd seen television detectives attach lights to the top of unmarked cars so they could cruise through traffic to a crime scene. I hadn't seen it in real life until tonight, when Theo whipped one out.

"What exactly are we going to do with whatever we find in Grant Park?" I asked, and checked the side mirror just in case Connor was following. I was a little disappointed he and Thelma weren't behind us. We probably could have used them.

"We handle it, or we call in backup," Theo said. "And we hope they get there on time."

It was late, at least by human standards, and traffic was light, mostly Autos shuttling the tired through the Loop. Even Grant Park, usually crowded with tourists or festivals, was quiet.

Theo drove north on Columbus, pulled the vehicle to a stop at the curb in front of the wide brick plaza and fountain beyond it. There was a low pool with monstrous sculptures that reached through the water and three tiers of pink marble that glowed in the darkness.

We climbed out of the car, looked around, and saw no one. In silence, we made a large circle around the fountain, scanning the park for anything unusual. But there were no nymphs, no humans, no fairies. Just the fine spray of water across the bricks as the wind blew through the fountain's towering spray.

And then the world shifted.

I felt it before I heard it, the vibration beneath my feet. Not a literal shaking, but a ring of power.

The monster felt it, too, and woke suddenly, stretching beneath

my skin, reaching for the magic. Not because it seemed familiar—
this wasn't the Egregore that called from my mother's sword. But
because the power was enormous.

The second vibration was even stronger, like the earth was con-
tracting beneath my feet. "Damn," I murmured, and braced a
hand against one of the metal supports around the fountain to
stay upright.

"Elisa? What is it?"

"You can't feel it?"

"No. It is the vibrations?"

"Yeah. Magic under our feet." The rippling grew more violent
still, like a train was bearing down on us. "And I'd say something's on its way. Get ready."

They appeared like ghosts, solidifying out of darkness. At least
a hundred fairies in two straight lines that stretched out across the
brick plaza.

Theo's voice was quiet as he spoke into his screen. "We found
the fairies."

Or they'd found us.

They stood in two tight lines that formed a V, all in green tunics.
All of them were fit. None too old; none too young. I guessed
these were the soldiers—the warriors—and all of them had weapons. Straight swords, longbows, and daggers. Not a single gun or
modern weapon, at least that I could see.

At the junction of the lines, facing us directly, their apparent
master. Ruadan.

Claudia was nowhere in sight, which made me wonder: Was
Ruadan here because Claudia had directed him, or because he'd
overridden her command? Dragged her from her room in the
castle and put himself in charge? And, maybe more important,
were the fairies behind him loyal to Claudia or to Ruadan? How
many rules were they willing to break for their would-be king?

"I'm alerting the CPD," Theo quietly said, and tapped fingers. against his screen even as he kept his gaze on the fairies. "Requesting significant backup."

"Good plan," I said quietly.

"Ruadan," Theo said, when he'd put the screen away again, "what are you doing here?"

"Is this not a public park?" Ruadan asked with a sneer. "Are we not entitled to use it?"

"Is that all you're doing?" Theo asked. "Planning an evening picnic?"

"Or maybe a group photo?" I offered, trying for bravado I didn't really feel. Because while there was a part of me that wanted to fight—and the monster was eager for it—we were severely outnumbered.

"Oh, nice," Theo said with a smile. "A group photo." He looked around. "But I don't see a photographer."

"You dare mock me." Ruadan's expression was hard, furious magic beginning to pump from the fairies with almost the same ferocity as the vibrations beneath the street. "In that case, we claim this land—what you call Grant Park—for ourselves."

"Who, exactly, is 'we'?" I asked, and Ruadan's gaze shifted to me, and his lips curled into a smile that made me want to shrink back into my skin. It was that look I'd seen before, the interest I didn't like.

"I speak for the fairies," he said.

"Does that include Claudia?" I asked.

His expression didn't change. But there was a twitch at the corner of his eye that said he didn't like the question.

"Where is she, Ruadan?" I asked, but kept my gaze on the fairies, wondering how they'd respond.

"Her location is not relevant," Ruadan said. And the fairies' expressions stayed blank. Maybe they didn't know where she was. . . . Or maybe they didn't care.

"It is relevant, because one hundred fairies have taken what appears to be a very aggressive position against the City of Chicago." Theo slid his hands into his pockets like a man only mildly interested in the conversation. For the first time, I could see the former cop in Theo's eyes.

"You mock us," he continued. "You're not here for enjoyment. Your people are armed. You've demanded property owned by the city, and I'm pretty sure you've already decided to fight. You know I'm not going to hand Grant Park over to you."

Ruadan's lip curled in obvious disgust. "We are older than your species, than your nation. We are better than you in every conceivable way."

"But you need a few acres of brick and grass?"

"For reasons that are ours to know."

"The Ombudsman's office would disagree with you."

"We have spoken with your Ombudsman," Ruadan said, spitting out the word. "We expressed our displeasure with your breach and found a sympathetic ear." And then he murmured something low and threatening.

With shocking speed, her movements blurred by it, the fairy behind Ruadan—pale skin, paler hair, and a narrow face that ended in a pointed chin—launched forward at Theo.

She looked so delicate, but there was nothing delicate about the blade she flipped from her tunic and held at Theo's throat. His eyes flashed to the blade, then up to me. But he didn't move. He might have been human, but he had vampire-level chill. Unlike the fairies, who'd become blade-happy.

"If you will not give this land to us," Ruadan said, "we will take it." Then he settled his gaze on me. "We were unsatisfied by our last encounter. Shedding blood here would provide much-needed resolution."

I looked at the fairy who held Theo. "A human isn't much of a conquest, is it? I'd be a much more interesting opponent."

She apparently agreed, as her blade was suddenly airborne and flying toward me.

I reached out and slapped my palms against the flat of the blade, the gleaming point barely an inch from my face. My heart beat so hard I could see the pulse throbbing in my wrists. And then I shifted my gaze around it to the fairy who'd thrown it.

"You missed," I said.

She took the bait, pushing Theo backward and jumping toward me.

I flipped the blade to grab the handle, then thrust it down toward her. The fairy spun away at the last minute, so it glanced off her shoulder, scratching fabric but not drawing blood.

She kicked back, sending pain through my knee that was sharp as a hammer strike. I fell to my knees but grabbed her ankle on the way down, yanked it backward. She fell forward, caught herself on her palms, then twisted from the waist like a break-dancer, flipping her legs up and over until she was on her feet.

As if sensing the danger, the monster beat inside me with fists, wanting to join the battle, angry at being restrained when there was fighting to be had.

I pushed it down, which took more than a little energy. I nearly considered, just for a moment, letting it loose to have its way with Ruadan and the rest of them. But I didn't want Ruadan to see, didn't want to see victory or validation in his eyes. And if I let it go, let it join the fight—let it kick and punch and spill more blood onto the ground—what kind of monster would that make me?

The fairy kicked, and I fell and rolled across hard brick, then popped to my feet again, sweeping with the knife in front of me. Her chin dipped, and I realized that was her tell, the signal she intended to move. This time she went for the knife and grabbed my wrist. I kicked out, tried to pull away. . . . And the world erupted with noise and wind.

The cavalry had arrived, in the form of two CPD helicopters, spotlights spearing toward the ground. And beneath them, drones with cameras, marked by the television stations that piloted them.

"Supernaturals," came the call from one of the copters. "Put your hands in the air."

The fairy dropped her hold, sending me nearly stumbling backward. The spotlight followed as she stepped back into line with the others.

Ruadan looked more irritated than angry or afraid they'd been caught. And when the ground began to rumble again, the buzz of magic flowing up through the ground, I knew why.

"Theo!" I called out over the blades, my hair whipping into my eyes. "They're using the magic again."

"You will see," Ruadan said. "You will see our power and you will fear."

The world shuddered hard, an earthquake only sups could feel. It threw me off my feet, sending me to my knees, which knocked hard against brick.

Light flashed above me, brilliant and white, leaving a stripe of color seared on my retinas.

And when I could blink again . . . they were gone.

For a full minute, Theo and I stayed in place, just staring at the empty spot where the fairies had been.

"That was . . . weird," I said, pushing chopper-blown hair out of my eyes.

"Very weird," Theo said. "And anticlimactic."

The monster was equally disturbed, and seemed to pace beneath my skin. The fight had been cut short, the enemies disappearing. Much like the fairies, it didn't like being denied. And it didn't respect their cowardice.

At least we had that in common.

EIGHTEEN

We were offered bottles of water and checks from EMTs, which we declined. Instead, we sent messages to the people who'd probably seen us on video—or would eventually—to let them know we were fine.

"You'll want more patrols here," Theo said to the CPD officer who questioned us. "They'll probably come back."

"Great," the man said. "Just what we freakin' need right now." His voice was coated in a thick Chicago accent, and the familiarity made me feel a little better.

"We'll go to the office," Theo said, when they'd left us alone.

"Fine by me," I said, and we walked back to his car.

Theo unlocked the doors, looked at me over the roof. "Are you aware that you can be scary?" He said it with a smile, so I took it as a compliment.

"I'm a vampire," I said, with the most casual shrug I could manage. "It's our thing."

Mr. Pettiway looked up from a large paperback as we entered, but his expression stayed somber.

"Fairies," he said, the single word holding a wealth of concern.

"Fairies," Theo agreed. "Is he here?"

"Oh, he's here." And he didn't sound thrilled about it. "And he isn't very happy."

"I appreciate the warning." Theo glanced at the book. "You finished up *The Odyssey*?"

"It was my third time," he said with a smile. "I breezed through it." He showed us the cover of his current read, which featured an enormous golden crown. "Thought I'd lose myself in a little fantasy for a few days."

"Any fairies in that one?" Theo asked.

"Plenty. Your high fae, your low fae, and everything in between."

"If it gives you any ideas about dealing with them, let us know."

Mr. Pettiway grinned. "You know I will."

"Who is 'he'?" I asked, as we walked through the main building. "Dearborn?"

"Yeah. Mr. Pettiway isn't a fan. I believe he compares everyone to your great-grandfather. He wanted Yuen to get the job, but Dearborn has better connections." He pressed his hand to a sensor beside a door and a "Briefing Room" sign.

The door slid open, revealing a long and narrow room with several rows of tables and chairs in a neat grid facing a large glass screen in the front of the room. Yuen stood in front of the screen, arms crossed as he watched Petra rearrange electronic images with a wave of her hand. Petra, like Yuen, wore a tidy suit and shiny shoes, which was quite a contrast to Theo's shirt, now dotted with blood from the faint scrape of the fairy's knife against his neck.

"Hey," she said, glancing back.

"Hey, Petra." I reached out to shake the bare hand she offered, and a bright blue spark jumped between our fingers, sending a literal shock of pain through me.

I yelped and yanked my hand back, rubbed the needlelike sting from my skin.

"Damn it. Sorry about that," she said, and rubbed her own

palm. "I forgot I wasn't wearing gloves. I can't use them when I use the damn screen. And the static doesn't help," she said, casting a sour glance at the carpet.

"We're getting a humidifier," Yuen said with a smile. "As soon as the budget's approved."

"Can't be soon enough," she said. "I'm a walking occupational hazard."

Pounding footsteps echoed down the hallway, and Petra slid her gaze toward the open door. "And speaking of occupational hazards."

Dearborn, wearing a tank top, running shorts, and tennis shoes, as if he'd been disturbed mid-run, strode into the room. "What the hell happened in Grant Park? I don't appreciate hearing about supernatural goddamned drama on the radio. And I certainly do not want to brief the mayor on another disturbance caused by Chicago's supernaturals."

Just like with the fairies, Theo looked totally unperturbed. "The fairies appeared via some magical mechanism in Grant Park. They attacked, we defended, and they disappeared."

"What do you mean, they appeared and disappeared? They can't suddenly transport themselves with magic."

"Actually, that's precisely what it looked like. We don't know how—this is new behavior for fairies."

Dearborn cursed under his breath. "And why were they in my park?"

I guessed everyone apparently had a claim on Grant Park these days.

"We don't know," Theo said, glancing at Yuen. Theo might have been answering Dearborn's questions, but I had the sense he was also reporting to the man who did the bulk of the work. "We asked, and they didn't answer. But they were in formation, had weapons, and tried to claim the park. They had something planned, but we don't yet know what that is. And we're lucky the

nymphs were there to feel the magic—and that we got there in
time, before they did something destructive."

"'Lucky,'" Dearborn said, "is the operative word. We can't afford further destabilization or bad publicity right now, any more
than we can afford to deal with speculation about a crisis involving the fairies."

"It's not speculation," Theo said. "The crisis is here. If it wasn't
for me and Elisa, they might have attacked, damaged property—
who knows?"

"Are you asking for my thanks?" Dearborn asked. "Because
you won't get it."

"No, sir," Theo said. And for the first time, he looked unhappy
with his boss. "I'm advising you that they're preparing for something."

"And they've probably been preparing for something since
their interruption at the peace talks," I added.

His brows lifted. "Their appearance at Grant Park tonight has
no obvious connection to the peace talks, and I won't accept speculation in that regard. They have no bearing on the matter of the
death of Tomas Cardona. An arrest has been made in that case."

"Riley Sixkiller didn't kill Tomas," I said. "A fairy did."

"You have a fairy's confession?" he asked. "You have direct,
forensic evidence tying a fairy to the crime?"

I glanced at Yuen, who shook his head slightly. I guessed he
didn't want to elaborate in front of Dearborn, and reminded myself to follow up later.

"No," I said.

"Ms. Sullivan," Dearborn said, rubbing the spot between his
eyebrows. "Even assuming your analysis is correct, there is a reason that I am the Ombudsman and you are not. I have the training. I have the resources. I have authority of the city of Chicago.
My methods do not damage property. My methods do not send

fairies from their homes. My methods do not end up with fairies in the middle of Grant Park."

"Neither do mine," I muttered.

"We have someone in custody. He has motive, opportunity, and means. And there's physical evidence that links him to the crime."

"He didn't do it. And the Pack's demands that he be released are only going to get louder."

"The Pack isn't in charge," Dearborn shot back.

"No, it isn't," I agreed. "But it's their city, too, and they're entitled to the same rights as humans. Including being considered innocent until proven guilty."

"That's surprisingly naive for a vampire."

"It's not naive," I said. "It's the ideal. If we don't live up to it, we've failed."

Dearborn held up a hand. "I don't have time for this. I'll need to shower, change, communicate with the mayor, and figure out how to spin this debacle."

"It's not a debacle," I said. "But if we aren't careful, it's the beginning of a war."

His eyes were hard and sharp, his pointing figure accusatory. "That is precisely the kind of hysteria we do not need." He took a step forward. "If you so much as suggest to the media that a war is at hand, your father and I will have a long talk about Cadogan House's continued existence in this city."

My blood began to speed, the monster to stir.

But before I could speak, Yuen said Dearborn's name. "We have enough threats from the outside. We are allies, and should act like it."

"Yes," Dearborn said, eyes glinting as he stared at me. "We should."

With that, he turned on his heel and strode down the hall again.

"You know," I said, when the echoes of his footsteps faded away, "for a thin man and a runner, he's quite a stomper."

"Ego," Theo said. "Makes the soul heavy." He looked at Yuen. "Methinks he's losing it."

"His cool," Yuen said. "Not his authority. That remains, regardless of how much we respect him."

"Or how little," Petra said, her tone utterly bland. "I will say again that you should have his job."

"He might have it in the near future," Theo said. "Dearborn bet his job on Riley, on this being a minor issue that he fixed by arresting a shifter. If it turns out all these pretty fairies are involved, he's going to lose a lot of face."

"That is for the mayor to deal with," Yuen said. "We deal with the details. Tell me what happened, from the beginning."

We walked him through the events at Grant Park, giving him every detail we could remember, while Petra made notes on a smaller screen paired to the larger one, so her words appeared in tidy rows behind us.

"I don't understand how they could simply appear and reappear," Yuen said.

"They must have learned a new skill," Theo said. "That wouldn't surprise me, given Ruadan seems to be pushing them in a new direction."

"But what direction?" I asked. "Shifters are blamed for Tomas's death. The peace talks fall apart, and fairies are trying to make big magic in Grant Park. How do those things connect?"

"Fairies," Petra said. "They're the common thread."

"And Ruadan specifically," I said. "He was at the sessions, the party, the castle, Grant Park."

"And without Claudia for the latter events," Yuen said. "You said her room was disheveled, and she's apparently missing. Why?"

"Ruadan likes violence," I said, thinking of his expressions at the castle and Grant Park. "He wants trouble. Maybe he wanted a real fight at the peace talks, and was angry when Claudia agreed to a seat at the table."

"What about the pin?" Theo asked.

"Forensic tests haven't been completed yet," Yuen said. "Surveillance video of the party is still being reviewed at Cadogan."

"How's Riley doing?" I asked, feeling a stab of guilt since I hadn't visited him again.

Yuen's eyes went dark, concern etched in his face. "For now, he's handling it. For now."

"Has his memory improved?"

Yuen shook his head. "We've tried meds, meditation, and magic. Nothing has helped. He still has pain when he tries to remember."

"What about the knife?" I asked. "I know his fingerprints were on it, but do we know where it came from?"

"We don't," Theo said. "At least, not specifically. It was a mass-produced hunting-style knife."

"Hard to trace," I said.

"Exactly. The blood on Riley's shirt was Tomas's. But the quantity wasn't nearly as much as should have been there given the nature of the wound."

I had to kick away the memory of Tomas's disconnected head.

"So the actual perp was probably covered in blood," Theo said. "There'd have been soiled clothes."

"The CPD's going through the castle?" I asked.

"They are," Yuen said. "They haven't reported anything yet, but if there's anything to find, they'll let us know."

"We have to figure out where the fairies are," I said. "Aren't there security cameras all over the place these days?"

"There are more cameras than there used to be," was all Yuen would confirm. "Petra?"

"I'm on it," she said, pulling off her gloves and working the main screen again, logging into some kind of a city portal. She pulled up a map, then zoomed in on the river's south fork, where the castle was located. The area was covered in dots.

"Those aren't all cameras," I said.

"Oh, they are," she said. "Welcome to the Internet of Things. Traffic-light cameras, speeding cameras, security cameras, laptop cams, body cams. Always wear your good underwear, because someone is probably filming you."

"Sound advice," Yuen said with a smile.

There were four traffic cameras near the castle. It took only a few moments to find video of the castle's gatehouse and front drive, and only a few minutes longer to speed through the window of time between our first and second visits to the castle.

Unfortunately, not a single fairy showed up. The only visible change in the time period was darkness; the torches hadn't been lit the second evening, so the castle stayed dark as the sun fell.

"Either they've got a secret way out of the castle," Theo said, "or they left by magic. And there's no way to tell that from the video."

"There might have been magical vibrations," I said. "But the castle grounds are enormous, so the ripples might not have spread any farther than that."

"So we assume they left by magic, as a group," Yuen said, studying the video. "And they took Claudia with them?"

"Maybe," I said. "But Claudia wasn't with Ruadan the night Lulu and I visited. It's possible she was already gone by then." And given the condition of her room, that they'd dragged her out in a much more conspicuous style.

"Go farther back," I said. "Find the period between the Cadogan party and our visit." If we couldn't find the fairies leaving, maybe we could find Claudia.

We searched video of the castle for nearly an hour. And still didn't have what we were looking for.

"Maybe we don't have the right angle on the castle," Theo said.

"There are more cameras in the sector," Petra said. "But unless we can narrow down a place or a window, it would take days to go through all the video."

"Zoom out on the map," Theo said. "Let's check our options."

On the screen, the square of green that held the castle became one block in the larger quilt of the city.

And there was an unusual bundle of cameras just up the street from the castle.

"What's on that corner?" I asked, pointing.

"Gas station," Petra said after a pause. "Lots of security cameras, including on the pumps themselves."

"Fairies have vehicles," Yuen said. "Good thought, Elisa. Pull it up."

The gas station was busy. Autos and driven vehicles pulling in for gas, people pulling in for snacks or necessities. They all looked human, or humanlike, at least until a large black SUV pulled up to a pump. The passenger's side opened and a fairy stepped out, looked around cagily, and moved to the pump.

While he waited for the tank to fill, he pulled open the back door. There in the backseat, hands tied in front of her and a vacant expression on her face, was Claudia. She was visible for only a second before the door was closed again.

"Well, well, well," Yuen said quietly.

The SUV drove off again, giving us a clear view of the license plate.

"I'm pulling the license," Petra said, logging into another information portal. "And . . . it's licensed to Claudia, no last name given, and the address is the castle, so no help there. Permission to track?"

"Track it," Yuen said.

Petra pressed a hand to her screen for some kind of security clearance, then did more swiping and typing. The overhead monitor flashed, and a map of the city replaced the camera footage.

"There's now a tag on the vehicle," Yuen explained. "If it's spotted by a person or camera, we'll get an alert, and we can track its movements."

"That's handy and terrifying," I said.

"It is," Yuen agreed. "In equal measure."

Petra looked back at us. "Now that we've got that underway, do you want to talk about the ley lines?"

"The what?" I asked.

Petra glanced at me. "Rivers of magical power that run through the earth's outer crust. Possibly remnants from changes in the earth's magnetic field."

"*Theoretically,*" Theo said. "There's no evidence they actually exist."

"Spoken like a tool of the Deep State. Bet you don't believe in aliens, either. Hot tip," she said in a whisper, "they're real."

"Let's just stick to planetary subjects for the time being," Yuen said with a smile.

"Fine by me," she said, but slid me a glance. "Ley lines are completely legitimate, but the government doesn't want you to know they exist."

"And why not?" I asked.

"Big Petroleum. Oil companies go out of business if humans figure out how to utilize the ley lines to run our vehicles, heat our homes, energize our tech. So they keep the knowledge very carefully guarded. But some of us know better."

"What does Grant Park have to do with ley lines?" Theo asked.

She gave him a flat stare. "Are you serious?"

"Yes?" he asked, his voice now uncertain.

Petra rolled her eyes. "I guess I'll need to lay it out for you."

"Please do," Yuen said, amusement in his dark eyes. "And nice pun."

"Yes, it was." She used her smaller screen to direct the large one, flipping through faded drawings to find a scratchy sketch of what I thought was Lake Michigan.

"*The North American Journals of Prince Maximillian*," she said. "He traveled the US in the 1830s, did these amazing natural-history journals where he recorded plants, animals, food, people, landscapes. Not much of Chicago at that point. But he didn't need the buildings to see this."

She zoomed in to reveal three lines that ran across the edge of the lake near where I guessed Chicago sat today. One crossed the city from east to west. The others were angled, one running southwest to northeast, nearly vertically, through the middle of the city, the other running northwest to southeast at a shallower angle.

"Two of the lines cross near downtown Chicago," Petra said, pointing at the map. "But the actual ley lines are only a couple of feet wide, so the scale is totally wrong on this map."

She swiped a screen and pulled up more data, and the overhead monitor showed a satellite image of Chicago marked by three glowing, intersecting lines.

"These are Chicago's ley lines," Petra said, beaming like a student who'd just nailed a recital. "I used satellite images, surface temps, wind data, and jet-stream movement, along with a sprinkle of human activity, and these are the lines predicted by that formula."

"They're real," Theo said, looking back at her with awe. "And you actually found them."

"It's more accurate to say I found the *echo* of them, the place they're algorithmically predicted to be. We don't have the knowledge to detect them per se, so this is the next best option."

She zoomed in, and the lines grew clearer, crisper, thinner, until they crossed just off Michigan Avenue, just south of the river.

And right over Grant Park.

"There's a ley line conjunction beneath Grant Park," Theo said, gaze intent on the screen.

"There is," Petra said, then looked at us. "Have you figured it out yet?"

We looked at her, then the map, trying to figure out where she was leading us.

"No?" Theo said.

With a heavy sigh, Petra pulled up another photo. This one was an overhead shot of the fairies at Grant Park, the careful lines in a V configuration, with Theo and me tiny dots in front of them.

The fairies' formation matched the ley lines perfectly.

"That's why they were in that V configuration," she said. "They were standing over one of the angles created by the conjunction."

"Damn good work," Yuen said, and his smile was as wide as Petra's had been. He seemed genuinely proud of her work, which I suspected wouldn't have been Dearborn's reaction.

"Thank you," she said.

"So the fairies wanted to use the ley lines for something," I asked. "And they figured the conjunction—two ley lines crossing—would give them the biggest bang for the buck."

"Maybe," Petra said. "We don't know much about the mechanism of ley lines because of—"

"*Big Petroleum,*" we finished for her.

"Hilarious," she said without a hint of humor. "And correct. But presumably they want the power."

"Ruadan wants the power," I murmured, stepping closer to the map and wondering what he had planned.

"If they wanted the conjunction," Theo said, "they might try Grant Park again. Or the next best thing, which I guess would be anywhere else along the ley lines?"

I nodded. "So if we search the ley lines, we might find the fairies." And then the obvious thing hit me. "Can you put the Potter Park tower and the castle on that map?"

Petra looked at me, grinned. "Of course," she said with a nod. "Of course they did that."

She knew what I was looking for. And when she plotted the two structures on the map, she showed my instinct had been right.

"They're positioned over ley lines," Theo said.

"Claudia probably selected the Potter Park tower because of the location over the north-south line," I said, "and bought the castle property for the same reason."

"We'll get CPD officers to travel the lines, look for any sign of them. Can you get me a scalable version of the map and the course of the ley lines to pass along? Perhaps one that, just in case of Big Petroleum, doesn't actually say 'ley lines'?"

"Sure," she said. "No one has to know what the lines represent. We can call them . . . fairy migratory routes or something."

"That's good," I said.

She smiled, which crinkled her nose. "Yeah, I like it, too."

Yuen's screen buzzed, and he pulled it out. "I think our luck is changing," he said, and swept a finger across the screen to send an image to the larger monitor.

The image was dark, but it showed side-by-side images of a fairy. In the first, the neck of his tunic was pinned with a gold pin. In the second, the pin was gone.

"Cadogan House surveillance video," Yuen said. "These images are from the evening of the party. And, interestingly, they are the only images of him at the event. There are none of him entering through the front gate or speaking to the other guests."

"Like he was there for a very short time," Theo said, "and a very specific purpose."

"Precisely," Yuen said.

I closed my eyes and walked through the scene, trying to put myself in the fairy's place. "He wants to stay undetected, so he avoids the front gate. Instead, he comes in over the wall. He kills Tomas, magicks Riley and gives him the knife, then sneaks out over the wall again, leaving his pin behind, then disposes of his bloody clothes."

"And the only evidence we have of any of that is circumstantial," Yuen said.

I nodded, opened my eyes again. We were getting closer. But we weren't there yet.

"We'll put out an APB," Yuen said. "But I suspect we won't find him until we find the rest of them."

"You'll let me know if you find him?" I asked. "And the SUV?" At worst, Claudia was in danger. At best, getting her back might help stop whatever the fairies were trying to do."

"We will," Yuen said. "While I'm still not entirely convinced by your Rogue-vampire argument, it would be wrong of me to discount your contributions. So thank you."

"You're welcome."

"If we don't find anything before dawn," Theo said, "we should get together at dusk. Give everyone an update."

"Arrange it," Yuen said, then glanced at me. "And in the meantime, if you could stay out of Dearborn's line of sight, all the better."

I left the Ombuds to their work and took an Auto back to Lulu's place, where I'd had my mother messenger the suitcase I'd left at the House.

She'd seen the news about Grant Park and had waited up for me. Even Eleanor of Aquitaine seemed a little mellower—hissing at me only once as I walked past her.

We turned on some Blondie, sat down in the rainbow of light that reflected off the windows, and worked on a box of crappy wine.

She sipped her mug of rosé. "Times like this make me wish I'd chosen the magic route," she said, ankles crossed on the coffee table. "That I could snap my fingers, and everyone would act the way I wanted them to. No one would get hurt."

The rosé was terrible. So I drank some more. "I don't think magic works that way."

"Do you know why I say no to magic?"

"Because of your mom?"

"That's part of it. Because magic—the entire world of supernatural drama—makes me feel powerless. It makes me feel like that little kid who was mortified by her evil-villain mother, who didn't have a choice."

"Your mother is a good person."

"With an addiction, and who hurt a lot of people because of it."

"No denying it," I said. "I think it's all about choice. About decisions. For a really long time, I felt like I didn't have any. So I decided to make some, starting with going to Paris. And, I guess, staying here while the rest of them ran back. Those are just choices. You make the choice, and you take the next step."

She nodded. "And what's the next step? Using the magic? Staying away from it? Being myself or being someone's daughter?"

I regretted that I'd brought these questions to her door, that my coming home forced her to face questions and issues she'd clearly tried to put aside.

"I think," I said after a minute, "that the next step is just to be Lulu. Whatever that means to you. Whatever feels right to you. I like you either way." I looked at her, smiled. "And, to be honest, it's kind of nice to have a safe place without magic. Where Steve and Eleanor of Aquitaine are the only disturbing things."

"Hell of a night," she said again.

And I thought that summed it up pretty well.

NINETEEN

I woke to pounding on the bedroom door.

"What?" My voice sounded as irritable as I felt.

Lulu looked in. "You awake?"

I swore under my breath. "I am now. What time is it?"

"Dusk. Get your ass up. We have stuff to do."

"Saving the city from mysterious fairies?"

"Chores."

"What?"

"This isn't a hostel for underprivileged vampires. You stay in my house, you work for the privilege."

I opened my mouth, itching to argue, but couldn't really think of anything to say. "Please don't make me clean a toilet."

No toilets, and no cleaning. But there was an assemblage of bowls and ingredients and a steaming waffle iron on the kitchen island.

"Waffles? Nice." I sat down on a stool, then frowned at her, because her expression was very serious. "Are you making me breakfast, or are you preparing me for something?"

"Both, kind of." A buzzer sounded, and she opened the waffle iron, pulled the waffle out with a pair of tongs, and put it on a plate that she slid to me across the island.

Then she poured batter into the iron's now-empty wells from a large glass measuring cup. She closed the lid, turned the dial on a timer, and looked at me.

"I've done some thinking," she said, then lifted her gaze to me. "If you're going to live here, we need to have some ground rules."

I lifted my brows. "Am I going to live here?"

Her lips quirked. "Do you have a better alternative at the moment?"

"I do not. I mean, I'm not even entirely sure if I'm going to stay in Chicago. I promised Dumas a year, assuming they'd actually take me back, and who knows about that? Their leaving without me wasn't exactly a vote of confidence."

"But you made a promise, and that matters to you."

"Yeah."

"Let's assume for the purposes of this conversation that you're going to live here." The timer buzzed again, and she pulled out the second waffle, then proceeded to bury it under syrup.

"So assumed," I said with a smile as she passed me the syrup, began to cut into her breakfast.

"One, no more pity parties. We might be emotionally damaged, but we aren't going to dwell on it. We're going to be who we are, and that's fine."

Lulu didn't have a clue how much I was grappling with that.

"Two, you're going to share the work, the rent, and the responsibilities."

"Okay. How much is the rent?"

"Less than it could be, more than it should be."

"That is vague and unhelpful."

"Three," she said, "Steve lives here. And so does Eleanor of Aquitaine."

"They're going to gang up and murder us in our sleep."

"So assumed," she said with a grin, and then chewed contemplatively. "And finally, we get to have some normal." She cut another cube of waffle, held it up. "Breakfast. Conversations. Food we cook ourselves. Trips to the zoo. Self-damn-care. Stuff that's completely mundane. We both grew up surrounded by supernaturals and magic. If we live together, we're probably signing up for more of it. I'm probably committing to more of it."

I frowned, put down my fork. "Lulu, I don't want to put you—"

But she held up a hand. "I can't run from it, Elisa. I can't hide away and pretend it's not out there. I don't have to use my magic. But I have to acknowledge it exists. Maybe I can live on the outskirts of it. We can be roommates, and you can tell me about your adventures. I get the good stories, but don't actually have to immerse myself in the drama."

She flipped off the waffle iron. "I think we're entitled to some normal. And I think maybe that's the kind of thing I can help with. I can do the normal. I can try to make sure you have breakfast and all that other stuff."

I smiled at her. "Are we dating now?"

Lulu snorted a laugh. "Girl, you are not my type. And you've only got eyes for Connor Keene."

"I do not have eyes for Connor Keene." But I didn't even sound convincing to me.

"Liar," she said, taking another bite. "You are a dirty, stinking liar."

I put down my fork, appetite gone. "He touched my wrist yesterday."

She paused midchew. "Is that a euphemism for . . . anything?"

I shook my head. "We were talking, and he took my wrist and looked at me, and he's so damn sexy, and he cares about the Pack and his family and . . . I'm falling for him."

"No shit, Watson."

I ignored her. "He's leaving. And I'm maybe going back to Paris—or who knows—but he's definitely leaving for Alaska. Twenty years I've known him, Lulu. Twenty damn years, and I hated him for most of those. Arrogant little punk who drove me crazy just because he could."

"You can't drive someone crazy unless there's emotion there to begin with. Otherwise, you wouldn't have cared."

I gave her a narrowed stare. "Is that intended to make me feel better? Because it doesn't."

"I'm just over here, eating my waffle," she said, taking another enormous bite.

"Why did he have to get so hot? And why did he have to get so damn noble?"

"Fucking shifters," she said.

"Fucking shifters," I agreed.

My screen buzzed, and I checked it. "That's my Auto. I have to get to Cadogan House." I rose, stuffed a final bite of waffle in my mouth. "I'll keep you posted."

"Have a good evening, honey!"

"You too, sugar. Don't wait up."

When I'd been a kid, my father's office had been a place for play-time, for watching television while my father held open-office hours, or for just taking in a few innings of a Cubs game with the House's senior staff. If I'd gotten in trouble, my parents handled it in our apartments. They hadn't wanted me to dread being in the office—or dread talking to my father if something came up.

Despite all that prep work, I stood outside his door for a full five minutes, not yet able to walk in.

All the while, I could feel my mother's sword buzzing, which was one of the reasons I hadn't yet knocked. Not the only reason, but one of them.

"You should have learned by now," I murmured to the monster, "that I'm not going to let happen what you want to happen."

I don't know if it was chastised or merely biding its time, but the throb of magic turned to a dull roar that I could manage. As ready as I was likely to be, I knocked.

"Come in," he said, and I opened it, found him alone and at his desk. He wore a dark suit with a crisp white shirt beneath, the top button opened to reveal the gleam of his Cadogan medal.

He smiled when I walked in, but there was caution in his eyes that I hadn't seen before. And that broke my heart a little.

"Is it already time for the meeting?" he asked, and glanced at his wristwatch. As with his vehicles, he preferred the old-fashioned kind.

"Not yet. I'm a little early." I closed the door. "Can we talk?"

"Of course." He rose, came around the desk, and gestured to the sitting area.

There was something formal in his manner that made me sad and uncomfortable. Had I completely screwed up our relationship?

He sat down on the leather couch, and I did the same, sitting at an angle so I could see him.

"I wanted to apologize for the Cadogan House Novitiate thing. I'd meant to talk to you about it before it came up with the Ombudsman, but I didn't, and that was my fault, and it was a really crappy thing to do. And I'm really sorry."

"I appreciate that," he said.

And a heavy and awkward silence filled the room.

"Did you have a good childhood?"

The question startled and appalled me. "What? Of course I did."

"We didn't exactly have good role models for parenting, your mother and I. And we tried so carefully to think of everything a human child would need, and everything a vampire child might."

Tears blossomed and I worked to push them back, afraid if they fell I'd slip into full sobbing. "I had a great childhood," I said again. "I know I was loved and supported. That if I fell, you'd help me back up. Mom helped me get past my chocolate chip cookie phase and learn the joy of a balanced diet, and you helped me understand the joy of rules and procedures."

He knew I meant that mostly seriously, and his grin was full and utterly relieved. "Without rules, chaos."

"No argument," I said, thinking of Connor and his penchant, at least as a kid, for doing whatever the hell he wanted.

"I was thrown," my father said. "We didn't fail to Commend you because of an oversight, because we forgot. We believed—considered—you to be a full member of the House. And I am monumentally sorry that we were wrong, even if only technically."

He cleared his throat. "Do you want to be Commended?"

And I thought we'd gotten through the awkward part. For a moment, silence hung heavily in the air. I didn't have an honest answer, and I didn't want to lie.

Finally, he held up a hand, smiled. "Don't answer that. I will apologize for putting you on the spot. I love you and I love your mother with all my heart. I love this House, as well. It is neither my child nor my wife, but it is . . ." He seemed to struggle with the word.

"It's yours," I said simply, and offered him a smile. "And that's all there is to it."

"Yes," he said with a relieved smile. "It is mine. And while your mother and I would both love to have you as an official member of this House, that decision is yours to make as you prefer."

"And if I choose Navarre?" I asked with a grin.

He was silent for a moment, lip curled just a little bit. "There's no accounting for taste."

I grinned at him. "Typical Cadogan response."

"Come here," my father said, and opened his arms. And I went willingly.

The tension had evaporated when Margot, the House's chef, rolled a wheeled cart into my father's office. It was stacked with gorgeous trays of food and smelled like sugar and bacon.

My mother stepped into the room behind her.

"As always," my father said, "your mother's timing is impeccable."

"She followed the scent of bacon," Margot said, offering me a wink as she began placing trays and baskets on the conference table.

"You're all hilarious," she said, snatching a piece of bacon from one of Margot's baskets. She glanced at us as she chewed, and I gave her a nod and a smile.

Outside there was chaos. But our family was okay.

Since coffee would only improve things, I fixed myself a mug and moved to the sitting area while we waited for the cavalry to arrive. They showed up in increments. Petra and Yuen, then Theo, then Gabriel, Connor, and Miranda.

I wasn't sad to see that Dearborn had skipped the meeting, and assumed we'd have to invite the press and the mayor to get him to actually attend. I hadn't expected to see Miranda, and was surprised she'd walk willingly into a House of vampires, given her issues with us.

Connor wore his uniform again today: jeans, boots, and a snug T-shirt under a fitted motorcycle jacket. There was dark stubble on his face, which made his eyes glow brighter. And he carried his dark motorcycle helmet.

He headed straight for me, and I wasn't entirely surprised by the quick flash of emotion in Miranda's eyes. Suspicion, anger, and maybe some hurt. So Miranda had feelings for Connor, the man she wanted to best for control of the Pack. Or maybe *share* control of the Pack.

I could sympathize, and shifted my gaze back to Connor. He looked like a model in a cologne ad. Sexy and seductive and arrogant. These were not comfortable feelings for me, especially in my father's office.

He put his helmet on the coffee table and looked down at me, expression unfathomable. "You keep taking on the fairies."

"Not by choice. What's wrong?"

He sat down on the opposite couch. "With what?"

"With you. You look tired, and you sound grouchy."

"It's been a long night." He ran a hand through his hair, which shifted muscles in his arms. "Riley's managing, but that's putting a shine on it. It's not a great situation."

"I think we're getting closer. We just need a little more time." And a little more luck wouldn't hurt.

Gabriel walked to the sitting area, stirred his coffee with the familiar *clink* of spoon against ceramic. "Facing down fairies on network television?"

"Wrong place, wrong time," I said.

"Or right place, right time," Yuen said, smiling as he walked toward us. He glanced at my parents. "You have a very thoughtful and capable daughter."

"And she's a very good fighter," Theo added with a grin.

"Agreed on all counts," my father said, then nodded at Yuen. "We're here to support your efforts, so we're ready when you are."

"We're ready," Yuen said. Then he nodded at Theo, passing the figurative torch.

"I'll go," Theo said. He verbally reviewed our visit to the castle, the fight in Grant Park, and what we'd seen on the surveillance video.

"We need to find Claudia," Connor said, and Yuen nodded.

"We suspect this might be Ruadan's reaction to the fairies' diminishing magic," Yuen said. "Maybe he isn't satisfied with how Claudia's managed the fairies since the Egregore, and thinks they should be doing more to increase their power, not let it slip away."

Gabriel looked at the photograph of the chained fairy queen Petra had uploaded to the monitor. "And he's shoved her aside so he can do what he wants."

"That's the current theory," Yuen said.

"It's logical," my mother said. "But why the ley line conjunction? Why do they need that much power? What are they planning to use it for?"

"A weapon?" Connor suggested. "A spell?"

"Whatever it is," Yuen said, "it's big. Something that requires a lot of power, and something it appears they haven't yet managed to pull off. They do appear to have figured out how to move along the ley lines—to appear and disappear by accessing the lines' power."

"That's a new skill," my father agreed. "I've never seen it. I presume you haven't been able to narrow down their location?"

"Not yet," Yuen said. "The castle and tower are empty. Officers have traversed the city above the ley lines several times, but the fairies haven't been spotted inside the city limits, or outside it in the jurisdictions we've convinced to check."

"They have to be somewhere," Connor said. "They can't just disappear."

"They'll go back to Grant Park," Gabriel said. "If they need the conjunction, the power, to pull off whatever they're planning for, they'll try again."

Yuen nodded. "Anticipating that, we've posted guards."

"Guards may not be enough," my father said. "Notwithstanding their disappearing act, they have no compunction about violence. They would have only backed off tonight because they chose to do so—because they decided that's what was in their best interest. Not because they were afraid of a fight."

"Precautions will be taken," Yuen said. "But we can't simply concede the ground and let them make their magic, especially when we don't know what magic it is. That puts humans, supernaturals, and the city itself at risk."

"The Pack is aware of the situation," Gabriel said. "We've kept them apprised in the event they need to be ready to respond."

"Good," Yuen said.

"When are you leaving?" my father asked.

"Tomorrow," Gabriel said, and the word settled in my gut like a stone. "But I'm not leaving. Other members of the Pack are, and Connor is leading them. And they've expressed some concerns about leaving before Riley's exonerated."

"We need direct evidence," Yuen said.

"So you've said." This time Gabriel's tone was short.

"What about the European delegates?" Theo asked.

"We have not been able to convince the delegates to reconvene the talks," my father said. "Since the most recent attacks occurred in France, they believe the French Houses need to be present for any further discussions to be productive. I'm inclined to agree with them. But they haven't left yet, so there is still a chance."

Petra's pocket began to buzz. She pulled out her screen, checked it. "They found the fairies' SUV—the one we saw Claudia in. It's parked outside"—she paused to swipe and review—"looks like St. Adelphus Church."

"She's in a church?" I wondered. "That seems odd. I mean, fairies aren't religious, are they?"

"St. Adelphus is abandoned," Theo said, rising. "I've been inside on an architecture tour. There's legal wrangling about its disposition, so it hasn't been torn down yet, but it's not in good shape."

"Where is it?" Yuen asked.

"Near West Side," Theo said, "not far from the United Center."

"The vehicle hasn't moved since it parked there," Petra said, gaze on her screen.

"Did they really abandon the vehicle?" I wondered. "Or are they staying there to keep an eye on her?"

"It's not unusual to keep alive the regent you've deposed," my father said. "Killing her risks turning the rebellion against them."

"So they're keeping an eye on her," Yuen said, "taking care of her, at least minimally. And keeping her out of Ruadan's way."

"We go in quietly," Theo offered. "No CPD, no uniforms. We incapacitate the guards, get her out, get gone."

"Do it," Yuen said, nodding at Theo.

"Sending tracking data to you," Petra said, and Theo's pocket beeped.

"I could use backup," Theo said, and looked at me.

"Sure, I'll go," I agreed. I'd started this and was ready to finish it. And I didn't mind getting out of Cadogan sooner rather than later. There was too much magic here.

I looked at my parents, who'd managed to stay silent at my offer. "I can help."

"It's not our objection to make," my mother said, putting a hand over my father's and squeezing. "You're an adult, and it's your decision." She slid her gaze to Yuen. "Assuming the Ombudsman's office approves."

"Go," Yuen said with a nod. "But try to stay out of trouble. And away from cameras."

We got coffee to go, checked weapons, and coordinated reporting. Theo was popping his screen onto the dashboard of his car while I slid my scabbarded katana inside. I looked up, found Connor a dozen feet away, putting his helmet on his bike.

I realized this was probably the last time I'd see him before he left for Alaska. It might be the last time I'd see him at all. And that possibility put a hollow feeling in my chest.

"I'll be right back," I told Theo, and walked toward Connor.

"Hey," I said when I reached him, and kept a safe distance between us. Not that it mattered. Magic still buzzed in the air between us, tense and heated and angry and sad.

"Hey," he said.

"You're leaving tomorrow."

He looked at me. "The Pack needs to go, and they need someone to lead. That's me." His tone was defensive.

"Because you want to be Apex."

"Because I *will be* Apex," he said.

I tried for a smile. "There will probably be wine, women, and song on the way. So that doesn't hurt."

I'd meant it as a joke, as a way to loosen the tension between us. But I regretted the words the instant I'd said them, and especially when I saw heat flash in his eyes.

"You know this isn't about partying."

"I know," I said. "I'm sorry. It was— I'm sorry. I find myself saying that a lot lately, because I'm feeling a little unbalanced here."

"You aren't the only one," he said. "I didn't expect . . . I didn't expect you, Lis."

"Not a big deal," I said with a smile I forced into position. "I'll probably be heading back to Paris soon, and you've got the Pack to focus on. I hope you find what you're looking for."

His jaw clenched, but he didn't speak.

"Elisa?"

I glanced back at Theo.

"You ready?" he asked. "We don't know how long the SUV will be there. We need to go."

"Yeah," I said, then looked back at Connor, gave him as much of a smile as I could manage. Which wasn't much. "Goodbye, Connor. Stay safe out there."

His eyes were dark, stormy, and unfathomable. And he didn't say a word.

TWENTY

Seconds later, I was in Theo's car, replaying every word I'd said to Connor and wondering if they'd sounded as lame aloud as they did in my head.

And berating myself for sounding ridiculous was somehow easier than dealing with the possibility I might not see Connor again. So I stayed in that space.

"Are you all right?"

"I'm fine," I said. We were driving west on Madison, the United Center a long, hulking building in front of us. It was time to focus.

Just as I made up my mind to do that, the road ahead seemed to shimmer. I looked at the sky, thinking clouds had passed over the full moon and I'd just seen a mirage, some kind of optical trick. But the moon was high and clear.

I blinked, looked down again . . . and watched solid asphalt ripple like water.

"Theo," I quietly said, leaning forward with hands on the dashboard.

"I see it," he said, and leaned forward over the steering wheel to peer into the darkness.

The ripple started again thirty feet in front of us, and the road waved . . . just like grass.

"What the hell is that?" Theo asked.

"I don't know."

He pulled the car to a stop, and we both climbed out and walked into the path of the headlights.

"Oh, shit," Theo said quietly.

A carpet of thick and waving grass had grown over the road, which was no longer really a road, but a soft and undulating hill that stretched a full quarter mile in front of us.

In that stretch, the streetlights were gone. The electric poles, the asphalt, the sidewalk, the yellow lines. All of it replaced with waving grass and air that felt like magic.

"We are not seeing this," I said quietly. "We are not seeing this."

"Elisa."

I ripped my gaze away to look at Theo, followed the direction of his gaze.

The problem wasn't just this quarter mile of Madison. The grass, the hill, the absence of everything modern, was spreading. It reached the United Center, and the building began to simply . . . disappear. Floor by floor, the concrete and glass were replaced by waving grass, then empty air. Another hill, soft and rounded, began to rise, arcing into the space where the enormous arena had stood.

And above it all, the cold and heavy weight of old magic.

"That's not . . . this can't be real." I didn't dare move close enough to touch the grass, afraid the magic would infect me, just as it had spread down the road, across the street, and over the building.

"Do you know what this is?" Theo asked quietly. His tone said he already knew.

I didn't know, not for sure, because I couldn't figure out how I was seeing what I was seeing. But hadn't we heard my mother's story? Hadn't she told us about exactly this? And hadn't the fairies been trying to work some unknown, big magic?

"It's the green land," I said quietly, afraid the words would disturb it, would make it aware of our presence, and we'd be sucked into the spell. "The ancient home of the fairies."

Theo pulled out his screen, scanned what had been the eastern-most half of the building, sent pictures and video to Yuen.

We ran back to the car. With the squeal of rubber on asphalt, Theo made a U-turn and hauled back down Madison until he found a clear path north toward the church.

"Is this why they were in Grant Park?" I asked, gripping the tiny dashboard as the car swung around. "Using the ley lines? To bring the green land here?"

"I don't know," Theo said. He found a strip of asphalt, and we skirted the hills in silence, watching. "Maybe. But the fairies aren't in Grant Park right now. So how are they doing it?"

"A different ley line? A different conjunction?"

"There isn't another conjunction near Chicago. There's the ve-hicle," he said as the light on the tracking program blinked faster.

The church, a rectangle of white stone with a domed top, squat-ted in the corner of a two-block span of parking lot. In the front, two pairs of columns flanked the front doors and were topped by a triangular pediment. The entrance faced a park. The side of the church faced another parking lot, which made the building—with its boarded windows and overgrown trees—seem even lonelier.

The SUV sat outside, dark and empty.

Theo parked a block down, and we climbed quietly out of the car. I belted on my katana in the light of the moon. And that was a disadvantage on this cover-free street. We wouldn't be able to hug the shadows to get closer to the building. On the other hand, no lights shone from inside the church, so it might give us more visibility once we made it in.

Theo checked the chamber on the gun he'd holstered at his waist.

"What's the layout of the church?" I asked quietly.

"Doors on the front, east side. Doors open into a lobby, and the sanctuary's directly behind that. It's a big space with a domed ceiling and arches along the sides. The basement has classrooms and offices."

"Most likely location?"

"I'm honestly not sure," he said, hands on his hips as he looked over the church. "What's the most likely place to store the fairy queen you're attempting to peacefully depose?"

"Fair point."

"Side door?"

I scanned the building, looking for easy ingress. An open window, missing plywood—something that would get me in quietly. "Let me get closer. I might be able to work something."

"Then let's move," he said quietly. And we got low and jogged quickly toward the building, hands on our weapons to keep them from bouncing.

We crossed the street, ducked into the shadow of the building. "Follow me," I said, and slipped quietly down the sidewalk. Everything on this side of the building looked carefully boarded, so I turned the corner. There'd once been a fire escape, but it stood in a hulking pile of steel behind the church, the exits boarded. But fairies had gotten into the building, and with Claudia, so there had to be a way.

If it were me, I'd have found a way to sneak in, then unlocked the front doors from the inside so she could be carried in. That's what I was looking for: the sneak.

I found it around the next corner. A plywood sheet covering a basement window had been pulled away. It still leaned against the window, but wasn't attached. The fairy had probably taken it down, slipped inside, then come back later to move it back into position, but hadn't bothered to reaffix it to the facade.

That's all we needed.

We each picked up a side, maneuvered it away from the window. The glass was dirty, and the room behind it was dark.

It was a single-hung window with a simple sliding lock. Theo offered a pocket knife before I could ask for it. I flipped it out, inserted the blade between the sash and the lock. Old paint chipped away and fluttered to the ground like snow, until I heard the click, then handed the knife back to Theo.

I confirmed he was ready, and pushed open the sash.

The window's screech was loud as a banshee's cry. Instinctively, we flattened ourselves against the building, waited for the bob of a flashlight, the sound of movement and investigation. But there was only silence, only darkness.

Surely the fairies weren't all sleeping. Not when they were supposed to be guarding Claudia—or imprisoning her.

I slipped into the window, dropped soundlessly to the floor, offered a hand as Theo followed. It was a classroom for kids. The toys and materials were long gone, but there were still marks on a chalkboard that stood in the corner, still a faded wallpaper border of cartoon pencils along the top of the wall. It smelled like dust and mold and rain.

We emerged into the hallway, cleared each room as we moved toward the stairs. There was no sign of the fairies down here. No movement, no sound, no footsteps in the dust and detritus on the floor.

They weren't in the basement, so they had to be upstairs. We waited at the edge of the staircase, straining to listen for sounds.

And then I heard singing somewhere above us. A man's voice, too far away to figure out the words. But the sound was sad and quiet, like an old-fashioned lullaby. And it made standing in this dilapidated church basement, with the remnants of childhood, even creepier.

I looked at Theo, cupped a hand behind my ear.

He nodded, and looked as disturbed as I felt.

"I'm going to need a drink after this," Theo whispered, then put a hand on the butt of his weapon and pointed to the stairs.

Being immortal, I took point. I wasn't about to sacrifice Theo—or incur Yuen's wrath—if the fairies heard us coming.

The stairs opened into the back of the sanctuary. The room was large and open, moonlight filtering through the stained glass in the dome to spread red and gold and green across the floor. There was no furniture, just detritus and decay. Paint flaked away from murals on the walls, tufts of drywall where animals had scraped through, and scraps of paper that blew in from other parts of the building.

Claudia lay on a cot in the middle of the room, strawberry blond hair spilling onto the floor, hands pressed together atop her chest like a princess waiting for a kiss to interrupt her slumber. There were tall candelabra at the end of the cot, probably borrowed from the church. A fairy in black fatigues and boots and carrying a very large gun stood between Claudia and the front door, body alert.

He was the only guard I saw. But it was unlikely there'd be only one. Even fairies had to sleep; there'd have to be someone to take a shift here and there.

I didn't realize where the second fairy was until a muzzle was pressed against my back. "Hello, bloodletter." The voice was female, and carried a whisper of Ireland in it.

Theo was only a couple of feet away but was steady enough to watch, to wait. I met his gaze, gave him a small smile.

"Move forward," she said. "Both of you."

We stepped into the sanctuary, her gun still at my back, Theo beside me.

"Two feet to your left," I said quietly.

He didn't need to ask why. Theo was moving before the fairy understood what I'd asked for: space to move. I turned with lightning speed, slapped away the fairy's gun, and threw up a side kick that had her stumbling forward in surprise.

"I think you've got this," Theo asked, picking up the gun. "You want?"

"I'm good," I said, and used a forearm to block the jab the fairy attempted with her left hand.

Theo pulled out his weapon, strode toward the other fairy and the queen who lay before him.

The fairy advanced, fury tightening her features, as I moved backward into the sanctuary. If we were going to fight, I wanted more room to do it.

"You won't win this," she said, with what sounded like deep-felt loathing. "Bloodletters never do. Not when we're involved."

She stepped forward, tried a right cross. I bobbed to avoid it, then turned into a crescent kick that she met with a high-handed block.

Bone met bone and sent pain ringing up my shin. But the monster didn't mind pain. Pain was proof of life, of existence. A reminder that it *was*, even if it was trapped inside me.

"You've got some skills," she said, advancing again. She was a sturdy woman with pale skin, dark hair in a sleek bun, and brown eyes. Barrel-chested and strong, she put some force behind her blocks. "But so do we. And we need it more."

"Need what?"

"Our lives back. Our kingdom back. We've been under your thumb too long."

By "kingdom," I assumed she meant the green land.

"How are you under our thumb?" I asked, stepping backward. She was moving me closer to the wall, and I was fine with letting her believe she was controlling my retreat.

"Bloodletters rule Chicago," she said, a corner of her mouth lifting.

"Humans rule Chicago. Mayor, city council, population."

"They're manipulated by vampires. Controlled by blood-letters."

"That's absolutely incorrect." If it had been true, I'd be giving Yuen directions, not the other way around.

My back hit the wall, and her smile grew wider.

"A brave little vampire to walk in here, but not brave enough to fight?"

The anger that flooded me pushed the monster forward. *Maybe I should give it a chance*, I thought. *Give it an opportunity to fight and play.*

So I let the monster step into me, and I slid back inside and watched it happen.

I pivoted, pushed a foot against the wall, flipped backward over the fairy. She turned, her breath a shocked exhalation, and watched me land to face her again.

"Some skills," I said, smiling fiercely. The monster moved forward with a right hook the fairy didn't manage to avoid, then an uppercut to the jaw that snapped the fairy's head back. She roared in pain, and it took her a moment to find her balance again.

The monster wasn't interested in waiting, and advanced. A kick to move the fairy backward, to give the fairy her turn against the wall. And then the real work began.

Punches to the gut, the jaw. A kick to the ribs, then another. The fairy tried to get a foot between mine, to twist me up and bring me down, but I managed to stay on my feet. A jab that knocked her head back.

The fairy's head bobbled, and she fell to her knees. But that didn't stop the monster. Not even when the fairy's eyes rolled back. One kick to the ribs, then two, then another.

"Elisa."

Chicago didn't belong to fairies or vampires. It belonged to the Egregore, and the fairies didn't have a right to destroy it.

"*Elisa*. Stop!"

Theo's hand gripped tightly around my arm, and he yanked me away. I stumbled, also not quite solid on my feet, and had to bend over, hands on my knees, to keep bile from rising.

"I'm all right," I said, and held up a hand to keep him back. "Give me a minute."

Go back, I willed it, demanded, but the monster fought me, waves of anger and aggression spearing forward. I closed my eyes, had to concentrate fiercely to keep my stomach from heaving and my mind in place. To take back control and keep it in my hands.

This was a price of the power. The monster didn't like being pushed back down again, into the place where it had to question its own existence.

When the nausea passed, I stood up again, glanced back.

The fairy was on the ground, unconscious. Her right eye swollen and dark, her lip bleeding, but her chest rising and falling.

I hadn't killed her. While I understood death, and understood now that it was inevitable in war, I found that to be a relief.

My hands stung with pain. I looked down, found the knuckles battered and bleeding. But I was a vampire, and the wounds would heal quickly enough.

"Are you okay?" Theo asked. The look on his face said he genuinely wasn't sure.

"I'm fine." I looked back, found the fairy he'd also knocked unconscious.

That made me feel so much better, it nearly brought tears to my eyes.

"We need to get Claudia out of here," Theo said, and I nodded.

"I'll get the door," I said, and took his hand when he offered one, pulled me to my feet.

Theo went to Claudia. I went to the small lobby and found the front door barred from the inside. I pulled up the long piece of steel, tossed it aside, turned deadbolts in the rotting wood, and pushed the door open.

The wash of fresh air, of air that was mostly free of magic, felt glorious.

"Cadogan House is closer than the Ombuds' office," I said as Theo carried Claudia through. "And we've got a doctor."

"Then that's where we'll go. You'd better make the call."

"Car first," I said, and glanced back. "Just in case they wake up sooner than we'd like."

The green land hadn't diminished. But it hadn't grown, either.

The United Center was still a field of grass, although now with CPD cruisers running crime-scene tape and barricades around Chicago's newest park. I gave credit to Yuen for moving quickly.

As we drove by, I regretted for an instant that I hadn't had a chance to walk through it, to see what the fairies' land really looked like from the inside. Even as I knew that anything touched by fairy hands was dangerous—tricky and seductive and usually a trap for the unwary.

"Would you like to tell me about your . . . skills?"

The question jerked me from my reverie. Theo said the word with uncertainty, as if he wasn't entirely committed to the idea it was a blessing, and not a curse.

"No," I said.

I could feel his gaze on me for a moment. "Okay," he finally said. "It's useful, for what it's worth. And I don't think anyone would fault you that."

Maybe. Maybe not. But this wasn't the time to debate it. "I'm going to call the House," I said, and pulled out my screen.

"Elisa," my father answered.

"I need a favor."

There was a heavy pause, and I could only guess at the questions he was asking himself.

"What do you need?"

Rain or shine, he was reliable. "Theo and I are en route. If you could have the garage open and meet us there, that would be best."

"What are you doing?"

"You're not going to like it," I said. "So it's best if we deal with it when we get there. Bring Delia, if she's available." Delia was the House doctor.

"Elisa—"

"I need you to trust me on this. I won't do anything to harm Cadogan. But we need help."

There was a pause.

"We'll be waiting," he said, and hung up.

I glanced back at Claudia, still unconscious on the backseat, realized there might not be enough macaroni drawings in the world to make up for this one.

The gate lifted when we drove up to it, the door into the basement garage sliding open. Theo drove down into the House, then into a space near the door where my father, my mother, and Kelley waited for us. She opened the door for Theo, and he lifted Claudia into his arms.

"Jesus," my father said, brow furrowed as Theo carried her to the door that Kelley rushed to pull open.

She was still limp, hair cascading nearly to the floor. And she looked worse in the fluorescent lights, dark shadows beneath her eyes, a bruise across her jaw, and a paleness to her skin that rivaled vampires'.

"Second parlor," my father said, and I pointed Theo toward the stairs. We followed him up, then into the pretty sitting room, where vampires scooted out of the way to give him the couch.

Theo placed her down, then stepped back into the foyer, where we watched her warily.

"Yuen's not here yet?" he asked.

"He's on his way," my father said. "Stuck in traffic."

"Delia's on her way, too," Kelley said. "She was at the hospital."

In the meantime, my mother stepped forward, checked Claudia's temperature, her pulse. "Alive, but unconscious. I really don't know how much we can do for her outside the castle. Her power, her magic, is tied to place."

"She was at the church?" my father asked.

"She was," Theo said, arms crossed as he looked down at Claudia. "Guarded by two fairies. She was bound, unconscious."

"And the fairies?" my father asked, the tension clear in his voice.

"Alive," Theo said. "But displeased."

My father nodded.

"Ruadan did this," I explained. "He wanted to get her out of the way in order to bring their kingdom back."

"Their kingdom?" my mother asked.

"The green land," Theo said.

My parents' stares were blank.

"I don't understand," my mother said. "The green land is a place. It can't be brought here. Deposited here."

"That's no longer the case," Theo said, and pulled out his screen.

They watched the United Center become hills and flowing grass, the fairy mound in the middle of it all. My mother's face, already porcelain-pale, seemed to lose all remaining color.

"They did it," she quietly said. "But how? How could they do it?" The question was quiet, as if she was speaking to herself, had forgotten we were there.

"She took us into that world," my father said. "And it's a world of magic. By logical extension, perhaps they could bring that world here." But he didn't sound convinced.

"Liege," Kelley said, "what are we going to do with Claudia? This may not be a popular opinion at the moment, but she's dangerous. I don't know that we want her in the House."

"I agree."

We looked back to find Yuen in the doorway, Petra behind him. They were becoming Cadogan House regulars. And there were no shifters in their wake on this trip.

"She shouldn't be here," he said. "I realize you didn't have any better options at the time, but her being here is problematic."

"It is problematic," my father said, then walked to the window and looked out, hands on his hips. He did that when he was trying to figure out an angle or a solution. "But I want her here."

"Liege," Kelley said, "I'm with the Ombudsman. It's dangerous. If they figure out she's here . . ."

"They may leave her be," he said. "If Ruadan wants her out of the way, she is out of the way. She's our problem now, which actually works for him.

"She's dangerous," he added. "No argument. But Chicago is disappearing before her eyes, and she's tied to that magic somehow. I want her where I can see her."

"I could overrule you," Yuen said.

"You could try," my father said. "And I mean that with all due respect. You could cite the deal with the city, and I could cite the sovereignty of this House." He glanced around at the other vampires in the foyer. "We fight when we must, and render aid when we can. She will be guarded."

A long moment passed, and then Yuen nodded. "Dearborn will be told you made an unassailable legal argument regarding the sovereignty of your House."

My father smiled approvingly. "So I did." Then he looked at Kelley. "Increase security outside the House. Double the guards."

"Liege," Kelley said with a nod.

"When Delia arrives, ask where she'd like to treat Claudia. Perhaps the guest suite or one of the empty Novitiate rooms would be best. Restrain her, and put two guards inside, another on the door."

"And video feed into the Ops Room," my mother said. "Just in case she gets creative with the magic."

A corner of Kelley's mouth lifted. "Sentinel," she acknowledged.

"She wakes up, or stirs magic, or anyone disturbs the House, I want an immediate report."

"Liege," Kelley said again. "We'll let you know when everything's in place."

"My office," my father said, and we followed him down the hall.

TWENTY-ONE

"The fairies at the church?" Theo asked, when we were in my father's office and the door was closed.

"In custody," Yuen said. "They're on their way to the brick factory, but for now are refusing to speak."

"If they were willing to depose their queen, they'll probably stay silent," my father said.

Yuen nodded. "I suspect you're right. But at least they're two we won't have to deal with at the immediate time."

"What happened to the people?" I asked.

"What do you mean?" my mother asked.

"The parking lots around the United Center were empty, so there probably weren't many people in the building," I said. "But there might have been guards, maintenance staff. There was no one, not a single person, in the green land, at least the parts that we could see. What happened to them?"

"We're thinking it's a kind of phase shift," Petra said. "The green land is a world of magic that exists in, for lack of a better term, a bubble. Outside our normal physical realm. The fairies want the green land here, which would require an immense amount of energy. They draw on the power of the ley lines, and they make the shift—they switch the green land for our world."

"And, theoretically, Chicago goes into the bubble," Yuen said.

"Exactly. An exchange of matter. When the United Center is

replaced, it pops into the bubble, along with anyone else who happened to be there at the time."

"So, they're alive," I said, and felt a flood of relief.

"They're alive," Theo agreed, but I didn't like his somber tone. "But their entire world is now the boundary of the United Center. No contact with our world, with those they loved."

"Wait," Yuen said, holding up a hand. "If the conjunction is in Grant Park, why did the green land appear at the United Center?"

"We aren't sure about that, either," Petra said. "But we have a theory." She looked at me. "You said the fairies at Grant Park didn't have guns."

"Right," I said. "Knives, bows—that kind of thing."

"So no modern technology."

I opened my mouth, closed it again. "Yeah. You're right." And I knew where she was going. "They didn't mean to disappear in Grant Park—they were trying to work magic, to bring the green land forward, so that's why they had bows and swords and tunics."

Petra nodded, obviously pleased I'd gotten the right answer. "Exactly. We think Grant Park was a failure. They wanted to pop the green land into place right over the conjunction, but they couldn't make it work. Instead of using the ley lines' power to move the green land in, they moved themselves out."

"Into the green land?" I asked.

"It's possible," Theo said. "We've been up and down the ley lines' tracks, and we haven't been able to find them." He looked at my mother. "Claudia was able to shift you into the green land, and they're able to shift part of the green land here. It stands to reason they can shift themselves, too."

"United Center may be another error," I said. "They tried again to pull the green land here, this time without the conjunction, and they only made it halfway."

"They got the green land," Theo agreed with a nod. "But not in the right place."

"There's no ley line near United," Petra said. "But Claudia was at the church. That might have been enough of an anchor to make the switch happen there."

"Why are they failing?" my father asked.

"This is big magic," Petra said. "It would take skill and expertise to make and control."

"And Ruadan is young," Yuen added. "He's discarded their queen, who's lived long enough to have seen the green land when it existed in our world. She'd have been an asset to the process. Instead, they pushed her away."

"She probably told them not to do it," I said, looking at my mother. "It's her realm, right? If she thought it could be done correctly, wouldn't she have already done it?"

"Probably," my mother said.

The office door opened again, and Kelley stepped inside.

"Claudia?" my father asked.

"Nothing yet," she said. She walked to the monitor, switched the view from the map of Chicago to the twenty-four-hour news station. And we watched grass creep slowly up Lake Shore Drive.

Traffic was stopped, and the grass inched toward the vehicle in the back of the line. Then the grass reached the tire, and the tire began to disappear, like a drawing being methodically erased. Trunk, back seat, front seat, engine, tires.

The car was subsumed, along with everyone in it. And the grass still crept forward, the stalks undulating in a breeze that undoubtedly smelled like salt and time.

People realized what was happening, began abandoning their vehicles, confused or screaming, and running to get away from the danger that crept toward them.

The Ombudsmen's screens began buzzing. And then the office phone began to ring.

Yuen pulled out his screen. "It's Dearborn. I'll be back." He stepped into the hallway.

"We have to evacuate Chicago," Theo said. "There's no avoiding it."

"First," I said, "we have to talk to Claudia."

While Yuen talked to his boss, Theo and I walked upstairs to the room where Delia watched over Claudia.

Delia stood in the hallway outside the closed door, bright pink scrubs a contrast against dark skin and hair, chatting quietly with one of the assigned guards.

"How is she?" Theo asked.

"She's stable, as far as I can tell. But she's away from the castle, from the magic. She's not fading as quickly as she once would have because of the Egregore's infusion, but she won't last forever. She needs to be with her people."

"At the moment, her people are trying to destroy Chicago," I said.

Delia didn't look the slightest bit fazed by that announcement, which was probably because she was a vampire, a physician, and a member of Cadogan House's staff. I'd bet there wasn't much that surprised her anymore.

"I presume you're here to make sure she doesn't involve herself in those efforts?"

"We'd like to talk to her about it," I said. "Has she said anything about what's happening?"

"Not that I've heard. She's been in and out of consciousness. I'm not certain, but I believe they dosed her for transport, and then relied on her absence from the castle to keep her weak. I'm going to get some supplies while you talk to her," she said. "I'll be back."

She walked down the hall, and we waited for the guard to open the door. Two more stood inside—one human, one vampire.

"We need to ask her some questions," I said. "And she might not talk with you here. Can you give us a few minutes?"

The human looked at the vampire, who nodded. "We'll be outside."

"That's fine. Thank you."

Then the door closed behind us, leaving us in silence.

The room was small, with pale walls and wood floors. There was a simple wooden bed, a nightstand, a dresser, and a bookshelf. Doors that led to a bathroom and closet. Most rooms had the same layout. Simple accommodations for the Cadogan vampires who chose to live in the House.

Claudia lay in the bed in the same dress we'd brought her in. She was still pale, but her color seemed to have evened out a little.

Her eyes opened. She looked at me. "You brought me from the church."

"We did. You're in Cadogan House. Ruadan attempted to depose you. He's trying to bring the green land to Chicago."

Her eyes opened wide and she tried to sit up, but her arms had been tied to the bed with leather restraints. If she were stronger, I suspected she'd be able to use magic to unbuckle them.

"They cannot."

"They are," I said. "They've shifted it here, or parts of it, into two places in the city."

"*No,*" she said with desperation, and dropped her head again. "Bringing it here will not cause it to thrive. I have told him so many times."

"What do you mean, it won't thrive?" Theo asked.

"The green land should not exist here. It exists only in its realm. While that realm has touched the human world before, it is to be separate. It should remain so."

She turned her head to look at us. "If you are speaking true, he has done a great wrong. Pulling the realm into this world stretches the warp and weft of our world and of yours. If that fabric is pulled too hard, it will tear. A hole will be wrought, and place and time will mix." She swallowed hard. "That cannot be allowed. You must convince him."

"I don't think they're going to be open to what we have to say." Theo's voice was dry.

"Make them understand. Keep the world as it is. Keep the green land hidden away. That is the only way you will save your city."

"How do we do that, Claudia?" I asked. "Help us save your people."

But her lips went tight.

"You'll tell us they're creating a danger," I said, "but you won't help us stop them?"

"They are mine," she said, and turned her head away. "Helping their destruction would be treachery and betrayal."

"They will destroy the green land," I said quietly.

"You are a bloodletter," she muttered. "You would lie."

"I'm a bloodletter who saved your life," I reminded her, and then recalled how much fairies loved bargains. "I am owed a boon."

She looked at me, and there was ferocity in her face. Her cheekbones sharper, her lips thinner, her eyes a void of darkness. Not just a beautiful queen or frail regent. But a creature of magic and power and terror.

"The *Ephemeris*," she said, looking away again as if disgusted by her weakness. "He found it . . . in the green land. It tells of the rivers of magic, and how to make use of them."

And then her eyes closed again.

"The mayor will be instituting an immediate relocation of Chicago residents," Yuen said when he returned. "Beginning with the neighborhoods closest to the . . . we'll call them intrusion sites. Centers for those displaced will be established using the protocols established during Sorcha's attack. The Illinois National Guard will be called in."

"The Pack may also be helpful," my father said. "Or what remains of it. And the other Masters may be able to assist with the relocation efforts. They also have experience in large-scale disruptions."

"We'll contact them," Yuen agreed. "Can you work with the delegates?"

"We will," my father said. "We can house any who wish to stay here, and assist those who want to return to Europe."

And no need to discuss the city's prior agreement with Cadogan, I thought, *because the Houses are already involved in the peace talks.*

"Riley should be released," I said, gesturing toward the monitor, which still showed images of the grassy LSD. "It's obvious this is bigger than him, that he was set up by the fairies."

"I've talked to the prosecutor. They aren't willing to release him, because there's still no physical evidence linking the murder to anyone else. For the moment, we have to focus on the fairies. They don't get to destroy Chicago, and they don't get to send its people into magical exile."

He looked at Theo. "Where are we on that?"

"Right this way," Theo said, and gestured for us to follow him to the conference table, where a thin, open box held a stack of thick paper sheets with illuminated letters, careful script, and small sketches. "Claudia told us Ruadan found the *Ephemeris* in the green land. Turns out, the *Ephemeris* is a book currently stored in the National Library of Ireland. This is a facsimile of the pages from the Cadogan library. Which is impressive," Theo added, with a smile for my father.

"What kind of book?" my mother asked, leaning forward.

"A fairy almanac," Theo said. "The information ranges from the basic—building charms, coordinating magic with phases of the moon, understanding natural signs—to the complex." He flipped through the pages to a sheet with a simple drawing of what looked like rivers winding through a forest.

"We don't have any experts in the language of fairies in house other than Claudia, and she's unconscious again. But this appears to be an explanation of ley lines and how to use them."

"There are a lot of steps," Petra said. "Charms and steps and procedures."

"Anything about the green land?" Yuen asked.

"Not that we can tell without a full translation," Theo said. "Ruadan must have figured that out on his own."

"Or he could have been pulling information from Claudia incrementally," I said quietly. "Waiting for his moment."

"And when she didn't do what Ruadan wanted at the peace talks," Theo said, "he decided the fairies needed a different approach."

"I don't know if all the other fairies agree with him, but he has at least some allies," I said with a nod. "The fairy who killed Tomas. The fairies who got Claudia into the vehicle and guarded her at the church. The fairies who supported him at the castle and Grant Park."

"To summarize," Theo said, counting on his fingers, "Ruadan learned how to manipulate ley lines and tossed away his queen, and is trying to use those ley lines to tug the green land into this world. He hasn't yet nailed the process, or what he believes the process to be, and his failures and successes are dangerous to the rest of us." He looked up. "What do we do about it?"

At that, the room went silent.

"Can we bomb it?" Petra asked.

We all looked at her.

"I'm not being bloodthirsty," she said in her slightly kooky, matter-of-fact way. "Okay, maybe a little bloodthirsty, although I think that's appropriate and deserved right now. Is there some way we can bomb the green land and not have it affect Chicago?"

"This is outside my expertise," Yuen said, "but if the green land and the missing parts of Chicago are still linked by the bubble, so to speak, I would think an explosion would affect both."

"Could we take out the fairies working the magic?" Theo asked.

"I think that presents the same problem," Petra said. "You take them out while the magic is in play, and you risk making things worse. Sealing off the bubble, putting the green land here permanently."

"So, what do we do?" I asked.

Silence fell again.

After a moment, Yuen looked at my father. "I believe there was some mention of a library?"

It was my mother's favorite room in the House, the two-story library where Cadogan's collection of vampire law books, magical history, and modern fiction was stored. The first floor had long rows of books and space for library tables, where I knew my parents had plotted some of their escapades. A wrought-iron balcony made up the second floor, where more books were stored.

A face, handsome and topped by a messy thatch of dark hair, popped out from an aisle, gave me a narrow-eyed stare. "No food, no beverages."

The Librarian was picky about his books.

"We don't have any food or beverages."

He gave us a head-to-toe looking-over. "Good," he said, then winked at me. "Nice to see you, Elisa." Then he disappeared back into the stacks.

I looked back at Petra, who stared, openmouthed, at the room.

"Reference books about sups are over there," I said, pointing to the several rows in the first floor's back corner. "So grab a table and get to reading, and let's figure out how to stop these people."

They nodded, and Petra wandered into the books with huge, glazed eyes.

"I always end up in Ravenclaw," I murmured, and headed in.

Two hours later, Theo was working with Yuen on the relocation, Petra was back at the Ombudsman's office, and I needed a break.

I pushed back the stack of books and scrubbed my hands over my eyes.

I'd worked through two dozen books, learned about wee folk, hidden people, fairy courts, and fairy hills. I'd read about the fairies' expulsion from Europe, mostly in response to fairies using their cunning to fool unsuspecting humans—to lure them into thorny woods, seduce away their secrets, or switch a healthy human child for the sick child of a fairy.

Unfortunately, none of it had helped me come up with a plan to reverse what was happening now.

I was tired, physically and emotionally. I'd fought a literal battle tonight, and my energy was gone. I needed blood and sleep, and I didn't want to leave Lulu unprotected in case the green land spread farther north and west.

So I said my goodbyes, agreed to meet the Ombudsmen at their office at dusk, and took an Auto back to the loft, stopping for blood along the way.

I found Lulu asleep on the couch, Eleanor of Aquitaine curled at her feet. The cat opened a single eye as I passed, closed it again quickly enough. I assumed that meant I wasn't enough of an enemy now to merit a full growl, which I considered an improvement.

I walked to my spare room, found a coloring book featuring a pretty pink fairy with her hair in a bun, her wings shimmering with holographic stickers, propped on the pillow, topped by a paint-smeared sticky note.

"Maybe this will help," it said.

I snorted, pushed the coloring book aside, and fell into bed.

TWENTY-TWO

I'd slept through what I assumed was a day of horror, so I pulled out my screen as soon as the sun set again and checked the latest video feed.

There was another green-land bubble in Lincoln Park, and the two existing sites—United Center and Lake Shore Drive—were complete hills and valleys of green.

Evacuation across the city was under way, humans streaming out of high-rises, carrying children and suitcases, purses and laptops, trying to escape before the fairies' wall of green overtook the rest of the city. And because the evacuees were mostly human, there was traffic, looting, and marching against supernaturals.

Not that I could entirely blame them.

I got dressed and walked into the loft. And there she was.

Lulu Bell, whom I'd known since the day she was born, leaned against the island in a T-shirt, running shorts, and sneakers. And she was stretching out her calves.

"What the hell is this?"

She jerked and looked back. "Shit. I was hoping I'd beat you out the door."

"I thought we agreed running was only appropriate if someone was chasing you."

She sighed dramatically. "It's probably time for a full confession. I've been running for two years now."

I narrowed my gaze.

"I've run four half-marathons since you've been gone."

"How dare you?"

She grinned, adjusted the laces on one shoe. "I also own a skort."

"You monster."

"Running's not all bad, Lis," she said, and began to bounce from foot to foot to warm up. "Just because your mother dragged you to a 5K once upon a time."

"It was eight 5Ks and it was ridiculous."

She winked at me. "I've run twelve."

I threw up my hands.

Living together was going to be a test of our relationship.

I grabbed a banana and a cup of the coffee Lulu had left when she went for her run, and called an Auto to the Ombudsman's office. By the time I'd grabbed my katana and made it downstairs, the vehicle was waiting at the curb.

I jumped in automatically. And it wasn't until I'd belted myself into the front passenger seat that I saw I wasn't alone.

The fairy who'd killed Tomas, who I recognized from the surveillance video, sat in the usually empty driver's seat, checking the point of a lethal-looking dagger.

My heart began to piston.

"He wishes to see you," the fairy said. "Resist, and you'll become intimately acquainted with my blade. I'm sure you know by now that I'm very good with it."

Before I could respond, a fairy outside the car grabbed my katana, and before I could launch myself after him, kicked the door closed. Then we were speeding away.

The Auto's screen showed the destination: We were headed back to the castle. The fairies must have figured I'd take a car this morning, and had hacked my system to give it a new destination.

But I wasn't sure why. If Ruadan wanted to take me out, there were easier and faster ways to do it. I thought of the covetous look in his eyes, the consideration and interest, and a dark and heavy fear settled in my belly. Not even the monster could push through that.

I had to ignore it, to ignore emotions, and think how to get out of this.

I considered trying to force my way out of the car, trying to survive a rolling stop outside it. But assuming I could do that on crowded streets without killing myself or someone else, I'd still be weaponless and facing down fairies.

Trying to free myself at the castle seemed like my best option. I knew the building relatively well now, and I'd hopefully be able to use that to my advantage. And given I was supposed to be at the Ombudsman's office, it seemed likely someone would eventually figure out I was gone.

Until then, self-rescue. And hope that I wouldn't have to gnaw off an arm.

The gate was open, the castle dark. The Auto drove over the gravel path, even though it was too narrow for a vehicle, and came to a stop outside the gatehouse.

"Out," Tomas's murderer said, dagger pointed at me as another fairy opened the door and pulled me out. Three more, this time with a mix of guns and blades, waited.

He strode toward the building, and I followed, the rest of the fairies walking behind us with weapons pointed. I needed a weapon of my own.

The gatehouse was dark and empty, but the doors into the courtyard were open and light streamed through—along with the prickle of fairy magic.

Ruadan stood in the yard with several dozen fairies. This time, instead of the V formation they'd taken at Grant Park, they stood in a long, straight line that cut across the courtyard, and probably traced the ley line that ran below it.

They'd abandoned the castle because they'd thought they could bring the green land here from Grant Park. And when that hadn't worked, they'd come back to the castle to try again.

Firelight from the torches they'd reinstalled shifted across their bodies as they waited to work their magic. They were in tunics, although like the fairies outside, some had switched their blades and bows for guns. I guess they weren't so concerned about being authentic anymore.

"She's here," Tomas's murderer said as one of the fairies behind me pushed me forward.

Ruadan turned and looked at me, and the excitement in his eyes made my skin crawl.

"Kidnapping is illegal," I said. "You have no right to hold me here."

"I don't think you'll want to walk away." He walked forward, arrogance in his stride, and looked down at me, the scent of green decay lifting in the air with his movements.

"Trust me," I said. "I want to walk away."

"Not when you learn of my plan. It was you who inspired it, after all."

That made the knot in my belly flip over. "What?"

"You see, bloodletter, the magic is old and complex, and the ley lines are not strong enough. The rivers not nearly deep enough to accomplish our goal."

"To bring the green land here."

"To bring the green land *alive*," he corrected. "There is a finite supply of magic in the world. Fairies used to control much of it, but the world changed. Djinn. Demons. Vampires. Shifters. Goblins, even the elves, who share some of our biology. More creatures, but no more magic. And we suffer because of it."

"You can't destroy Chicago because your magic has faded. That's not our fault."

He spun around, and his eyes had gone to angry slits. "Then

whose fault is it if not yours? Humans'?" He gave a considering nod. "Maybe. So we take from them."

"And you toss aside your own queen?"

His eyes flashed hot again. "She would rather we die than renew our kingdom."

"You told her there was a vampire-shifter conspiracy," I said. "Convinced her the peace talks were some kind of revolution. You're the reason she broke into the session."

"She should have fought then and there. We made it inside the room. You were outnumbered and outarmed. But your father spoke, and she lost her nerve . . . as she ever does."

"And Tomas? The vampire you killed at Cadogan House?" I shifted my gaze to the fairy who'd killed him. "You wanted to implicate the shifters to disrupt the process more?"

Ruadan's smile was thin. "Disruption is the first step toward revolution. And revolution—upsetting the current order—is the first step toward getting the power and recognition we deserve." His smile fell away, replaced by a pouty look that would have been better suited to a teenager. "Claudia believes magic and history have sealed our fate. We disagree, and sentimentality is not a weakness we share."

I thought I'd seen desire in Ruadan's eyes when he'd looked at Claudia. Maybe he was lying, or maybe it hadn't been romantic desire at all. Just want and need for something he thought she could provide.

He moved closer, until his magic surrounded us both and I was forced to look up at him, and could see the shadows under his eyes and the fear that lived in them.

"I am too young to fade away, to become a shell of myself. A husk. So we put aside the obstacle to our resurrection."

"Your queen."

"She was wrong about this magic. But when we succeed, she will see that we were right, and she will celebrate it."

"Given you kidnapped her and stuck her in an abandoned church, I doubt that. She's not nearly as grateful as you seem to think she should be."

His dark eyes flashed. "She will thank us."

"For what? Your plan failed. Look around, Ruadan. We aren't in the green land, and she knows it." I tried to remember what Claudia had told us, what tampering with the green land would do. "Trying to bring the green land here will only screw up this world. She wanted us to convince you to stop."

His eyes were mean. "Lies fall from your lips, bloodletter. We haven't failed. We merely have not yet been successful." He took a step forward, voice low and menacing. "I saw what you were at Cadogan House, when our magic enhanced the natural blood-thirst of your kind. I saw the red of your eyes, the magic that flows through you. We cannot do this on our own. But we can do it with you."

Fear was a vise around my heart, a vicious, sharp-tipped hand. I didn't want Ruadan knowing anything about me, much less about the monster.

"You and I were born at the same time," he continued. "We were brought here by the same magic, the power that Sorcha spread across the city. That power allowed fairies and vampires to breed again. You and I were born of that same power. That means you can help us."

For a moment, I simply stared at him, and then nearly laughed in relief.

He'd gotten it wrong. Never mind that I'd been kidnapped, didn't have a weapon, and was completely outnumbered. The fact that he didn't know about the Egregore and only thought I was different because Sorcha had sprinkled around some pixie dust loosened that knot in my belly. And I wasn't about to correct him.

"You think the ley lines aren't strong enough, but a twenty-three-year-old vampire can help you?"

"I think you don't give yourself enough credit."

"I don't even know how to do that. How to access magic."

"Oh, that won't be a problem," Ruadan said. "We're going to do it for you. Put her in position," he ordered, and the fairies behind me prodded me forward again.

Magic began to tingle as thin green vines began to curl between the stones ahead of us. They'd tie me again, and this time there'd be no wolf to cut me free. So it was now or never.

I gasped, pretended to stumble forward. The fairy on my right stepped forward, reached for my arm. I grabbed his wrist, twisted it back, and reached for the knife belted at his waist.

"Secure her!" Ruadan yelled, and the other two fairies moved forward, grabbing my arms and pinning them behind me before I could take the weapon. They pushed me forward toward the crawling vines on the stones, and I began to feel very pessimistic about my chances.

"Begin!" Ruadan ordered, and the fairies held my arms wide while the tendrils curled into place around my left wrist.

The ground began to ripple as they began their magic. Ruadan stepped in front of me and pressed his hand to my wrist.

"*Now,*" he said, and the world became a blur.

It was like bees had taken up space in my body, an entire hive vibrating and moving beneath my skin as Ruadan sought to pull from me the magic he believed I possessed. But he hadn't been right about the monster. He'd guessed wrong. And instead of convincing it to link its magic to theirs, he'd only made it angry. It climbed to the surface, claw over claw, and began to scream back its own vibration of magic.

I squeezed my eyes shut, trying to drown out the roaring tornado of noise in my head, trying to keep from losing my sanity in the vortex.

The monster flexed arm and muscle, and the tendrils at my right wrist snapped, and the magic fluttered in response.

"ATTENTION. ATTENTION."

Was that Theo's voice on a loudspeaker?

"YOU ARE SURROUNDED. RELEASE YOUR HOS-TAGE AND PROCEED IN AN ORDERLY FASHION TO-WARD THE GATE!"

"Do not stop!" Ruadan said as the magic stuttered around us. "Complete the charm!"

Before they could respond, the ground shook. And this time, it didn't have anything to do with magic. Stones crumbled through the lower part of the outer wall about forty feet away, sending a ball of fire through the gap. Smoke began to pour into the court-yard, and chaos erupted.

I tried to make myself focus despite the spinning in my head and punched out, caught the closest fairy beneath the chin. He hit the ground and I fell on top of him, trying to wrap my fingers around his knife. I began to saw at the vines on my other wrist. But my vision was double, and I struck the ground twice—sending shocks of pain through my arm—before managing to break through a single strand.

Someone grabbed my arm and I swung back, struck out.

"Elisa! It's me! It's Theo!"

I stared at him, waiting for his face to come into focus. "Theo?"

"Yeah. Let's get the hell out of here, okay?"

I blinked, nodded, offered him the knife. "Can you get this one? They magicked me, and I think my aim is off."

"Sure," he said, and sawed through the vines.

"What . . . was the noise?" I asked, opening and closing my eyes again until he had only a single head.

"I sacrificed the Auto parked outside."

"They hacked my Auto account."

"Yep. You didn't show this morning, and we couldn't reach you. Lulu found your katana outside her apartment when she came back from a run, called me. And then Petra checked your account and learned they brought you here. She says she's sorry about the hacking. And you should change your password. But not until she makes sure you aren't charged for the entire car."

"I will do that . . . at the first opportunity. What's a little privacy violation between friends?"

"My thought," he said with a smile. "We reported this to the CPD, but dispatch is overwhelmed because of Lincoln Park and the looting and the protests. But let's discuss that elsewhere."

We ran across the yard, fairies shouting behind us.

"Doors!" I said, when we got into the gatehouse, and we grunted as we pushed them closed, then flipped the steel bar down to give us more time. Then we ran through the building to the outer wall. And I stared at the empty lawn.

"Where's your car?"

"Outside the gate," Theo said as we took off down the stone path.

"You couldn't park next to the door?" I asked.

"I didn't want to drive on their lawn. That seemed rude."

"They *kidnapped* me."

"We don't all have to be assholes."

We'd made it twenty feet when something whistled over us. We both covered our heads, then stared when an arrow pierced the grass in front of us, still quivering with energy.

Another whistle, and a second arrow pierced the grass a few feet to our right.

"Figures they've got damn arrows," Theo muttered. "Let's haul ass."

We pushed harder, arms pumping as arrows whistled through the air like angry hornets. I was faster than Theo, and I was working up a nice lead when I heard the muffled scream of pain behind me.

I looked back. Theo was on the ground, an arrow through his thigh, pinning him to the ground.

"*Oh, damn,*" I said, and ran back, sidestepping another arrow that nearly tagged my calf.

"Shit," Theo said as I went to my knees beside him. "Shit."

"Yeah, you've got a little bit of a problem," I said, and looked it over. The arrow had gone right through the middle of his thigh, spilling blood across the ground. *Not enough,* I thought, *to have nicked his femoral artery.* But enough to worry about.

Blood scented the air like wine. And that was enough to silver my eyes.

"Oh, damn," Theo said, his pupils enormous. Shock was going to be a concern if I didn't hurry. "You're not going to—"

"Bite you?" I said with a grin, trying to keep the mood as light as possible. "No. It's just a reaction to the blood."

I fought to keep my fangs from descending, as I didn't want his heart pumping harder than it already was. The point was to keep the blood inside him. Not on the ground, and not in me.

An arrow whistled above us. I ignored it, made myself focus on the arrow that had already become a problem. The shaft was probably a quarter-inch in diameter, and the diameter stayed the same from top to bottom. Based on the length of the other arrows around us, it embedded in the ground four or five inches.

There wasn't going to be an easy way to do this. Not without pain, and not without risking further injury or keeping him in the open for longer than was safe.

"Theo, I'm going to hold on to the arrow and lift your leg to raise the arrow out of the ground." Sliding the arrow out of the dirt and threading it through his leg seemed like an injury risk, and while I might be able to snap the arrow in half, I didn't want to hurt him further.

"As soon as you're free, I'm going to pick you up and carry you to the car and drive us the hell away from here."

He swallowed hard. "You're going to leave the arrow in my leg?"

"For now, yeah. I want someone more skilled to remove it. Someone trained in keeping the blood actually inside your body. My expertise is kind of the opposite."

"Okay," he said with a forced smile. "Okay."

I wiped my hands on my pants, smearing blood and dirt, then reached beneath his leg and gripped the arrow. I put the other hand beneath his knee, prepared to lift his leg straight up. I pulled, but my fingers slipped away, and I ended up slamming my hand into his leg.

"Damn," he said through his teeth. "Oh, damn."

"I'm sorry, Theo. One more time, okay? For all the marbles. Brace yourself." He sucked in a breath, readying himself for the pain. And I didn't make him wait. I gripped the arrow again. With Theo rigid and shaking beside me, I lifted his leg and managed to keep the arrow in place, removing it from the soil one slow inch at a time.

A volley of arrows made a quick ring around us, a Stonehenge of armament.

"Almost there," I told Theo, ignoring the flash of an arrow in my peripheral vision. I grabbed his leg, the arrow, and pulled.

He stifled a scream as he was freed.

"Hold the arrow," I said, then climbed to my feet, pulled him up.

"Put your arm around me," I said, putting an arm around him and trying to avoid jarring the arrow that still stuck sickeningly through his leg.

"Lean on me," I said.

"I'm bigger than you," he said, chin trembling as he fought against the pain.

"I'm a vampire," I said as we hobbled across the yard toward his car. "But are you made of Adamantium, by chance?"

"No."

"Or possibly dark matter?"

"No," he said, the word falling to a grunt as he stumbled a little. "I sure as hell would like to see the goddamn getaway car right now."

I thought I was losing him, that he was going loopy because of the blood loss, because there wasn't a single siren on the wind.

Until the enormous black SUV burst through the open gate. It roared toward us, then spun to a stop with a spray of dirt and grass.

And then Connor was throwing open the back door.

"'Bout time," Theo muttered, and his head slumped against my shoulder.

"I'll get him," Connor said, casting a curious glance at the arrow and then picking up Theo with a grunt and loading him into the back of the SUV. He closed the door just as an arrow buried itself in the door panel.

Connor swore. "Eli is not going to like that."

Another arrow flew overhead, but I couldn't stop staring. Or smiling. "What the hell are you doing here? You should be in, I don't know, Iowa by now."

"Good to see you, too, Lis," Connor said, and his smile was as cocky as his tone. "Get in the vehicle."

"I called Connor, too," Theo said in a singsong voice from the backseat. "And he rode to the rescue again. Really screwed up the lawn, though."

I called Yuen as Connor drove to the nearest hospital, explaining what had happened and arranging to meet him at Cadogan House when Theo was on the mend.

We got Theo situated in the ER, which was full even in the middle of the night, and walked outside to get some air. And talk. Because we needed to talk.

"I thought you were leaving," I said, when we sat on a bench in a small garden area.

Connor leaned forward, elbows on his knees. "I was. And then Theo called, said you'd been taken to the castle. So I borrowed Eli's SUV, and there you go."

That this gorgeous man who'd had his pick of women for years seemed flustered in this moment made me relax.

"I guess I owe you for the second rescue."

He slid a glance my way. "Maybe you do."

We looked at each other, years of memories and history and insults between us. "What— What is this?" I asked.

"I don't have the foggiest idea, brat." He looked down at his linked fingers. "Confusing?"

"Yeah," I said.

"But also maybe . . ." He trailed off, and then he turned to me again, and then his hand was on my cheek, pulling me closer, and his mouth was on mine, hard and hot and possessive.

I am kissing Connor Keene.

I tried not to think about that, tried not to think about anything, tried not to let rules or roles take me out of the moment. Instead, I put a hand against his chest, grabbed a handful of T-shirt, and pulled him toward me.

He growled happily and deepened the kiss, slipping his tongue between my lips, wicked and teasing.

"Brat," he said against my mouth.

"Yes?" My voice sounded husky, even to me, and I could feel his smile against mine.

"I've got to take care of something," Connor said. He pulled back and looked at me, and his eyes were swirling and stormy blue. He was almost unfairly gorgeous, like every line had been carefully and intentionally carved.

"You are . . . beautiful," he said, then kissed me again, softer this time. "I have to get the vehicle back to Eli." He stood and looked down at me. "Take care of Theo, Lis. I'll see you."

I didn't have the courage to ask him when.

*   *   *

Three hours later, Theo hobbled on crutches, his leg thoroughly bandaged, into the waiting room.

"You really should stay overnight," said the doctor who followed him, and who looked barely older than me.

"Things to do," Theo said, swinging into the room. "It didn't hit anything vital, and you gave me some fluids, and I'm now at one hundred percent. And she's a vampire. You don't let us go, she might give your blood bank an extra look."

The doctor gave me a skeptical look before sighing and heading back through swinging doors.

"Ready when you are," Theo said.

"There's an Auto outside." We walked outside, and I got him settled in the backseat. The Auto was too small for his crutches, so the ends stuck through the open windows. But at least we were getting the hell out of the hospital.

"Why did you call Connor?" I asked Theo on the way back to Cadogan House.

"He was the only person I could reach."

"My parents?"

"Deal with the Ombudsman's office," he said. "Sending them to the castle to accost fairies seemed a little over the line, even for me. But they're so busy, anyway, and the story had a happy ending." He glanced at me. "I take it he left for Alaska?"

"I'm not entirely sure." And I didn't like that I wasn't sure. But there was nothing to do about that now. "Either way, probably better not to mention that he helped us. At least until he talks to Gabriel or whatever."

"Not a problem. They tricked you, huh?"

"What?"

"The fairies. They tricked you." He yawned, dropped his head back on the seat. "You didn't know they were in the car."

"Yeah, I guess they did." And that had me thinking. . . .

"Typical Big Fairy," Theo said, closing his eyes. "Could you maybe keep it down a little? I'd like to rest a little bit."

I hadn't made a sound, but I didn't argue. I let him sleep, and I thought about fairy tricks . . . and whether they'd work in reverse.

We were greeted at Cadogan House like heroes, or Theo was, anyway, as my mother proceeded to ply him with food and drink. Lulu had dropped off my katana, and it felt good to belt it on again. Gabriel and Miranda waited with my parents in my father's office, and I felt a momentary pang that Connor wasn't with them.

He'll come back, I told myself. *He said he would, and he will.* But he wasn't here yet, and I had to put that out of my mind.

"You don't need to thank me," Theo said. "Your daughter did the heavy lifting."

"Literally," I said. "And I owe you for showing up in the first place."

"The OMB owes you one," Yuen argued.

I looked at him, nodded. I was enough of a Sullivan to accept a good offer. "Okay. I'll take that on credit."

"Let's start with the fact that Riley will be released within the hour," Yuen said with a smile. And a little of the weight that had pressed down on my shoulders fell away.

I closed my eyes in relief.

"The pin you found tested positive for Tomas's blood," Yuen said. "Adding that to the surveillance video from Cadogan House, the fairies' subsequent activities, and the remains of a bloody tunic found by the CPD in the castle's keep's main fireplace, the prosecutor became convinced she had the wrong man."

I opened my eyes again. "He burned the tunic in the castle?"

"He did," Yuen said with a smile that said he was less than impressed by the fairy's effort to conceal evidence. "Most of the tunic was destroyed, but scraps of the fabric near the collar remained. They tested positive for blood—and there are visible holes from the pin."

My only regret was that I hadn't found it myself, since I'd walked right by that damn fireplace.

"The fairies were gone when the CPD got to the castle," Yuen said. "Presumably hiding in the green land again."

"Ruadan wants to complete his plan," I said, "and he hasn't been able to do that yet because the ley lines weren't strong enough. He kidnapped me because he thought I could provide the missing power."

"Why?" my father asked.

"Because we were born around the same time, right after Sorcha, during the fairy Renaissance. He thinks that makes me magically similar to the fairies, and that he could use that power to complete the switch. He started the magic, but didn't finish it before Theo showed up. And he'll try again, because he's convinced that's the only way fairies will survive."

I hadn't told my parents the entire truth about me, but I'd been honest about what Ruadan had said. I decided that didn't make me entirely a liar.

"In order to do that," Theo continued, "they're going to have to show themselves again. Pop back into this world."

"Yeah," I said. "And when they do, I think we should take advantage of it."

"How so?" my father asked.

"Fairies like to play tricks. They like cons and games, because they think they're innately smarter, braver, and more talented than any other supernatural. I say we turn the tables against them. We trick them into believing we have something they need."

"Which is?" Yuen asked.

I smiled. "A solution to their magical problem. We give them one. We give them Claudia."

*   *   *

An hour later, after the idea had been talked and argued through, and Yuen had secured Dearborn's and the mayor's approval, my mother opened the door of my father's office to the fairy queen who stood in the hall.

Her hair fell loose in waves over pink scrubs, and she was escorted by Delia on her left and Kelley on her right. The vampires in the room looked curious. The shifters still looked dubious. The humans looked amazed.

Claudia tossed her head. She might have been physically and magically weak, but the woman knew how to get attention.

Since she was in my father's House, he and Yuen had decided my father would take the lead. While the rest of us looked on, he stood with his hands in his pockets, wearing his coldest—and, to my mind, scariest—expression.

"Claudia," my father said.

"Bloodletter. I am being held against my will. I wish to be released."

"Excellent news, as we are here to offer you the terms for your release. Your protégé has tried again to shift the green land to Chicago. Thus far, he's tried and failed. And, as a result, he has spread, shall we say, bubbles of your world around ours. Theo," he prompted, and Theo sent images of the affected areas to the wall screen.

Claudia's gaze flicked to the grasses that waved in the pockets of Chicago. Her eyes widened instantaneously. "He is no protégé of mine."

But the lie showed clearly in her eyes.

My father didn't comment on it. "Ruadan is destroying our world. He kidnapped my daughter this night in an effort to try it again. He was thwarted, and your castle was damaged in the process."

Her eyes flared. "He dare not."

"Oh, he dared," my father said. "And now he will be stopped. You can assist in that process, with a result that is beneficial to your interests, or we can do it without you."

Silence fell heavy, a curtain drawn forward, interrupted only by the *tick* of the clock on the other side of the room.

"How do you propose to stop him?" she finally asked.

"You will send a message to Ruadan that you were captured by vampires and cruelly treated. You now see that he was correct, that the fairies must bring the green land here, whatever the cost. After studying the *Ephemeris* yourself, stolen from the Cadogan library, you have identified the optimal location for the process. You will wait for him there, and you will work the magic together and rule as king and queen."

Her eyes were hard. "I am queen of the fae. I rule with no man."

"Get it, girl," Petra muttered.

"You don't have to rule with him," my father said coolly. "You only need tell him that you will. The humans will arrest him and his allies. You will be returned to your castle to live in peace with the fairies who chose not to join him."

"I owe you no boon."

"My daughter was kidnapped by one of your people," my father reminded her. "A boon is owed, as you will recognize. But moreover"—my father moved closer, and there was no mistaking the cold anger glinting in his eyes—"you will help stop Ruadan, or you will lose what's left of your people and your kingdom. You help us, and you will regain them. And we will deliver him to you to be punished as you wish."

Yuen hadn't been thrilled about that part of the plan, but he knew my father would need room to negotiate.

Claudia walked to my father's desk, ran a fingertip across a chunk of quartz that held down papers. "And what do you seek in return for delivering him to me?"

"You will reverse the damage he's done."

"I could tell you that's impossible."

"You're a powerful queen," he said. "That would be a lie."

She lifted her gaze to him again. "I could betray you."

"You could. But you won't. You may not like or respect us, but you hate him more. He has sought to depose you. To harm your subjects. To ruin your castle. To destroy your world. To harm what you have built here. You have no love of Ruadan."

A pause. "They will be suspicious." She looked at me. "You told him that I believed he was wrong? That he would harm this world?"

I glanced at Yuen, my father, got their nods before answering. And when I did, said, "Yes. But he didn't believe me. And I think you could convince him pretty easily that I was lying to drive a wedge between you. That you weren't sure it could be done, but the *Ephemeris* changed your mind."

"You are their queen," my father said, the words a challenge. "Make them believe."

Claudia walked back to him, and my mother moved a hand to her katana, just in case.

"Your blade is not needed," Claudia said, without looking at her. She looked down at her scrubs. "But I need garments befitting royalty. Something that will . . . inspire him."

"That," my father said with a slow smile, "can be arranged."

TWENTY-THREE

Claudia was escorted back to her room, and we got to work on the details.

"We need a location," Yuen said. "We need to ensure that area is evacuated. We need CPD personnel in place to capture the fairies, and transportation to get them to the facility."

"Faster to just kill them all," Miranda muttered.

"Mass murder isn't the most diplomatic solution," Gabriel said.

"We have time," I said. "Because this is our con."

"And I think I have a place."

We all looked at Theo.

"Lake Shore East Park," he said, gaze on the monitor.

He'd pulled up a satellite image of downtown Chicago that showed the small park north of the river and just west of Lake Michigan.

Walkways swept through a rectangle of grass in dramatic arcs. There was a playground near the lake end, and a water feature that moved downhill toward it. The walkways were lined with trees and shrubs, as were the outer edges of the park.

"It's over the north-south ley line. It's a manageable area, and it's bounded by buildings. But it's also near Lake Shore Drive, so most of the humans have already been evacuated. We've got the lake nearby if we need to make a quick escape. And it's fancy."

"It's fancy?" my father asked.

Theo lifted a shoulder. "It's a nice park. A modern park. It looks like the kind of place Ruadan would want to take a stand."

"Now that you mention it," my father said, nodding his agreement.

Yuen was already working on his screen. "I'll contact Dearborn. Then we'll work on getting everything else in place."

"I'll help."

We looked back.

The prince of wolves stood in the doorway in jeans and a T-shirt, leather motorcycle jacket over it. Helmet in hand, Connor strode toward us, but kept his gaze on me. The look in his eyes was like lightning, and it sent a bolt of heat through my body and a frisson of magic into the room.

That magic was matched by Miranda's rage.

She strode forward and grabbed his arm with painted fingers, fury radiating in her wake. "What the hell are you doing here? You were supposed to leave hours ago. You have responsibilities!"

Connor's expression went hard, his gaze very cool. "I'm well aware of my responsibilities, Miranda. And you're going to want to remove your hand. As much as you might want to be, you aren't Apex of this Pack."

Her eyes fired, but she pulled back her hand. "Neither are you."

"I'm aware of that, too." He looked back at his father, his competitor. "If the Pack determines they don't want me, that will be their decision to make. But I'll be damned if I'll run away now."

Miranda pressed on. "So you're abdicating your responsibility to lead them to Alaska?"

"No. I'm taking on the responsibility of leading them here. There's a battle to be fought on the road, and there's a battle to be fought in Chicago." He looked at me, his gaze searing right through my soul. "I'm joining this battle."

"And Alaska?" Gabriel asked.

"I've found a replacement."

Gabriel just lifted his brows.

"Aunt Fallon," Connor said with a smile. "She and Uncle Jeff decided to take a vacation."

Only a shifter would refer to a several-thousand-mile drive though enemies as a vacation.

"I'm here now," he said, and slid his gaze to my father. "And I understand you've got a plan."

It took hours to get the CPD team in place, the remaining residents evacuated. And, of course, to get Claudia suitably dressed.

When she walked back into my father's office, her hair was gleaming and plaited and crowned with a golden diadem, the scrubs exchanged for a gown of stunning crimson with beading along the scoop neck and long, draping sleeves.

"Claudia," my father said, walking to her, "you are a vision."

As if the dress had restored her confidence, her acknowledging smile was haughty. "I am a queen," she said.

"Of course."

"Where'd you get the outfit?" I whispered to my mother.

"Lindsey's been doing cosplay," she said with a grin. Lindsey was her best vampire friend, and a whiz at reinventing herself.

Yuen showed Claudia the park, explained the general plan, then looked back at her. "The CPD team is in place and waiting. The rest of the team will move into place when you can get an invitation to Ruadan."

She slid her gaze to Petra. "May I borrow your hand, aeromancer?"

Petra glanced at Yuen, got his nod, and walked toward her. She pulled off her glove and presented her hand, palm up, to Claudia.

Her eyes fixed on Petra's, Claudia put her hand above it, then closed her eyes, murmured something that had magic lifting in the room and sparks crackling between their fingers.

Her lips spreading in a smile that had my mother putting a hand on her weapon, Claudia touched a fingertip to Petra's palm. The resulting spark was enough to make even Petra jump.

"The message is sent," Claudia said, opening her eyes again and shifting her gaze back to the rippling grass on the monitor. "We will see if he agrees to play your game."

Transportation was arranged. Weapons were checked. And Connor walked to me, his expression unfathomable, and gestured to the hallway.

"Can I talk to you?"

I nodded and followed him into the hallway, then down the corridor to a quiet spot behind the main stairwell.

I wanted to tell him I was glad that he'd stayed, but I didn't think I was ready for that admission.

"I brought you something." As I lifted my brows in surprise, he opened his jacket, fished for something in an interior pocket. He pulled out a toy sword.

I stared at it. "That's my sword. Why do you have my sword?" I narrowed my gaze. "How do you have my sword?"

"I stole it from Cadogan House."

I blinked. "You did what?"

"Four years ago, I snuck into Cadogan House and I took it."

"Why would you do that?"

He lifted a shoulder and grinned in Classic Teenage Connor style. "I wanted to see if I could."

"You are such a punk." But I couldn't help being a little impressed. He might have been reckless, but he was undeniably brave.

His grin was wide, confident. "I should get points for bringing it back to you."

"Why should you get points for returning something you stole in the first place?"

"Because I think you need a reminder about who you are."

"And who is that?" I asked cautiously.

He watched me for a minute, as if carefully choosing his words. "You're different, Elisa. You're different than you were, and you're different from the rest of them. You aren't just a vampire, and you aren't just their kid."

"No, I'm the monster nobody knows about."

"*No*," he said, and the word was forceful. "That's my point. You're thinking about rules and biology and what vampires are supposed to be. They don't apply here, because there's nothing else like you out there.

"I don't know what happens in your head," he said, moving a step closer, his voice growing deeper with each word. "Because you won't let any of us in. But I've seen you fight."

I swallowed hard against the desire to argue, to reject what he was telling me. To shake him off, because that's how I'd dealt with the monster. By not thinking about it. By pushing it down and away.

"Trust a shifter, Elisa. Claws don't make you unclean. They make you strong."

"Calling a girl's murderous inner urges one of her strengths isn't going to win you friends."

"Are they murderous?"

"They're violent."

"I'm violent."

"It's not the same."

"Isn't it? It's all magic in some form or other."

"We don't have time for this right now," I said, anger and impatience growing. "We have to get ready for the fight."

"We absolutely have time for this, because we *are* getting ready for the fight. This is a conversation you need to have. Why did you let it hurt the man who hurt Lulu? Because you wanted it to."

My blood sped, my eyes silvering at the rush of fury. "Take it back." Every word was bitter and bitten off.

"No," he said. "Because it's the truth. There may be foreign magic inside of you, Elisa. But there's no foreign magic in control of you. If you gave it control, it's because you wanted it. Stop justifying it and stop overthinking it."

Connor moved a step closer, close enough that our toes nearly touched. And now his voice was a whisper.

He put a fingertip beneath my chin, lifted it so our eyes met. "You've been in control for a long time. And you've always had your rules. You've always known the way things are done. Maybe, with Lulu's attacker, it was time to do what you wanted."

The idea made something clench in my abdomen. "To hurt people?"

His eyes were equally kind and fierce. "No, Lis. To *save* people. To fight because violence had been done against people you cared about."

I didn't know what to say about that . . . or what to feel.

"The next time you feel the monster, as you call it, the urge to fight—instead of pushing it down or letting it go or pretending it's not you, accept that it is. And fight the good fight."

I thought about the church, about my attack on the fairy. "I've tried to manage it. I can't. I just went berserker again. I hurt a fairy when we were rescuing Claudia."

"Why did you go berserker, then?"

"Because the fairy would have killed me and Theo if she'd had a chance."

"Is the monster in control right now?"

"No."

His smile was sly. "So you managed to force it back after that fight?"

"You make it sound so easy."

"Oh, I'm not saying it's easy. I'm a shifter, and I know about managing those two minds. The point is this: You're in control, and you always were. And yeah, that thought may not be comfortable. But there is nothing wrong with you."

His eyes darkened, the blue swirling like dark ocean water. "You are exactly who you should be."

Thirty minutes later, Petra, Connor, and I were in an SUV and approaching the site. Yuen, Theo, Claudia, and Gabriel would travel separately, and we'd rendezvous at Aqua, one of the skyscrapers that edged the park. They'd handle the magic and keep an eye on Claudia. We were responsible for helping round up the fairies—or taking Claudia down if this all went bad.

"Nearly there," said the driver, a vampire named Brody, who was also one of Cadogan's guards.

Adrenaline began to pump, speeding my blood. The monster knew a fight was brewing, and it knew what I'd been thinking. What I'd been feeling. It waited and it wondered.

We'd had to avoid Lake Shore Drive because of the intrusion, and he cruised up Michigan, which was nearly empty of people because of the relocation. We made it nearly to Randolph when the world rose in front of us.

Michigan Avenue became a hill, soft and green—and right in front of the SUV.

Petra screamed, and Brody slammed on the brakes—and we slammed directly into dirt and grass, the impact throwing all of us forward.

Air bags inflated, and the world went silent but for the roar of blood in my ears.

The prickle of magic and the scent of blood filled the car.

"Is everyone okay?" I asked.

"I'm good," Connor said, working on his seat belt. "But my neck may never be the same. Check on Petra."

I fumbled trying to unclip my seat belt, finally managed it, then lurched over the second-row seat to check on her.

There was no visible blood, but her eyes were closed. "Petra?" I patted her cheeks. "Petra? Are you all right?"

She opened one eye. "I'm fine. Why are you yelling at me? Ow."

"Brody? You okay up there?"

"I'm—" He put a hand to his head, drew it back to find blood. "I'm just cut, I think. But everything's attached."

"Warn the other SUV," I said. "Tell them Michigan is blocked. And let's get the hell out of this vehicle."

Connor wrenched open the door, helped Petra and me out of the car. My head spun when my feet touched pavement, but my legs held.

"You're all right?" Connor asked, tipping up my chin to check my eyes.

"Immortal," I reminded him.

"But not unbreakable."

"I'm going to try not to get broken." It was the best I could do.

While Millennium Park was fine, skyscrapers were becoming hills east of Michigan and south of the river. These hills were rockier than we'd seen near the United Center, a mix of grassy fields and craggy hills, moving slowly west.

"You've told them?" I asked Brody, staring at a craggy peak that rose over State Street.

"I told them. They're changing routes."

"Then we'll meet them at the rendezvous. We'll go the rest of the way on foot."

We walked through Millennium Park, Cloud Gate shooting our reflections back at us, then over to Randolph and up Columbus to Aqua, which rose nearly nine hundred feet above our heads. Its undulating edges looked more organic than glass and steel, like a bridge between the two worlds we faced right now.

Yuen wore a black jacket with OMBUDSMAN in white letters, and he directed members of the CPD into action.

"No Dearborn?" Connor asked, glancing around.

"He's monitoring with the mayor," Yuen said dryly. "You're all okay?" he asked, looking us over.

"Dented, but fine," I said. "The SUV's a total loss. The fairies?"

"Claudia is waiting. No sign of Ruadan."

"The trembling is starting," Connor said, and we all went quiet. The vibration was subtle, but it grew stronger. "They'll be here soon."

"Then we'll be quick," Yuen said. "Connor, Elisa, this is Hammett. His people will be backing you up out there."

Hammett was short but stocky, with muscle packed into dark fatigues. His hair was cropped, his eyes bright blue. A dozen men and women in the same ensembles stood behind him.

"Hammett," he said, shaking my hand, then Connor's. "I saw the footage from Grant Park," he said, smiling at me. "You have nice moves."

"I had good teachers."

He nodded approvingly. "Good answer. We've got Tasers"—he pointed to the weapon belted at his waist—"and guns if we need them. But we're hoping to incapacitate if we can."

"Always a good strategy," I said. "Once they figure out what's happening, they might try to rush Claudia."

"We can stay on them, let you run the field."

I nodded, glanced at Connor.

"Fine by me," he said with a nod. He lifted his shirt, showed the gun holstered there. "I'm fighting in this form. There's going to be too much confusion otherwise, and too much magic."

"Understood," Hammett said. He gestured toward another group of uniformed cops. "That's the round-up team. Off to the brick factory they'll go."

"Here's the lay of the land," Yuen said, and offered a larger screen with an overhead plan of the park.

"Claudia's here," Yuen said, pointing to the largest spot of open lawn.

"She said it's possible there will be some stuttering," Petra said. "You should be prepared."

"What do you mean by 'stuttering'?" I asked.

"Incomplete phase shifting," she said. "Ruadan is going to try to bring more of the green land here, while she tries to reverse it. In the meantime, the green land might stutter in and out of existence."

"So, you're saying you could be on a bridge over the river," Gabriel said, "then it's a nice, green hill, then it's a bridge again, and you might or might not end up in the water?"

Petra smiled at him. "Yep."

Gabriel just shook his head. "At least I know how to swim."

Connor and I crept in from the west, came to a stop behind a copse of trees while Claudia waited in the grass, looking perfectly serene in her gown. Petra and Theo were on the other side of the park, and members of the CPD's SWAT team surrounded it.

The earth was vibrating harder now, an unnerving sensation since the leaves above us didn't so much as rustle.

"You can feel that, right?" I whispered.

"Yeah. I don't like it."

Magic flashed, and the fairies appeared in their single-file formation over the ley line, Ruadan in front.

He walked forward, confident and calm, and looked over his queen. "You are well."

"No thanks to you." Claudia let her gaze dance along the fairies behind him, then back to Ruadan. "You sought to dethrone me. Your betrayal, Ruadan, was keenly felt."

"I have proven—have I not?—that it was necessary. We have done what was required of us, what was necessary to bring back our kingdom. To place our kingdom here, in this world, where it should be."

"And you have succeeded . . . in part," she said, the phrase perfectly calibrated not to compliment. His face didn't register it.

"Ouch," Connor murmured beside me.

"Seriously," I agreed.

"I did not think this much was possible," Claudia said. "And so I was wrong. But I believe there are . . . improvements to be made in the process."

"And you would show us how to correct them? To fully repair our world?"

"That would depend on what you have to offer."

"Your kingdom," he said. "And our fealty." He took a step forward. "We would rule together, as in old times. As queen and king."

She closed the distance between them, lifted her hand to his face. He leaned into her, and I saw that same desire in his eyes, recognized it for what it was now. Not for love, but for power.

"There would be power between us," she said. "Such as the world has never seen. My magic is ancient and wise. Yours is young and vigorous. Together, they would be . . . unprecedented."

"She's going to betray us," Connor said, but I put a hand on his arm to keep him from running forward.

"I don't think so." I thought of Claudia at the reception, the arrogance and confidence, the seeming refusal to acknowledge Ruadan as anything other than her companion. "I don't think she really wants to share power."

"Then let us begin," he said, and offered his hand to her. She placed her hand atop his.

Power began to ripple through the park again, in slow undulations that were different from the frenzied vibrations Ruadan had managed.

"Yes," Ruadan said as light began to glow between her hands. "Yes."

But in the gap between the buildings, we could see the grass that had been Lake Shore Drive. And once again, as Claudia began to reverse the magic he'd wrought, well-lit concrete took its place.

Ruadan saw it, too, and stared back at her, looking confused.

"If you're going to attempt to depose your queen," Claudia said, her voice darker and rougher, "you should be more careful. The fae have never needed a king before, and they do not need one now."

Ruadan screamed, and his magic faltered as fairies stared at their powerful queen and the man who would depose her, uncertain what to do.

"No!" Ruadan screamed, holding a hand behind him, pointing at those who looked more than willing to run. "You will stay and we will finish what we have wrought."

"We will finish it together," Claudia said, and grabbed Ruadan's wrist.

Ruadan might not have been as ancient as Claudia, but he was still capable and skilled. The burning fury in his eyes said he knew that he'd been beaten, but he wasn't going down without a fight.

Magic filled the park, thick enough to fog the air, as they battled for control. I'd wanted Ruadan for myself. But I'd known that wasn't going to happen. Not when Claudia could get to him first.

The world paid the price for the war that they waged. The neat lines of sidewalk across the park lifted and fractured, then spread with a thick carpet of undulating grass. Trees disappeared, reappeared.

The stuttering had begun, and the rest of the fairies wanted none of it. They scattered, trying to leave the field of battle to the generals. And we were there to meet them. Humans and super-naturals emerged from their positions on the edge of the park.

Connor and I stepped out of the trees, into the paths of two running fairies.

"I'll take the right," I said, heart speeding as I unsheathed my katana.

"I'll take left," Connor said, pulling a dagger from his boot.

The monster clawed at me. And this time, instead of pushing it down or giving it control, I let the monster step beside me. It didn't so much as hesitate. Two consciousnesses in one body, with all the combined strength and power.

I looked back at Connor, saw the acceptance—the encouragement—in his eyes.

"Use it!" he yelled to me, before turning to avoid the downward thrust of a dagger.

If the fairy understood what the scarlet shade of my eyes meant, he didn't mention it. And he didn't wait for me. He advanced, horn-handled blade held aloft and ready to strike.

"I guess we're skipping the preliminaries," I said, and met his blade with mine. He was strong, and the force rattled my bones nearly as effectively as the magic.

I lunged forward at the fairy, blade raised, and sliced a line of red across his shoulder as he pivoted away. He screamed with pain and stabbed out again, the tip of his blade catching the edge of my hip and sending searing heat through my abdomen.

Together we pushed forward and swung our katana, tearing skin and muscle across the fairy's calf and sending him to the ground.

Part of me was afraid. Part of me was thrilled.

Another fairy came toward us, and we spun the katana and sent the man sprawling to the ground.

"LSD is back!" said the voice reporting through my comm. "United Center is stuttering."

"No!"

The scream was sharp and shrill. I glanced over, saw a fairy with his blade at the neck of an officer he'd grabbed from behind. The fairy slit the officer's throat and let him drop to the ground. Then he looked up and met my gaze. He was the fairy who'd killed Tomas, who'd held the knife on me.

He turned to run and saw a woman at the edge of the park, a human who hadn't relocated or who'd come back to see what was becoming of her city, camera aimed at the unfolding drama.

"Stop!" I screamed.

He grabbed her, started running, dragging her along. So I ran, too.

"Elisa!" I heard Connor's voice behind me as I darted toward the edge of the park.

The ground rumbled beneath me. A hill of grass bubbled up, disappeared, then bubbled up again as the masters fought for superiority.

The woman screamed, and I ran harder, but the fairy was fast.

The hill just got larger, the grass spreading as Aqua shrank and disappeared beneath a carpet of stone and sky. And then the stones rose, a dozen of them. Four feet wide and growing taller with each second, atop the mound where humans had once lived.

The fairy spun, tried to avoid them, came face-to-face with a new stone. He turned around, his back to it, his thin fingers around the wrist of the screaming woman.

"Let her go."

The fairy looked back at me, eyes all but spitting with rage. "Bloodletter," he muttered.

"Let her go," I said as we swung the katana. "Or learn what a bloodletter is."

His eyes narrowed. He shoved her behind him but kept a grip on her wrist, the blade—still scented with human blood—in his free hand.

"I see what you are," he said, and sliced forward. But he was literally fighting with one hand behind his back, and it was an easy dodge.

I grabbed his wrist, twisted until he dropped the knife, and loosened his hold on the woman. She skittered back.

He kicked, caught the back of my knee, and sent me sprawling. I grabbed a tuft of grass to keep from falling down the hill, and when he lunged again, I lifted my katana. He spun across it, ripping a wound across his abdomen, then fell to the ground and rolled down the hill.

And then he was still.

Chest heaving, I looked back at the human, could feel the monster looking, watching, through my eyes. "Are you all right?"

The human screamed. "Don't touch me! You're as crazy as he is!" She scrambled to her feet and ran down the hill.

I sat there for a moment, dew seeping through the knees of my jeans.

Connor strode toward me. "Lis! Are you okay?"

"I'm fine." I took the hand he offered and climbed to my feet. "The human saw what I am."

He glanced at her disappearing form, then back at me. His expression was flat. "You put your life on the line because the fairy would have killed her. And instead of thanking you, she insulted you. She's the monster. Not you."

I didn't have time to argue. And I had only a moment to look down, to realize where we stood, when the world began to shift again.

The soft hill grew harder, and we rose so quickly my ears popped, like a phoenix hurtling toward the stars on feathers of steel and glass.

We came to a bouncing stop on a thin strip of concrete between waving balconies on the Aqua building.

There was a scream, and then Connor disappeared over the edge.

* * *

The world went silent except for the roar of blood in my ears. The world went still except for the hot pulse of fear that twisted my gut.

"Connor!" I screamed, dropping to my knees. I caught the edge of fingers gripping the six-inch-wide lip of concrete.

His face was a study in focus and concentration, his gaze on his fingers as his body dangled four hundred feet above the street below.

He grunted, and I went down on my stomach, wedged one foot into the railing on the edge of the next apartment's balcony and prayed the railing would hold. "Don't you dare fall, because I am not breaking that news to the Pack."

His forehead was beaded with sweat, muscles corded with effort. "And you'd have to live without my charm and devastatingly good looks."

I blew out a breath between pursed lips. "The world would probably stop turning.

"On three," I said. "We're going to pull like there's no tomorrow. One . . . two . . . three!"

I pulled and he heaved, turning as he lunged over the edge and landed on top of me.

His body above mine, we both hovered on the two-foot wide strip of concrete, with moonlight and darkness below us.

"We have to stop meeting like this," I said.

"Shut up, brat."

And then his hand was at my neck and his mouth was on mine, his lips insistent, his body hard and hot above mine. Heat and magic rose so quickly, surrounded me so completely, that I gasped against his mouth . . . and then tunneled my fingers through his hair and pulled him closer.

His groan was masculine, satisfied, possessive. "Lis," he said quietly, before ravaging my mouth again.

When my body was warm and my lips were swollen, Connor pulled back, and the chill that replaced his mouth was equally startling, even though his lips hovered just above mine.

And in his eyes was surprise . . . and certainty.

I didn't dare move, uncertain whether he'd let me go—or whether I wanted him to.

"Um, hello?"

We both looked over at the woman who stood on the balcony, eyes wide as she stared down at us. "Do you . . . Maybe you need help getting down?"

The woman's name was Jolie Brennan, and she'd decided not to evacuate. She'd been mightily surprised to learn her condo had become a rolling hill, and we'd been grateful when we were able to slip inside the condo and take the elevator back to the ground.

Or Connor had been. I'd been a little disappointed that I wouldn't get to jump.

When we finally made our way back outside, some of the fairies were being restrained and dragged into buses that lined the edge of the park. The CPD and supernaturals were being treated for their injuries.

Petra and Theo sat on the grass, and they climbed to their feet as we limped toward them.

"You okay?" Theo asked.

"We're good," I said.

I looked around at the park. Trees had been toppled, boulders were plentiful as thorns, and there was a long line of cracked and scorched earth above what I assumed was the route of the ley lines. Claudia stood near it, her expression defiant but sadness lining her eyes. She'd been betrayed by her people, or at least some of them. She'd be escorted back to the castle, where I guess she'd see what there was to rebuild of her community.

"Ruadan?" I asked, since I didn't see him.

"Claudia imprisoned him in the green land," Petra said. "He'll live there, alone, for the rest of his natural life."

"Cut off from her and the rest of them," Connor said. "No one to fight for him, or stroke his ego. He won't like that one little bit."

No, he wouldn't. It was a fitting punishment that he'd probably see as a victory, at least for a little while.

Gabriel walked over, looked at his son, at me. "You both look solid."

"We are," Connor said. "You good?"

"I am," Gabriel said. "But I could use a drink."

"A-fucking-men."

As it turned out, the European delegates hadn't needed a fancy party, formal talks, or expensive, fancy hors d'oeuvres. They just needed to be thrown together into the Cadogan House ballroom with chaos swirling outside—and my father's best Scotch.

My father had opened Cadogan to all the delegates who'd wanted shelter, thinking the House's stash of food and weapons would at least give them some respite and protection if Hyde Park shifted to the green land. While we'd been working on the plan to trick Ruadan, they'd cobbled together a rough plan for a new vampire council. They'd still have to get the French and Spanish delegates' okay, but it was a start.

And when that was done, they'd all but taken over the House. They poured champagne and mingled with vampires in Cadogan T-shirts, shifters, and nymphs to celebrate Chicago's return. The television monitors were tuned to the celebration, where people emerged from cars on the LSD, embracing one another and thrilled to be stuck in traffic again.

Theo flirted with a nymph. Petra and Lulu—who figured the magic was done so the party was just a party—chatted in a corner.

Connor talked to his uncles, drinking bottled beer and occasionally casting glances my way. We'd need to talk about the kiss . . . about everything. But for now, we could just be.

I'd skipped the champagne for blood—I needed the boost—and watched revelers run up and down the House's main hallway. My father would probably rein them in tomorrow. But for tonight, everyone was happy.

EPILOGUE

The night was warm, the air sweet with the last growth of summer. And on the breeze, the first chill of fall.

Two men sat in low chairs, the fire pit between them. Inside it, wood popped and sparked and flame flickered and danced beneath the slowly spinning rotisserie.

Father and son with fire and charring meat, reenacting the same moment that had been played a million times over the course of history. Gabriel and Connor Keene. Alpha and heir apparent, preparing for another historic moment.

"Alaska," the son said. "You pissed?"

The father stretched out his long legs, crossed them at the ankles. "I wasn't angry you were going to Alaska, and I'm not angry you're staying. Those are your decisions to make."

"You said I had responsibilities. That I couldn't shirk my duties to do what was easier."

"You doing what's easier by staying here?"

"Fuck, no. Easier would be hitting the road. Feeling the sun, the wind. Sunrises, sunsets, and everything in between." He smiled slyly. "And if I was lucky, a chance to . . . work out some aggression."

Gabriel smiled. "Coyotes can pack a punch. Might have been easier, but you'd have been bloody for a few miles."

"I don't mind a fight."

"So I've seen. And you don't mind jumping into one, either. Even if the fight isn't yours."

"Chicago is our home."

"And that's all you're interested in? The city. Not the girl?"

Silence rang through the room.

Without comment, Gabriel sipped his beer. "Alpha isn't taking the hard road or the easy road. Alpha is doing the thing that needs to be done. Sometimes that decision will be for you. Sometimes that decision will be for the Pack. And sometimes you have to decide between them."

He looked over at his son. "Miranda will fight you for the Pack. Her and maybe others. They want the Pack, and they'll fight for it using whatever weapons they need to use."

Connor's body went rigid, protective. His father was no threat, but he'd mentioned the possibility, and that had his instincts working. "They can try. But the Pack's mine."

Gabriel's eyes gleamed. "You're mine," he said. "And I'm proud of you. But watch your back. And hers."

Knowledge swirled in Gabriel's eyes, magic shifting and shimmering. He knew something. And that put Connor on alert. But he didn't bother asking which "her" his father meant.

After that kiss, there'd been no doubt for him at all. And his father would have known that, would have felt the truth of it. "Why do I need to watch her back? What's coming?"

But his father shook his head. "You know it doesn't work that way."

"If there's a prophecy, I deserve to know it."

"Not if it's not her prophecy."

Connor's jaw worked. Anger, flame surrounding a core of icy terror, burned in his eyes when he looked at his father. "If she's in danger—"

"We're all in danger," Gabriel said, then took another drink of beer. "'Dying since the day we're born.'"

"Don't give me song lyrics, and don't test me. Not about this."

"I can't give you information. Just be careful of her. She has enemies."

Connor sat back again. He could deal with enemies. Enjoyed dealing with them. What was the point of being alpha otherwise?

"Doesn't matter if the road is hard," Connor finally said. "The road is the road." He gave his father a glinting look. "Didn't you teach me that?"

"I'm shocked to learn you listened, whelp. Your head's as hard as a damn rock most of the time."

"Built-in helmet," Connor said, the same joke he'd been making for fifteen years.

Gabriel rolled his eyes. "No funnier today than it was the first forty times."

"But accurate," Connor said.

"Decisions will have to be made. Between love and responsibility."

"They always do. That's the road, too. And the only way to reach the destination." Connor took a drink.

"Are we done with this conversation?"

"I think we've covered it sufficiently."

"Good," Gabriel said, shifting in his chair. "I feel like I'm in a therapist's office."

Connor snorted. "No member of the NAC Pack has ever willingly walked into a therapist's office. Court order? Maybe. But not willingly."

"That's because we're surrounded by things that comfort," Gabriel said, moving closer to the fire and crossing his ankles on the fire pit's stone surround. "You have darkness, stars, booze, fire. There is nothing more that you need. Except possibly a good woman."

And, by his reckoning, his son was moving closer to that particular goal.

Read on for an excerpt from the first
Chicagoland Vampires Novel,

SOME GIRLS BITE

Available now

ONE

The Change

At first, I wondered if it was karmic punishment. I'd sneered at the fancy vampires, and as some kind of cosmic retribution, I'd been made one. Vampire. Predator. Initiate into one of the oldest of the twelve vampire Houses in the United States.

And I wasn't just *one* of them.

I was one of the best.

But I'm getting ahead of myself. Let me begin by telling you how I became a vampire, a story that starts weeks before my twenty-eighth birthday, the night I completed the transition. The night I awoke in the back of a limousine, three days after I'd been attacked walking across the University of Chicago campus.

I didn't remember all the details of the attack. But I remembered enough to be thrilled to be alive. To be shocked to be alive.

In the back of the limousine, I squeezed my eyes shut and tried to unpack the memory of the attack. I'd heard footsteps, the sound muffled by dewy grass, before he grabbed me. I'd screamed and kicked, tried to fight my way out, but he pushed me down. He was preternaturally strong—supernaturally strong—and he bit my neck with a predatory ferocity that left little doubt about who he was. What he was.

Vampire.

But while he tore into skin and muscle, he didn't drink; he didn't have time. Without warning, he'd stopped and jumped away, running between buildings at the edge of the main quad.

My attacker temporarily vanquished, I'd raised a hand to the crux of my neck and shoulder, felt the sticky warmth. My vision was dimming, but I could see the wine-colored stain across my fingers clearly enough.

Then there was movement around me. Two men.

The men my attacker had been afraid of.

The first of them had sounded anxious. "He was fast. You'll need to hurry, Liege."

The second had been unerringly confident. "I'll get it done."

He pulled me up to my knees, and knelt behind me, a supportive arm around my waist. He wore cologne—soapy and clean.

I tried to move, to give some struggle, but I was fading.

"Be still."

"She's lovely."

"Yes," he agreed. He suckled the wound at my neck. I twitched again, and he stroked my hair. "Be still."

I recalled very little of the next three days, of the genetic restructuring that transformed me into a vampire. Even now, I only carry a handful of memories. Deep-seated, dull pain—shocks of it that bowed my body. Numbing cold. Darkness. A pair of intensely green eyes.

In the limo, I felt for the scars that should have marred my neck and shoulders. The vampire that attacked me hadn't taken a clean bite—he'd torn at the skin at my neck like a starved animal. But the skin was smooth. No scars. No bumps. No bandages. I pulled my hand away and stared at the clean pale skin—and the short nails, perfectly painted cherry red.

The blood was gone—and I'd been manicured.

Staving off a wash of dizziness, I sat up. I was wearing different clothes. I'd been in jeans and a T-shirt. Now I wore a black cocktail dress, a sheath that fell to just below my knees, and three-inch-high black heels.

That made me a twenty-seven-year-old attack victim, clean and absurdly scar-free, wearing a cocktail dress that wasn't mine. I knew, then and there, that they'd made me one of them.

The Chicagoland Vampires.

It had started eight months ago with a letter, a kind of vampire manifesto first published in the *Sun-Times* and *Trib*, then picked up by papers across the country. It was a coming-out, an announcement to the world of their existence. Some humans believed it a hoax, at least until the press conference that followed, in which three of them displayed their fangs. Human panic led to four days of riots in the Windy City and a run on water and canned goods sparked by public fear of a vampire apocalypse. The feds finally stepped in, ordering Congressional investigations, the hearings obsessively filmed and televised in order to pluck out every detail of the vampires' existence. And even though they'd been the ones to step forward, the vamps were tight-lipped about those details—the fang bearing, blood drinking, and night walking the only facts the public could be sure about.

Eight months later, some humans were still afraid. Others were obsessed. With the lifestyle, with the lure of immortality, with the vampires themselves. In particular, with Celina Desaulniers, the glamorous Windy City she-vamp who'd apparently orchestrated the coming-out, and who'd made her debut during the first day of the Congressional hearings.

Celina was tall and slim and sable-haired, and that day she wore a black suit snug enough to give the illusion that it had been poured onto her body. Looks aside, she was obviously smart and savvy, and she knew how to twist humans around her fingers. To wit: The senior senator from Idaho had asked her what she planned to do now that vampires had come out of the closet.

She'd famously replied in dulcet tones, "I'll be making the most of the dark."

The twenty-year Congressional veteran had smiled with such dopey-eyed lust that a picture of him made the front page of the *New York Times*.

No such reaction from me. I'd rolled my eyes and flipped off the television.

I'd made fun of them, of her, of their pretensions.

And in return, they'd made me like them.

Wasn't karma a bitch?

Now they were sending me back home, but returning me differently. Notwithstanding the changes my body had endured, they'd glammed me up, cleaned me of blood, stripped me of clothing, and repackaged me in their image.

They killed me. They healed me. They changed me.

The tiny seed, that kernel of distrust of the ones who'd made me, rooted.

I was still dizzy when the limousine stopped in front of the Wicker Park brownstone I shared with my roommate, Mallory. I wasn't sleepy, but groggy, mired in a haze across my consciousness that felt thick enough to wade through. Drugs, maybe, or a residual effect of the transition from human to vampire.

Mallory stood on the stoop, her shoulder-length ice blue hair shining beneath the bare bulb of the overhead light. She looked anxious, but seemed to be expecting me. She wore flannel pajamas patterned with sock monkeys. I realized it was late.

The limousine door opened, and I looked toward the house and then into the face of a man in a black uniform and cap who'd peeked into the backseat.

"Ma'am?" He held out a hand expectantly.

My fingers in his palm, I stepped onto the asphalt, my ankles wobbly in the stilettos. I rarely wore heels, jeans being my preferred uniform. Grad school didn't require much else.

I heard a door shut. Seconds later, a hand gripped my elbow. My gaze traveled up the pale, slender arm to the bespectacled face it belonged to. She smiled at me, the woman who held my arm, the woman who must have emerged from the limo's front seat.

"Hello, dear. We're home now. I'll help you inside, and we'll get you settled."

Grogginess making me acquiescent, and not really having a good reason to argue anyway, I nodded to the woman, who looked to be in her late fifties. She had a short, sensible bob of steel gray hair and wore a tidy suit on her trim figure, carrying herself with a professional confidence. As we progressed down the sidewalk, Mallory moved cautiously down the first step, then the second, toward us.

"Merit?"

The woman patted my back. "She'll be fine, dear. She's just a little dizzy. I'm Helen. You must be Mallory?"

Mallory nodded, but kept her gaze on me.

"Lovely home. Can we go inside?"

Mallory nodded again and traveled back up the steps. I began to follow, but the woman's grip on my arm stopped me. "You go by Merit, dear? Although that's your last name?"

I nodded at her.

She smiled patiently. "The newly risen utilize only a single name. Merit, if that's what you go by, would be yours. Only the Masters of each House are allowed to retain their last names. That's just one of the rules you'll need to remember." She leaned in conspiratorially. "And it's considered déclassé to break the rules."

Her soft admonition sparked something in my mind, like the

beam of a flashlight in the dark. I blinked at her. "Some would consider changing a person without their consent déclassé, Helen."

The smile Helen fixed on her face didn't quite reach her eyes. "You were made a vampire in order to save your life, Merit. Consent is irrelevant." She glanced at Mallory. "She could probably use a glass of water. I'll give you two a moment."

Mallory nodded, and Helen, who carried an ancient-looking leather satchel, moved past her into the brownstone. I walked up the remaining stairs on my own, but stopped when I reached Mallory. Her blue eyes swam with tears, a frown curving her cupid's bow mouth. She was extraordinarily, classically pretty, which was the reason she'd given for tinting her hair with packets of blue Kool-Aid. She claimed it was a way for her to distinguish herself. It was unusual, sure, but it wasn't a bad look for an ad executive, for a woman defined by her creativity.

"You're—" She shook her head, then started again. "It's been three days. I didn't know where you were. I called your parents when you didn't come home. Your dad said he'd handle it. He told me not to call the police. He said someone had called him, told him you'd been attacked but were okay. That you were healing. They told your dad they'd bring you home when you were ready. I got a call a few minutes ago. They said you were on your way home." She pulled me into a fierce hug. "I'm gonna beat the shit out of you for not calling."

Mal pulled back, gave me a head-to-toe evaluation. "They said—you'd been changed."

I nodded, tears threatening to spill over.

"So you're a vampire?" she asked.

"I think. I just woke up or . . . I don't know."

"Do you feel any different?"

"I feel . . . slow."

Mallory nodded with confidence. "Effects of the change, probably. They say that happens. Things will settle." Mallory would know; unlike me, she followed all the vamp-related news. She offered a weak smile. "Hey, you're still Merit, right?"

Weirdly, I felt a prickle in the air emanating from my best friend and roommate. A tingle of something electric. But still sleepy, dizzy, I dismissed it.

"I'm still me," I told her.

And I hoped that was true.

The brownstone had been owned by Mallory's great-aunt until her death four years ago. Mallory, who lost her parents in a car accident when she was young, inherited the house and everything in it, from the chintzy rugs that covered the hardwood floors, to the antique furniture, to the oil paintings of flower vases. It wasn't chic, but it was home, and it smelled like it— lemon-scented wood polish, cookies, dusty coziness. It smelled the same as it had three days go, but I realized that the scent was deeper. Richer.

Improved vampire senses, maybe?

When we entered the living room, Helen was sitting at the edge of our gingham-patterned sofa, her legs crossed at the ankles. A glass of water sat on the coffee table in front of her.

"Come in, ladies. Have a seat." She smiled and patted the couch. Mallory and I exchanged a glance and sat down. I took the seat next to Helen. Mallory sat on the matching love seat that faced the couch. Helen handed me the glass of water.

I brought it to my lips, but paused before sipping. "I can—eat and drink things other than blood?"

Helen's laugh tinkled. "Of course, dear. You can eat whatever you'd like. But you'll need blood for its nutritional value." She leaned toward me, touched my bare knee with the tips of her fingers. "And I daresay you'll enjoy it!" She said the words like she was imparting a delicious secret, sharing scandalous gossip about her next-door neighbor.

I sipped, discovered that water still tasted like water. I put the glass back on the table.

Helen tapped her hands against her knees, then favored us both with a bright smile. "Well, let's get to it, shall we?" She reached into the satchel at her feet and pulled out a dictionary-sized leather-bound book. The deep burgundy cover was inscribed in embossed gold letters—*Canon of the North American Houses, Desk Reference.* "This is everything you need to know about joining Cadogan House. It's not the full *Canon*, obviously, as the series is voluminous, but this will cover the basics."

"Cadogan House?" Mallory asked. "Seriously?"

I blinked at Mallory, then Helen. "What's Cadogan House?"

Helen looked at me over the top of her horn-rimmed glasses. "That's the House that you'll be Commended into. One of Chicago's three vampire Houses—Navarre, Cadogan, Grey. Only the Master of each House has the privilege of turning new vampires. You were turned by Cadogan's Master—"

"Ethan Sullivan," Mallory finished.

Helen nodded approvingly. "That's right."

I lifted brows at Mallory.

"Internet," she said. "You'd be amazed."

Photo by Dana Damewood Photography

Chloe Neill—*New York Times* bestselling author of the Chicagoland Vampires novels (*Blade Bound, Midnight Marked, Dark Debt*), the Dark Elite novels (*Charmfall, Hexbound, Firespell*), and the Devil's Isle novels (*The Sight, The Veil*)—was born and raised in the South but now makes her home in the Midwest, just close enough to Cadogan House to keep an eye on things. When not transcribing her heroine's adventures, she bakes, works, and scours the Internet for good recipes and great graphic design. Chloe also maintains her sanity by spending time with her boys—her favorite landscape photographer (her husband) and their dogs, Baxter and Scout. (Both she and the photographer understand the dogs are in charge.)

CONNECT ONLINE

chloeneill.com
facebook.com/authorchloeneill
twitter.com/chloeneill